Butterfly Barn

KAREN POWER

COMERAGH PUBLISHING

First published in 2014 by
Comeragh Publishing
Co. Waterford
www.karenpowerauthor.com

CreateSpace paperback   ISBN: 978 1 909483 76 7
Paperback   ISBN: 978 1 909483 73 6
eBook – mobi format   ISBN: 978 1 909483 74 3
eBook – ePub format   ISBN: 978 1 909483 75 0

Produced by Kazoo Independent Publishing Services
222 Beech Park, Lucan, Co. Dublin
www.kazoopublishing.com

Kazoo Independent Publishing Services is not the publisher of this work. All rights and responsibilities pertaining to this work remain with Comeragh Publishing.

Kazoo offers independent authors a full range of publishing services. For further details visit www.kazoopublishing.com

Cover design by Andrew Brown
Printed in the EU

Butterfly Barn

For Michael, Aisling, Eoghan and our twin boys, Aidan and Michael.

Karen Power lives with her family in County Waterford. She has spent many years working in the travel industry and currently delivers training in communications and tourism. *Butterfly Barn* is her first novel.

Chapter One

Sheets of rain beat against the windscreen as a wiper began to break loose from its rubber band. The shrill ring of Grace's mobile added to her frustration. She had left it in her handbag, which was lying on the floor on the passenger side, too far to reach. She was already running late, and pulling over could mean the difference between making the flight to New York or not.

It was probably Dirk and she really didn't want to talk to him. Why couldn't he understand that this was her dream? Yesterday morning when the cruise liner docked in Bayrush Harbour, it had been the best feeling. All of her hard work had been worth it. But then Dirk had started on about setting a date again ... Why couldn't she commit? She was wearing his ring. She was already in deep – three and a half years and a house together deep.

"Stop," she said out loud, surprising herself. "Focus on what's ahead. JESUS!" She narrowly missed the bumper of the car in front. The sooner she got to the airport the better.

What if the call was from Eoghan, her business partner? A great deal depended on the meeting she was to attend later. Maybe he'd forgotten to tell her something? He was supposed to be with her but had woken earlier with an ear infection and couldn't possibly fly. At sixty years old Eoghan was in excellent health but today it had let him down. It meant she'd have to make the pitch of her life, alone! The nearer Grace got to Dublin Airport the worse she felt. Nerves mixed with excitement filled her.

Waiting at the traffic lights on the dual carriageway, she looked into the rear-view mirror. "If it's to be it's up to me," she said, trying to quell the many doubts she had about herself. She looked across towards the lane beside her and sure enough, there were two lads in a minivan grinning at her. Thankfully the light changed so she stuck her foot to the floor, laughing.

Grace had sent an email explaining about Eoghan's sudden illness and had asked if they would agree to him making a conference call. The time difference meant she'd had no reply, but at least they'd be aware of the circumstances. Eoghan was an expert at all things nautical while excursions and activities were her areas. If they could sign Pal Pacific to their books it meant they could stay in business. If not, well … that wasn't a thought she could afford to have!

Sophia sat in the back of the taxi. The radio was playing one of her favourite songs, "The Way We Were". Barbra Streisand's voice said it all.

"What time is your flight luv?" asked the driver, breaking her reverie with a thick Dublin accent that she knew so well from her many trips.

"Oh not until one-thirty, I've got plenty of time."

"Well you certainly got the weather until now," he said nodding towards the window as the rain bucketed down. "The best we've had in years! What part of America are you from?"

"New York."

"The Big Apple! Me and the missus went there a few years ago. In the good times. Sure I couldn't get her outta the shops. I got lost in that Macy's more times."

Sophia smiled, noticing two twinkling brown eyes looking at her through the driver's mirror. The way he spoke about his wife saddened her. She would never be Bill's missus again.

"So, were you here long?" He seemed determined to keep chatting.

"Just four days this time."

"Oh, so you're a regular. Well, is there any Irish blood in ya?"

"None."

"Jaysus that makes a change! I don't think I ever had an American in the taxi that didn't have a drop in them." He paused, obviously waiting for an explanation.

"I'm an original then." This seemed to stop him in his tracks. He fiddled with the radio and changed the channel. Sophia looked out the window and wondered would the emptiness she felt inside ever leave her. The taxi driver was nice but she'd had enough of idle chatter.

Sitting in Mr Morrison's waiting room in Bayrush, Jessie could feel her heart racing. She looked across at another couple; the woman seemed to not have a care in the world as she browsed through VIP magazine. Jessie could feel Geoff shifting uncomfortably in the seat beside her, a sure sign he was just as nervous as she was. She picked up a magazine and flicked through the pages, anything to distract her.

"Did you see the match last night?" asked Geoff, directing his attention to the fellow sitting across from him beside a heavily pregnant woman.

"Ah stop, it'd break your heart," the guy replied. Their voices became a background noise to Jessie's nerves. She turned the magazine page and saw a picture of a mother kissing a chuckling baby on its cheek. Its beautiful round eyes seemed to look straight into Jessie's heart. She was terrified. Twenty years together and they had been blessed with six-year-old Sam. She was afraid to think about what had happened four years ago.

"Mr and Mrs McGrath," announced the secretary, breaking Jessie's thoughts. She touched her tummy and felt so grateful for the little life inside. She was so looking forward to seeing the baby for the first time. She knew it would just be a blob on a monitor but it would be their little, long-awaited blob, and she was looking forward to showing Sam the print-out. He was so excited. "Only another twenty-eight weeks to go," Geoff had told him this morning at breakfast.

Jessie heard the rain outside and hoped that Grace would make it safely to the airport. All her hard work was paying off. If the deal went through Grace could finally make wedding plans. Just then Geoff looked at her and gave her that sweet, private smile he saved for her. She relaxed; he was right to smile. She had made it to twelve weeks. Their dreams were coming true.

Jack Leslie looked out of the aeroplane window. They were circling over Dublin. The view was incredible, even on a rainy day. He had loved Dubai but since the shock of finding out about Lynda's betrayal, he hadn't been functioning properly. He'd never suspected a thing. He had actually thought they were trying for a baby. What a fool she'd made of him! Women, he was finished with them, devious, conniving and cold. The jolt of the aeroplane touching the tarmac bought him back.

"Fáilte romhat go hÉireann, and thank you for flying with us today." He loved the sound of the Irish accent. He had missed it. Over the years he had been back and forth for holidays. But could he actually live in Ireland again? Or did he even want to?

"Miss Grace Fitzgerald, travelling to New York, please report to the Aer Lingus customer service desk immediately!"

Oh no, thought Grace as she weaved her way through the June holiday crowds. She joined the queue at the desk. Her mind was working overtime. What could it be? *Oh please God it's not Jessie; stop being such a pessimist*, she told herself. Grace was so anxious about her best friend's scan. Please God everything would go well for her this time. Grace was virtually hopping from one foot to the other; she was already short on time. She settled herself and continued waiting her turn.

"I'm terribly sorry," said the perfectly made-up ground hostess. "We actually have a small problem with the flight to New York. It is overbooked but we have taken the liberty of upgrading you to our premier service."

"Oh my God, that's fantastic. Thank you so much. I'd better get a move on or I'll never get through security."

"Here is your boarding card and have some champagne on us. Enjoy!"

"Thanks a million," Grace said, picking up her hand luggage and rushing towards the security gate.

After passing through security she made her way along the series of corridors to the gate, thrilled to be travelling first class. She could hardly keep the smile from her face. Eoghan not being able to travel had been such a blow. Being upgraded certainly made up for it.

Standing on the moving sidewalk she looked through the glass wall dividing the arrivals from the departures. "Oh my God. Jack!" she said out loud, spinning around and nearly tripping over her carry-on luggage and crashing into the woman behind her.

"I'm so sorry," she said, completely flustered.

"No probs, whoever he is … he's very cute! Don't you think you might be heading in the wrong direction?" The woman laughed.

Grace smiled but the man she had taken for Jack had been swallowed in the crowd so she couldn't be sure it was him. "An old friend," she said, taking the handle of her carry-on and pulling it off the moving sidewalk. The woman smiled too knowingly for Grace's comfort so she decided to walk along the corridor instead.

Jack Leslie had been such a good friend when she had badly needed one. She had seen his wedding photograph in the local paper nine years ago. He had looked so happy her heart had nearly broken all over again. Underneath the photograph it had said he was living in Dubai and that the dark-haired girl beaming beside him was from Chicago. What's wrong with you, Grace? Focus, she told herself, shaking her head from side to side as if willing all her issues and concerns away.

Jack walked along the arrivals corridor. Dublin Airport had changed so much over the years, he thought. He could see the departures passengers through the glass wall. Part of him wanted to change his mind. Was he crazy to come back?

He spotted a tall, blonde girl and for a brief moment he thought he recognised her. Could it be Grace? He dismissed the thought as quickly as it came. Somewhere in the back of his mind had he always compared every other woman to her? Was that why he was coming home? He ran a hand through his curly brown hair, settled the holdall on his shoulder and kept on walking.

Dr Morrisson stood up and walked around his desk. "Jessie, Geoff, it's so good to see you both again." He kissed Jessie on the cheek and shook Geoff's hand. "Congratulations," he said warmly.

"So far so good," smiled Geoff, "she's been keeping well and taking it easy. Haven't you Jess?"

She nodded and smiled, noting that Geoff was as nervous as she was. He always talked more when he was anxious, but who could blame him. He hadn't been keen to try for another baby when she had miscarried four years ago. He had said, "isn't Sam enough?" But she had desperately wanted a brother or sister for Sam. It hadn't happened so she had stopped hoping. She hadn't noticed missing a period, not until she had been feeling off a few mornings in a row. Then she had been violently sick the following day. The pregnancy test had confirmed it. When she told Geoff he had simply taken her in his arms and held her tight, reassuring her that everything would be all right.

"That's good to hear. Unfortunately the ultrasound just went on the blink a few minutes ago. I won't be able to scan you today, Jessie."

"It's no problem, these things happen," said Geoff, squeezing Jessie's hand to reassure her. She smiled, trying to hide her dismay.

"I know how much you've been looking forward to the scan but I can check for a heartbeat using this machine. I'll take a listen?"

"Can you fit us in on Monday for a scan?" asked Jessie as she rolled up her top.

"It's Friday afternoon so I can't promise. Jennifer is getting in touch with the technician as we speak. We will, of course, make you a priority."

Dr Morrison placed the listening device on her bump and moments later the room was filled with the wonderful, magical sound of the baby's heartbeat.

"That's a nice solid heartbeat Jessie," declared the doctor, smiling.

"Fantastic," said Geoff, grinning from ear to ear.

"Thank you, Dr Morrison," said Jessie, closing her eyes and relishing the sound as the two men chatted. If she could stay like this for the rest of her pregnancy – wouldn't it be fantastic! Too quickly Dr Morrison disconnected the equipment and the sound stopped. So much for that thought she smiled as Geoff helped her back into a sitting position.

"Jennifer will arrange another appointment for you as soon as possible. Again I'm terribly sorry for the inconvenience."

"No problem. We'll see you then," replied Geoff.

Having arranged to come back next Wednesday they walked hand in hand to the jeep.

"Now that we're in town let's go for lunch," beamed Jessie. "I can eat for two."

Geoff laughed and threw his eyes to heaven. "You always could!"

"Geoff McGrath, the cheek of you." She laughed as she climbed into the jeep. "It's a good job I'm not sensitive."

Grace sat sipping champagne from a crystal flute. The seat beside her was still free. She gazed around the cabin. So far she hadn't spotted anyone famous or anyone even vaguely interesting-looking for that matter. Between being upgraded, and thinking she had seen Jack, she had completely forgotten to check her mobile for its missed call. Just then her attention was drawn to the entrance of the cabin.

"Good afternoon Mrs Wynthrope. It's good to see you again," said the air steward.

"Thank you. It's always a pleasure to fly with your airline!"

He took the red cashmere shawl she proffered. Meanwhile, another hostess handed the woman a glass of champagne while the steward guided her to the free seat beside Grace.

"Hi, I'm Sophia," she said with an American accent.

Not anticipating an introduction Grace stuttered, "Eh, I'm Grace, and I'm not supposed to be here."

"Lately I'm not quite sure where I'm supposed to be either, so cheers," said Sophia, clicking her glass to Grace's with a perfectly manicured hand and then sitting.

"Sláinte, that's what we say here. But you probably knew that."

"Ah sure and I do. Before you say it … that was a terrible attempt at an Irish accent."

"I won't disagree," laughed Grace, holding up her glass. "It's a pity I can't have a few more of these."

"Why ever not? You've been upgraded. They're free!"

"I suppose these gave me away," said Grace, pointing to her jeans.

"No, it was the 'I'm not supposed to be here' statement. You could pass for a model or a movie star with that bone structure. People no longer dress for premier class. It's not like the old days. So tell me why only the one glass?"

Grace reddened at the by-the-way compliment and she was glad the cabin steward distracted them by collecting their glasses and checking seat belts for take-off.

"So …" Sophia remarked, encouraging Grace to expand.

"I'm making a presentation at five-thirty today to Pal Pacific."

"Wow, Pal Pacific, one of the biggest cruise companies in the world. Are you crazy? Why didn't you fly yesterday?"

"You see that's the thing, our business is small. Yesterday we had a cruise ship in so I had to be there. We handle the ground arrangements for visiting cruise liners."

"Fascinating, tell me more?"

"Well, there are two of us, myself and Eoghan Forrester. The business is called Ireland for Real. We contract tour guides on the days the ships dock. The company is only four years old but hey, we're getting there. So you can imagine our excitement to get a call from these guys!" Grace was on a roll because Sophia was taking so much interest. "Anyway enough about me! What do you do?"

"How do you know that I *do* anything? Maybe I could have married well?"

Grace had put her foot in it so she decided to plough on. She was never going to meet Sophia again. "Okay, this might sound cheeky but … you don't look the type."

Sophia laughed a deep, sexy laugh that caught the steward's attention. She called for another champagne adding, "And a soda for my friend." He looked quizzically at Grace.

"A diet coke would be great, thanks," she said, relieved that Sophia obviously hadn't taken offence.

"Now tell me about the excursions your company offers," said Sophia, settling herself into the comfortable aircraft seat.

"Good to see you Bro," said Jack, hitting shoulders with his older brother. He had a sudden urge to hug him tight, but Conor would think he was losing it if he did that, they weren't that kind of family. Conor had been stunned to silence when Jack rang to say he was coming home indefinitely. He had been grateful that his brother hadn't grilled him as to why the sudden decision; instead he had offered to pick him up from the airport.

Jack planned to crash at his mother's until he found a place to rent.

He had told his mother that Lynda needed to go back to the States for a while and so he was taking the opportunity to come home to see if he could get some work away from the heat of Dubai.

He knew that his mother wasn't convinced by his story but she had gone along with him and for that he was glad. The last thing he needed from anyone was pity.

"What's in the bag? A dead body?" joked Conor, lifting the large suitcase into the boot.

Jack laughed, swallowing a lump that had formed in his throat. It was good to be home. When his father had been alive he hadn't been able to get away fast enough. Life had been hell for them all.

Was it crazy to come back? Could Bayrush ever be enough for him? Could he honestly see himself working as a vet in a small town in the south-east of Ireland?

"You know, Sophia, I'm grateful to be working at something I enjoy – especially in the present economic climate. God, I sound all mushy and stupid!"

"My grandmother once said when you earn a living doing something you love you'll never work another day of your life."

"I like the sound of your granny," said Grace, just as the steward passed them the dinner menus. The two of them spent the next while discussing them in detail. They discovered a shared love of food and both agreed that they didn't cook half as much as they would like to.

"I'm glad you're not a member of the lettuce leaf brigade," said Sophia.

"With these hips you must be joking," said Grace, slapping each hip with her hands.

"They're curves. You know, I'm glad I met you. It feels like being in premier class for the first time."

Just then, Grace accidentally hit one of the buttons on the seat and sent herself flying.

"Sophia, if you don't stop laughing they'll throw us out," said Grace. But that only made Sophia laugh harder. "I have to admit I was thrilled about the upgrade. But if I had to pretend all the way to New York that this is what I'm used to it wouldn't be half as much fun."

"I'm going to have another glass of champagne because, Grace, it's a long time since I laughed so much and meant it."

"Go for it girl," Grace smiled, wondering what it was that had made this lovely woman so sad.

After a delicious dinner of crab cake and lamb for Grace, and pate and salmon for Sophia, they were sipping coffee when Sophia asked. "So when is the big day?" She inclined her head towards Grace's left hand. Immediately Grace began to spin the lone diamond set on its platinum band with her thumb. She flushed and then answered quietly. "I don't know."

Sophia shifted in her seat, forcing Grace to look at her. Her silence was almost deafening. "It's the truth," Grace heard herself say and then added, "I really don't know."

"How long have you been engaged?"

"A year."

"So what's the problem?"

It was Grace's turn to shift in her seat. She couldn't believe she had got into this conversation especially with a total stranger but her mouth hadn't quite connected with her brain. "I'm scared. I really don't know if he's 'the one'."

"Oh my dear ..." The genuine sympathy in Sophia's voice made her continue.

"We've been together three and a half years. We bought a house together two years ago. He thinks I'm holding back because I want a big wedding ... and to be honest I've allowed him to believe that. But ... oh Sophia. Oh God. I'm sometimes so scared at the thought of marrying that I feel paralysed. I can't believe I'm telling you this ..."

"Grace, it's a huge decision and I'm actually honoured that you are sharing with me. In my life I have found that when I actually voice my concerns it helps me to be clearer in my decision-making. It's simply because I begin to hear it aloud."

"It's been in my head for so long Sophia. I was afraid that if I said it I would be judged harshly. Why would I lead Dirk on? What if he heard it back? I do love him. It's just ... well my father left a note on the kitchen table when I was sixteen and we haven't seen him since."

"Oh Grace, I'm so sorry."

"That happened such a long time ago I thought I was over it. But when Dirk proposed ... well ... I so want us to be together but a part of me keeps thinking that being married didn't make my dad stay." She bent down to retrieve her handbag to search for her mobile phone; looking at the screen it showed Dirk's missed call. "Oh God, Sophia. Dirk tried to reach me on the way to the airport and I completely forgot to ring him back."

"Don't be so hard on yourself! I'm sure he understands this meeting is a big deal to you," said Sophia, her voice was so full of understanding it made Grace relax. "Now didn't you say you needed to relook at your presentation?"

"Absolutely, and thanks, Sophia," she said as she began to set up her laptop.

Grace was so grateful that Sophia hadn't started to dish out advice or push her for more information. She hadn't even seemed to judge her. The world hadn't stopped turning now that she had actually said how she felt. Working took her mind off everything and she became so engrossed that the time slipped away. Meanwhile, Sophia had begun to read her book.

Thirty minutes or so later Grace noticed Sophia was fast asleep with her half-moon reading glasses perched on her nose. Her perfectly cut and coloured honey blonde bob drew attention to high cheek bones. It was hard to tell how old she was – mid-fifties maybe. But her eyes were her best feature. They were so full of genuine interest. She had a way of extracting information at a great rate but told nothing about herself. A nagging suspicion that something awful had happened to her wouldn't go away.

Shutting down her laptop, Grace's thoughts drifted back to the more important task at hand. "If it's to be it's up to me" ran the little mantra in her head again.

When the flight landed they walked together to the baggage claim area.

"I only have carry-on luggage so I'd better get a move on. Well, it's been lovely meeting you Sophia. Take good care," said Grace.

"Oh no, you don't, young lady. How do you plan on getting to your meeting?"

"A taxi, of course!"

"You're in my town now and I plan to get you to that meeting with time to spare."

"No really Sophia, I'll be fine. I'm going to the ladies, to freshen up. I won't inconvenience you."

"You are already by objecting. Now off you go and I'll meet you over there," she said, pointing towards a seat opposite the baggage carousel.

"Ah, thanks a million Sophia. I won't be long."

Ten minutes later Sophia watched as Grace made her way through the crowds. Because of the importance of the meeting she was about to attend, Sophia had steered her away from talking about the dilemma Grace was in. She had been so touched by her. Of course she'd have commitment issues. Who could blame her?

She noted Grace's change of clothes. She wore a light pink, silk blouse which softened the sophisticated look of her beautifully tailored, high-waisted grey skirt. Her shoulder length blonde hair was newly brushed and tied in a knot at the nape of her slender neck and her full lips had been given a fresh gloss. Sophia noted the admiring glances Grace received, yet she seemed completely unaware of the attention.

"You look stylish with an edge of sexy," remarked Sophia as they made their way to the arrivals hall.

"I should hang around with you more often. You're great for a girl's ego," laughed Grace.

Moments later a perfectly dressed chauffeur greeted Sophia.

"Good afternoon Mrs Wynthrope. I hope you had a pleasant flight," said the driver, tucking his cap under his arm.

"Yes thank you, George. It was made all the more pleasant by my young travelling companion," she replied, taking Grace by the arm.

"Ladies, you won't mind waiting a moment while I drive the limousine around to meet you."

Sophia could see that Grace was struggling to be cool and not ask any questions. Minutes later George opened the trunk and placed Grace's small overnight bag along with Sophia's set of Louis Vuittons inside.

"Okay, I give up," declared Grace, putting her hands up in the air. Sophia laughed as Grace sat into the limo. It had cream leather seats and thick, dark carpet underfoot. There was a TV monitor and a drinks cabinet.

"So what are you thinking?"

"That this could only happen in America and I'm impressed."

"Not half as much as you have impressed me!"

Grace felt the colour rise in her cheeks. It had to be a record-breaking day for blushing, she thought. "I did go on a bit. Maybe I needed to talk to a stranger today. I'm glad we met and thank you for the 'ride' as you Americans call it."

They arrived at the skyscraper housing the headquarters of Pal Pacific.

"Let's keep in touch. I'd like to hear how your meeting goes. Here's my card. Have you got one?"

"Of course," Grace took a card from her purse and handed it to Sophia.

"Thank you, Grace Fitzgerald, for reminding me of how it felt starting out in business."

"And thank you for making the journey feel so short. I didn't have time to feel nervous. My stomach is doing somersaults at the moment."

Sophia smiled and said in her terrible impression of an Irish accent. "May the luck of the Irish go with ya!"

"Ah Sophia, if you insist on doing the accent, will you for God's sake practise it!"

Sophia burst out laughing. "I'm being nice to you and that's the thanks I get."

Grace laughed and declared, "Do you know it's been a pleasure meeting you, Sophia?"

Then Sophia reached over and gave Grace a quick hug and wished her luck again.

Moments later the sleek black limousine rejoined the New York traffic.

Sophia entered her penthouse building on Park Avenue.

"Welcome back, Mrs Wynthrope. It's so good to see you," said Tyler, the doorman. He had been working in the building since the year after they'd bought in. Twenty-six years ago.

"Thank you, Tyler, and I hope your grandson's christening went well."

"It was a great success and my daughter-in-law was so pleased with your gift. You really shouldn't have," he smiled. His kindness to her could never be repaid. It was the small things that you remember when your life falls apart. Tyler's genuine sincerity had shone through when she had most needed it.

"It was just a small token. I'm glad she liked it," she answered, getting into the lift.

Moments later she alighted at the top floor. She opened the door and walked into the beautifully furnished penthouse. As always her eyes fell upon the antique Chinese marble-topped hall table which she had been admiring when Bill had first approached her forty years ago. As she stroked her fingers along the pink-hued marble she could hear his voice in her head as though it were yesterday.

"It's sold. But if you want to see it again you can always come visit," he had said.

"And who would have thought a man so arrogant could have such good taste," she had retorted and had walked straight out of the antique shop onto Warren Street. He had followed her, smiling and saying, "I meant my *mother's* house."

"You don't even know my name and you expect me to meet your mother," she had replied, really enjoying his crazy sense of humour.

"We might as well get straight to it because it's gonna happen sooner or later. I'm William Wynthrope Junior."

"I'm Sophia Campolo and I don't date strangers." She had continued walking up the street smiling as he called after her.

"We'll meet again Sophia. I just know it. Arrivederci."

The tears trickled down her cheeks as she remembered those words. He had kept his promise. It had taken a massive heart attack to part them. No chance to say "Arrivederci" ever again. The cold feeling of the marble seemed to travel up her arm and enclose her heart. Ten months, three weeks and four days and the hollow, empty feelings were as strong as ever. Some days she wondered why she bothered to get out of bed. Going to Ireland had been a flight of fancy. They had always talked about buying a place there. Part of her had still wanted to, but when it came to signing the contract she hadn't been able to do it. Her loneliness had been too overwhelming.

She picked up her cell phone and pressed Richard's number. It went straight to voice mail. Her only child was a busy man running Wynthrope Communication Inc., the company she and Bill had built together. Bill had had the finance and business acumen while she had had the vision and passion. Her plane journey had awakened her a little. Listening to the young Irish girl so full of enthusiasm had been a breath of fresh air. She really hoped Grace's meeting went well. She had surprised herself by asking for Grace's card. It had been a long time since she had been genuinely interested in anything or anyone.

Grace took a deep breath and then pushed the heavy glass door open.

An hour later she emerged onto the sidewalk punching the air with excitement. A man in a business suit commented, "I'm glad someone is having a good day."

"The best," she said as he returned her smile. She rang Dirk. He answered on the fifth ring.

"Hello," he said in a preoccupied tone. It was ten-thirty in the evening in Ireland and she knew he was busy with a wedding party at The Meadows Country Club he managed.

"Oh Dirk, can you believe it! The cruise company's on-shore team were so happy with the range of excursions I offered they're prepared to sign for two years. They've heard …"

"Listen that all sounds great but I have to go. You know how it is around here."

"Okay …"

"Bye," he said, clicking off before she had time to reply. She stood looking at the phone. Talk about bursting her bubble. He knew how much it meant to her – why couldn't he be genuinely glad for her? Okay, she should have called him back earlier but to hell with him, she thought scrolling to look for Eoghan's number. "Eoghan, that was fantastic. Thank God for technology. You were great at answering all their queries."

"No, Grace, it was you. They really bought into the picture you painted of Ireland. We have so much to offer and you presented it well. So take a bow, I'm so proud of you. Let's keep it small and tight, Grace, overheads at a minimum."

"I know, Eoghan, but …" she answered.

"No buts, Grace. We have to be realistic."

"Okay, okay, but I'm going to celebrate tonight."

"God help Manhattan with you and the mad Lisa. You can charge it to me," he laughed.

"Hey, I bet you're going out on the town too."

"Sure am girly. I'll be heading down to Nutties in a few minutes – 'tis a far cry from Manhattan."

"Don't going buying a round on me!" she laughed, clicking off. She was so glad to have her old school-friend to celebrate with. A part of her wanted to ring Sophia but … it might be a tad forward of her, maybe Sophia was just being polite.

Chapter Two

*A*nybody home?" called Grace, stepping over mucky riding boots abandoned at the back door of Jessie's cottage on the outskirts of Bayrush. There was no answer.

She placed the kettle on the range, which Jessie never turned off no matter what the season, and wandered out the back door. As she crossed the cobbled courtyard, the morning sun broke through the oak trees beyond the stables, which were built with the same old stone as the cottage. The yard was well washed down and the air smelt of horses and leather where Monique and a few others were oiling their saddles and tack.

"Hi girls, have you seen Jessie this morning?"

"Yes, she's giving a lesson in the sand arena and Kate is here too. She brought a group out on the trek about an hour ago," said Monique.

"It's a perfect day for it. Is it mucky by the sand arena?"

"No, the weather has been great while you were away. Hey Gracey, I love your sandals!"

"Yeah so do I!" laughed Grace. "And I don't want to get them ruined."

She had bought them on discount in Macy's, deciding she deserved a treat. Around the corner Jessie was instructing a group of children including her son, Sam. Beside the arena horses grazed in the meadow as sunlight sparkled off the lake beyond. Grace could see the mountains far off in the distance, an iridescent mixture of greys, browns and greens. God, she never tired of this view.

"Hey Gracey, wouldn't you think after all these years you'd know what to wear coming to see us. Loving them though," said Jessie, looking towards her feet.

"I'm a townie and you're never gonna change me," Grace laughed, pleased to see Jessie looking so well.

"And I wouldn't want to. I'm nearly finished here."

Grace leaned against the stud fencing and watched the kids. Sam was riding a grey pony and jumping him very well. He was so like Jessie with his dark red, curly hair and his mother's cheeky grin. Grace smiled, remembering the old days, when Jessie's smile had got them out of trouble more times than she could count.

Fifteen minutes later the riders finished and began to take off the tack.

"Oh Jess I hope I haven't burnt the ass out of your kettle," said Grace running back towards the house.

"Sure it won't be the first time," Jessie called after her as she helped one of the kids with her pony. When Jessie arrived in the kitchen Grace was already filling two mugs. "Now tell me about the scan. I can't wait to see the print-out."

"Oh Grace, the bloody thing broke down just as we were about to go in."

"Ah Jess."

"I tried so hard to hide my disappointment. I'm so worried Gracey. What if it happens again?"

"It won't Jess," said Grace, covering Jessie's hand with her own. "You have to think positively. This is the best news. It's so exciting that Sam will be getting a brother or sister."

Jessie smiled gratefully. "Thanks for the reassurance. I've spent the past few days pretending not to be worried for Geoff and Sam's sake. But … ah … sometimes it gets a bit overwhelming. Anyway it doesn't help that as my pregnancy progresses Geoff is going to be under more pressure."

"Are things bad?"

"Numbers are falling. Horse-riding is a luxury Grace. We have to watch every penny. Ah look, I'm not complaining. Aren't we blessed?" She smiled, rubbing her tummy. "Anyway we have another appointment on Wednesday. So … my high-flying friend. Did you nail another contract or what?"

Understanding that Jessie wanted to change the subject, Grace launched into her story. "Oh Jess, it was fantastic. Pal Pacific owns a couple of lines, one is called Silver Blue Cruises and they have signed to dock three times both next year and the year after. Their sister company Platinum Lines is planning to make two visits over the next two years. The good news for us is that P.L. owns one of the largest cruise ships in the world. It's called 'The Traveller' and it carries 3500 passengers and 1700 crew. Imagine Jess, nearly a crew member for every two passengers, what luxury!"

"And Gracey, you are going to organise day trips for that amount of people?" Jessie asked incredulously.

"And why not? Haven't I been doing it already on a smaller scale?"

"But it will be the biggest one ever to dock here!"

"Yes, it sure will be, so I'll need all the support I can get from coach companies, restaurants, golf courses, tourist attractions and of course, the Port Authority. This will bring plenty of revenue to the area. The cruise passengers are good spenders. It's a great opportunity to build a bigger profile for the business."

"God, I never appreciated how much was involved. Will you be able to hire Kate full-time now?"

"Oh Jess I'm excited and disappointed at the same time. Eoghan says we have to keep costs down but I am hoping I can change his mind about taking on Kate."

"I wish her past wasn't such a block to her moving on. She's been clean for how long now?"

"Coming up to four years but because her problem started at sixteen and she has a gaping hole in her CV, living in a small town … well, it's hard to hide your past."

"How is a person supposed to change their life if everybody continues to harp backwards?"

Grace stared into the coffee cup and began swirling the remains around. "It's thanks to you that she's involved with horses. It gave her focus when she badly needed it, and you accepted her back every time she fell off the wagon. I'll never be able to repay you."

"We're friends Gracey, that's what we do. None of us is perfect, as you always say, 'shit happens', all we can do is be here for one another. I'd love Kate to follow her creative side. She's brilliant at art but has no self-belief."

"That's so true. She was just eight when Dad left. Being the youngest he had doted on her. Who knows why or how it happened to her? Lots of people experiment with drugs and don't become addicts. Sometimes I feel like screaming. I suppose I blame Dad, he was an addict to the drink. Ah look, let's not go there today."

"How's Dirk?" asked Jessie, topping up Grace's mug with coffee.

"He's still a bit cool."

"I suppose he's wondering are you ever going to set a date."

"I think you might be right. I'm not being fair to him. God Jessie, I do love him …"

Jessie's green eyes were looking straight into hers.

"Hello the house!" said Kate, taking her riding boots off at the back door. "Well sis, I saw your car outside. Isn't she some woman, Jess?"

"She is," said Jessie. Grace looked at Jessie and smiled. She was glad Kate hadn't arrived earlier and happy for the interruption.

"And the stupid ultrasound machine broke just when Jessie was about to climb aboard," smiled Kate.

"Jessie just told me. Bummer or what!"

"Ah look, it'll be all grand," said Jessie. "Have you decided to jump Kelpie at the show tomorrow?"

Whenever Jessie and Kate got together the subject turned to horses. Grace was relieved the focus was away from her. Later all three of them wandered back out to the busy yard. Geoff and Sam arrived in the tractor.

"Hey Gracey, do you want to see the new foal down in the well field?" asked Sam.

"I'd love a spin. But I'm not exactly dressed for it!"

"Yeah, Dad. Can Grace have a turn?" asked Sam, completely missing the point.

"She's great with kids," remarked Kate, watching as her sister climbed awkwardly aboard the tractor.

"She sure is! Only I wish she could see it too," muttered Jessie wistfully.

Jack's mother had left earlier for a night away with her bridge club. For the past few days she had been fussing over him and had even suggested cancelling her night away. He had insisted she go, happy to be alone. He took the stairs two at a time and smiled at the fact his mother still hadn't taken his Liverpool FC posters from his bedroom wall. He searched his old CD collection and picked U2's *The Unforgettable Fire* album, turning it over to read through the playlist. The first song was "A Sort of Homecoming". Perfect, he thought. He hadn't been able to sleep when he had heard about Lynda's betrayal. Three months of anger and frustration at her for leaving him for a man old enough to be her father. But since coming home he had slept like a baby. He heard his mobile and ran back downstairs, but it rang out. It was Conor; he'd ring him back later.

He opened the fridge and got himself a beer and popped the CD into the player. He turned it up loud and continued out through the French doors to the patio. Sitting on a white, cast-iron chair he lit a Marlboro. A habit he had picked up again recently. It felt so good to be away from the incessant heat of Dubai. Making rings with smoke he let his mind wander to the memories of ten days he had spent with Grace Fitzgerald when he was twenty years old.

He had been walking across the fields one evening with Benji, his springer spaniel, on his way to catch a bay mare. That particular evening he had been glad to get out because his father had just returned from another of his "benders".

Benji, his rabbit-mad dog, had found a young girl instead. She had been sitting high on a rock surrounded by gorse and heather. When he had climbed up he noticed that she had been crying and she hid it by being full of attitude. He had liked her immediately. There was a sense of sadness about her that he could empathise with.

Over the following days they became friends; he had taught her how to drive a tractor, cut corn, and ride a horse. Finally on the last day she had confided in him that the reason she'd been upset that first day was because her father had left home. She had thanked Jack for keeping her busy, because although the family had been through so much because of her father's drinking, she still loved him. Jack had understood and had confided in her about his own dad. Although he couldn't say he felt anything but resentment towards his father.

At barely sixteen to his twenty, he hadn't seen Grace as anything more until the moment it came to saying goodbye. She had kissed him briefly on the lips and had run down the road calling back, "Have a great life, Jack Leslie."

And that was when he had known she'd always have a place in his heart.

He had had big plans back then and he had fulfilled those ambitions but at what cost he wondered? His mobile rang. It was Conor again asking him over to his house for a bite to eat.

"Sounds good, I'll walk across the field to you. I fancy a few beers tonight, are you on?"

"Count me in," said Conor.

Thankfully they could enjoy a few drinks without it being a problem. It was something that both of them were painfully aware of; neither had inherited their father's gene for alcohol. Strolling across the fields he thought of Sunny Rock, the name they had given the place he and Grace had first met. It was long gone; the land had been developed for housing.

Maybe he'd ask Conor about Grace? He or Marie his wife might have crossed paths with her over the years. The thought of seeing her again lightened his mood.

Later that evening Jessie sat in the living room reading *Horse and Hound* with her feet perched on a pouffe. She looked up when Geoff arrived in. "Grace was in good form today. How did her meeting go in New York?" asked Geoff, dropping into his recliner where he began to flick through *The Racing Post*.

"Really well, the company committed to two seasons. She's thrilled about it but I'm afraid I ruined it by talking about settling down."

"Ah Jess."

"I know. It's just that I worry about her that's all." She sighed. "Life is short, Geoff. I wish ... Oh I don't know. I wish she'd see ..."

"See what?"

"I don't want her to waste her life if he's not 'the one'. I just want her to be happy ..."

"She is. It's not your version of happy, honey. Everyone is different. The business is her baby. Now do you fancy a cup of tea? You look tired."

"Yeah I am. That'd be lovely, thanks."

He came over, bent down and dropped a kiss on her head.

"Don't worry so much. Do me a favour and take it easy tomorrow. You can watch. Let the lads take some responsibility. You need to take it easy."

"I will."

Grace parked in the drive of their two-storey, red-brick townhouse. Dirk's car wasn't in the drive. She had managed to get out of going to the regatta with him earlier. She found it boring to watch people rowing up and down the river and she wasn't in the mood to listen to Dirk regaling his buddies with his stories in the clubhouse tonight.

He had sent her a text to meet him there but she had replied that she was jetlagged. She knew he'd be disappointed but he'd get over it. She opened the yellow front door and was met with the sight of her carry-on bag. She had been so keen to share her news with Jessie she hadn't bothered to unpack it earlier which was so unlike her. She brought it to the utility room where she put on a colour wash.

The house was so quiet after the hustle and bustle of Jessie's place. Grace had fallen in love with the house from the first moment she saw it and was grateful to spend her days working from one of the high-ceiling bedrooms which she had had converted into an office. At night it was especially beautiful when the Bayrush Castle lights reflected on the bay below.

When she finished putting the wash on she went back into the kitchen to switch on the kettle. Waiting for it to boil she realised she was standing on the very spot where Dirk had asked her to marry him for the first time. It was the evening they'd got the keys of their new house. She had brushed him off saying he was too young – being four years younger than her. She had joked that he'd only felt obliged to ask. He had laughed and agreed but she had seen the momentary hurt in his eyes before he had grabbed her and swung her around the empty kitchen, and planting her back on the ground he had added, "Whew, that saved us a few bob." She had laughed too loudly such was the relief. Seeing Jack Leslie or someone she imagined he would look like, twenty years on, had unsettled her. But Jack was married and Dirk wouldn't wait forever.

"Grow up, Grace," she muttered, opening the fridge door and pouring a glass of wine instead. She'd watch some TV; maybe it would take her mind off things.

"Any luck with the job hunting?" Conor asked, handing Jack a beer which he took, joining his sister-in-law in the living room.

"Yeah, actually. Remember George Brown? He was a few years ahead of me in college."

"Mmm, I think so."

"He set up a practice here a few years back. It's a mixed one, large and small animal." Jack could see the sceptical look on his brother's face but chose to ignore it. "He offered me maternity cover."

"Why, when are you due?"

"Very funny!"

"Don't mind your brother. I'm glad you're home, Jack. You've been away far too long and your mother is thrilled."

Conor threw his eyes to heaven. "Marie, he's one of the best vets on the horse racing circuit and he's going to be fixing cats, dogs and probably hamsters. Come on. Am I the only one wondering what exactly is going on here?"

"Conor, if Jack wants to come home for a while that's his choice."

"Hey guys, I'm actually here," laughed Jack. He knew his brother was just being concerned so instead of turning it into an argument, he changed the subject. "Anyway Marie, do you know Grace Fitzgerald? She might have gone to school with your sister Mairéad."

"I never heard Mairéad talking about a Grace." She took a sip from her wine glass. "Wait now, I've heard that name before. Isn't she the woman who brings in cruise liners to Bayrush."

"What? You have cruise liners coming in here!"

"Yeah, we're out of the ark," said Conor, still a bit disgruntled.

"Oh shut up, Conor," said Marie. "He's been like this for days. Just ignore him Jack. Anyway about Grace, yes, she's a real go-getter. I heard her being interviewed on the radio a few times. She really loves Bayrush and wants the best for the area. Isn't she right, we have so much to offer?"

Marie was on a roll talking about tourism so Jack sat back, listening. He really should tell Conor the truth about why he was back. He'd tell him tomorrow when they were alone. For now he wanted to find a way to contact Grace, so he asked, "What's the name of the business?"

"Is Grace with you?" Kate asked, coming up to the bar counter in Nutties where Dirk was chatting with Sandra Payne, a little too friendly for Kate's liking.

"No, she sent a text when I was at the clubhouse to say she was jetlagged."

"Oh! I thought she'd be out celebrating her incredible achievement. Landing a contract like that is just so wow."

"Yeah right, maybe she should get a real job. It's taking over her life. It's not like I can't afford to keep her." He smirked in the direction of Sandra, who was all ears and probably gloating on every word. Sandra had been in school with Grace and they had never seen eye to eye. Propping up the bar with Dirk at her side made for great gossip. As she walked away she could hear his sneering laugh as one of his friends called, "Ah come on Dirk, quit chatting up women. We're dying of thirst here."

"Ye lot would drink Ireland dry," he retorted. Kate knew by the sound of his voice he was well on and his veneer was down. He was Mr Bloody Charming around Grace and he even had their mother fooled, which was no mean achievement.

Grace made breakfast, which was Dirk's usual Sunday morning treat to her, but she had felt guilty for not meeting up with him last night. She brought the tray upstairs and laid it on the dresser. She could hear him singing in the shower, a habit she found endearing. She opened the shower door.

"And here's me thinking you were making breakfast," he smiled, holding out his hand as she stepped in to join him.

"Let's set a date," she said, wrapping her arms around his perfectly toned body.

"Well it's about time, woman. I was nearly giving up on us."

In his arms she could feel all her anxiety drain away. Jessie had been right.

In the early hours of Wednesday morning Jessie sat in the kitchen with Buzz, their old black Labrador, who was lying in his dog basket in front of the stove. She couldn't sleep because no matter how hard she tried her thoughts kept returning to that terrible time. Being pregnant with Sam had been so very different from this one. She had never once thought that she might lose him. Whereas now ... well ... "Stop," she said aloud and then remembered what Grace had said earlier: "Think positive." Making it to twelve weeks was a blessing; she had miscarried in the ninth week of her last pregnancy.

She got up from the kitchen table, touched her tummy and walked towards the patio doors. The sky was a vision of burnt orange mixed with purple hues and at its centre was a huge bright, yellowy, ball of fire. It felt almost like it was sending a message of hope and lightness to her soul. "Thank you," she muttered, and then sipped the last of her tea. She placed the cup in the dishwasher, patted Buzz who as usual hadn't moved an inch. His name so didn't suit him, she thought. Smiling, she went back to bed. Her sense of peace had been restored.

Dr Morrison moved the ultrasound across her bump. Jessie's eyes were glued to the screen but it was almost impossible to read it. She could hardly breathe in anticipation.

"Can you see here?" said Dr Morrison, pointing to a white blob. "This is the head and here is the rest of the body. And look here is another head ..."

"Oh my God, Geoff ..." said Jessie, shocked but thrilled too.

"Did I hear you right ...?" Geoff beamed, his eyes beginning to fill up. "How will we cope ... can you imagine Sam's face? This is the best news ever. Two for the price of one. I can hear the slagging already." He hugged her and shook hands with the doctor.

"Congratulations, I'm absolutely delighted for you both."

"Can we have some prints to show Sam? He'll be so pleased. Oh Geoff, can you imagine telling our parents? There'll be such excitement."

"I can't wait to tell everyone," said Geoff. His mobile rang so he excused himself while Jessie got dressed. "Hi Monique, is everything okay?"

"Geoff, Beauty is acting a bit strange. She's lying down in her stable. She has a temperature and I can't get her to stand up."

"I'm on my way." He clicked off. Jessie opened the door and both of them thanked the doctor again. Walking along the corridor Geoff filled her in about Beauty. "Let's hold the news until we've sorted this out eh?"

Twenty-five minutes later back at the yard Geoff rang the vet's office.

"Hi Aoife, do you have any vets working in our area at the moment?"

"We have a new guy on the team and he's not far from your place. He specialises in horses."

"Good, as I have an awful feeling the horse has colic."

Geoff had managed to get Beauty up and was walking her around the yard when a silver jeep arrived. Jessie, Monique and a few of the livery owners were all gathered near Beauty's stable door when the vet climbed out of the jeep and strode towards Geoff.

"Jezz, who's he?" asked one of the ladies gathered. There were mumblings; nobody seemed to know. Jessie saw him shaking hands with Geoff and heard him saying "John Leslie, but most people call me Jack." I'm sure they do, she thought and a lot of other things with it. The guy was tall and broad shouldered with slightly long, curly brown hair and eyes a woman could get lost in. He had an air of a man who was sure of himself but didn't flaunt it. From the growing interest around the place she wasn't the only one who thought so. Geoff led Beauty into the stable and Jack followed.

Five minutes later, Jessie heard a car door close and saw Grace walking across the yard just as Monique was diplomatically trying to get everybody to go back to what they were doing.

"Is everything okay, Jessie?" Grace called, concerned by all the activity.

"I hope so. Geoff had to call the vet for Beauty. They're in the stable and he's doing some tests on her. We think it's colic."

"What is that?" asked Grace.

"An infection in the abdomen. If it's serious it may require surgery."

Grace, Jessie and Monique peered over the stable door.

Just then Jack stood up, and turning towards them, he spoke with Geoff. "Yes, you were right. It's colic. I'll give her some painkillers and I may have to lubricate the tract. It's best to keep an eye on her through the night and I'll call again tomorrow. Hopefully there won't be any further complications."

"Thanks, Jack," said Geoff. Jessie was relieved. With the proper care and attention colic could be treated. She was so busy listening that she hadn't noticed Grace had turned away and was walking back towards her car. "Hey, Grace where are you going?"

"My phone is ringing."

"Jeez, she's obsessed with that phone. God bless her hearing because I can't hear it. Can you?" she asked Monique, who laughed and said, "When the vet is finished I'll walk Beauty around the yard again. You go and have a cuppa. I just heard Geoff offering the cute guy one."

"He is way too old for you, my girl. I'll tell your Gran." Jessie laughed as Monique went in search of a lead rope, calling back, "You'd never tell on me."

"Want to bet. Grace, are you coming in for a coffee?" Jessie called across the yard.

"No, I have to go."

"But you only just got here!"

"That was Dirk. We have to be in Butlers by seven. They're having a barbeque. I forgot about it. I'll catch you tomorrow I promise."

"Okay, see you tomorrow," said Jessie, but she was sorely disappointed as it would have been the ideal opportunity to tell Grace about the twins face to face. Ah well, she thought.

As Grace reversed out of the yard she saw him again in the rear-view mirror walking beside Geoff towards the house. When she was halfway down Jessie's avenue she had to pull over. She thought she was going to pass out. She actually had to tell herself to breathe. She'd never had a panic attack in her life but she figured it must be like this. It was crazy. How could a man have such an effect on her?

She had nearly done herself an injury the last time and that was only because she had thought she'd seen him and now that he was actually here she might just about die from lack of oxygen. "Get a grip, Grace," she said. "Flip, if Jessie looks out and sees the car, she'll surely call me back." She put the car into gear and pressed the accelerator so hard she skidded. "Now I'm going to kill myself in a car crash. Oh God get me out of here." She drove towards Bayrush beach.

It was six-thirty in the evening and the weather was so good the beach was still buzzing. Bayrush beach was so wide and long that even on a busy day its expanse allowed freedom to be alone. Grace locked the car. Her hands were still trembling. Actually all of her was as she headed towards the sand dunes. Glad of the slight breeze on her face, she could see surfers and kite-surfers in the distance.

Had Jack remembered their time together? That summer twenty years ago had been horrendous. Her father had left her mother a note on the kitchen table and had never returned. Jessie had been at Irish college and she had been so lonely. She had spent most of her time trespassing on the local farmer's land and had been in constant fear of being caught. But when she had eventually been found it had been the best thing that had ever happened in her short life. From the moment she laid eyes on Jack Leslie she was in love.

Being four years older than her and in college he had shown zero interest in her but it hadn't stopped her from dreaming. Instead they had become unlikely friends, spending the last ten days of the summer holidays hanging out together. He had even taught her how to drive a tractor. Meeting Jack had distracted her from the nightmare that summer had become. On their last day together she had confided in him about her dad's drinking and how he had left. She hadn't added how much hanging out with him during that awful time had meant to her. She had thrown caution to the wind by kissing him that last day and she had never regretted it. He was most definitely her first true love. Her most treasured possession from that time were the photographs they had taken in a photo booth. They had split them. She wondered if he had kept his two.

She stopped and looked out towards the sea. She could see a ship on the horizon and thought for a moment. Our ship has sailed Jack, you're a married man and it's time I let you go. Dirk is my future.

She had never told Jessie about Jack because that summer Jessie had met Geoff at Irish college and Jess had been so full up on love that Grace's story didn't compare. What was there to tell? Jack didn't think about her in that way and he had had big plans back then. Bayrush had been too small for him.

Grace pressed Jessie's number. "Hey Jess I'm so sorry for not asking about the scan. There was so much going on when I called." In more ways than one, she thought. "What ...? Twins! Oh my God. That's fantastic. Oh Jessie ... that's the best news ever. I'm on my way back. What barbeque? Oh that. Eh ... I'm on my way ..." She hung up and began running back up the beach. She'd even lied to her best friend in all her fluster. Twins! That was the best news ever! She couldn't wait to see the printout. "Oh wow," she shouted as she ran, giving a jump for joy. She must look a right eejit but she didn't care.

Chapter Three

I'm so happy it is August bank holiday weekend," said Grace, just as Jessie's back door opened.

"Not saying anything, Jess. But you're huge," said Kate, taking her riding boots off in the back porch.

"Well don't hold back Kate!" laughed Grace, from the kitchen table where Jessie had laid out a lovely lunch for them.

"I'm twenty weeks pregnant and you're not getting anything to eat after saying that," said Jessie, pretending to be put out but delighted. Her last visit to the GP had gone well.

"Ah you know I don't mean it in a bad way. It is twins, so you're bound to be big!"

"Quit while you're ahead eh, Kate!" laughed Grace, reaching for the salad bowl. "The time is flying along. Imagine you're halfway there now!"

"Speaking of time flying. Any word from Donal – is his band available for Grace's wedding?" said Jessie.

"Actually he rang last night. They're going on tour but will be back in Ireland around the end of May."

"Are you sure he's okay about playing at a wedding? I mean the band is beginning to make a name!" asked Jessie.

"It's for my sister! Of course he'll do it," laughed Kate, putting a great big lump of ham into a blaa, and taking a big bite out of it.

"Kate, you couldn't be any sloppier. Look at you, you've got flour all around your mouth," said Grace, handing her some kitchen roll. "What are you like!"

"I'm in a rush."

Listening to the sisters' banter, Jessie couldn't help thinking how uninterested Grace was in any element of her wedding.

Kate put her riding boots back on in the back porch and said, "Have things to do and people to see, bye girls."

"Thanks, Kate," Jessie called after her.

"You're welcome, Jess! Sure, aren't I having a great time chatting with the tourists and taking in the views?"

"And you're getting paid for that?" laughed Grace. "She'll never do a day's work for me again Jess." Jessie could hear Kate laughing as the door closed and Grace rejoined her at the table.

"I'd be lost without her," she said seriously to Grace. "And she won't take any money."

"She's great Jess, but it's also her way of helping you just like you were there to support her," said Grace, with eyes filled with concern.

"I just can't manage the physical work. The sciatic pain is unbearable at times. But enough about me, how are you doing?"

"Busy, but it's how I like things to be."

"I didn't mean work, Grace."

"I know you didn't." Grace averted her gaze. But Jessie continued.

"Are you really sure … about the wedding?" The moment Jessie asked, Grace got up and put her mug in the dishwasher.

"Yes, I am, Jess."

"Okay … I'm sorry I asked."

Grace walked behind Jessie's kitchen chair and put her arms around her and said, "You only asked because you love me, I know that. See you tomorrow and let me know how the twenty-week scan goes."

"Will do," said Jessie, feeling guilty for questioning her.

As Grace walked across Jessie's yard, a silver jeep pulled into the vacant place beside her car. *Oh my God*; her heart began to pound – it was Jack Leslie. He got out of the jeep and with a big smile on his face he walked towards her.

"Well if it isn't Grace Fitzgerald," he said, his grey-green eyes sparkling in the sunlight. Never caught for words, she was completely overwhelmed by the force of his presence. She moved slightly towards him and he seemed to think she had intended to kiss him in greeting. They kind of bumped off one another and then both laughed, embarrassed by it all. "Jack, err, emm. It's good to see you," she managed to say.

"And you." She noticed he was looking at her left hand. She twiddled her ring with her fingers and dropped it out of sight.

"You're engaged, congrats. Who's the lucky man?" he asked. She thought or maybe she wished she could see a hint of regret on his face. No it was only her imagination. How could there be? He was married. She was engaged, what was she playing at?

"Dirk Fleischer, he's not originally from here."

"I could have guessed with a name like that." He laughed and the lines around his eyes crinkled just like she remembered, making him even more handsome. There was still a sureness about him that had always attracted her. She immediately felt protected even though the last feeling he provoked in her was safety. None of it made sense to her. She just had to get away. He being a memory was one thing, but not this. "Well, eh. It's been lovely to see you. Take care." She sounded so formal even to her own ears.

"You too," he said.

Getting into her car she noticed he hadn't moved and in her fluster she couldn't start the car. He walked towards it.

"Shit," she muttered but thankfully it started on her second attempt. She gave a wave through the window and drove away at speed, leaving a cloud of dust behind her, so much so she could only barely make him out in the rear-view mirror. She hit a pothole and nearly lost control. "Slow down, you big eejit." Oh God this can't be normal, she thought. He's just a man. Oh but what a man!

Jack watched her drive away in her silver Golf convertible. God, he thought, she was even more beautiful than he'd remembered. He'd been home nine weeks and hadn't tried to contact her. He had heard she was engaged. But seeing her he couldn't believe the effect she had on him. He actually couldn't stop looking at the car as she drove away. She'd think he was some kind of weirdo staring after it. "Get a grip," he muttered.

"Hey Jack," called Geoff, coming out of the American barn. "We're just about to tack up."

"I'm looking forward to this. It's been a while since I rode out."

"You'll have aches and pains tomorrow so," laughed Geoff. "This is Jay, he's coming with us."

"How's it goin?" the young lad said, continuing to tack up.

"Jay's got his amateur jockey's licence recently. He's some man at the point-to-points."

"What am I letting myself in for?" laughed Jack.

"Ah we'll go easy on you, won't we Jay!" said Geoff, slapping him on the back. The young lad smiled.

At nine-fifteen on Monday morning, Geoff helped Jessie as she wiggled her way into the jeep.

"They're going to be fine strapping babies," he joked.

"And this is you being supportive. I'm so big now I'd give the Michelin man a run for his money. I'm so looking forward to the twenty-week scan. The babies will be much clearer on it," said Jessie, beaming.

Thirty minutes later, Geoff pulled into the drop-off point at the hospital entrance. "Save you walking from the car park, pet." He smiled as he ran around the jeep to help her out.

"Thanks, Geoff," she said. As the pregnancy progressed her sciatic pain was getting worse. She did her best not to complain, she was so grateful to be pregnant. It was a small price to pay. Sitting in the lobby, she watched the comings and goings of people. She noticed a group of people gathered who seemed to have been given bad news, God love them, she thought as Geoff arrived. "Are you okay, honey?" he asked. But rather than explain what she had noticed, she said, "Ah, it's just my sciatica acting up again."

"We'll take our time," said Geoff kindly.

They walked through the maze of corridors to the outpatients' clinic. Eventually her name was called. She lay down on the plinth and the nurse spread the gooey stuff and then her two beautiful babies appeared, clearly visible on the monitor.

"It's fascinating," said Geoff, beaming.

"Yes, babies are little miracles. They are so clear and so easy to see," the nurse remarked. Dr Morrison began to take measurements. Suddenly there was a palpable tension in the room. Jessie wondered was she imagining it. Everything was going to be fine, wasn't it?

He asked them to go across the hall to another room. He said he'd be with them shortly. A few minutes later the door opened and when she saw the doctor's ashen face she knew there was something seriously wrong. He sat in the chair opposite them and began to speak. "I'm sorry," he paused. Then he spoke again. "Your babies are doing fine but unfortunately your placenta is creating too much water. This could bring on premature labour. Hydropic pregnancy is a rare condition, but can occur in twin pregnancy. It is happening early in your pregnancy. It may or may not stop."

Jessie looked at Geoff who was staring at the doctor in disbelief. She wondered had she heard him properly. What was he saying? What did he mean? The babies were fine, she had just seen them and she felt them moving all the time. What was he talking about?

"Can't we do something?" she whispered. "Surely, I ... can *do* something. My babies are fine you said. I will take it easier. Please tell me what I can do to make it stop?"

"I'm sorry. It is just one of those things. It may or may not stop," the doctor repeated. "There is nothing we can do this early in the pregnancy.

I have to be truthful with you … if I were a gambling man the odds are stacked very gravely against you."

"What are they, Doctor?" Geoff asked.

"Ninety-nine per cent against," answered the doctor, shifting uncomfortabley in his chair as he spoke. She looked at Geoff. She could see her own pain reflected on his face.

"Well," she said, her voice filled with desperation. "You did say there is a one per cent chance. We'll take those odds, won't we, Geoff?" Geoff just nodded his head.

"Rest and do as little as possible, and call me if you have any unusual pain. I'm always here for you," advised Dr Morrison as he walked them to the door. She linked Geoff because her legs had turned to jelly and she was afraid she'd fall to the floor. How could this be happening to them? It wasn't until she eventually sat into the jeep that the full impact of what the doctor had said hit her.

She wouldn't cry because that would be giving up and as long as she had her babies she'd never give up. "It's okay, Geoff, it's going to stop. I know it. Why would God give us two babies when we thought we were only having one? He won't take them, Geoff. It's just not going to happen."

Geoff sat frozen in the driver's seat. He said nothing at all and then he took her hand in his and squeezed it gently. Moments later he started the jeep.

"Let's not tell anyone about this because they'll just worry, okay," she said, trying desperately not to cry.

"Okay," he replied.

Later that evening when Geoff and Sam were in the living room watching TV Jessie went to her bedroom. Lying on the bed her mobile phone kept ringing so she turned it to silent.

She had thought getting past twelve weeks was all that she'd had to worry about and now this. It was so unfair. She couldn't answer the texts or calls. What could she say? The scan went great – that would be a lie. But she'd be damned before she'd tell anyone, not even Grace, what the doctor had said. She turned her face into the pillow to bury the sound of the sobs that racked her body. How could this be happening? Why, God? Why me? She thought it was so unfair.

Four weeks later, Grace woke to the sound of Dirk walking into the bedroom with a tray laden with freshly squeezed orange juice, coffee buttered hot croissants with the Sunday papers tucked under his arm. "Wakey, wakey!"

Grace smiled up at him. God, she thought, he was good-looking, with his broad shoulders, blond hair and sallow skin inherited from his German father and the most piercing blue eyes. She had been right to set a date. They lazed on the bed munching and sipping with the newspapers spread across it.

"I missed this last weekend when I was in Poole at the regatta."

Grace laughed. "Nothing to the hangover you don't miss. For a fit bunch of lads into rowing they sure know how to drink."

Dirk just smiled. "I'm glad you don't make a big deal about me going away with the lads. Some of the women go crazy. I hope you're not going to change when we get married."

"Dirk, I have no intention of being joined at the hip by a ring. Thank you very much."

"Good," he said, stretching over to kiss her.

"The summer seems to have flown by. It's hard to believe we're in the middle of August already. Hey Dirk, remember I told you I met an American lady on the aeroplane back in June?"

"Yes," he said, flicking through the newspaper.

"She's coming here on Friday. I've booked her in to The Meadows."

"I'll sort out an upgrade, eh!" he said, absently. "Hey, I forgot to tell you I arranged for us to go kayaking with Paul and Anna today."

"Ah Dirk, I'm wrecked. Why didn't you ask me first?"

"Because I knew you'd say that. Anyway as you've just said the summer is nearly over. We have to make the most of the good weather. Ah come on, Grace, we'll have some fun. Get ready, they'll be along in fifteen minutes." He laughed, hopping up and going into the bathroom.

"You're such a plonker!"

"I heard that." He laughed again from inside the bathroom. She smiled. Life was never dull around Dirk.

"This is absolutely fabulous," said Grace as a school of dolphins splashed and played right up close to her kayak. It was one of the most exhilarating experiences of her life although terrifying too because she was so afraid of capsizing.

"I knew you'd love it!" said Dirk, paddling up beside her. His blond hair fell into his eyes and he flicked his head back to clear his vision. He could so easily have been a model. Sometimes she wondered what he saw in her. She was four years older and not bad looking but he could have had anyone and yet he had chosen her. He leaned towards her and managed to plant a kiss on her lips.

"Hey, get a room," a voice called from a passing fishing boat. They all laughed.

As they paddled back towards the beach passing the pier she heard someone call the name Jack. Startled by the effect the name alone had on her, when she realised it was actually Jack Leslie, she nearly capsized. He was standing high up on the storm wall. A group of teenagers were joking and laughing up at him. What the hell was he doing up there, she thought? There was a young blonde girl in a bikini shouting up, "Don't do it Jack!"

She stopped paddling and Dirk nearly crashed into her. "Grace, sorry about that but what did you stop for?"

"Hey Dirk, yer man is going to do a back flip. He's a bit long in the tooth for that," remarked Paul.

"He's not *that* old," she muttered, not realising she had said it out loud.

"Let's watch," said Anna. Grace was filled with concern. It was a long way down and she hoped he knew what he was doing. And who was the blonde girl, she wondered. His wife had had dark hair in the wedding photograph and she hadn't looked that much younger than him.

Grace watched as he walked to the edge and back-flipped off the pier, but there was no sign of him coming back up. Oh God, she thought, and then there was a burst of applause mixed with laughter from the crowd gathered.

"Nice one," said Paul as he and Anna continued to paddle towards the beach. Grace was all flustered and tried to organise her paddle.

"Ah come on Grace, you had it going perfectly. What's the matter?" asked Dirk.

Between the wetsuit, the life jacket and the paddle she felt like a drowned rat and she was exhausted. "Go ahead. Am I stopping you?" she said with more than a hint of irritation.

"Fine so," he said, paddling off after the others.

"Hi there …"

"What the …!" It was Jack treading the water beside her kayak, smiling up at her. It was the last thing she needed. "For God's sake Jack, are you crazy diving off that storm wall? Do you think you're twenty all over again?

"You'll never know how much I'd like to be twenty again." He grinned cheekily up at her. "Anyway, why are you so concerned?"

She gave him a withering look and tried desperately to make a decent exit. She said, "I'm not."

"Do you want a push?" he said, still treading the water.

"Don't you have somewhere to be?" she said, directing her gaze to the blonde bombshell on the pier who was waiting anxiously for him.

"See ya so," he said, gliding through the water like bloody Tarzan.

Meanwhile she felt like a big rubber blob with straw for hair plonked on a big piece of orange plastic. She paddled off with as much dignity as she could muster. She looked ridiculous while the blonde could have starred in Baywatch. Then she thought miserably, she probably wasn't even born when Baywatch was a hit.

Dirk came over to help her pull the kayak on to the beach while Paul chatted with a fisherman who offered them mackerel from his little gas stove. The man was waxing lyrical about the joys of the simple things in life.

"Do you know that guy?" whispered Dirk, standing right beside her as she listened to the fisherman. "Him?" she said, looking at the fisherman. "No."

Dirk looked at her questioningly and then walked over to the stove, saying, "They look lovely. I didn't realise how hungry I was. Can't beat exercise!"

She turned away and peeled off the top of the wetsuit, leaving it hanging around her waist. Why was she being so short with Dirk? She wasn't being fair. Earlier they had left their towels, clothes and a picnic in the boot of her car but now she just wanted to leave. But Dirk and the others were enjoying themselves. And the plan had been to spend the rest of day swimming and relaxing on the beach.

"I'm going to the car," she said to nobody in particular. They were all so busy chatting and tasting mackerel none of them took any notice. Looking towards where Jack and his friends were sitting she thought she had been so right to say yes to Dirk. Her memory of Jack was so far from how he was. He was such a huge flirt. Climbing the cliff-side steps to where the car was parked along the roadside, she glanced again in Jack's direction and noticed there was a dark-haired woman in the group as well. She must be his wife, she thought and just then Jack waved up at her, smiling. She tripped and with cheeks burning she managed to get up but didn't dare look back in his direction. She was absolutely mortified.

When she got to her car she took her mobile from the glove

compartment and checking it she thought just how much she'd love not to have to go back to the beach. But when she heard her voice mail, without a single thought she jumped into the driver's seat and drove away at speed.

Geoff had left a message to ask Grace to come urgently. Thankfully he had just hung up when Grace rang back to say she was on her way. He needed her to take care of Sam while he brought Jessie to the hospital. He told her Jessie was in unbearable pain and had had a bleed. She was so bloated she could hardly move.

Seven minutes later when Grace arrived at the cottage, Geoff was already helping Jessie into the jeep.

"Gracey, you look funny," said Sam, running towards her. She bent down on her knees with the wetsuit half-on-half-off and said. "I have a great idea. Let's get your swimming togs and go back to the beach. We'll have great fun."

"Okay, see you later, Mum," he said, running to find his swimming gear.

"I didn't tell him we're going to the hospital. He already knows something is wrong. I don't want to worry him any more than necessary," whispered Geoff. "Thanks for this Grace, keep him busy and distracted."

She nodded and went around to the passenger's side and opened the door. Jessie's face was grey and anxious. Grace simply brushed her hand along Jessie's head and shoulder and said, "I'll take good care of him." Jessie nodded as Geoff started the engine and then the jeep disappeared at speed down the driveway.

The private jet from New York landed in Shannon. Sophia was glad to be greeted by a warm, sunny, August day unlike the rainy June day she had left Ireland. She and Grace had been in regular contact by email and her plan to travel to the south east was a new departure for her. She had become quite fascinated by what the young woman was trying to achieve in a small town called Bayrush.

Over the years she had visited Dublin, Belfast and Cork, and she and Bill had driven the entire Western seaboard. As much as she had loved it she was glad to be travelling to a new part. So often her memories overwhelmed her. She wondered would it ever get easier, glad to be distracted from her reverie by the young man from the car rental company. "There you go, Mrs Wynthrope," he said, handing her the keys of a C-class Mercedes.

"Thank you," she replied.

"You sure you're okay driving on the left-hand side? Take your time now. It takes a bit of getting used to." He seemed particularly worried, possibly because she was old enough to be his grandmother. "I'm glad you chose an automatic. Will I run through how the satellite navigator works?"

"No, it's fine thanks. I'll figure it out."

"Ah grand," he said, clearly impressed and a little more relieved. "Enjoy your holiday so!" He smiled as he held the car door open for her. She sat in and waited until he disappeared from sight. Then, smiling to herself, she spread the map she'd picked up earlier across the steering wheel. Tipperary, the name popped out at her. What was the song called? 'It's a long way to Tipperary.' She sat foolishly humming and then declared. "That's it Tipperary, here I come."

About an hour and a half and lots of wrong turns later she saw a bed and breakfast. From the front drive she could see a spectacular group of medieval buildings in the distance with what seemed to be a round tower. Rolling green fields cascaded down into the valley beneath. It had never crossed her mind to stay anywhere but a five star hotel but for some reason unknown to her she had pulled into the drive. Moments later she rang the doorbell. A lady with a round, friendly face answered it.

"Come in, come in. My name is Rita and yes we have a room I hope you'll like – it's en suite! You can see if it suits you. Now we don't have a TV in any of our bedrooms. But we do have a communal living room with a TV, books and newspapers. We like people to enjoy our home."

The lady smiled. Sophia guessed she was in her sixties. She followed her up the mahogany staircase.

"The room is very pretty."

"Now I can recommend some restaurants or if you like I offer an evening meal."

"An evening meal would be perfect, thank you."

"Gracey, is my mommy going to be okay? They think I don't know that Daddy is bringing her to the hospital."

Oh God, thought Grace, how can I answer this? "Sometimes they just have to check things out. But hey Sam, Dirk has a kayak and he's dying to bring you for a spin in it, just within the harbour walls. It'll be fun."

"I'm big enough to go right out to sea," he declared from his booster on the back seat of her car. Great, thought Grace, that had sidetracked him.

"I'm sure you are, little man. Now you can help me carry the picnic basket down. I'm so glad you're here," she said, ruffling his red curls as she took the basket and a rug out of the boot. She could see the concerned look on Dirk's face when he saw her coming down the cliff steps. He ran up towards them. "Is everything okay, Grace?" he asked.

She was behind Sam so she shook her head but said, "Fine, I just thought Sam might like to join us and go for a spin in the kayak with you."

"Great idea, buddy," said Dirk, taking the basket from Grace and continuing back down the steps, chatting away with Sam. She was so grateful that he had got the hint immediately and now that he had taken over she could feel a weakness descend on her.

She sat beside Anna and watched as Dirk managed to borrow a child's life jacket from a parent on the beach. He'd make a great dad, she thought, as she watched him paddling around the harbour with a very happy Sam.

"Oh Anna, I just don't know what to think. Why? Why is life so unfair? Jessie has already been through a miscarriage. And when she unexpectedly became pregnant with twins, well, it was just so exciting."

"Everything will be fine," said Anna, trying to sound reassuring. "Sure she's well over twelve weeks. They're just being extra careful." Grace nodded, knowing that Anna had even less experience of pregnancy than her.

"Isn't Dirk fantastic with Sam, well who would have thought?" remarked Paul, coming in from the sea and picking up a towel to dry himself.

"And you finally set a date. Good for ye!" said Anna. "I'm looking forward to it already."

"Mmmnn, sorry, Anna, I'm just ... well ..."

Paul looked at her quizzically. "Oh no ... Not about the wedding. I'm just distracted, my mind is at the hospital imagining all kinds of scenarios."

"Of course, we can take care of Sam if you want to go ..."

"Oh no, no. Thank you for offering. I wouldn't dream of leaving him. I'll think I'll swim out to join them. It might help to take my mind off things."

"Do," agreed Anna, touching her husband's shoulder as he sat down beside her on the rug. They had been married three years and Grace knew how much they wanted a baby but it hadn't happened yet. It must be upsetting for them too. Why was life never straightforward, she wondered as she dived into the cool blue sea.

After the initial investigations Jessie had finally got a bed in the hospital and the doctor had told her to rest. She had been dozing when she woke to the sound of someone in the room. She looked up in a half-dazed state.

"My name is Fr. Albert," said the monk dressed in brown friar's robes. "I thought you might like some company for a minute."

"Hi," she muttered. "Is it going to be okay?"

He looked at her and paused for a minute and then said, "I don't know. But I do know that God will be with you one way or the other and he will help you deal with this. Even when you think he doesn't exist he will find a way to help all of you."

She looked into his sincere, round brown eyes and said, "Thanks, I needed to hear that." Moments later Geoff arrived from the hospital shop with water and a newspaper. "Who was that?"

"An angel, just when I needed one …"

At seven Sophia went downstairs to the large living room. There were some tables set near a large window overlooking a well-tended garden.

"Would you like a glass of white wine?" asked Rita, coming in a door leading from where Sophia presumed the kitchen might be.

"Thank you, Rita."

"Make yourself at home," she said, handing Sophia a crystal glass filled to the brim. Sophia smiled, thinking if she was in a hotel the large glass would be half filled. "Now I have chicken liver pate with melba toast for starter and lamb shank to follow."

"Sounds wonderful, do you have other guests tonight?"

Sophia smiled as she listened to Rita. She loved the Irish accent. It was the way they spoke, their turn of phrase. Over time Sophia had noticed the variation in accents around the country and Rita's was completely new to her. She always had to concentrate hard because people spoke at a much quicker pace.

"Not tonight but we have four due on Saturday night as part of a coach tour group. It's slower since the recession but sure we make the best of it. Now you must be starvin'. I'll be back in a sec," she said, retreating through the door she had come in. There was music playing softly in the background and Sophia sipped her wine and perused the daily newspaper as she waited.

After dinner, Sophia sat on the comfortable couch.

"Would you like tea or coffee, Sophia?"

"Tea, please, but are you free to join me?"

"I will so, just give me a few minutes." Rita smiled, taking the dessert plate that had previously been filled with the most tasteful fresh fruit pavlova.

"No rush at all. I haven't felt this relaxed in a long time. Thank you so much for the wonderful meal."

"You're very welcome, Sophia."

When Rita came back she placed a tray on the coffee table, and plopped down beside Sophia.

"The room is beautiful," Sophia said, adding, "You must collect antique furniture!"

Pouring the tea Rita began to chat about how she had decided to open a bed and breakfast. Sophia found her hugely entertaining as she recounted little anecdotes of her experiences over the years. Eventually she asked, "So what brings you to Ireland, Sophia?"

"I'm thinking of moving here for a while." The question had been so unexpected that Sophia had shocked herself by her answer.

"Oh and why in God's name would you want to do that? The weather is terrible; the country is collapsing around us. Not to mention the health service and as for crime …"

"Rita, you're in the tourism business!"

"If the tourism people heard me, I'd be struck off the approved list," she laughed and then carried on. "But do you know Sophia, if the truth be told, I wouldn't live anywhere else. A few years back we even went on one of those organised trips in the good times to buy an apartment in Spain. My Jimmy was all talk about it. But when push came to shove we couldn't do it."

"Why not?"

"Sure, I love Ireland and we've a granddaughter. She's three years old. Sure isn't that what it's all about? I'll let you off to bed Sophia before you drop off in front of my eyes."

"Thanks for the chat, Rita," said Sophia, getting up. As she began to climb the staircase she noticed a photograph of Rita sitting proudly with her little granddaughter perched on her lap, surrounded by her family. The loneliness overwhelmed her. Richard was right. She was running but it was better than doing nothing. Or shutting down like him.

Chapter Four

Grace couldn't help checking her phone constantly. There was still no news. She supposed that was a good thing. Today had been the longest day and it was still only nine-thirty. She stole a glance at Dirk who was driving her car along Jessie's avenue; only for him she'd have been lost. He had been so good with Sam, keeping him occupied all day. She leaned across and put her hand on his knee. "Thanks," she said. He smiled and glanced in the rear-view mirror.

"He's out for the count."

She turned to see little Sam fast asleep on his booster seat. Her phone bleeped. "It's a text from Geoff. He's asked me to stay the night so that he can stay as long as possible with Jess. If you'd prefer to head home, I don't mind."

"Of course I'll stay," said Dirk, patting her knee. "Don't worry, darling. Everything will be all right. He's a great kid, I'm glad he ate the chips on the promenade. At least he won't wake up hungry. What about you? You haven't eaten all day …"

"I'm grand," she said, getting out of the car as it drew up outside the cottage. Food was the furthest thing from her mind. She was way too anxious to eat.

"Hey, little man," said Dirk, picking up Sam and carrying him inside. He followed Grace to Sam's bedroom where she took off his crocs and shorts. Leaving his tee-shirt on, she tucked the duvet up and kissed him on the forehead. She then crept quietly out leaving the door ajar.

Dirk had gone down to the sitting room and was already watching golf. "Cup of tea or coffee?" she asked, unable to sit still.

"Coffee. Thanks."

She filled the kettle and waited as it boiled. What a day it had been and it wasn't nearly over.

"Honey, maybe you should go home. I'll be fine, I promise," said Jessie.

Geoff was sitting beside her bed. "I rang Grace while you were dozing. They brought Sam to the promenade for chips and they're going to stay over."

"She's the best. Honey I'm fine now. Go home and get some sleep, you're wrecked."

Geoff shifted in his seat. She knew he was anxious although he was trying his best not to show it. "I'll stay another while …"

At midnight, Grace heard Geoff's jeep drive into the yard. She rushed to the kitchen and when she saw his ashen face she had to do everything in her power not to crumble. Instead she went to the kettle to boil it. Why did she always boil the kettle in a crisis, she wondered? She placed two mugs on the butcher-block table and took milk from the fridge. Geoff sat down despairingly. Years of friendship allowed the companionable silence.

"Well," she said, pouring tea into his mug.

"The doctor said it's a waiting game. We didn't tell anyone, Grace, but we've known since the twenty-week scan that there was a problem."

"Oh my God, why didn't you?"

"Because talking about it would make it real, and we couldn't give up. The doctor gave us a one per cent chance and we took it."

Grace nodded, completely understanding. The last thing anyone in that circumstance would need was an opinion or pity.

"But what I'm most concerned with now is Jessie. She is so bloated her lungs are under pressure making her breathing shallow. It's very worrying and I know she is unaware of the impact it's having on her body. She is just so focused on the babies. She keeps saying as long as they are in her womb they are safe."

"Jesus, Geoff, did you get to speak with a doctor?"

"Yes, he's been excellent. Very supportive but because she's twenty-four weeks, the babies' lungs aren't formed enough to survive. If she can hold on or another week they'd having a fighting chance … but … Jesus …" He put his head down and buried his face in his hands. Thankfully, she thought, Dirk had had the good sense to stay in the living room.

"I'll just go up to check on Sam. Thanks for everything, Grace," he said, getting up wearily.

Grace lay in Jessie's spare bedroom, tossing and turning. She could hear Geoff walking around downstairs. The poor man mustn't be able to sleep, she thought. She couldn't imagine what Geoff must be feeling. What if anything happened to Jessie? She tossed and turned so much, Dirk reached out. "Darling, come here," he said, pulling her close to him. They lay in spoons. She used to laugh when she saw people do that on TV, thinking it was the most uncomfortable position, ever but tonight it was comforting. Eventually she slept.

No matter which way Jessie turned she couldn't get comfortable. One nurse had even brought in a lava lamp and another had given her lavender for her pillow. Their kindness was incredible. Pain shot through her body. Sam had been overdue and she had had a Caesarean section so she'd never experienced labour pain. The nurses kept calling it pressure pain and God it was excruciating. She told herself that everything would be fine when daylight came.

She turned on the television in an attempt to distract herself. That didn't work. She tried to read to no avail.

She was crying with the pain when at four a.m. the nurse brought in a Tens machine to help relieve it. She eventually managed to sleep and woke two hours later feeling a little less anxious. Daylight, thank God, she thought. Geoff would be back soon. She had made him promise not to tell their parents she was in hospital unless he had to. She didn't want to worry them. "Oh please God help me."

Jack was on the road at seven. He hadn't slept well and was blaming it on too much coffee but the truth was he couldn't stop thinking about Grace. He had been pleased she'd been concerned about him diving off the storm wall. The weather had been so hot yesterday when Conor rang to say he was going to the beach. It had been a no-brainer. Garvan, his nephew and his pals were also there jumping and diving off the pier. And then Conor had dared him to dive off the storm wall backwards like they used to do. Never one to back down he had won twenty quid for his trouble.

The last person he had expected to see in a kayak was Grace. He couldn't stop smiling at the get-up of her as she had tried to manoeuvre away, she had been hilarious. And when she had tripped walking up the cliff steps he had had to stop himself from running up to help her. God he wished she wasn't engaged, and when he saw how happy she was frolicking about in the sea with the little boy and Dirk, the Adonis, it had been a blow.

Jessie touched her tummy – it was rock hard. She was finding it increasingly hard to breathe but was glad that the awful pain was gone. She needed to use the loo, so she managed to wriggle her way out of bed and waddle slowly the few paces to the bathroom. Everything was going to be all right, she thought. No pain had to be a good thing. She sat on the toilet and began to wee when the most awful thing happened. Something appeared between her legs. She touched it and screamed. It was a tiny limb. She reached for the bell and kept pulling but nobody came. She struggled to open the bathroom door but the bedroom door was closed too. Lying on the floor she began to howl.

Minutes later a nurse came, and within seconds the room was in chaos with nurses trying to get her from the bathroom floor onto a trolley. The ward sister arrived. She was a big strong woman who wrapped her arms under Jessie's armpits. Three other nurses picked up the rest of her and managed somehow to get her onto the trolley. They rushed her to the labour ward. "Ring Geoff, please somebody, I need him," she cried.

Their first baby boy was born at 8.23am. He took a gasp and then left the world as the tears streamed down Jessie's face. He was perfect with all his little fingers and toes and he had the most beautiful little face.

Twenty minutes later Geoff burst into the labour ward. He must have broken every speed limit in the county. What could he say or do? He just held her in his arms and cried with her.

"Can we call him Anthony – after my granddad?" she asked through her tears. Geoff could only nod through his.

Forty minutes later it happened again. Anthony's brother took a gasp and left just as Anthony had.

The nurse handed Geoff the baby and holding him in his arms he said with eyes filled with tears, "I'd like to call him Geoff." It was her turn to nod.

She kept hoping it wasn't real and that she'd wake up and everything would be the same as before. She'd still have her babies. Oh God, why?

Grace made breakfast and tried to act normal. She was so grateful to Dirk. He kept chatting to Sam as they munched their cornflakes. She was on tenterhooks waiting for the phone call she knew would come. It had happened and she had no idea what to do or say. She needed air.

"I'm just going to see if Monique has arrived yet."

Dirk looked up with eyes full of concern. "Okay, darling. Sam has challenged me to a game of soccer on the console, and I told him he's going to lose."

"No way!" said Sam, grinning from ear to ear. She smiled and went out the back door. Monique was mucking out Jasper's stable. Grace thought how very grateful Jessie had been to have her and Kate to help. Monique looked up and brushed a strand of chestnut hair that had fallen from her usual ponytail.

"I can't believe this is happening. Why Grace, it's so unfair? Jessie is like a mother to me. I don't know what would have become of me if she had not pleaded with me to come up here."

"We will have to be strong for her. I heard Geoff speeding down the drive about an hour ago. I'm so afraid to ring him. It can't be good. Come here," said Grace, wrapping her arms around the young French girl who was sobbing inconsolably.

"I'm so sorry Grace. I will get myself together for Sam. I do not want him to see me crying. Un moment!"

Poor Monique, she had only turned thirteen when her parents had been killed in a car crash in Paris. Having no other relatives she had come to Ireland to live with her grandmother, Nora. Filled with grief, Monique had refused to come out of her bedroom until Jessie had coaxed her to visit the stables. And since that day Monique had fallen in love with horses. Grace kept thinking of all the people Jessie had helped over the years including Kate, her sister. Why, God, she thought, why when she is such a natural mother?

"Let's go back to the house," said Grace.

"I'll be in soon. I need to finish cleaning this stable."

"Thanks, Monique, for all your help. I know Jess is very grateful."

"Jess."

"Yes."

"I think we got the names wrong. Look," said Geoff, pointing to Anthony.

"He's so like you." She smiled through her tears. "And look." She pointed at baby Geoff's fingers. "They are just like my granddad's."

"What are we like?" Geoff smiled but his heartbreak was laid bare to her.

"Come here," she said. Geoff bent over her and laid his tear-stained cheek next to hers. "I'm sorry, honey. So, so sorry." She ran her hand through his hair and felt him shaking.

He gathered himself and pulled away. He wiped his tears with the back of his hand and said, "I'll go and make the phone calls, Jess. I'll be back in a few minutes."

Lying on the bed, she watched as her strong, manly husband walked forlornly out of the labour ward. How would they ever get over this? What were they going to tell Sam? The babies he had told everybody about were … she couldn't say the word. When the door was firmly closed she finally broke down. She cried and the pain wracked her body, every sob physically hurt her but that didn't matter. The midwife who had left to give them some privacy came rushing back. She simply held Jessie in her arms and let her cry.

"I'm sorry. I'll get it together," said Jessie, wiping her tears with her hands. The midwife nodded but stayed sitting on the side of the bed. Then she stretched over and picked up a box of tissues and said, "It's going to be hard but as long as you have one another, that's what counts. Keep talking to one another." Jessie was so grateful for the woman's kindness.

Grace arrived at the hospital. She managed to get into the labour ward. Jessie was behind the curtains in a cubicle being washed down by the nurses.

"And who are you?" asked the sister on duty in a not very pleasant tone.

"I'm Grace McGrath, Jessie McGrath's sister. I'm sorry to be any bother but I need to see her."

Jessie guffawed. "Gracey, don't attempt to come in here. I'm not a show it all kind of girl. I haven't a stitch on."

Everyone laughed, the sister included. When the curtain was finally drawn back Grace was shocked to silence at the sight of Jessie. It was like somebody had turned off the lights inside her friend. The sparkle that was Jessie had disappeared. Thankfully, the nurse spoke. "Come on, you might as well make yourself useful now that you're here. You can help wheel your sister back to the ward."

"You'd get in anywhere, you know," Jessie whispered, giving her a watery smile.

"Always could," replied Grace, leaning down and kissing her best friend on her forehead. She whispered, "I love you, sis."

Jessie's eyes filled up and the tears trickled down the sides of her face into her ears. "I know you do but thanks for saying it. And you big eejit – how can you be my sister by calling yourself McGrath!" she mumbled.

"Oh yeah, feck it, but it worked, didn't it!" Grace gathered herself and with tears still in her eyes she pushed the bed along the corridor.

A few hours later a nurse called Mary spoke to Jessie about how to approach telling Sam. "Include him. He's nearly six years old. Let him see the babies. It's only my advice, of course. Talk about it together, it might not be what you feel comfortable with."

Later that evening Geoff brought Sam to the hospital where he was the first person to see his baby brothers. Jessie told him that they were asleep and would be going up to Holy God in Heaven who'd look after them and then they would become little angels.

"Can I hold my baby brothers?" asked Sam unexpectedly.

Geoff looked at her in amazement. All Jessie could do was to nod her head.

"Of course you can, son," said Geoff, walking over to the cot where their two baby sons lay together. He picked up baby Anthony and placed him in Sam's arms.

As he did this the hospital room door opened and both Jessie's and Geoff's parents came in – all their faces were grief-stricken. Sam turned towards them and said in a matter of fact voice that only a child could have under the circumstances, "Do you want to hold my baby brothers?" And Jessie thought there were reasons for everything because she'd never have suggested that.

Later that night after all the visitors had left and Geoff had taken Sam home, Mary, the nurse, offered to leave the babies in the room with Jessie overnight. It would be the only night she'd ever spend with them. She cried as she held a baby in each arm – her tears dropped on their little white baby-grows making big wet blobs. The realisation that they would never grow up, never run and play and fight with their big brother broke her.

The picture Sam had drawn earlier lay on the bedside locker. It had a man and a woman, a small boy and a baby in each of the adults' arms and he had even included Buzz, their dog. Sam had asked could he put it in the coffin with them to remind them that they had a big brother. He had said he didn't want them to forget him. She had tried so hard earlier not to cry when he said that because he was so earnest but now the tears just wouldn't stop. And when Geoff had brought him for a walk earlier Sam had asked Geoff to buy them a cuddle toy each. He had decided that they wouldn't want the same ones "coz then they'd get them mixed up in heaven." Geoff had whispered to her, "I'm sorry but these are all his ideas."

Cradling her perfect babies in her arms she couldn't understand why. How could God do this? It didn't make any sense. Why give her two babies and then take them away?

On Tuesday morning just as Kate arrived at Grace's house the front door opened.

"Morning Kate, you're out and about early for a Monday morning," said Dirk, getting into his Audi.

"Yeah you're right Dirk, I'm not usually out and about so early. So this is what it's like in the real world?" she replied, with an underlying tone in her voice.

"Got to keep her in the style she's used to now," he laughed as he placed his briefcase on the front seat of his car.

"Ass," she muttered under her breath, continuing in the front door. "Grace, is the kettle boiled?" she called. "I badly need a coffee. How is she?" Kate asked.

"The funeral is tomorrow. I'm dreading it so I can't imagine how she feels. Kate, they are so beautiful. Can't you go and see her? She'd love to see you."

"I can't Grace, I ... I wouldn't be any good for her and what if she asked me to see them. I wouldn't be able for it."

"I know it's hard, but it's important to Jessie and Geoff that people know that they were babies, perfectly formed. They called them Anthony and Geoff."

"I'll think about it."

"You mean so much to Jessie, Kate."

"Grace, I said I'll think about it okay?"

"Just don't take too long," muttered Grace, trying to accept that people were different and everyone had their own way of dealing with things. She changed the subject. "Remember the lady I met on the flight to New York in June."

"Yeah," said Kate, absently taking a sip from her coffee cup.

"Well she's in Ireland and wants to meet. She mentioned something about staying around here for a while."

"Did you reply?"

"I enjoyed chatting with her and everything but ..."

"But what ..."

"But I'd feel awkward."

"Ah lighten up Grace, from what you said she sounded like a lovely lady. Doesn't your curiosity get to you? Wouldn't you love to know more about her?"

"I suppose. The card she gave me was a personal one with only her name and mobile number on it."

"Well if your curiosity doesn't get to you, mine does. So do me a favour. Meet her!"

"You're a gas woman, Kate Fitzgerald."

"No, I was just born nosy. I'll go up to the office and start filing. Where's Eoghan?"

"He's meeting the tour guides to brief them on Saturday's itineraries. I'll clean up here and I'll be up to you in a few minutes."

Grace felt guilty for pressuring Kate to go to see Jessie. And the truth was she really could do without a visit from Sophia at the moment. There was just so much going on. She wiped down the counter and went upstairs to the office. Kate was on the phone.

"Yeah, I'll be there at about seven after I finish here." Kate paused, hanging the phone between her ear and shoulder as she stretched across the desk looking for a file. "Okay so, see you there." She hung up. "That was Monique. She needs a hand at the yard. It's so unfair Grace. First a miscarriage and now this. What did Jess and Geoff do to deserve this? I don't get it."

"Look, I'm sorry about earlier, putting you under pressure to go to the hospital …"

"It's not that I don't want to. But Jessie is the person I go to for a laugh. She's the one who helped me through my problems. God knows where I'd be if she hadn't immersed me in horses."

"It's hard to see her so down. But Kate, we need to stay positive and be here for her, okay," said Grace, getting up from the desk to give her sister, who had tears flowing down her cheeks, a hug.

"It's time," said Geoff, gently. Jessie looked at the white coffin her babies had been placed in together. Beside it lay another coffin with a baby in it. It was more common than she had imagined. In the five days she had spent in the hospital she had heard so many sad stories.

She remembered the joy and happiness they had experienced the day Sam was born, the flowers, the cards, the balloons, the teddies and the feelings of pure love that no words can ever explain. And yet somebody else would have been going through this. She stood up and put a letter she had written to her babies into the coffin. Then Geoff put in a set of child's rosary beads his mother had given him.

"Mammy, we have to fit these in," said Sam, picking up the cuddly toys he had chosen for his brothers. It was too much; she began to cry, great big sobs. How could she allow the coffin to be closed, her babies would be gone forever. It was so final.

"I'm sorry, Mammy, I didn't mean to make you cry." She took her little boy into her arms and held him tight. "You didn't honey. I'm just so sad."

Geoff took over placing the furry animals gently on either side of the babies. "Sam, will we put in your picture?" he asked.

Sam just nodded and taking it from his dad he placed it carefully on top. "Bye brothers," he said.

"I think we'll go outside and leave your mammy and daddy for a while, okay?" Jessie's mother said, leading the little boy to the door. Geoff passed a grateful look to his mother-in-law as all the grandparents left, leaving Jessie and Geoff alone in silence. She felt numb. Geoff leaned down and kissed his babies for the last time. He put out his hand to help her up to do the same. She touched each tiny face with her fingers as if imprinting them to her memory, and bending, she brushed her lips to each little cold face and whispered, "Goodbye." Just as Geoff closed the lid a huge indescribable sound came from somewhere deep within her. Her whole body shook but Geoff wrapped his strong arms around her to quell her and they stayed like that for what seemed an age. Then he turned and picked up the white coffin and carried it as he had been told he must, down the stairs and out the hospital emergency doors.

Geoff's father was double-parked outside waiting for them. Sam travelled with her parents while she and Geoff sat in the back seat of Geoff's dad's car with a white coffin across their laps. It was surreal. A part of her wanted the drive to last forever. Although it was August, it began to rain, then it poured, and by the time they got to the church it was torrential. Both of their families were gathered there, along with their closest friends. After the small service they walked through the torrential rain to the graveside where Jessie felt her legs give way as Geoff placed the little white coffin into the rain-sodden hole in the ground. Grace caught her on one side and her mother linked her on the other side. "Why ... why, it's not fair," she whispered as Sam threw two red roses onto the little white coffin.

"Come away, Jessie," her mother said, gently guiding her away. Grace tried desperately to hold an umbrella over them as a cold north-easterly wind blew.

"Oh Mammy, what am I going to do?"

Aoife, the vet's receptionist, had asked Jack to call to the McGraths' place because a pony had cut its leg. When he got out of the jeep he was surprised to be met by an elderly man he'd never seen before.

"I'm Tom Phelan, a neighbour farmer of Geoff's. Jaysus, it's tough news! Look I'll bring you to the young horse and let you at it. I'll crack on with the feeding okay."

"Sorry, but what's tough news?" asked Jack, lost. What was going on?

"Ah you mustn't've heard. Ah well, poor Jessie lost the little 'uns. They're at the funeral. Jaysus boy, it'd break your heart. 'Twas twin boys. Ah sure." He was walking away clearly upset. So Jack didn't ask any more questions. Geoff had been so proud when he had told him Jessie was having twins. They must be heartbroken.

"Hey girl," he said to the chestnut filly, taking a polo mint from his pocket. "Let's take a look at that leg of yours." But he couldn't stop thinking of the McGraths.

Grace wasn't feeling well. The last thing she needed was a social evening. But Sophia had arrived in Bayrush and had checked in to The Meadows.

Grace parked and tottered across the drive in her high heels. Bloody pea gravel, she thought. It looked lovely but it was a hell to walk on, her high heels would be ruined. Wearing a sky blue linen dress, she wondered was she a tad overdressed. She felt strangely nervous. They had exchanged emails and it had been easy to talk to Sophia on the aeroplane but that was because Grace had never expected to meet her again.

Sophia was sitting in the bay window of the lobby. The moment Grace walked in she stood up to greet her. "Hi there, I've been so looking forward to this," said Sophia, kissing her continental style.

Grace relaxed immediately; maybe being with Sophia was exactly what she needed after all.

"It's great to see you again, Sophia. I never imagined we'd meet again especially so soon."

"We used to visit at least once a year," said Sophia, wistfully sitting back down. The sadness Grace had noticed on the aeroplane was still there. Grace wondered who "we" was but didn't dare to pry. Sophia continued. "Shall we order some drinks here or would you like to eat? We have so much to talk about. This place is so pretty and thank you so much for the room upgrade. It was very thoughtful of you."

"You're welcome, it was Dirk's doing," Grace smiled. "Let's have a drink. I'll go and get some menus. What will you have?"

"A gin and tonic, thanks." Fiona, the receptionist overheard her, and said. "I'll get it. What would you like to drink, Grace?"

"Just a sparkling water for me, thanks a mill, Fiona."

"Wow, that's what I call service," remarked Sophia, smiling at Fiona.

"Anything for the boss's future wife," joked Fiona, heading towards the bar.

Grace laughed but blushed too. "Anyway tell me how has your trip been so far?"

Sophia began to talk about her stay in Cashel.

"So far so good then. Are there any places in particular you'd like to visit while you're here?"

"Kilkenny Castle and Lismore Castle." Sophia laughed. "I'm an American, I have a fascination for castles. And, of course, the House of Waterford Crystal, I'd like to see how they create those magnificent trophy pieces."

"Consider it done. Now let's take a look at the menu before my tummy thinks my throat is cut."

"You have the most unusual turn of phrase here. Does anybody ever say what they mean?"

"No, that's why we leave a trail of confusion," laughed Grace, choosing salad to start and chicken for the main. She dearly hoped her tummy would settle.

"So, you've set a date?" said Sophia. "I'm looking forward to meeting your fiancé."

"Yes, he's hoping to join us after dinner."

"Wonderful. It's a busy place," remarked Sophia just as a crowd arrived into the lobby. The noise level had risen significantly.

"Yes, the races must be just over and it's the nearest hotel to the …" Grace could feel the colour rising in her cheeks. Jack Leslie was in the middle of the group and he was heading in her direction just as someone stopped him.

"Are you … okay, Grace?" asked Sophia, following Grace's gaze.

"Yes, yes … em."

"Hi Grace, it seems we keep meeting in the most unlikely places."

"Hello again, Jack." She could feel Sophia watching her. "This is my friend, Sophia."

"Hi Sophia, it's nice to meet you," said Jack, shaking Sophia's hand.

"Very nice to meet you too, Jack."

"You're American. What part of the States are you from?"

"New York."

"I love New York …" said Jack, launching into a full-scale chat with Sophia. Relieved that he wasn't directing any conversation towards her, Grace began twiddling with her earring. The bloody thing fell out. She was feeling around the floor for it when he turned towards her again.

"Lose something Grace?" He raised his eyebrows.

"Eh, no …" she said, putting her hand up to her other ear to hide it. Why did she turn into a nervous wreck when he was around? *I'm so over you*, she thought.

"You sure?" he said, bending down to pick up the earring. As he handed it to her, their fingers barely touched but it was like an electric shock. She pulled her hand away quickly. She could see by the look in his eyes that he had noticed too. He was still squatting beside her seat when he almost whispered, "You look fabulous." Standing back up he added. "Sophia, last time Grace and I met she was wearing a wet suit and paddling like a mad thing to ..."

"Quit while you're ahead Jack," she said, smirking at him. "At least I don't still think I'm a teenager back-flipping from storm walls." He threw his head back and laughed.

"Did you guys grow up together?" asked Sophia.

"Well I wouldn't quite say that ... but well ... we do go back ..." He was looking at her as though it was just the two of them in the room.

"Jack is married," she cut across him but couldn't take her eyes away from his. It actually sounded like an accusation even to her.

"There you are. I've been looking all over for you. I thought you'd be in the restaurant by now ..." said Dirk. He stood behind her chair and put his hands on her shoulders. "This place is crazy busy all of the sudden."

"Hi honey," said Grace turning towards Dirk. "Sophia, this is Dirk, my fiancé."

"It's so nice to meet you finally. Grace has told me so much about you." Dirk looked at Jack quizzically.

"Bye Grace, it was nice to meet you, Sophia." He nodded at Dirk and turned to re-join his friends.

"So ladies, I've been told your table awaits you." said Dirk. Grace stood up, picking up her handbag as she glanced in Jack's direction. He was deep in conversation. *What are you doing?* she reprimanded herself – *I'm engaged to be married. I'm happy. Why did he have to come back?* She could feel Dirk's hand around her lower back. The guilt she felt was making her nausea worse by the minute.

Jack couldn't help watching her walk across the lobby. He sighed.

"What's eating you?" asked Conor, handing him a beer. "It's jammers in there." Conor nodded towards the bar. "Who was the babe you were talking to?"

"Grace Fitzgerald ... she's engaged to the asshole who owns this place," Nick, a friend of Conor's, cut in before Jack had a chance to reply.

"Shhh," said Conor, "someone will hear you, Nick."

"What do I care? She's too good for him. She might be from the wrong-side-of-the-tracks but she has more class in her little finger than most I know. He's a jumped-up mammy's boy," Nick said, just as somebody called him away.

"Come on, let's go into the bar. I can't be listening to that fella. He's worse than a woman," said Conor, under his breath to Jack.

Nick's remarks were exactly what bugged Jack about small town Ireland. Why can't people be judged by their deeds and not their address? To hear Grace being talked about rattled him.

"I must say this salmon is wonderful," said Sophia, noticing that although Grace looked fabulous, she was clearly not herself. She had picked at her starter and was moving her food around the plate instead of eating.

"The food is always great here," she remarked but Sophia looked pointedly at her plate. "I know. Oh Sophia, I don't like to moan. Especially since it's the first time we've met again. But I'm feeling awful. My tummy is in knots. I must be coming down with something."

Sophia raised her eyebrows but it was not the time or the place to ask questions about what she had witnessed in the lobby. Was that the cause of Grace's anxiety, she wondered? Sophia was sure that Dirk had noticed too.

"Order some peppermint tea, it will help. We can make it an early night Grace. We'll have plenty of time to catch up. I'm planning to stay a week or two."

"That's great news," said Grace, putting down her knife and fork. She tried to get the attention of the waiter.

"Can you recommend a place, maybe self-catering? I'd like to look after myself while I'm here."

"There are some self-catering thatched cottages near Bayrush Beach which is a wonderful, long, golden sand beach. I can check availability in the morning."

"It sounds perfect Grace."

Later over a decaf coffee to Grace's peppermint tea, Sophia began to talk about Bill and how devastated she was by his sudden death.

"Oh Sophia, I'm so glad you're staying around for a while. And thanks for sharing with me about Bill. I can't imagine what you are going through but I just know you'll love it here. There's so much I want to tell you about. But tomorrow is another day," said Grace.

"Grace …" said Sophia, with tears in her eyes. "Thanks for listening.

And for letting me in to your world."

"I'm not going to ask you to explain that to me. But tonight was just lovely."

"For me too. I hope you'll feel better after a good night's sleep."

"God Sophia if anybody overhears us there'll be a rumour about us." Sophia burst out laughing.

Walking out to the lobby, Grace said, "Let me find Dirk to tell him I'm going home. Oh, there he is."

Sophia watched as they spoke together and was about to turn away when she spotted Jack leaving. He smiled and waved at her. She waved back, but his attention was on Grace who was pecking Dirk on the cheek. Jack accidentally bumped into the door. So, thought Sophia. What was that about? It was all very intriguing, she thought as Grace rejoined her.

"I'll walk you to your car. I could do with some fresh air," said Sophia, walking out into the cool night air. At the car Grace climbed in, and Sophia added, "Talk to you tomorrow. Arrivederci." The word had simply rolled off her tongue for the first time since Bill had died.

"And to you too," said Grace, from the open window. Sophia watched as the car disappeared down the long avenue. Turning back towards The Meadows she noticed its beautiful façade. She walked to a garden bench and sat, looking upwards. The sky was awash with stars. Bill had once said he loved Ireland so much because heaven felt close to the earth.

I know you're up there, Bill, she thought. *I can feel you near me. And tonight I truly understand what you had meant. Oh Bill, I miss you so much.*

Chapter Five

It was September and two weeks since the twins' funeral. Grace drove into Jessie's yard after another long day. She had just helped Sophia settle into her holiday cottage. Every day Grace lived in hope that Jessie would be her old self again. But she knew that was an impossible wish. All she could hope for was a glimmer of the old Jessie. As she parked, Geoff came over to her.

"I'm glad I caught you before you go in, Grace."

"Is everything okay?"

"I just don't know what to do. The house is constantly busy, the phone never stops … look I'm not complaining … but … she won't leave the house."

"Geoff, I don't know what to say or do either but … I suppose we have to just give her time."

"She hardly sleeps. Most nights she walks around the house. I found her kneeling beside Sam's bed at three o'clock this morning checking his breathing," said Geoff, rubbing the top of his head. "I just don't know what to do …" His voice broke.

"It's hard on all of you. Sam was so excited …"

"Look, I have to go. I didn't mean to dump on you." She watched him walk towards the yard with his shoulders slumped and head down. She opened the back door and could hear Nora, Monique's grandmother who was a great friend and always had a few wise words.

"You timed that well," said Nora, pouring tea for Grace.

"How is she?"

"Take a look."

Grace looked over to the far end of the kitchen where Jessie sat in an armchair staring out the window. She hadn't even noticed her coming in.

"She's so disinterested. The only time she lightens up is when Sam is here."

"What are we going to do, Nora?"

"Just be here, talk to her even if you're getting nothing back."

"Hey Jess," said Grace, sitting down in the chair opposite her.

"Oh, sorry Grace, I didn't hear you coming in."

Grace could feel the tears coming and bit her lip to stop them. Jessie had lost so much weight and her face had a grey pallor to it. Her hair was dull and lifeless. "Do you fancy a walk? We could look around the yard."

"Another day, maybe."

"Okay ..."

"Minnie Madden from across the road sent this over," said Nora, offering Jessie a slice of carrot cake.

"That was kind. No thanks."

"I'll have a slice, thanks Nora," said Grace, as Nora passed her a sympathetic look.

"I think I will too," said Nora, pulling over a kitchen chair to join them. "I'm looking forward to the next cruise visit. I can't wait to guide the group around The Vee and some of the gardens of West Waterford." Grace sat back and listened as Nora waffled on and Jessie stared out the window. Thank God for Nora, she was a retired librarian and an avid gardener. She also loved her stint as a tour guide on the occasions the cruises came in.

On Thursday morning Sophia wandered around the farmers' market in Bayrush's busy square. The stalls offered a wonderful array of food from organic vegetables locally grown to cordials and chutneys in pretty little glass jars. There was a selection of cheeses to be had at another stall. Ooh, she thought, she'd definitely be back next week. Then she noticed a leaflet offering cookery courses in the evening time. Maybe she'd sign up for that. Why not? she thought as she walked towards the harbour. Earlier as she'd driven by she'd noticed a public library with a big window overlooking the bay. She'd go in to take a look around it on her way back to the car.

Strolling along the dockside Sophia could smell seaweed mingled with fresh fish. From the sound of the fishermen chatting they might have been speaking a different language. It was then that she realised they were. It sounded guttural to her ears. She sat on a bench and pretended to text as she listened intently. They most definitely were not speaking English, but yet they looked Irish. Curiosity got the better of her.

"Excuse me, are you speaking Gaelic?" she asked one of them. He wore a navy jumper and on close inspection had a handsome face. Sophia reckoned he was in his early sixties.

"Yes, are you looking for directions?"

Was she so obviously a tourist, she wondered. "Oh, you speak English."

He threw his head back and laughed as one of the others said, "He likes to think he can speak Irish."

"It sure sounded wonderful to me," she remarked in his defence.

"The lads here are from the Gaeltacht, the Irish speaking area across the bay there." He pointed to his left. "And sure I can only speak a little but I love trying it out. It gives them a good laugh. I get more wrong than right."

The two men were smiling over at her and one said, "He's not lying there. Sure isn't he a Jackeen!"

"She's American lads – that means nothing to her."

She smiled and said, "It means you're from Dublin."

"Well now my apologies." He even had the good grace to blush slightly as she stood up to leave.

"You're forgiven," she said, smiling as she continued walking along the dockside. Looking at the many boats reminded her of how much she missed sailing! She and Bill used to sail regularly when they went to the Hamptons for weekends and summer breaks. Already it seemed like another lifetime ago. Stop, she told herself, opening the glass door of the library. Browsing through books might help curb the loneliness that constantly flooded her.

"I'm proud of you," said Dirk, taking her in his arms in public and kissing her. Grace could feel her face flushing. They were in Nutties where she had arranged to have a buffet for all the tour guides and people who had helped especially.

"I mean, two cruise ships docking here in little old Bayrush on the same day. That's a fantastic achievement. I've never seen so many locals out taking photographs and video footage. It was brilliant. Well done." He held his pint glass up in the air and shouted, "Here's to Grace Fitzgerald for having the vision and courage to do what she did today."

Jesus, she thought, how much had he had to drink? It was coming to the end of the season and seemed only fitting to celebrate today more than any. They were all on such a high; everybody had come straight to the pub from the dockside.

"Speech, speech!" cried a voice from the bar.

Grace was absolutely mortified, but had no choice. Laughing she said, "Thanks a million to everybody who has helped make today and every day that a cruise liner docks here possible. None of it would ever have happened if I hadn't been fortunate enough to meet Mr Eoghan Forrester."

A big cheer went up for Eoghan, who raised his pint of Guinness in her direction with a big beaming smile on his face. He said, "Enjoy the night and don't forget we have another cruise liner on the 28th of September. And Nuttie we'll have a round of drinks for everyone here." Everyone cheered again.

"Are you okay?" asked Grace quietly. Dirk had been acting a little strange since the night she had met Sophia for dinner.

"Yeah, of course … this is a big day for you."

Just then Paul and Anna arrived in to join them so the moment was lost. She watched him as he chatted with his best friend. Was she trying to find problems? Dirk was being hugely supportive and it was nice of his friends to come along too. Although having them here made her miss Jessie all the more – she was becoming increasingly withdrawn.

Grace looked towards Sophia who was sitting at the bar chatting with Eoghan and a group of locals. She seemed happy. Grace wondered often what was it that she was hiding besides the fact that she had lost her husband. Maybe someday she'd trust her enough to talk to her; for now Grace simply enjoyed her company.

"So Grace, you've had a great day."

"Sorry, Anna, I was miles away … Yes." She began to fill Anna in on the day.

"Isn't that just a good one that we met at the harbour last week? What are the odds?" laughed Eoghan, twirling his creamy pint.

"It was a surprise. I presumed you were a fisherman," Sophia smiled.

"Ah sure, I love the sea. I have a small boat that I take out every so often. But hey, thanks for taking the couple who missed their coach to Waterford's Viking Triangle," said Eoghan. "It was a hairy moment. Juan, the shore excursions manager, was so grateful to you because it was his fault he'd put them on the wrong tender."

"Not a problem, I took the opportunity to join in the Walking Tour of the city. I didn't know Waterford was Ireland's oldest city. It's steeped in wonderful history and the guide was such a character, the passengers loved him."

"Although I'm just a blow-in, I love it here. And since the day I met young Grace, well let's just say she has given me a new lease of life."

"How did you meet?" asked Sophia.

"Over coffee and across two tables," he chuckled. "I recognised her from the Tourist Office. Some friends of mine wanted me to arrange accommodation, a reliable coach company and to recommend some restaurants. I was new to the place and had no idea where to start. Grace offered to do it for me and it was such a success. Not long after Grace came to me with an idea and here we are. Now I work more than I ever did but I love it."

"What did you work at?"

"I was a marine biologist."

Just then the man beside her nudged her.

"Did you hear about the fella that fell off the horse in McGraths' today?" Mossy, a regular in Nuttie's, asked, coming dangerously close to falling off the bar stool himself. "That's the thing about you Americans; ye never seem to realise how old ye are. He was in his seventies at least, so Kate said. One minute he was riding along and the next he was on the ground. A fella from Dallas and there was I thinking all those Texans were born cowboys."

"So you reckon seventy is past it, Mossy?" Sophia said, with mischief in her eyes.

"Ah, you're taking me up wrong now Sophia. There's plenty of life left in this old dog." He winked at her. And Sophia burst out laughing just as Kate came over to join them.

"How was Jessie today?" asked Eoghan, concerned.

Kate shook her head. "To be honest, she's physically still very weak but I'm even more worried because she seems to have lost interest in everything except Sam. Mam looked after things while Monique and I brought the group trekking. And her home baking and jams with great big dollops of cream went down a treat."

"Ah good, was the Texan all right?" asked Eoghan, nodding his head in the direction of Mossy.

"The only thing hurt was his dignity," smiled Kate. "He was stuffing himself with Mam's scones last I saw of him."

"Sure that's grand so," smiled Eoghan.

"Hey Kate, come 'ere," a voice called from the other end of the bar.

"Catch ye later," she said, leaving them alone again.

"She's a great kid. Hopefully we'll be able to take her on full-time in the future, if things continue to go well. Have you ever seen her art though? Bloody fantastic! Will you have another?"

"I will, thanks," said Sophia, thinking if any of her friends saw her they'd be amazed at her propping up the bar in a quaint Irish pub. But she was having a great time, and then Grace came over to join them.

"Eoghan, I just got a glowing email from Juan Moreno to say that there was a positive buzz on the tenders heading back to the liner. He'll provide us with the passenger satisfaction scores as soon as possible."

"Sure that's fantastic. Oh, the power of technology. What'll you have?"

"A sparkling water, thanks. Sophia, I was wondering if you're free in the morning, I'd like to introduce you to someone."

"Absolutely."

"Pick you up at ten-thirty so."

"Grace!" called Dirk.

"Sorry guys, see ye later," she said, going back to join Dirk and the others.

At ten-thirty a.m. the next morning, Grace turned the quaint ivory doorknob of Sophia's pretty little summer house.

"Hello the house," she called.

"Are we having coffee first?"

"No, we'll have one in my mother's house. I'd love you to meet her. I know you two will get along."

"I'd imagine we will but give me a break with your terrible imitation of my accent. Yours is worse than Kate's. She sounds more like an Indian – the Eastern kind."

"True, I'll give you that. Anyway Mam is expecting us. You've been here so long I'm embarrassed that you two haven't met yet. By the way what do you think of Eoghan?" Grace smiled knowingly.

"Well now Missy, the living cheek of ya!" Sophia chuckled.

"Now look who's talking about accents? You're still no better, Sophia Wynthrope. Come on, life definitely begins at what age did you say you are? Seventy," Grace joked.

"My gosh, the nerve of you. And I count you as a friend …" laughed Sophia, getting into the passenger seat of Grace's silver Golf.

Twenty minutes later Grace pulled up outside the small terraced house in which Grace had grown up. She opened the front door with her key.

"Mam, we're here. Oh, the smell is lovely," said Grace, adding, "we're in for a treat, my mother bakes the best fruit scones in Ireland."

"Come in, come in, you're very welcome," said Grace's mother, coming out from the kitchen into the tiny hallway.

"Sophia, I'd like you to meet Molly, my mam."

"It's a pleasure to meet you Molly. I'm delighted to be invited to your home."

"Sophia, I've heard so much about you from Grace I feel I know you already. Grace, bring Sophia into the sitting room. I've set up a tray."

Grace smiled. Her mother liked to use the "good" room. All the family had chipped in a few years back and they had completely redecorated the inside and outside of the house. Marilyn, their eldest sister, had wanted her mother to move away. Marilyn had married well and wasn't exactly proud of her humble beginnings. But her mother was contented, surrounded by lovely friends and neighbours and a community spirit second to none.

"So, Molly, how many children do you have?" asked Sophia.

"Seven, it was crazy in those days, but sure everyone was in the same boat. We had the four girls in the big room and the three boys in the next one and myself and himself in the box room."

"My goodness."

"What about yerself Sophia? Where did you grow up?"

Grace had never asked Sophia any questions about herself and was intrigued to hear the answer.

"My Italian grandmother raised me in the Bronx ..." She paused and Grace wondered should she fill the momentary silence. But then Sophia continued. "My mother was ... let's just say 'a handful', I never knew who my father was, she refused to say. And when I was around six years old my mother disappeared and we never saw her again."

"Oh my Lord, you poor thing," said Molly. Grace was stunned to silence that Sophia had opened up to her mother in this way. She wanted to leave the room to allow them to chat but she couldn't move.

"Molly, strangely it was for the best because my life settled down. Gran and I had a great relationship, she didn't have much but she was hard-working and I was loved. She used to work as a housekeeper for a wealthy family in the city and she believed in education. She never spoke to me in Italian, wanting me to have perfect English. I obtained a scholarship and became a journalist. So things worked out for me."

Grace had never asked Sophia about the limousine experience and was still no wiser as to what Sophia actually did for a living but she certainly knew that being a journalist wouldn't cover the cost of that life.

"Come on. Let's go out into the garden. Sure, aren't we missing the bit of good weather we're getting?" Molly suggested. Grace smiled, knowing her mother wanted to lighten the mood and of course show off the deck her brothers had built at the end of the garden. Her garden was her passion; it had kept her sane in times of great trauma.

They were sitting on the deck at the end of the garden in the shade of the old apple tree her father had planted years back, when Grace heard the doorbell.

"I'll get it, Mam."

"It's probably Lauren and the kids. Lovely. Sophia, you'll get to meet some of my ten grandchildren," said Molly.

"Ten, my goodness, that's wonderful!"

"Do you have children?"

"I have one son, his name is Richard."

"Lovely," said Molly, stretching to pour more tea. Meanwhile Grace stood gaping at the person on her mother's doorstep.

"What are *you* doing here?"

"I can explain. I recognised the car. I was on my way back from a call when I spotted it. So I thought to hell with it. I'll call and say hello. Hello." He smiled that deadly smile of his. She was completely lost for words. "Aren't you going to invite me in?"

"It's my mother's house."

"I'd love to meet her."

"Are you for real?" But she couldn't help laughing.

"Ah, sure why not? I'd murder a cup of tea."

"Em …" She had never felt so unnerved in her life and was grateful when she heard her mother's voice call from the kitchen. "Is that Lauren?"

"No, Mam, just an old friend of mine."

"Bring her in so."

She looked straight into the green-grey eyes that so unnerved her. He grinned and said. "Can I borrow a skirt?"

She laughed and held the door wider to allow him to pass. Her heart was pounding so much she was afraid he'd hear it in the confines of the tiny hall. "My mother is in the back garden with Sophia." He was already nearly out the back door before she finished the sentence.

"Get a grip," she told herself.

"Hello again, Sophia. And you must be Grace's mam," he said.

In different circumstances Grace would have laughed when she saw the look of confusion on her mother's face. "Mam, this is Jack Leslie. Em, an old friend of mine." Grace looked at Sophia, who seemed equally confused.

"Oh … hello Jack. Come over. Sit down with us. Grace, make a fresh brew, will you? Jack …" Molly said, pondering "I can't remember Grace ever talking about a Jack. But sure there were so many in this family it was hard to keep up with them all."

"I probably wasn't worth remembering," he laughed. "You must be into the garden … it's very beautiful."

"Jack, I love it. It's small but it suits me now. What with my age and all!"

"You couldn't be a day over sixty."

"Oh, go on outta that," she said to Sophia. "We have a right charmer here, don't you think?"

Sophia laughed along. Grace watched from the kitchen where she could hear the whole conversation as she waited for the kettle. She was glad of the reprieve. What was going on with her? She was a happily engaged woman. She set out a tray with a fresh pot of tea and more scones and took them to the garden.

"They look delicious. I'll bet they are homemade," said Jack, his eyes twinkling mischievously up at her. "Thanks," he said, buttering one. Why did he have such an effect on her? "So, Grace, when is the big day?"

"The 26th of May next year, please God," Molly answered for her. "We're looking forward to it. She's living with the grandest chap. Ah, but I'm wicked old-fashioned and so I'm delighted he's making an honest woman of her." She nodded towards Sophia. Leave it to her mother to tell all, thought Grace. No one could get a word in as she continued blabbering on.

"What about you, Jack?" her mother asked. "Are you married?"

"It's a long story," he answered, taking a bite from the scone.

"Are you just back from vacation Jack? You have a wonderful sun tan," remarked Sophia, looking sympathetically at Grace, who wondered was she that obviously disconcerted? She was grateful to Sophia for her attempt to change the subject.

"Actually I came back nearly three months ago. I was living in Dubai for the last nine years. I'm always out in the weather so I guess I'm holding the tan."

It was then that Grace noticed he wasn't wearing a wedding ring.

"That sounds very exciting. What do you work at?" asked Sophia.

"I'm a vet. Grace and I actually met one summer. It was great, wasn't it?" He looked straight into Grace's eyes.

"It was a long time ago," Grace replied, avoiding his gaze. It was just too much.

"Twenty years," he said as Grace felt the blood rush to her cheeks.

"Where was I that summer? Oh, yes, we went to London for the first time. Oh my, what a city," remarked Sophia.

Oh thank you, Sophia, thought Grace as she watched her mother staring dubiously at the stranger in her garden. But her mother loved to talk and was easily distracted by the mention of London.

"London, I loved it. Grace brought me there a few years ago. Thanks to Ryanair and my family I've been to quite a few European cities," Molly reminisced. Her mother was losing the run of herself, thought Grace, as they chatted on about cities and other inconsequential things until finally Jack decided to go. Grace walked behind him through the kitchen and into the small hallway.

"I'm glad I took the chance today. It was nice. Maybe we can catch up again," he said, turning around unexpectedly in the hallway.

She caught her heel in the hall mat and fell forward into his arms. He held her for a moment. Neither of them spoke until she broke the silence. "Jack, I don't think that would be a good idea," she said, pulling away, but her heart was thumping so loudly she could almost hear it.

"I didn't mean it like that. Jeez Grace I'm sorry I've offended you. I just thought we could be friends, like we used to be."

"We can't be friends Jack. Let's just leave it as the nice memory it is."

"Goodbye Gracey, take good care of yourself." He turned, opened the door and left. She closed it and leaned against it to gather herself. Thinking about Jack made her feel out of control, not to mention being near him. She needed steady and reliable not this … what … what was she feeling? Whatever it was she didn't like it. She brushed herself down, shook her head and walked into the garden as if nothing had happened.

"Are you coming in for a while?" asked Sophia, when Grace pulled up outside her summer house.

"No, I think I'll go for a walk on the beach now that I'm down this way," said Grace. Her head was miles away. She needed to focus. She had a million things to do for work and she was worried about Jess.

"If you want to talk you know where I am."

"Thanks, Sophia, but I'm okay." Sophia looked doubtfully at her but didn't say another word. "See you tomorrow."

Grace parked the car at the beach and leaned back in the driver's seat, glad to be alone. She was so tired. It was mid-September and it had been a busy season. But none of that had fazed her in the way Jack Leslie had. She locked the car and strolled over towards the sand bank. When she was at the top she took in the view. The sun was going down and the sky was a purplish pink. It was breathtakingly beautiful. She loved the expanse of the bay. She could see for miles. Being near the sea always made her feel less alone in the world and that there was something greater guiding it.

She took off her flip-flops and rolled up her white linen trousers. If only she wasn't tired all the time. Walking along the water's edge she felt the waves breaking gently against her bare feet. Jack Leslie, oh how she had wished that he would come back and be her knight in shining armour all those years ago. Now she didn't need one. She was right to say she didn't want to see him again. She loved Dirk, he was her world. Steady and reliable.

"Thanks, Geoff," Jessie said, as her husband handed her a cup of tea. They were sitting outside on the patio watching Sam playing with Buzz in the garden.

"How are you doing?" Geoff asked.

"Tired," she replied. "I'm glad the summer is over. Sam is settling well in school."

"You've lost so much weight." She gave him a withering look. "Seriously, you were never heavy Jess but you're under what you were before you were pregnant. It's just I notice you're not eating or sleeping properly ..."

"Neither are you!" she said, sipping the tea. "I saw the letter from the bank."

"I didn't want to worry you."

"Honey, I'm not fragile. We have a responsibility for this place, together. I need to know about things."

"I'm sorry. It's just, well, I just want you to get better." He looked at her with eyes full of anxiety. "Jess, you walk around the house at all hours of the night ..."

"How are you doing?"

He shrugged his shoulders and looked towards Sam. He said, "What I wouldn't do to have them here with us. Sometimes when I'm in the tractor the tears start to flow and I just can't stop them."

Jessie listened, afraid to move in case he'd stop talking.

"I was so excited. I couldn't believe how blessed we were to be having twins. 'Two for the price of one', they'd say. People would think they were original when they'd say it." He smiled forlornly and took a sip of beer. "I'd love more children but when people say, 'you're young ye can try again,' I feel like screaming, 'that won't bring our babies back'. I know they're trying their best to be consoling but ... they didn't see them. They were so perfect and so different looking. I felt they had personalities. I reckon that Anthony would have been a tough little cookie and, well, Geoff, he'd be …" He coughed, to hide his emotions. "Ah that's life. What can we do? I'm sorry for upsetting you." He got up and touched her on the shoulder. "I won't hide anything again." He walked past to join Sam. "Fancy a game of hurling, son?"

The tears rolled down her cheeks. She remembered the nurse saying, talk to one another. They hadn't because she couldn't and she didn't want to upset Geoff. She needed to hear him. As a woman she got plenty of support, whether she wanted it or not. She'd have to get her act together. Face the world, teach the riding lessons again, otherwise they'd lose their regulars. She also needed to attract new people and the last person they'd want to be near was a mope. She'd have to get herself going again. Facing people at the school gate on Monday would be a huge challenge, but one that would have to be done.

Sophia opened the door leading to the terrace of her rental. Her holiday was nearly over. Chatting with Molly had reminded her so much of her grandmother. There was such a genuine humbleness about Molly that Sophia had almost felt moved to tears.

Wandering around the mature gardens of the complex she felt a sense of peace that she hadn't experienced in a long, long time. She still had trouble sleeping but her days were filled. She had visited almost every historical place within a thirty-mile radius. And she had met some lovely people through Grace. She was regretful that she hadn't met Jessie, Grace's best friend who had lost her baby twins. It was such a heartbreaking thing to have happened. Her phone rang, bringing her back from her contemplation.

"Hi Grace," she said, seeing her picture pop up.

"Hey Soph, Mam was wondering if you'd like to go to bingo with her tonight?"

"Why not!" said Sophia, smiling.

"She said she'll pick you up at seven. Have to fly."

The girl was like a whirlwind, thought Sophia. She worked so hard and managed to visit Jessie and include her. Sophia had assured her countless times that there was no need to, but Grace had simply replied, "You're in my town now." The same words Sophia had used to her that first day in New York. Sophia had laughed but she had also noted how exhausted Grace was. Thankfully the cruise season was coming to an end with the final one arriving next week. She was seriously considering extending her stay to see it. There was such a buzz around when the ships docked.

Sophia walked back to the little house and placed her coffee cup in the sink. Running the tap to wash it she was suddenly overwhelmed by memories of her first home with Bill – a tiny bedsit in a rough area of the city. It had been all they could afford at the time. Bill's parents had disinherited him for marrying her, saying she wasn't good enough for their son. He had never forgiven them and nor had they asked for it. He had given up everything to be with her and Richard. If only she could hold him in her arms again.

She wiped the tears that had begun to flow with the back of her hand. They were never far away. Why ... oh why? She gathered herself and picked up her cell phone. It would be nine a.m. in New York.

"Hi Colleen, is Richard available?"

"Hi Mrs Wynthrope ... How is Ireland?"

"Wonderful Colleen, much better than I expected."

"Someday I'll get to the land of my ancestors."

"I hope you will Colleen."

"I'm putting you through, bye for now."

"Hi Mom, it's good to hear you. But is everything okay?"

"I just wanted to hear your voice. You sound so like your dad."

"Mom ... are you sure you want to be all the way over there? You know how I feel about it."

"Richard ... it's actually doing me the world of good. Truly." She tried to reassure him.

"Mom, you never call in the middle of a working day."

"I've joined a cookery class, and I've met some really genuine people. It's fun and yes I'm ... happy. Well as happy as one can be ..."

"Okay, if you're sure."

"Richard, I'd like to extend my stay. What do you think?" There was silence. "Are you still there?"

"Yes, yes of course, as long as you're happy ..." She could hear someone in the background. "Sorry, Mom, I have to go ... you know how it is around here. I'll call you later and we can chat."

"Maybe you'll visit."

"Have to go. But I promise I'll ring you back later."

"Of course," she said, clicking off. It had been unfair to ring him at the office. He was always so crazy busy. But she felt better for having spoken with him. Her next call was to her letting agent where the lady assured her that she could stay for as long as she liked.

Chapter Six

I'm warning you, Dirk, you tell her or I will," said Kate.

"Do you think she'll believe you over me?" Kate could hear the sneering tone in his voice on the other end of the phone. Kate had heard a rumour from Pat Twomey that when Dirk was away with the rowing team in Poole he had been seen with a woman. The problem was that she didn't know the full story.

"There's a witness."

"Pat was drunk. He's making things up. He's always been jealous of me." He changed his tone to one of placating. "Honestly Kate, do you think I would do anything to hurt Grace? We've finally set a date, for God's sake. Twomey is lying."

Dirk sounded so genuinely upset she began to wonder if maybe Joe had only made it up to cause trouble. "Well then tell her what's being said because it will be all over Bayrush soon and I won't have you making a fool of my sister."

She hung up. Jesus, maybe it was all lies. And the last thing she wanted was to upset Grace unnecessarily.

Jessie held Sam's hand as she walked towards the school gate. Sally, Oliver's mum, had been doing the school run for her. She could tell he was delighted that she was bringing him this morning. He chatted away happily beside her.

"Teacher promised to change our places today."

"Isn't that great!" she said, only half listening. She was terrified anyone would say anything to her that might make her cry. Sally waved and walked towards her.

"Morning Sam," Sally smiled.

"I hope me and Oliver get to sit together," said Sam. "Teacher promised to move us." Jessie smiled and mouthed a thanks to Sally. Sally had been a rock over the past weeks, inviting Sam over for play dates with Ollie when she really needed the support.

"It's going to be fine, chin up," Sally whispered to her and then she said to Sam and Oliver, "Don't be too disappointed if it doesn't happen, okay guys?"

"Hi Jessie, I haven't seen you all summer. What did you call your babies?" asked another mother. Seeing the look on Sally's face the poor woman apologised and kept on walking.

"Sam and Ollie, run along into the playground now! Enjoy the day," said Sally.

But Sam just stood looking up at Jessie; his big brown eyes began to well up. She hugged him tightly and then kissed his forehead and said, "Have a great day honey. See you at two."

"Okay, see you later. You will be here, won't you?"

"I promise."

He ran off with his pal while she did everything in her power to hold it together.

"I'm glad you made him that promise Jess. It will get easier. People haven't heard because it happened during the holidays. Come back to my house for a coffee. You're as pale as a ghost."

"Thanks, Sal, for everything. I will so." She climbed into the jeep but she was shaking. It took all of her power to follow Sally, she really just wanted to go home and curl up in a ball and cry.

"Grace, I heard about a group who are into dressing up as Vikings. They're having a night upstairs in Walton's in Waterford. Will you come with me?" asked Kate, closing the laptop she had set up on the office table.

"Can I come?" asked Sophia, who was helping with filing.

"Brill, the more the merrier," said Kate.

"What time?" asked Grace, busy sending an email from her laptop.

"Seven."

"Yes, sounds interesting."

At seven Sophia parked outside Walton's and they were greeted by a Viking.

"Welcome ladies, follow the signs," said a voice, from behind the masked helmet. They began to giggle like schoolgirls.

"What have you got us into Kate Fitzgerald?" laughed Grace as they climbed the stairs.

The room was full. It was a talk on the history of Ireland's oldest city and its Viking Triangle. "A thousand years of history in a thousand paces." The talk was very informative with a questions and answers session, after which they provided tea and coffee and time to view the work of the re-enactment group. Sophia was enthralled, chatting to a lady who had sourced and made her costume. She had even made the dye from berries, exactly as they had done in the old days. Some men wore battle armour and had made shields and the chain mail themselves.

"You really do plan to ignore me!" one of the warriors said, taking off his helmet.

"I'm sorry," said Grace, and then she burst out laughing. "Jack, in all fairness how could I have known you, I never thought you to be the dress up type."

"I got roped in."

"Chained, you mean."

They both laughed.

"I enjoyed the talk. The area is so full of history and folklore," said Grace, taken aback by how sexy he looked in costume.

"To be honest, it's terrible to think that I'm from here and yet I didn't know that the Irish flag was flown for the first time here. Are you into history?"

"I'm interested in tourism. I worked in the Tourist Office for a few years."

"So that's why you're here. You're representing them."

"No, about four years ago I set up a business with a friend. We organise ground arrangements for cruise line passengers and other groups who stay in the area."

"So you did make it." He smiled, his grey-green eyes looking deeply into hers, completely disconcerting her.

"Hello again," said Sophia, joining them. "I'd hardly have recognised you. What a warrior you make!"

Grace laughed, happy to be interrupted.

"Who's he? Gorgeous in a rugged kinda way," Kate whispered into her ear. "I think I'll join this group. There are a few fine-looking fellows around. They're doing a re-enactment battle scene in the yard in a few minutes, all swords and shields and testosterone. Are you coming?"

"I'll follow you in a minute," said Grace, but Jack was engrossed in conversation with Sophia so she wandered over to a table where some women were displaying knitwear and braids. She began talking to them about the group. Her mind was working overtime. Wouldn't it be great to arrange a Viking banquet scene for a cruise group? She discovered they were all volunteers who wanted to raise awareness about how the Vikings had lived. And they planned to invite other Viking groups from Northern Europe to Waterford. Some of the group had been to Norway and had had a great time exchanging ideas.

She spotted Kate in the middle of a group heading downstairs; she was laughing and in her element. Kate was so artistic and creative; this could be a great interest for her. Grace worried so much about her.

"Penny for them."

"You really have a thing about creeping up on me."

"Big ego or what?" He laughed. She felt the colour rise in her face.

"Hi Jack." A pretty, blonde girl passed dressed in a linen dress of Viking times. She looked very like the girl Grace had seen on the beach. Grace felt a pang of jealousy she had never experienced before and wasn't in the least bit happy about. What was coming over her? She looked around, desperate to leave, but Kate had gone to the yard and Sophia was talking with the historian who had given the presentation. Jack was chatting with the blonde still, so she took out her mobile and began texting the two to let them know she would see them at the car. She couldn't stay any longer.

"Fancy a coffee," Jack asked, coming towards her and inclining his head towards the bar, "or something stronger?"

Sophia had driven them and lately Grace had noticed even a whiff of coffee made her feel sick. "A glass of white wine would be nice, thanks." She couldn't believe she was doing this. Everything told her to stop. She was in a relationship. She was very happy. What the hell was she playing at … *It's a glass of wine, Grace*, she told herself as she watched him walk to the bar. She'd never look at a Viking again in the same light. She sat on the bar stool while he ordered. She couldn't help studying his face in profile. He had hardly aged. He turned just then. Sensing she had been caught, she blushed.

"So how's what's-his-name?" he asked, smirking.

"You mean Dirk."

"What kind of name is Dirk?"

"His father is German, but he was born here."

"Bet he got some slanging over that name …"

"He never said. Why are you so interested anyway?" It was a dangerous question because she wasn't sure if she wanted to know the answer.

"Just wondered what kind of guy you'd choose – thought you might go for a bookworm."

"Why?"

"You being such a one yourself …"

"You think you know me just because we spent a few days together twenty years ago!"

"Thought I got a handle on you …"

"Listen Jack, just because I told you things that I never told anybody else doesn't mean you know me. We're grown-ups now, well at least, I am!" She looked him up and down in his costume but found she was blushing even more from either temper or attraction or the bloody wine.

"Jeez Grace, I'm sorry, I didn't mean to upset you and I never did or never will mention what you told me. I know what it's like. My father nearly cost my family the farm because of his drinking. Well, I'm sure you already knew …"

"Hey Jack, I'm finally finished. Where's that drink you offered me?" It was the pretty blonde again.

"This is Pam … Grace," he said, introducing them and calling for a vodka and slimline tonic.

"Hi Grace, did you enjoy the evening? Different isn't it!"

"Yes." She was completely flustered. It was becoming clearer as to who had "roped" him in.

"We're hoping to host a group from Norway soon, that's why the boys are practising their battle skills. I'm trying to convince this guy to get involved, but at least I managed to get him to dress up tonight. Doesn't he look the part?"

Grace didn't know where to look and just about managed to nod in agreement and finish her glass in the same movement. The girl was in her mid-twenties and gorgeous. Jack was beaming at her.

"Listen, I'd better go. Nice to meet you Pam!" she said, getting off the bar stool and praying she wouldn't trip as was her way when she was flustered.

"Take care, Grace," he said.

"You too, Jack." She couldn't get away fast enough. She didn't even look for Kate and Sophia. Instead she made her way downstairs to the main bar; it was busy so she went to the ladies'. Closing the cubicle she turned the toilet seat lid down and sat on it. She began to text Kate, hoping she was ready to leave too. She heard voices from the basin area – one of them was familiar. It was Sandra Payne's sister. Her husband was on the same rowing team as Dirk.

"Pat says he's always the same when they go away. Jesus, I can't understand why he can't keep it in his pants."

"Who are you talking about?" asked the other woman.

"Our coxswain, he only has to give a girl a nod and she'd go off with him. It's unbelievable!"

Grace's couldn't believe her ears. It could only be Dirk they were talking about; her head was thumping. She didn't want to hear another word but was afraid to move.

"Isn't he getting married next year?" asked the woman. Grace could hardly breathe now.

"Being engaged didn't stop him. I doubt a wedding ring will make any difference." The other woman sniggered.

"The poor girl. Someone should tell her."

"Sure she hasn't a clue. You'd want to see him when he's with her, falling under and over her, it would sicken you. Did you see the state of the dress on Kate Fitzgerald …?" The bathroom door closed and there was nothing left but the sound of silence.

"What bitches!" Grace muttered. Had they seen her coming in? The cheek of them for talking about her sister like that! And what the hell was going on? Dirk … could it be true? Surely someone would have told her. She was shaking from head to toe and she felt like puking; lifting the toilet-seat lid she did. Her mobile rang. She picked it up from the floor and saw a photo of Kate's smiling face. With hands still shaking she answered. "Where are you sis?"

"Outside, please say you're ready to go, Grace?"

"Be there in a sec." She clicked off, and trying to compose herself she decided not to tell Kate or Sophia what had happened. She just wanted to get home as soon as possible and after that she had no idea what the hell she was going to do.

When she walked into the living room, Dirk was lying on the couch watching TV.

"Hi darling, did you enjoy the evening?"

"Don't you DARLING me, you miserable, fucking bastard."

"What?" He jumped up. "What the hell is wrong? What has your sister being saying?"

"My sister … what's my sister got to do with it?"

"Well you were out with her tonight. I told her it was all lies. Pat Twomey has always had it in for me. Spreading lies and gossip about me."

She was shaking with rage. He was completely denying it.

"What lies Dirk? Tell me what you think I heard."

He paused; a look of complete confusion crossed his face. And then he came towards her.

"Listen to me. There are a lot of people jealous of us, of what we have, and now that we finally set a date, things are worse. They're saying things about me that just aren't true. I mean, Kate heard them and asked me about it and I assured her just like I'm assuring you. They are simply not true."

She slumped into the chair. Maybe he was telling the truth. He was always kind and supportive. It couldn't be true. He was her solid, reliable Dirk. She had never noticed him looking at other women. Was he really capable of giving a girl "the nod" and she would go off with him? Wasn't that all a bit childish, really? Could they have been talking about somebody else? She desperately wanted to believe that they were.

"Do you have a new coxswain?"

"What ... no. Why ... what are you talking about?" He was looking at her as if she'd lost it. She stood up slowly and as she walked past him, he reached for her, pleading. "Please, Grace ..."

"Don't touch me," she said. " And don't say another word?"

Her head was pounding as she rushed upstairs. When she reached the bedroom, she stood for a moment and looked around. Then, almost as though she had been taken over by someone else, she calmly took her carry-on bag from the wardrobe. She placed a few necessities in it. She picked up her laptop from the office and walked downstairs and out the front door, closing it to the sound of Dirk running along the hallway. The front door swung open.

"Come back Grace," he called after her. "We can talk about this. Don't be silly!"

But she was already in her car. She drove off. When she was a kilometre away she stopped and burst out crying. It was only nine-thirty; so much had happened in such a short space of time.

The phone rang, startling Jessie from her thoughts.

"It's on the worktop in the kitchen," Geoff called, from the living room.

"Jessie ... it's me." The line was breaking up a little.

"Grace, are you okay?"

"No."

"Where are you?"

"In the car."

"Oh my God, did you have an accident? Are you hurt?"

"No."

"Grace ... where are you and stop talking in riddles! I'm getting annoyed now."

Jessie could hear a kind of muffled cry. "Gracey, tell me please, where are you?"

"It's okay, don't worry about me. You have Geoff and Sam to worry about. How did school go today?"

"Long story. Where are you?"

"I'm on Bayrush beach."

"Why are you on the beach at this hour?"

"I always liked the beach."

"So do I but that's not the point. I'm on my way."

The line went dead. Geoff looked at Jessie who was still holding the phone in her hand.

"What's the matter? What was that all about?"

"It was Grace, she's on Bayrush beach."

"The beach?"

"I don't know how long I'll be. Will you sort Sam out?"

"Of course," said Geoff.

His face was full of concern but she didn't want to say too much in front of Sam so she kissed them both and ruffled Sam's hair. "I shouldn't be too long. Dad will read you a story eh! Go get ready for bed."

"Cool," said Sam, running upstairs.

"Be careful," said Geoff as she rushed out the door.

Less than ten minutes later, Jessie parked her jeep beside Grace's car and set off across the stones piled up against the storm wall. She could see a lone figure sitting on the wall. This is crazy, she thought.

"Gracey," she called out as she clambered up along the stones and sat beside her.

"What happened?"

The tears rolled down Grace's face and her body shook.

"It's okay, you don't have to talk. We'll just sit here, okay honey?"

Grace nodded just like a little girl and Jessie took her hand. They sat like that for ages, just watching the waves break gently onto the sand below them. Eventually Grace spoke.

"It's Dirk – it's over."

"What?"

"It's over Jessie. He cheated on me, on us."

"Are you sure? That's a pretty strong accusation."

"I couldn't be surer. It was on the rowing trip. The thought of him with someone else makes me feel sick, I had to get away."

Jessie was stunned; she'd never have thought that Dirk would cheat. She'd had her misgivings about him being the one but never that he'd cheat. After a while Jessie said, "My ass is sore. Is yours?"

"Yes."

"Come on back to my place. I'll make up the spare room."

"No, no, I'm okay. I'll go to Mam's."

Jessie gave her a look.

"Okay, you're right. I'm not up for the interrogation."

"Let's go."

Grace didn't object again. When they reached Jessie's house, Geoff made himself scarce while Jessie boiled the kettle. Grace kept looking at her phone. It was full of missed calls and texts from Dirk. She turned it off. She began to talk about what had happened and then she finally asked. "Did you ever hear rumours, Jess?"

"Never."

"Coz Kate did."

"Oh, and did Kate tell you?"

"No."

"Maybe you should ring her."

"Not tonight. I've had as much as I can take for one evening. I'm such a fool Jess. I mean to overhear people talking about him in the city – thirty kilometres from Bayrush. Oh Jess I love him. I never doubted him." She finished her tea. "I need sleep."

They made up the spare room together in silence. Jessie pulled the bedroom door closed and walked down the landing. She couldn't believe what had happened; how come they had never heard that Dirk was such a cheat? How two-faced could he be? She wondered was it actually true or just vicious rumours. He was one of those people you could love or hate. He was hard to be indifferent to. Maybe tomorrow would bring more clarity; they were all too upset to think straight tonight.

Kate arrived at Grace's house. Dirk's car was still in the drive, which was unusual. And Grace's wasn't. Not over thinking things, she parked her ten-year-old banger next to Dirk's shiny Audi. She really was taking the look off the place, she thought as she rang the doorbell. It swung open.

"You, you have the nerve to show your face here after all the trouble you've caused. I told you it was lies and yet you go and ruin mine and Grace's life. It wasn't enough for you to ruin your own with your pathetic drug taking. Jealousy … is a terrible trait, Kate Fitzgerald."

The door slammed. Kate stood transfixed to the spot. She couldn't believe her ears. She turned and fled to her car, shaking. She drove away wondering where in God's name was Grace. Automatically she drove towards Bayrush and Jessie's house. Jessie's jeep was coming down the drive as Kate drove up. They stopped beside one another.

"I'm dropping Sam to school," said Jessie, nodding towards the backseat where Sam was. "The kettle is boiled. She's in the kitchen."

"Cheers Jess, see you in a while." Kate knew that Jessie wouldn't say anything in front of Sam. Her heart was pounding. What had Dirk told Grace? How had all of this happened? Oh God, please let my sister be okay.

When she walked in the back door Grace and Geoff were sitting at the kitchen table drinking tea. Geoff got up.

"Hi Kate, I'm off to do a bit. See you later. There's tea in the pot. Help yourself."

Grateful, she took a mug from the rack and poured it, and then she joined Grace at the table. Grace looked up and she could see that her sister mustn't have slept a wink.

"You knew and didn't tell me, Kate."

"I didn't know for sure Grace. I rang him and told him to talk to you about a rumour I had heard."

"Well he didn't and I had to go through the indignity of overhearing about my fiancé's infidelity in a city thirty kilometres from Bayrush. And it's not the first time. I keep replaying the conversation I overheard in my head. Quote 'He's always the same when we go away. Jesus I can't understand why he can't keep it in his pants.' Did you know that too and think it wasn't important enough to tell me?"

"Hey, just wait a second Grace. I know you're angry but it's not me you should be angry with. All I heard was that when he was in Poole recently he was seen with a bargirl outside a club in a questionable situation. It's not exactly a lot to go on. And that asshole can talk his way out of most situations. That's why I rang him to ask him to explain it to you in case something like this happened."

Grace sat still with her shoulders slumped. Kate didn't know what to do next so she stayed quiet which was not her way.

"Kate, tell me it's not all around Bayrush that he's been making a fool of me for years."

"I can't answer that Grace because it was only by chance that I heard about that incident. I mean, let's be honest, who is going to tell me – I'm your sister. Anyway does it matter? Today's news – tomorrow's chip wrapping. Since when did you care what people say? It's what you're going to do next that's important."

"I feel such a fool Kate. How long has it taken me to finally set a date? Dad leaving … never really being sure of a man. I had so many trust issues. Always wondering would I be let down and now it's happened. I will never trust a man again. How stupid am I?"

"Stop, Gracey," said Kate, getting up to hug her big sister. "Don't be so hard on yourself. Look at me. I'm a jealous junkie or so your fiancé has just informed me. Now that's what I call issues."

Grace smiled through her tears. "When did that happen?"

"Oh, just this morning when my big sister forgot to inform me that the shit had hit the fan and I walked right in to it!"

"Oh Kate, nothing ever puts you down."

"Not any more. Gracey. Thanks to you and to Jessie. Never again. Life is too short. Now go up and get dressed, we have a shitload of work to do."

Grace had asked Jessie to collect some clothes, files and other essentials from the house. She knew she was being childish but she just couldn't face Dirk yet. She had stayed in Jessie's all week.

"My car is here so much, Jessie. People will talk."

"Let them. When they're talking about you they're leaving somebody else alone."

"No, seriously Jess, I'll have to move out. It's not fair on you and Geoff."

"Take all the time you need," Jessie assured her.

"Thanks, Jess. How are you doing? I heard you walking around again last night."

Jessie sighed. "I have a riding lesson now. I have to just get on with it Grace."

Grace just nodded as Jessie said, "See you later." And she disappeared quickly out the back door.

Tidying the breakfast dishes Grace thought so much had changed in both of their lives in just three months. The daytime wasn't so bad because she was busy. But her nights were awful. It felt like somebody had physically removed her heart. She was angry, hurt and confused and she could hardly eat. Breaking up was one hell of a way to lose weight, she thought. But it was time. She picked up her mobile phone and after three rings, he answered.

"Dirk."

"Oh, Grace," he stammered. "How are you …?"

"Can I call over sometime soon?"

"Yeah, great, how is tonight?"

"Seven o'clock."

"Okay, see you then."

She felt nauseous and ran to the bathroom to be sick.

"Come in," said Dirk. "Are you hungry? I have some food. It's your favourite, stuffed pork steak."

Grace threw her eyes to heaven and said, "Thanks but I've eaten, Dirk. We need to talk."

"Yes, we do."

"What about a tea or a coffee?"

"Tea, thanks."

She watched him walk across the kitchen to boil the kettle. The realisation hit her that she had given so much of herself to him and to this house. Buying it had been such a wonderful time in their relationship, shopping and decorating it together. He had been more into it than her and now they would have to sort it all out.

He placed the tray down on the kitchen table, and seeing the pottery mugs she remembered the day they bought them in a quaint little pottery workshop in the West of Ireland. Hold it together, she thought.

"Look Grace, can we please try again? I really am sorry but all the times you went on trips don't tell me you didn't ..."

She looked at him in amazement and jumped up. "Dirk, YOU ARE THE PITS. You bastard. Some crazy part of me hoped that none of it was true. You are so in the wrong you can't even defend yourself. You've called people liars and the way you spoke to my sister is unforgivable. IT IS SO OVER." She stormed down the hall. He ran after her, shouting.

"It would never have happened if you had agreed to marry me sooner."

She turned and with eyes blazing said, "I can't believe you Dirk. Do you honestly think that a wedding ring would have made you keep it in your pants? So this is NOW all my fault?"

"No, I'm not saying that ..."

"And for the record I never fooled around with anybody else ever. More fool me by the sounds of it!"

"Look, let's not do this. Can't we just try again? I love you, Grace. I always will. I am so sorry."

"Dirk, I am devastated by this. I can't sleep. I can't eat. But some day I will wake up and feel okay again. I will never forgive you. I'll pick up my clothes and things when you're not here. Sell this place." She walked out, slamming the door behind her.

It was a bright September evening and her life was falling apart. She knew moving out was a rash decision but she couldn't bear to be in that house for another second. They'd never get what they paid for it. She'd be in debt forever. It might even put her business in jeopardy but she didn't care. She could not stay there. She drove to Bayrush beach – it was her sanity. She opened the car door and an overwhelming feeling flooded her. She held onto the storm wall and then puked. "Oh my God," she said aloud.

"Are you all right love?" asked an elderly lady who had been walking her dog. Grace nodded. "If you're sure," the lady said but even as she walked away she kept looking back.

"Yes, yes, I'm fine thanks." Grace was mortified, making her way back to sit in the car until her equilibrium was restored. Looking out at the calm sea steadied her and after a few minutes she got out of the car again to walk along the shoreline.

She watched as two teenage boys set up their fishing stands on the sand and found herself wondering what kind of fish they would catch. There was so much she didn't know. She wanted to fill her mind with things of no consequence. Maybe that was why her stomach was in knots. Where was she going to live? What had she done? You weren't supposed to move out – wasn't that the advice that people gave? She hadn't done anything wrong and yet she was now homeless. "You are some fool Grace Fitzgerald," she muttered.

She was exhausted yet she'd hardly walked 500 metres. She sat down on a flat-topped rock. The stench of rotten seaweed added to her nausea. She had to get it together but it was too late; she vomited again.

"That's gross!" said one of the teenagers.

"Cut her a break boy," said the other, adding, "Hey lady are you okay?"

She waved a hand in his direction. "Just had a few too many last night!"

"Cool. I know the feeling." They both grinned at her, pleased with her explanation. What the hell was wrong with her, she wondered. She thought of Sophia; maybe she might have something to settle her tummy. She was staying just up the road. Her two-week vacation had run into four and she still didn't seem to have any plans to leave.

Ten minutes later Grace knocked on Sophia's door. "I just couldn't go back to Jessie's tonight, she has so much to deal with already. I didn't want Sam to see me upset and I don't have the strength to act. Not tonight anyway."

"You don't need an excuse to be here, Gracey." Sophia hugged her. "Come in, honey."

The turf fire was lighting in the open plan living area. Sophia went to the kitchenette and took two glasses from the press and a bottle of wine from the rack.

"None for me thanks, Sophia. My tummy isn't the best. It's cosy in here," remarked Grace.

"Yes, too cosy sometimes!"

"Are you staying around then?"

"Yes, at least for another few weeks. I'm enjoying my time here."

"Good, I'm glad."

"I'm glad you're glad."

"We're beginning to sound ridiculous," said Grace from where she lay on the couch with one of the throws Sophia had bought wrapped around her. "I'm going to look for a place to rent tomorrow."

"Do you want some company?"

"Yeah, that would be nice."

"Grace, you can stay here for a while. I could use the company."

"That's so kind of you, Sophia. Maybe I could take you up on the offer just for a few days. I'm not ready to tell Mam yet and it's not fair to intrude any longer on Jessie and Geoff. I was so angry this evening that I told Dirk to put the house up for sale. We'll never get what we paid for it. God, I just don't know what I'm going to do."

"Take your time, Grace. Don't make any rash decisions. Maybe there is some reasonable explanation. Have you talked it out?"

"Sophia, I thought maybe it was all lies. Some crazy part of me was nearly prepared to forgive him. I had thought that maybe the guy had mixed Dirk up with someone else. Instead I found out it wasn't just once. Dirk actually thinks it's okay to sleep around when he's away with the lads on weekends. That bastard even had the nerve to say that some women make a big deal about boys' weekends away and how he hoped that I wouldn't change when we were married. I trusted him completely. What a fool I am and a lousy judge of character. There is no turning back. I never want to see or speak to him again."

Chapter Seven

Half an hour later, Sophia sat in the armchair looking at the sleeping figure on her couch. There was something more going on with Grace. She was determined to get to the bottom of it. She picked up Grace's cell phone and looked for Jessie's number.

"Hi Jessie, my name is Sophia Wynthrope, I'm a friend of Grace's."

"Oh hi Sophia, is Grace okay?" said Jessie anxiously.

"I'm sorry to alarm you. It's just that I borrowed Grace's phone to let you know that she's fast asleep on my couch and I think I'll let her sleep."

"That's very kind of you Sophia. She's going through so much at the moment. Grace talks about you a lot and well … I haven't been around to meet you …"

"I was so sorry to hear about what happened to you and your family, Jessie. Life isn't easy at times."

"Thank you, Sophia. Maybe we might meet up soon."

"I'd love that. Jessie, can I ask if you've noticed anything else about Grace?"

"She's constantly tired and not eating properly and she spends most of her time in the bedroom. But you know how it is with breaking up."

"Break-ups are emotionally and physically tiring but I think there is more to it. Maybe I'm over reacting. She plans to look for a place to rent tomorrow but I don't think she'll have the energy."

"I'm glad she's with you tonight. She needs peace and quiet."

"I might suggest a visit to her GP."

"Good idea but I wish you luck. Grace can be a force to be reckoned with if she doesn't want to do something."

"It's worth a shot. Thanks for the chat Jessie."

"Good night Sophia and thanks for ringing. It would be nice to meet in person."

"I'd love to, Jessie. Good night."

The following morning Grace woke and couldn't believe she had fallen asleep on Sophia's couch.

"Ah, you're back with us. I was worried that you might fall off the couch during the night so I put cushions on the floor."

"You're too good to me, Sophia. I'm sorry for barging in on you last night and then falling asleep."

"Let's have some breakfast. I set the table outside on the patio, it's a lovely morning. I picked up some fresh croissants and juice on the way back from my walk, and how about some freshly ground coffee?"

"Everything sounds great except the coffee. I'll have tea if you have it. I'm gone right off coffee lately."

"I got the newspapers too."

"Thanks, Sophia, can I do anything to help?"

"No, go on out and relax."

Grace wandered out to the patio. She looked across towards the sea in the far distance and thought about how much her life had been changed by Dirk's revelation. Did all their friends know he was cheating? Were they laughing at her behind her back? Why hadn't anybody told her?

She hadn't even a toothbrush or a change of clothes. Everything had changed in a moment. She flicked her fingers towards the bright blue morning sky. I'm going to find a little place in the country and live the rest of my days quietly in peace, and alone, she thought. The last two words hurt. Oh, Dirk, why? Even the day she had found out her father was never coming back didn't compare to the hurt she felt right now.

"Here we are." Sophia's words broke her reverie, placing ham and a selection of cheese with the croissants and rolls.

"Thanks, Sophia. This is really kind of you."

"Eat up. I noticed you're losing weight, my girl. Weight you can't afford to lose."

She was glad that somebody was concerned for her. No that wasn't fair; she thought of Jessie immediately. "Oh no – I forgot to ring Jessie last night. She'll be worried sick." She made to get up.

"It's okay; I rang her when you fell asleep. I looked up her number on your cell. She knows where you are."

"Thank you so much, that was thoughtless of me. God, Sophia, I'd love you two to meet."

"We actually talked about that, maybe we can soon. She so understood … Grace, I was thinking maybe you might consider making a trip to see your GP."

"What makes you think I need to see a GP?"

"Lately you look awfully tired. She could recommend a vitamin treatment or, em, I've overstepped, and it's not my place."

"No, no, you're right, Sophia. I am so incredibly tired all the time. I actually feel like going to bed again. I didn't mean to sound so tetchy."

"I've already made up the spare room for you, eat up and go back to bed," said Sophia.

"Thanks, Sophia, I am so tired."

"Promise me that you'll arrange to see your GP soon."

"I promise. Sophia, are you sure about me staying here for a few days?"

"I wouldn't offer if I had any doubt."

"Thanks a million ... for everything. And if you're free later we could call to Jessie's house."

"I'd love that. Now off to bed with you."

When Grace went to bed Sophia set off to Bayrush. She had been reinventing herself since she came to Ireland. She smiled at the thought of making breakfast and arranging a bed for somebody else.

The only connection to her previous reality was the nightly call to her son, Richard. She loved to hear his voice. He had promised to visit sometime in the next few weeks. That was something to look forward to.

Walking along the harbour front she passed an estate agency. Her eyes were drawn to a photograph of a house she had often admired. She couldn't believe it was actually available to rent. Without a second thought she went inside.

Fifteen minutes later she continued walking along the harbour when she heard someone calling her name. She looked around and saw Eoghan waving from a boat moored beside the harbour wall.

"Hi Eoghan," she said, smiling at him.

"Sophia, I was wondering if you've seen Grace recently."

"Yes, as a matter of fact. I saw her this morning."

"Oh, d'ya mind me asking how did you find her?"

"Well ..."

"Look, it's just that I'm worried about her since the break-up."

"Do you have time for a coffee?" she surprised herself by asking.

"Em ... I suppose I do, why not! There's a nice coffee shop just around the corner in the square. Give me a minute to lock up and I'll be with you."

It was a beautiful, clear day. Too still for sailing, she thought, remembering all the times she and Bill had spent sailing in the Hamptons. That house was closed now; she couldn't face going there without him.

Eoghan walked towards her along the gangway and then locked the security gate. He chose a coffee shop that could have been located in New England; it was all white panelling with egg-shell-blue walls. They ordered lattes, and because it was lunchtime Eoghan suggested they order some food. She chose a chicken salad wrap, while Eoghan tucked into a tuna and cheese panini. Sitting opposite her in the comfortable armchairs he declared, "Well, isn't this the life."

Sophia didn't want to talk about Grace and her situation as she wasn't sure how much Eoghan knew, so she asked about his boat.

"Do you fish?"

"Oh yes, I love nothing more than spending my spare time on the sea. I used to have more of it until I met Grace. But sure I love what we do now."

"Bill and I sailed often at the weekends. I miss the sea."

"Oh really, well you're more than welcome to come out in the boat, it's not a sail boat, but sure you might enjoy the scenery … that is if … well I don't mean to be forward. You're married obviously …"

"Oh, em … my husband … died fourteen months ago." Her voice broke as she spoke.

"Oh Sophia, I'm so sorry. I didn't mean to upset you. It must be very difficult."

"We were married for thirty-six years and I have many happy memories. We've had heartache too of course. Life isn't easy."

"It never is, Sophia. We all have our crosses to bear; maybe that's what makes us enjoy the good times."

"I'm bringing down the mood on such a beautiful day."

"How about some dessert?"

"I shouldn't."

"Ah, go on. The apple and berry crumble is delicious here."

"You've twisted my arm." She smiled.

He went to the counter and turned back, making a gesture of drinking. She nodded. He returned with two more lattes and said, "Dessert is on the way."

Eoghan was so easy to talk to that they didn't emerge from the coffee shop until an hour and a half later.

"Well, it was nice chatting with you Sophia and if you ever fancy a trip around the Waterford coastline, send me a text before the weather gets hardy."

"I will thanks, Eoghan. See you again." She walked back to her car.

*

It's going well, thought Grace, as she cut some more lemon drizzle cake. She had brought Sophia to meet Jessie and the two of them were sitting in the armchairs in the corner of Jessie's kitchen. Already they were deep in conversation. There was something about Sophia that drew a person in. Grace was pleased because maybe Sophia could reach Jessie in a way that she couldn't. She had no experience with pregnancy or babies.

"Everybody keeps saying 'they're your angels now.' At first it bugged me, I just wanted my babies. But … well lately I found myself looking up the internet about angels and I even went to the bookshop. It's quite fascinating the amount of information available about angelic spirits."

"I'll tell you something, Jessie, that I have not told many people. I believe in angels," said Sophia, pouring milk into her tea.

"Why haven't you told people?"

"Because they might think I'm crazy."

Jessie raised her eyebrows. "You're right, they probably would. But it is helping me so I don't care what people think. Walk a day in my shoes and see how it feels," said Jessie, with a determination Grace hadn't heard in her in a very long time.

"So true. Whatever helps you make it through the day in one piece can't be bad," said Grace.

"It beats gin or something stronger," remarked Sophia. "I suppose I've always held them close to my heart. I actually can't believe I am having this conversation."

"Me neither, but I'm really glad we are. I knew from our phone conversation that I'd like you. Anyway this one is always singing your praises," said Jessie, tilting her head in Grace's direction. Sophia laughed.

"Our Jessie is nothing if she's not honest," laughed Grace.

"Me too," said Sophia, smiling, and clinked her mug to Jessie's.

Over the following days Grace had been too busy with work to make an appointment with the doctor. But another bout of being sick had forced her to fit one in. She shifted and picked at the foam sticking out from the well-worn leather armchair in the waiting room of the old townhouse surgery. She had been thankful to be swamped with work because it helped to distract her from the overwhelming loneliness and at other times the rage that engulfed her. Her emotions were like a rollercoaster. She really didn't have time for this. Anyway what could she say to the doctor? I'm getting violently sick at all times of the day since my asshole boyfriend told me he's been sleeping around for years. She was tired but couldn't sleep. What the hell was wrong with her? Her stomach was in knots, but that had to be normal. She had been betrayed by the person who was supposed to love her. What a lousy judge of character she was. She'd ask for sleeping tablets. If she got some sleep she might be able to think straight. That was it; a few nights' sleep would sort her out.

"Grace Fitzgerald," called the secretary.

She explained her symptoms to Jill, her doctor who was also an old school-friend. Jill handed her a pregnancy kit.

"What!" said Grace, looking incredulously at the box Jill was handing her. Somewhere in the back of her mind it made sense. She had been in denial. She knew even before she peed on it that it would confirm her worst fears.

"Just humour me."

"I can't be."

"But Grace, I thought you'd be pleased."

Obviously Jill hadn't heard the rumours. Kate was right, today's news tomorrow's chip paper wrapping. She had no intention of discussing her circumstances.

"I'm thirty-six years old. I'm not stupid but ..."

"I'm not saying you are Grace, but let's rule it out," said Jill, kindly.

Grace got up. "Back in a sec."

Moments later, when she walked back in, Jill looked up expectantly from behind her desk.

Grace nodded and slumped into the chair in front of it as Jill walked around and leaned against the desk.

"Oh Jill, how could I have been so stupid? I don't know what I'm going to do."

"Grace, it's not the end of the world. You're engaged ..."

"You obviously haven't heard. We've broken up ..."

"Oh Grace, I'm so sorry ..."

"Look, you've a surgery full of patients out there waiting on you. I'll be fine. Thanks, Jill," she said.

"Grace, you are okay about this?"

Grace gathered herself quickly. "Oh, yes, yes, of course. Why wouldn't I be? It's a baby! Of course I'll figure it out."

"That's okay, then. I thought ..."

"No, I'm, eh, delighted," Grace added before Jill launched into what would happen next. All about gynaecologists and dominoes, a service provided by midwifes to promote natural childbirth and loads of other stuff. Grace didn't take in any of it. All she could think of was that she couldn't have this baby. She couldn't – how would she cope? Having a baby ... mother of God. She was hardly capable of taking care of herself, never mind a baby. People say it's easy. It's nature, it's natural. But a baby ... she didn't even own a dog.

"Look, Jill, I'd like to keep this quiet for a while. Pregnancy can be very long if everybody knows too early."

"Of course, Grace."

"Thanks, Jill."

She walked out of the surgery in a complete haze. She couldn't think straight. She had a hundred and one things she should be doing; all of them related to work. And now she was possibly ten weeks pregnant. A scan on the 1st of October would give a clearer timeline. Hello, pregnant, she thought. Wandering aimlessly along the square she heard somebody call her name.

"Grace, hi Grace, over here."

She looked around. It was Anna, Paul's wife, waving like a mad thing. Grace pretended she didn't see her. But it was too late; Anna was already making her way across the busy square.

"Oh, Grace, I'm so glad I've met you. I've been trying your mobile, but you never answer. I'm probably ringing at all the wrong times. I was worried about you. I want you to know we're here for you. We're friends too, you know."

"I know, but ... I'm sorry I didn't return the calls, Anna. I've been so ... oh maybe in time we can meet up for coffee or something, but thanks Anna, thanks for caring. I'm sorry, I'm on my way to a meeting. I'll call you ... I will."

"Please do, Grace."

"See you."

She tried not to cry as she rushed along the street. This time she wasn't aimless. She wanted to get to her car as quickly as possible before she met anybody else she knew.

Sophia had been dreading this day, pushing it to the back of her mind. If only she could blot out the 24th of September, every year. She remembered people saying "give it time". She knew it was true to some extent. After three years the pain had become less sharp, more of a dull ache. She could still hear their voices in her head the last time she had spoken to them. Standing in the bathroom of Rose Cottage, Sophia looked at her reflection in the mirror and thought how much her life had changed in the intervening years. Tired from another sleepless night, she decided to set out for a walk, a long one. It was windy outside. It might help to blow the cobwebs from her over-active brain.

As she walked along the beach, she felt drawn towards the church spire of St Brigid's, the Catholic Church which was perched on the top of the hill overlooking the sea. She wandered around glancing at the names engraved on the tombstones. Some of them were barely readable, they were so blotted from the white lichen blown in from the surrounding countryside. One in particular caught her eye; it read:

In loving memory of Agnes Moran, aged 2 died 1892
daughter of Patrick Moran, aged 60 died 1926,
and his wife Bernadette, aged 61 died 1928.

There were no other inscriptions, leading her to think that maybe they had no other children. How sad. They had probably been surrounded by large families. She would have loved a large family. Month after month she had hoped and twice she had been devastated by miscarriages. Bill had been so disappointed too. And when Richard had met and married Heather they had been so delighted. Heather had been bright and bubbly and had brought out the best in Richard. When Billy Junior had been born, the excitement had been incredible.

Sophia felt an overwhelming sense of sadness engulf her as she sat on the low wall surrounding the graveyard. She needed to be here; she needed a place to share her grief.

Sophia had been so lost in her thoughts that she hadn't noticed the time. She had no idea how long she was actually sitting on the wall at the very back of the graveyard. From her viewing point she could see for miles across country to the mountains in one direction and the sea in the other. It was a beautiful clear but cold day; thankfully the wind had died down. The cows were grazing away, taking no notice of her. Behind her, the graveyard was neatly arranged with rows of footpaths ready and waiting to be filled with the bodies of other people's loved ones.

The sound of footsteps from behind brought her back to her reality. The feet had to be coming to see her because there was no other reason to bring a person to this end of the graveyard.

She didn't turn around, hoping that the person would get the hint that she wasn't in the mood for pleasantries. But no … the person leaned on the wall a few feet away looking out towards the view beyond. For a few moments neither of them spoke.

"How long has it been?"

Sophia turned to look. The woman was in her sixties and she had a full head of grey hair acting like a halo around her round face. She wore reading glasses around her neck, which led Sophia to think of her as bookish. Sophia had seen her around but they had never spoken before. Sophia looked away.

"I'm sorry, I shouldn't have invaded …"

With eyes filled with tears. Sophia replied, "Three years today." Silence again. Eventually, Sophia spoke. "And you?"

"Five years next week."

"Does it get any easier?"

"No."

"Great, you're exactly what I need."

The woman laughed a loud laugh. Sophia smiled.

"My name is Nora. I've heard of you, you're Grace's American friend."

"Sophia."

Sophia put out her hand and Nora took it, putting her other hand over both of theirs. "It doesn't get easier but you get used to it. You have to move on," she said, with such kindness that Sophia felt a strange comfort in it. "It's life. It's for the living," Nora continued. "There are times I would do anything to see my daughter again. But if I did I wouldn't have my lovely granddaughter, Monique, in my life. I would be turning back time, and time waits for no one."

Sophia felt the pain in her heart at the mention of grandchildren. "My eight-year-old grandson, Billy, and his mother were killed in an aeroplane crash." Looking at Nora's face, Sophia realised how the words must have sounded. But she continued, it was like a flood gate had opened and she needed to share. "Heather, my wonderful daughter-in-law, had planned to surprise Richard, my son. He was working in Grand Cayman at the time. They took a sea plane from Miami. It never reached the island. Do you know what I find so hard to accept?" Nora remained silent, but it was her kind face that made Sophia continue. "Their bodies were never recovered … Sometimes I wake in the night, having dreamt about them. For that first moment, I am so sure that none of what happened is true and then reality hits. It was easier to bear when my husband, Bill, was alive but since his passing … Oh God …"

"I'm sorry." Nora spoke again. "I'm so sorry to have invaded your …"

"Oh, no," Sophia cut in. "It's nice to think that you weren't afraid to come over. That's one of the things I like about Ireland. You're never really alone."

Nora smiled but didn't say anything. Sophia watched the cows graze.

After a few minutes, Nora spoke again.

"You know watching that lot graze is making me hungry. How about a cup of tea and some freshly baked scones? You've been here long enough for one day. Now come on, get down off that wall!"

Sophia felt like a sixteen-year-old being reprimanded. Her body reacted before her brain did and she found herself obliging. The two women walked along the path together. Sophia asked about the woman's family. Nora talked about how much she missed her daughter who had been killed in a car crash in Paris along with her husband. Nora had become a guardian to her granddaughter Monique, who helped out at Jessie McGrath's yard. Nora's husband had also died just a few months before her daughter.

"Do you believe? Do you think you'll meet them again, you know, up there?" asked Sophia.

"I don't know. I come here every day to have my chat with Eilish, although she is buried in Paris with her husband, and Mass is an outlet for me, a reason to get up in the morning to meet my neighbours and chat and the like. I'd like to think there is an afterlife," Nora replied.

"I grew up in the Catholic faith but I didn't practise for years. I guess I fell out of it. I can't say I go in for all the rules but it's nice to have something to believe in and a place to go. Like today I needed this place. To be honest, I don't think I could get through the day without thinking that someday I will see all of my family again."

"That's nice, Sophia."

"Nora, you gave me a chance to talk. Something I haven't done for a long while and had no intention of doing. Thank you so much."

"Come on, my cottage is not far from here. That is, if you have the time …"

"I have all the time in the world, thank you so much, Nora." Sophia smiled, struck by the kindness of a perfect stranger.

For the first time in her life Grace felt she couldn't turn to Jessie. Her friend had wanted her twin babies so much and now a baby couldn't have been further off her "to do" list.

She had driven out of town and was still aimless when she spotted the signpost for the mountain drive. She took the turn. There would be hardly anyone up in the mountains today. Her head was throbbing so she stopped at a service station. The whiff of food from the deli counter made her stomach turn. She picked up a box of paracetamol and a bottle of water, paid and sat back into the car and was about to pop the pills when she realised maybe she shouldn't. "So this is it, it's dictating my life already," she muttered. After reading the instructions she took the tablets.

She drove on. After a while she stopped at one of the empty viewing points on the roadside. It was a perfect day; she could see for miles, right down to the ocean. It's a pity I haven't a ship in today, she thought. She couldn't stop herself from thinking about business. Her life was falling apart and she was thinking about cruise liners. Her head was fit to explode.

She needed to sort herself out and fast. But what if she couldn't work – if she got sick during the pregnancy! She was self-employed. She couldn't stay with Sophia forever and her mother was nearly seventy. She couldn't expect her to help.

"What am I going to do? I'm a thirty-six-year-old pregnant person. I mean please. Jesus, how can I be pregnant?" she said, aloud to the sky.

She thought of Dirk – what would he say? She hadn't heard a word from him since that day. She felt the tears come. She got back into the car. Which way next? If she turned left she would end up back in Bayrush or right would lead her further into the mountains.

She turned right. After a few kilometres she saw a signpost for an old monastery and retreat centre. Some monks still lived and prayed there. She knew about it because she had organised tours to visit there. People always came back raving about how tranquil and peaceful it was.

Along the way she stopped at a grotto dedicated to Our Lady. It had become well known in the eighties when the moving statues phenomena had swept Ireland. She was still a little intrigued by all of that. Here goes nothing, she thought as she got out of her car. There was a handful of people either kneeling or sitting in complete silence. Grace sat too on a pew obviously donated from an old church. It was so peaceful. She felt her head begin to relax for the first time all day.

After a while a young girl came down the steep incline, carrying a baby in her arms. Grace watched as she gave the baby to an elderly woman, who had been kneeling in front of the grotto since Grace arrived. No words passed between them.

After a few moments the old woman walked towards the statue of Our Lady. She seemed to be praying and kind of swaying rhythmically at the same time with the little baby in her arms. Grace looked around for the young girl who was kneeling at one of the pews with her head in her hands. The girl's body was shaking – no, racking would be a better description.

The realisation hit Grace that this little baby was obviously ill in some way and the old woman seemed to be in some way gifted with prayer or faith. It didn't matter because whatever it was the young girl obviously believed in it and really needed her. Instinctively Grace put her hand on her belly protectively.

She knew in that moment that she would never give up this baby. She would be capable of loving it and caring for it. As Jessie always said, "there are reasons for everything" and maybe she had been meant to witness this.

She sat for a while longer, offering up a prayer for the young girl and her baby and for Jessie's little ones, Anthony and Geoff. The day she had held them in her arms had been heartbreaking. How could she not want this little life … her tummy rumbled.

Okay, okay, I get it – you're hungry.

Grace drove up to the monastery. She parked and walked across the paved courtyard which housed a café and a little gift shop. She ordered a chicken and stuffing panini and a cup of tea. It was a homely little place.

After eating, she pottered around the gift shop for a while. It was full of little ornaments – angels, fairies and statues along with prayers and cards inscribed with words of wisdom, bookmarkers, candles, crystals, and fridge magnets with thoughtful words.

She saw two little blue figures of boy angels and thought of Jessie. And then she saw a little plaque with the serenity prayer on it:

God grant me the serenity
To accept the things
I cannot change;
Courage to change
the things I can;
and the wisdom to know
the difference.

She felt those words were so appropriate for Jessie. Her friend was desperately trying to make sense of what had happened. Maybe she'd buy two because it spoke to her too.

She remembered listening to Nora in Jessie's kitchen recently. She had said, "If God told a group of people to lay their problems on the table and then choose one, most likely they would choose their own again because they are already learning to deal with them."

Nora was right. She'd take her problem over Jessie's. She placed her gifts on the wooden counter to pay.

"Lovely day," remarked the old man dressed in a long brown robe.

"It is," she said.

"Nice choices. Will I gift-wrap them for you?"

"Ah no, they're grand," she said. "Thank you."

"You're very welcome my dear."

She walked out of the shop into the wide-open space and wondered if the monk was lonely. She couldn't bear the thought of being alone forever. How would Dirk react when she told him about the baby? Oh God, please help me.

"Happy birthday, Jess," said Geoff, kissing her on the lips when she arrived down to the kitchen. He handed her an envelope. She opened it. She had told him she didn't need or want anything for her birthday but enclosed in the birthday card was a print-out of a plane reservation to Barcelona leaving on Tuesday next and back two days later.

"What's this about?" she said, trying not to sound pissed off, but doing everything to contain the anger inside.

"I picked midweek so that you won't miss lessons. You need a break Jess. I thought it would be nice for you to visit your sister. Jesus, can't I do anything right?"

He walked out the back door, leaving her standing in the kitchen holding the envelope wondering how it had all gone wrong. She was about to go after him to apologise when she looked out the kitchen window and saw him talking to Jack in the yard.

"Christ, that's all we need. Another vet's bill!" She threw the envelope on the counter and stormed up the stairs.

Jack had been passing near Geoff's place and decided to call to say hello.

"Bad time?" he asked, seeing the look on Geoff's face.

"Women," said Geoff.

"Tell me about it!" laughed Jack.

"I'm just heading up to move a couple of horses from the top of the farm. Come with me, we'll be safer out here," said Geoff.

The two of them set across the fields.

"It's good to get a walk in. I spend so much time in the jeep driving all around the place."

"Do you miss Dubai Jack? I mean the weather is so changeable here. You must miss the heat!"

"Yes and no, sometimes I miss the job and yeah the sunshine too, a bit. But I don't miss other stuff."

"A woman?"

"Wife."

"I didn't know you were married."

"Nine years and she went off with a man twice her age."

"Lovely. Any kids?"

"No, thank God. I would have loved one and she told me we were trying but that was a lie. I was sorry to hear about what happened."

"People are so good, you find out who your real friends are in times of crisis."

Jack nodded his head and thought he hadn't been so fortunate. Nobody had told him about Lynda's affair; he had found out later that it was the talk of the circuit. He wasn't ready to go back to Dubai, not yet. He missed the buzz of his work, but nothing else. It occurred to him he had hardly thought about Lynda since he had come home. His head was full of just one woman but that was doomed.

"What do you think of her?" asked Geoff, pointing towards a grey mare.

"She's a fine-looking horse," said Jack, momentarily startled. Had Geoff read his mind? Then, smiling, he walked towards the mare to take a closer look.

"And there's her three-year-old daughter. Now she's got great potential. I'm seriously thinking of applying for a training licence but it costs a few grand and I just don't have it at the moment."

"Really!" Jack watched as the young horse cantered around playfully. She was a beauty all right. "Geoff, are you interested in an investor? I miss the racing circuit."

"Let's talk some more but yeah, I'm certainly interested." They chatted about the finer details and shook hands, making a gentleman's agreement. Walking back towards the yard, Geoff said, "We'll have to work out a training schedule and young Jay Moynihan is a fine amateur jockey. Hey you can ride her out too, if you're up for it."

"Jeez, I'd love to but I'll leave the racing to Jay."

"Too right," laughed Geoff.

Jack loved coming over to McGraths'. Geoff was sound and now he'd have some involvement with horses, more than just when they were sick. Conor had been right; he wished he could just work with horses. But he was glad to have landed a job at all.

Chapter Eight

It was the beginning of October, only five weeks since Jessie had lost her babies. Maybe it was a good thing to get away, Jessie thought, as she looked out of the aeroplane window. The plane was beginning its descent into Barcelona. Physically she was getting stronger. She could handle things if she stuck to the humdrum of her life. Not having anything to do was what she avoided. That's why sleep was so hard – in the silence of the night her head had a free rein. And the subsequent tiredness made her exhausted and irritable. She still felt guilty about her reaction to Geoff when he had given her a present of the trip.

Catching sight of her younger sister, Cliona, in the arrivals hall gave her a slight lift. They hugged while Carlos, Cliona's Spanish husband, carried her bag and led the way through the terminal.

They stayed up late talking about everything and anything except what had happened. When Carlos went to bed, Cliona begged Jessie to try a therapist she had heard about.

"Just try it out. Look, Jess, I don't know what to say or do. But this lady is supposed to be very helpful. Lots of people have found a sense of peace from visiting her. Oh please, Jess, it's worth a shot," she said, taking a sip from her wine glass.

"Okay," agreed Jessie, just to shut Cliona up. She wished people would leave her alone. When she stood up she realised that the wine had gone to her head. "I'm off to bed. See you in the morning."

It was the way Cliona looked at her that made Jessie realise just how ungrateful she sounded. "I'm sorry, Cliona," she said. "I just ... well ... I'm trying ... but I can't get excited or interested in anything. I feel guilty all the time. I can see Geoff is doing everything to make me happy and Sam tries his best ..."

"Well then, do something for yourself. The only person who can help you is you Jess."

"If only it were that easy. Goodnight, Cliona, and thanks."

"Night, Jess," said Cliona as she took the glasses from the table to the kitchen sink.

*

The next evening Jessie knocked on the blue door of a small villa in a Spanish village about ten kilometres from Barcelona. What the hell was she doing here? Cliona was sitting in her car watching to make sure that she actually went in. Where else could she go? What choice did she have? She was angry with everyone, especially Geoff for sending her here in the first place.

"Hello, you come in …" said an elderly woman. She had a kind face but it still didn't quell the anxiety. What was she letting herself in for? She felt like choking Cliona. The woman didn't seem to have good English so she couldn't imagine them having any great big chat.

"You lie on massage bed."

"Do I take off my clothes?" asked Jessie awkwardly.

"No, no, no. Up, up," she said in a slightly exasperated tone.

I'm going to kill Cliona when I get my hands on her, thought Jessie, climbing onto the bed. The woman proceeded to place a pillow under her head and a fleece blanket over her. Candles flickered. Relaxing music played in the background although Jessie didn't feel even slightly relaxed. The scent of lavender filled the room; she hated the smell. It brought memories of the awful night before the babies were born. Okay, she thought, just close your eyes and it will all be over soon. She could feel her heart beating anxiously in her chest.

"You canna talk if you wanna. It up to you, just relaxa and enjoy this time. I worka with angels to helpa you."

Jesus, Jessie thought, the woman is mad.

Halfway through the session she actually cried for the first time in weeks. It was a huge release and she hadn't spoken a word.

"How did you get on?" asked an anxious Cliona when she got back into the car.

"Good," said Jessie. It was pointless saying any more because she couldn't explain what had happened. "Would you mind if I go to bed when we get back? The lady told me to drink water and get some sleep."

"Cool," said Cliona as she drove away.

Back at Cliona's house Jessie climbed into bed and slept through the night for the first time in months.

Grace ran to the bathroom and got sick for the second time that morning. She was terrified that Sophia would hear her. She couldn't face telling anyone about her pregnancy. She still felt so vulnerable about the break-up. What if Dirk heard about it? He might start to make demands. And nor could she deal with telling Jessie, not yet. She stood up from the toilet bowl and saw her face in the mirror. She was pale and her eyes were sunken in their sockets. She began to apply her make-up, a habit she had started since finding out she was pregnant. At least Sophia wouldn't see how she really looked.

She and Eoghan had a group of twenty German golfers staying at The Meadows, Dirk's Country House Hotel for a week. Thankfully Kate had offered to handle them because she couldn't bear the thought of meeting Dirk. She couldn't continue all the hiding. It was wearing her out but she still felt so foolish. "Just another while, Gracey," she muttered, putting concealer under her eyes. Sophia had been kind to let her stay. Tomorrow she had an appointment to view a place to rent. Then she planned to tell Dirk.

"Morning Sophia," Grace called, trying to sound cheerful while coming downstairs.

"Pop the kettle on while you're passing it, Gracey. I was hoping you might have an hour to spare."

"When?"

"As a matter of fact, in a half hour. Sorry about the short notice but I'm thrilled about this."

"About what?"

"Take a look!" She turned her laptop, which was on the kitchen table, towards Grace.

Rose Cottage is a dormer-style thatched cottage furnished to a high standard with all the conveniences of modern living. Its beachfront location allows access directly onto the golden sands of Bayrush Beach – a favourite with bathers, surfers, walkers and horseback riders alike.

The property is fully furnished and the owners are looking to rent on a long-term lease. The gardens are landscaped with pretty rose bushes to the front and herb garden to the side. There are three bedrooms one with en-suite bathroom. But its most attractive feature is an upstairs sitting room which opens out onto a Canadian cedar-wood deck and a fabulous view of the coastline."

"Oh, wow! It sounds fantastic and if it's the one I think it is ... Oh wow."

"I admire it every time I walk past it. Will you come with me?"

"You don't have to ask twice."

"Any other news?" asked Sophia.

"No, nothing strange." Grace averted her gaze. Sophia had a disconcerting way of asking a question as if she already knew the answer.

She hoped she hadn't heard her being sick earlier. To change the subject Grace said, "Did you enjoy the Bridge Club with Eoghan and Nora last night?"

"I had such a good time with them. Nora is really good and so patient at explaining the rules." She finished her tea. "I must get ready. Come on, shake a leg," she laughed, running upstairs.

Half an hour later, Sophia drove through the gates of Rose Cottage along a pebbled driveway through a pleasantly landscaped garden. Grace noted the large oak tree with a swing hanging from it and a wooden tree house with a climbing frame. The owners must have small children, she thought. It was absolutely fab. She loved it even before putting her foot inside the door.

Pretty white climbing roses grew around the front porch. Sharon, the leasing agent, shook hands with Sophia and led them in through the red half-door.

Inside the house was even more beautiful. It was open plan with exposed beams. The solid-oak kitchen was painted white with a granite counter separating it from the large living area, which was spacious enough to fit two cream couches. The white marble fireplace was a beautiful feature. Near the large picture window there was an antique dining table and six chairs which looked out towards the front garden. At the opposite end of the room French doors opened out to a patio and back garden. Beyond the garden a red cast-iron gate led to the golden sands of Bayrush beach.

Just as the description had said, the house had "all the modern conveniences of living", digital TV and WiFi. There was a bathroom and one bedroom downstairs and two more and another large bathroom upstairs. Its main feature was an old claw bath with a huge old showerhead. The bath was draped by a soft cream shower-curtain.

"It's fabulous," said Grace. She could only dream of ever owning a place like this.

"Grace, come and look at this!" said Sophia, standing in the master bedroom, which also had exposed beams and French doors opening onto a deck. "What a view!"

Grace could see the great expanse of beach and across the bay towards Everest Rock.

"Fab, I can't wait to see the upstairs sitting room. Come on."

Sophia laughed, following her along the landing. "You're like a child in a candy store."

"Don't you just love the hardwood floor? Oh my God, this is

fabulous. I didn't think it would be so spacious, and the view again. I love this beach so much." She opened the French doors and stepped onto the cedar wood deck. "Look Sophia, it runs the length of the back of the house. You can have the sun all day."

"Grace, we're in Ireland!"

"Ah sure I know but we can always dream."

Sophia laughed.

Grace rubbed her tummy in that protective way that new mothers did, confirming Sophia's suspicions even further. She had heard her being sick again this morning and many other mornings. She admired Grace's strength of character for trying to deal with her situation alone. She just wished she could help her.

"Hey Sophia, there's steps leading down into the garden." Grace disappeared from sight. Sophia smiled. Hearing footsteps behind her she turned around. It was Sharon, the agent.

"So, Sharon, can you draw up the necessary contracts? The owners have a deal. When can I move in?"

"It's available immediately."

"Great, thanks for your help."

"You're very welcome, Mrs Wynthrope."

"We're going to take a walk along the beach. We'll close the gates after us."

"That's no problem. I'll contact you later today regarding keys."

Sophia walked out to join Grace who was standing at the end of the garden looking towards the beach. The tide was out. It went out a long way. Sophia could see dots of people far in the distance walking along the water's edge. "We can move in tomorrow."

"We ... don't you mean you're moving in?" Grace turned around, stunned. "But I'm viewing a place later today."

"I hoped that you might consider staying here too. As you know this is only available on a long-term lease and as I'll be travelling back and forth to New York, it would be a shame to leave this place empty. I don't mean to impose but ... well ... I hoped you could caretake it for me. It does make sense. Doesn't it?" She had thought about this for a while. She didn't want to offend Grace.

"Oh Sophia, it's so beautiful here. I really can't accept that offer, but how about if I rent a room?"

Sophia smiled and put out her hand. "It's a deal."

Grace hugged her. "Congratulations to us."

"By the way, how did Jessie get on in Barcelona?" asked Sophia.

"She actually just sent a text inviting us over for a coffee now. We can tell her our great news!"

"Sounds good."

"It's good to see you both again," said Sophia. "I must say I enjoyed the trek the last time I was here, Geoff."

"Well, you're a fine horse woman Sophia," smiled Geoff, taking a sip from his mug. "Unlike so many of the cruise passengers who ride cowboy style."

"I'd love to go on one of those ranch holidays," declared Grace, stirring a half a sugar into her tea. Jessie burst out laughing. "What's so funny?"

"Sophia, don't you find that funny?" asked Jessie. Sophia laughed and nodded her head in agreement.

"You're too fond of your comforts, Gracey," laughed Geoff. "Can you image her sleeping under the stars and eating cold beans out of a tin?" They all laughed.

"Well I'm glad I'm such a source of amusement to you all and I consider ye lot friends!" she retorted, happy to see Jessie smiling again.

Since Barcelona something small had happened. It was just good to see her and Geoff both relaxed even if it was for Sophia's benefit.

"We have some news. Sophia has just taken a long-term lease on Rose Cottage."

Sophia was beaming.

"Do you mean that gorgeous thatched cottage right down on the beach?" said Jessie.

"The very one, I've been admiring it since I came here. I can't believe it came up for rent."

"So you're going to stick around a bit longer," said Geoff. Sophia nodded, smiling.

"That's fantastic news," said Jessie as Geoff got up and went to the wine rack in the kitchen. "It ain't champagne but Cava will do, I'm sure, coz it calls for a celebration. We have a new neighbour."

"Two kilometres away, Geoff," laughed Jessie.

"But only one on horseback."

Grace watched Sophia; she was thrilled by their reaction. The back door opened.

"What's going on here?" asked Kate. "What are we celebrating and why wasn't I called in? We're out there slaving away, aren't we Mon, and look at this lot." Monique appeared from behind her.

"Ah shut up complaining and grab a glass will ya! Sophia's staying on longer. She's renting Rose Cottage," declared Geoff.

"Way to go Soph," said Kate, clicking her glass to Sophia's.

Monique, being so much more demure, said, "This is very good news."

Grace smiled, thinking that this was the best day they had all had in a long while apart from the fact that it had begun with being sick. She'd tell Sophia about her pregnancy tonight.

Sophia was curled up on the couch reading as usual when Grace brought her in a mug of tea. It was nine o'clock. She smiled when Sophia felt around in search of the TV control.

"It's on the floor."

"Thanks," said Sophia, picking it up and aiming it at the TV to hear the evening news.

"We really are like an old married couple," remarked Grace, sitting into an armchair.

"Isn't it great that we've our packing done? Just a couple of suitcases and we're off in the morning." Sophia smiled at her and all of Grace's pent-up anxiety at her decision to tell Sophia burst from her.

"I'm pregnant," Grace blurted and then the tears came. "I don't know what I'm going to do. I feel so foolish. Dirk is seeing someone else already and I'm going to be alone for the rest of my life and now I'm sorry you're missing the news."

"Oh my darling, I'm so glad you've decided to tell me," said Sophia, sitting up, her expression full of concern. "You've been so sick, I've been worried but I didn't like to interfere. It will be okay, I promise. You're strong Grace. You have a wonderful family and great friends and you have me. Things have a way of working out."

"Oh Sophia, I can hear my mother already. 'I reared you to thirty-six and you go and get yourself pregnant.'" She was mimicking her mother's accent.

"It's hard not to laugh," said Sophia, smiling. "Because that is probably what she will say, but she'll support you all the way. She might have already guessed."

"But I'm not showing. Oh God, Grace, what if Dirk finds out? And how am I going to tell Jessie? The last thing I want is a baby. I feel guilty for saying that when Jessie so wanted hers."

"Grace, there are options. Maybe you need to talk to someone."

"Oh God no Sophia. I don't want an abortion."

"There are other solutions."

"You know just by saying it out loud I realise that no matter what ... I will keep this baby. Sometimes I wake in the dead of the night and think why ... why did it happen to me? The truth is that I knew Dirk wasn't 'the one' from the moment I saw Jack Leslie again. It was actually the same day I met you for the first time. I saw Jack through the glass partition wall, he was walking through arrivals and I was departing Dublin Airport. It seems to me that is the way with us. Timing is never right." She let out a huge sigh and Sophia remained silent. "He was married. I was engaged. He's ... I don't quite know what now. And now I'm pregnant."

"It's good to talk, Grace. You are voicing how you feel which makes it easier to find solutions. In just a few words you are clearer about what you want already."

"I am?"

"Yes, you said you want your baby and Dirk is not the person for you."

"You've been reading too many psychology books." Grace nodded in the direction of the book on the floor beside Sophia's stockinged feet.

Sophia smiled and said. "Nobody knows what the future holds. All we have is now. This moment, we can't fix the past, we just deal with the hand we have."

"Oh Sophia, I fall to pieces every time I think of Jack. He was so good to me the summer my dad left. He was four years older and didn't think of me as girlfriend material but it didn't stop me from dreaming. Did you ever love someone so much it hurt?"

Sophia nodded.

"Of course you did, that was stupid of me."

"It doesn't happen to everyone, Grace. It is something to be glad about. At least you know how it feels."

"But I don't want to feel like this."

"I wish I had all the answers. I can just tell you to cross each bridge as it comes."

"Thanks, Sophia, for listening to me and for inviting me to stay with you in Rose Cottage. You'll never know how much it means to me."

"How about an episode of CSI?"

Grace smiled through her bloodshot eyes. "Perfect, blood and gore is all we need."

"You set it up while I make a fresh brew."

"God Sophia, that was your worst attempt yet at our accent."

"I drive Richard crazy with it too." She laughed as she went to the kitchenette. "I can't wait to move in tomorrow."

Sitting in the passenger seat Jessie remained quiet as Geoff drove up the pebbled drive of Rose Cottage. The girls had decided to have a house-warming party. It was the last thing Jessie wanted to do but Grace had pleaded with her. Sophia had even been kind enough to include Sam's friend Oliver to keep him company and had invited his parents too. Sophia had met Sally at the yard and they had taken to going on regular treks together.

If it had been any other party she would have declined. It was enough to meet people at the yard. What if somebody said something to her? What if she cried? Her stomach was in knots. Maybe she could say she was feeling sick and leave the boys to enjoy the day. This was her first social event since she'd buried her babies. The feelings when she climbed exhausted into bed at night hadn't gone away. She was back to not sleeping properly. She was irritable and short-fused privately and spent the rest of the time pretending to be in good form for the people coming to the stables. Looking over at Geoff, she felt guilty; he needed to unwind too, she thought. So she'd make the effort for his sake.

It turned out to be a bigger affair than Jessie had anticipated. She was beginning to relax and chat with a few people she knew and was about to go to the buffet when Kate stopped her.

"Jim, did you meet Jessie?" asked Kate, leading a man with a beard in his mid-forties towards her. "Jim's a great friend of mine. He's a priest and a counsellor." Seeing the surprised look on Jessie's face, she said, "I know you'd never think it. We met years ago, you know that time when I had to have a chat with myself." Kate laughed; she had no hang-ups about what she had been through. "This guy is great. He really helped me ..."

They looked at one another and then at Kate who conveniently found someone else to talk to. "Nice to meet you, Jim ... I don't mean to be rude but you know ... eh. I'm not exactly into counselling!" Jessie planned on choking Kate when she got her alone.

"I know what you mean, neither was I," he replied, smiling warmly. "Sorry about that, I suppose Kate though she was doing the right thing." He chatted on about the music playing in the background. She began to relax. He wasn't going to psychoanalyse her after all. He was a really nice guy. "If you ever change your mind Kate has my mobile number."

"Thanks," she said graciously, but thinking, no bloody way. She wandered into the living room and found a place to sit. She noticed

Eoghan chatting with Sophia. He looked happy; she had known him five years now and had never seen him so animated. He was helping with the food and generally pottering about picking up glasses.

There was a time when Jessie would have been in the thick of it, not looking for a place to blend into the background. She just didn't have the energy or the heart for it all. Everything was a drag.

"Penny for them," said Sophia, joining her on the cream sofa.

"Oh, they're not worth even that much, Sophia."

"Thanks for coming."

"I didn't want to let Grace down because she's the best in the world. And she's going through so much. You're so good to her, Sophia."

"Jessie, life hasn't been easy for the last number of years, but I'm pushing through it. Spending time here with Grace has helped me, but I have to go back and well … face things."

"Sometimes I wish I could run away but the emptiness I have inside would still be here," said Jessie, holding her solar plexus. "Just look at those two." She inclined her head towards Geoff and Sam. Geoff was chatting to Eoghan and ruffling Sam's head at the same time. "I don't know what I would do without them. I'd have no reason to get out of bed in the morning."

"Jessie, I completely understand. So let's top up that glass of yours and be glad."

"Fair enough, Sophia. Cheers," she said as Sophia poured white wine into her glass. Jessie watched her walk towards the boys and wondered what darknesses Sophia held in her heart.

A few days later, Grace came downstairs from the living room cum office she had set up upstairs at Rose Cottage.

"Sophia, I have a small cruise ship coming in today. It's a theme ship," said Grace, taking the kettle and filling it with water from the kitchen sink.

"What does that mean?" Sophia asked, looking over her half-rim reading glasses from where she was sitting reading the papers at the kitchen counter.

"The passengers are interested in a certain subject. And theirs is history and heritage of ancient Ireland."

"So what do you have planned?" Sophia was intrigued. She folded the newspaper, giving Grace her full attention.

"I've organised a feast in a marquee on the river front where the passengers can watch a re-enactment between the Celts and the Vikings.

I even managed to get the Vikings to come up the river in a long boat."

"Good gracious, it sounds fantastic."

"I had thought of getting the passengers to dress in costumes but that might be a step too far," she laughed. "So are you coming with me or what?"

"I'm not missing this for the world. There's no doubt but you come up with some mad ideas." She took the stairs two at a time. It was going to be a sight – either a great success or an unmitigated disaster.

Having organised four coaches to transport two hundred people to the other side of the quay, Grace stood with Sophia, Eoghan and Kate welcoming the cruise passengers as they disembarked. Although she looked and acted relaxed Grace hadn't felt so nervous in a long time.

She had approached the Viking re-enactment group after attending their evening and together they had come up with an idea to act out a piece of drama – a fight between a Viking warrior and a Celt over a girl. She had also hired a local well-known chef to re-create a menu of the times. The marquee was big enough to seat everyone with space to house stalls to display craftwork from both cultures and how the clothes and weaponry were made, along with space at the centre of the marquee to act out the drama. Wanting audience participation she had arranged for Viking helmets on half the tables and Celtic crosses on the other half.

"They'd better be good actors," Eoghan whispered, "I must have been drinking when you got me to agree."

"No time for backing out now, mister. We're in this together remember. For better or worse," Grace said, out of the side of her mouth, and then she gave a beaming smile to a couple as they boarded the coach. "Welcome to Bayrush," she said.

Thankfully it was a bright, sunny day and within thirty minutes the passengers sat sipping a choice of wine, Guinness, Baileys or a soft drink on the plaza watching the Viking Longboat sail up the river.

Grace could see a Viking warrior standing at the bow of the boat and couldn't help thinking of Jack. He had looked so … stop, she thought. The warrior took off his helmet and greeted the crowd and the disappointment she felt inside that it wasn't Jack shocked her. God, she thought, get a grip.

After the meal, the drama began and the girl the two men were fighting over was Pam, the blonde whom Jack had introduced her to that night. Grace watched, enthralled. She glanced around the marquee and was delighted by the reaction from the audience. After the show the passengers wandered around the stands where they watched women making flour using a grinding wheel. Many of the male tourists were fascinated by the weaponry and were listening intently as one of the Vikings explained how they had made the various weapons.

"So has it been a success?" said a familiar voice from behind her. Her breath caught as she turned around.

"What are you doing here?" she asked, trying to regain her composure. He inclined his head towards Pam.

"Just being supportive!"

Grace felt a pang of jealousy, the same feeling she had had the last time when Pam had joined them at the bar.

"She was such a nervous wreck earlier. I thought it would be nice to stop by as I was passing."

"Do you treat many horses in the town then?" She sounded sharp. He looked amused and his smirk bugged her even more. She really did not like this feeling at all.

"Well, if you want the truth I knew you'd be here," he said without a hint of guile. Completely thrown by his comment she was glad of Sophia's interruption.

"Hi Jack, it's so nice to see you again. I was sure you'd dress for the occasion," said Sophia, clearly delighted to meet him.

"Ah Sophia, that was a once in a lifetime for me. As I told Grace I was just helping out that evening, Pam's boyfriend couldn't make it that night and they needed a doorman."

"So *you* were the doorman ..." laughed Sophia.

How could he chat and be so relaxed when he had just said those words? So he wasn't dating Pam. What did he mean? But it didn't change anything.

"Yeah and thank God he was able to be here today or I could have been roped in again. The thought of getting into that costume and acting, could you imagine me!"

"I thought you made a great Viking, although your surname suggests Norman ancestry."

"God Sophia, I never knew you were so informed about Irish history and names," remarked Grace, trying to steady her nerves.

"You're right, my ancestors are Norman."

"I'm just a mine of information. Ask me anything about the history of County Waterford. Go on." Sophia was clearly delighted with herself. Jack laughed.

"You're hanging out too much with tour guides and Eoghan," said

Grace, smiling, as Sophia laughed and wandered off back in the direction of the stalls.

"Does she live here?" asked Jack.

"She came for a fortnight in August and ended up renting a cottage in Bayrush. She loves it here."

"God and to think how much I couldn't wait to leave!"

"Are you settling back?" she asked, wanting desperately to continue chatting with him but knowing that her attention was needed.

"Yes and no. Look Grace, I really need to talk to you. I think you already know what I'm going to say. There is something, something well, you make me feel. I know you're engaged … I know this isn't the time or the place but can we meet?" She could feel the tears welling behind her eyes. He felt it too. *Oh my God …*

"Grace, Eoghan needs you." It was one of the tour guides. "He's over at the coach."

"Sorry about this … I have to take care of this." She ran before he had a chance to say another word. How could she tell him she felt the same when she was carrying another man's child?

"Grace," he called after her. When she looked back and saw his face she knew he would always be the only man in the world for her. Life was so unfair.

Jessie sat in Dr Brennan's modern waiting room. She remembered when she had come here as a child with her mum. He had made big changes since. She wished she had an infection or something straightforward to tell him. What was she going to say? Her head was full to the point of bursting. When she opened the door he looked up from behind his large desk and said, "I wondered how long it would take for you to come to see me."

"I'm sorry. I don't understand. Why did you say that?"

"Well, considering all you have been through …"

"I'm just finding it hard to sleep. I'm trying to work and get on with things. But I feel hormonal and tired all the time. I wouldn't put it down to any one particular thing."

"I see. Maybe you need to talk to somebody. It sounds to me like a touch of post-natal depression without the babies."

"Post-natal depression?"

"It can happen you know. Physically your body is trying to adjust and of course … the loss you have suffered is huge."

Jessie sat looking at him, not quite taking in what he was saying.

Dr Brennan proceeded to prescribe sleeping tablets and antidepressants and he wrote a couple of names on a piece of paper and handed it to her. "Give one of them a call."

Still slightly shell-shocked she took it from him. Had he actually said post-natal depression? She wasn't the type of person to suffer from depression. Depression – it was an unspoken word.

She walked out of the surgery holding the pieces of paper in her hand. She sat in the car and looked at the three names and numbers he had given her and then she rang Geoff.

"You are not going to believe what he said, Geoff. He said I have post-natal depression. The cheek of him. Well, I never heard the like. I'm sitting here with a prescription in my hand for … wait for it … antidepressants and sleeping tablets."

She paused to draw a breath when she heard Geoff say, "Well pet, he's the doctor. Maybe he's right."

"What? How can he be right? I was only in there for five bloody minutes. And he wants me to see a counsellor. When I looked at the names I realised I know all of those people. I'm not going to tell my deepest feelings to any of them."

"Calm down, Jessie. Just come home and we can have a chat."

She hung up and drove to the beach. The rain was beating down and the wind was howling. It was a terrible day. The car park was empty. Who in their right mind would want to go walking on the beach today? But she did. She got out of the car. She had no coat on and it didn't concern her. She ran against the wind, letting the rain beat into her face and body. After a few minutes, she let out a howl that was carried swiftly away as if it hadn't happened. Then another one.

"Why?" she screamed but it couldn't be heard. "What did I do? Why us? No don't give me any of your stupid fucking platitudes delivered by people who should know better. Come down here. Come down here," she roared at the sky as the tears of anger and rage streamed down her face. She wanted a fight and it felt like God was giving her one. It seemed like the wind was his representative pushing fiercely against her and the rain was its cohort. After a while she ran out of steam. What was the point? She couldn't win. He had her babies and if she kept going on at him he'd have St. Peter tipped off to block her entry at the pearly gates. She'd never see them again. The moment that thought hit her consciousness she dropped to her knees. "I'm sorry, I'm sorry," she muttered, wondering who exactly she was trying to fool, him or her. It was safer to be silent.

Chapter Nine

A mid-October wind gushed along the beach and the rain beat against the French doors of Rose Cottage as Grace worked. She stood up when she caught a glimpse of somebody on the beach. Who could be out walking on a day like today, she wondered, and then she saw the person dropping into the sand.

"Jesus, Mary and Joseph, what's that about!" she said, running downstairs. "Sophia, you're not going to believe it but some eejit is out walking in that weather with no coat on and whoever it is has fallen." She picked up a couple of raincoats as she spoke.

"Wait, I'll come with you."

"No point in the two of us getting wet!"

"Okay, but be careful."

"Ah Sophia, it's broad daylight," she smiled. She ran along the beach, getting soaked in the process.

"Jesus Christ, what the hell are you doing? Get up!" She couldn't believe her eyes. It was Jessie.

Jessie roared at her. "Leave me alone, for God's sake leave me alone. Why does everybody think they need to fix me? They can't. My heart is broken. It can't be fixed Grace …"

"Look Jess, I don't want to fix you. I want you to come in out of the rain. We can talk, okay? You need to TALK, if not to me to somebody. Jess, get up, honey. Come on," she shouted above the wind, trying to be heard.

Jessie got up and allowed Grace to drape the raincoat over her as they walked back along the beach in silence.

Grace led Jessie through the red half-door of Rose Cottage. Without saying a word, Grace gestured to Sophia to boil the kettle. Grace could see the shock on Sophia's face to see Jessie in such a state. She brought Jessie upstairs and straight into the bathroom. Neither of them spoke as Jessie sat on the downturned toilet lid. Grace began to run a bath for her friend. Jessie was soaked to the skin, her red curls were plastered to her head and her face was as pale as a ghost. She looked haunted.

"Give me those wet clothes and get in before you get pneumonia. I'll bring you up a cup of tea. I promise I won't look."

Jessie gave her a half-smile. "Thanks, Grace.

Grateful for the smile, Grace closed the bathroom door and went downstairs. She rang Geoff. He was worried sick – Jessie was supposed to have been home ages ago and she hadn't answered any of his calls. Grace told him where she had found Jessie and that she'd run her a bath. Geoff filled Grace in about the trip to the doctor who had prescribed medication and recommended a counsellor because Jessie was suffering some kind of post-natal depression without the babies.

"Okay, I'm glad I know that. I was wondering what in God's name had come over her." Grace felt guilty. She had been avoiding Jessie, speaking only on the phone for the past week in case she noticed that she was pregnant. She was having a baby that she hadn't wanted while Jessie had so desperately wanted hers.

After bringing Jessie tea, Grace joined Sophia, who was sitting at the kitchen counter. "What can I do to help her, Sophia?"

"Nothing," Sophia said simply. "You are going to do nothing but listen."

"Sophia, you don't understand, that's the problem. She won't bloody well talk so how can anyone listen?"

"She'll talk when she's ready. You will just have to wait." She spoke with such conviction it was impossible to dismiss her.

"Sophia, you don't understand. Jessie is a talker, she has never – not talked."

"Could this be the first time in her life that she has suffered, deeply suffered?"

Grace thought for a moment and answered simply. "Yes."

"Then give her time. Support her, be here but don't try to fix her. Nobody can do that except Jessie. She'll do it when she's ready. She'll find a way."

Sophia woke the following morning. The bad weather remained. She rose and walked to the bedroom window. She watched the rain dashing down in sheets. She'd have to put off her morning walk. It was hard to believe that she was still here. The weeks had run into one another and now she was renting this beautiful house. It just seemed so natural, normal even. Still it was time. She had booked a flight to return to New York next week but had made a promise to herself that before she left Ireland she was going to do something that she had watched every second Sunday since she'd come here. After that she would be ready to face things again. As her Italian grandmother once told her, "you can run, but remember when you stop, it is *yourself* that you will find." She had said those words when Sophia had complained about how hard their life was. Her grandmother had smiled and said, "All I want for you is happiness, Sophia? Things will never make you happy, people will."

Her words made sense. Richard was the only family she had left. Yesterday had been traumatic. Poor Jessie's circumstances had brought back memories of all the miscarriages she had been through. She had had hopes and dreams of a little brother or sister for Richard, but she had never reached past ten weeks. She couldn't imagine how it must have felt to give birth to perfectly formed little babies and then to bury them. It truly wasn't fair. She had every faith in Jessie; yesterday needed to happen. She needed to show a crack in the armour. At least now another person could reach in.

Jessie drove to another town to get the prescription filled; such was her shame about depression. She took the medication for the next three days. The doctor told her to take the sleeping tablets with the antidepressants for the first few days because sometimes it took a while for the tablets to take effect.

But she was still exhausted and after three nightmare-filled sleeps she rang the counsellor priest, Jim, the guy Kate had introduced her to at Sophia's house-warming. He lived miles away; she eventually found the seventies-style bungalow on the outskirts of the little fishing village.

"Come on in, you're very welcome," he said, leading her along the hallway. She felt awkward and self-conscious. She truly believed that she was supposed to be able to deal with her own problems. She was an adult and everybody had problems. Coming to a counsellor made her feel weak and inadequate.

She sat down in a comfortable armchair in the living room and busied herself with looking at the patterned carpet. It made her think of her childhood home. Jim sat opposite her. There was a big picture window to her left draped with net curtains.

"So, Jessie."

Silence. She sat looking at the pattern on the nets. She didn't know where to start or if she really wanted to.

"It must be difficult. We're not meant to lose our children," he said.

Finally she spoke. "It's my fault."

"Why do you think that?"

She didn't know why. She remained silent and then a few moments later she said, "My placenta was creating too much water. They were perfect. It was me. I let them down. I was supposed to be their mother. My body did it. Me. It was my fault."

"So, are you angry?"

"No."

"So you're not angry."

She was staring out the window. She turned and looked at him.

"I'm not angry. I'm just … irritated." She was ringing her hands. "I know that doesn't make sense. I just feel irritated by people. Older people say things like, 'Ah sure, it could have broken a bigger cross', meaning there might have been something wrong with them. Imagine people imply that kind of thing! I simply wanted our babies. I wanted to love them and bring them up. That's all. What did we ever do that was so bad that God took them away? Yeah … I am angry. But I'm scared to be."

"Why?"

She explained that she thought that if she got angry with God he might not "let her in" and then she would never see her babies again. But she said she felt so trapped in the silence.

"I was trying so hard not to scream at God. I did though. Last week I screamed at him but I stopped myself."

He told her that grieving was a process and that anger was part of that process.

"It's like a child throwing a tantrum. The best thing a parent can do is to hold the child in their arms until he or she stops kicking and screaming. Then the child will feel the arms of love around them. That's what God does. He lets us kick, scream and rail against him but he still loves us. He never turns his back on us. We may turn away from him but he is always open and always ready to forgive. It is okay to be angry Jessie. It really is."

She sat there in the big soft chair with tears pouring down her cheeks. "I feel stupid. I'm sorry. I can't stop the tears."

"Ah. Don't worry about it. I'd say that carpet could grow mushrooms all the tears spilled on it over the years."

She smiled through them and asked for some tissues. He passed a box and said, "When you think you are strong enough Jessie, you will find a place and a time to let them go. Imagine if you still had your baby boys, some day they would grow up and fly the nest. One might say –

Mum I'm going to Australia, the other might marry a girl you can't see eye to eye with, who knows. What I am saying is that we don't own our children. As parents we simply have a loan of them. All we can do is our best. Jessie, if you love somebody you have to set them free. With that freedom they will love you back tenfold. Think about this and when you find the strength, make a trip. Mark the occasion and place where you can finally let them go to their spiritual resting place. I assure you they will always be near you."

Jessie listened intently. A huge part of her struggled with what she was hearing. She realised she would need time to process what he was saying. Then maybe she could act on it.

"Oh my God, I've been here two and a half hours. How much do I owe you?"

"Nothing."

"No way!"

"No, really, I'm glad to help."

"I'm sorry I can't accept that. I want to give you something."

"Okay, pick a charity of your choice and make a donation to it if that makes you feel better." He smiled.

As Jessie drove away her faith in humanity was never stronger. She thought of the goodwill and kindness of her family and friends. Each of them had supported her in ways impossible to describe. They had brought casseroles, helped in the yard, and sometimes they had simply stayed around her even when she had nothing to say. She had to help herself for Geoff and Sam's sake as well as her own.

The long journey was a therapeutic experience. She had time to reflect on what Jim had said. She stopped and made a phone call. She had heard about a lady in Bayrush who gave treatments like the one she had experienced in Barcelona. She decided to give it a try; even if it only helped her to get some sleep again.

Jessie sat on a bench looking out to sea, waiting for Grace. She already knew what Grace was going to tell her.

"Hi, sorry I got delayed," Grace said, rushing towards her. Her voice was filled with apprehension.

"No problem, I was just admiring the view. The town council have done a great job along the harbour. It's a credit to them. Bayrush is looking very smart, even if we are in a recession. At least they spent the money well in the good times."

"Don't know if many would agree. What about health and …"

"Don't go there. Come on, let's get moving. I'm getting cold sitting here."

The two of them linked up and walked along the riverfront.

"I have something to tell you, Jess."

"I already know. I guessed a while ago." Jessie stopped and looked directly into Grace's eyes. "As long as you're okay that's all I care about, Gracey."

Grace began to pour her heart out. "Oh Jess, it was such a shock. I was afraid to tell you. Especially because well ... I wasn't happy about it."

"Grace, my wanting the babies shouldn't come into it. Nobody can ever replace them and it would be an awful place to be if I resented you for being pregnant. I'll be here to support you all the way."

Grace's eyes filled with tears as she hugged her best friend. "I always knew you would but I just felt ..."

"Stop, will you. I'm just so glad you told me because it was wrecking my head watching you and not feeling like I could say anything. Aren't we lucky we're going to have a new addition to our lives? Have you told your mother?"

"Yes, I told her the other night. She's ... well she's not exactly over the moon about it. Of course she threw in her oar about how in God's name did I manage to rear you this long and then at thirty-six you go and get pregnant and I thought you were the bright one."

"Sounds exactly like her." And then the two of them laughed as they made their way to Nutties for a pot of tea for Grace and a Bacardi for Jessie, along with a discussion about how Grace was going to tell Dirk.

Two days later Grace finally found the courage to contact Dirk. She sat on the same bench as Jessie had and waited looking out to sea. The sky was a mixture of red, blues and grey. The way the evening sun's rays broke through the clouds in beams made her feel that there was more to it all, something more powerful beyond just us. The wind blew in from the sea, leaving a taste of salt on her lips. Her stomach was in turmoil. She hadn't seen Dirk since the night she told him to sell the house, which was eight weeks ago. He hadn't tried to contact her and she hadn't felt strong enough physically or emotionally until now. She had heard so many rumours about him that she'd stopped listening. How would he react? Would he want to be involved? Or would he deny the baby? Had she ever known him at all? She had lived with him for three years and thought he was faithful, honest and caring, when it had all been nothing but lies. She was a lousy judge of character. Her belief in herself was so low sometimes she wondered how or if she'd ever trust a man again.

She spotted Dirk in the distance as he walked along the promenade towards her. He was as handsome as ever, but as he drew close there was coolness in his demeanour. She could feel his arrogance even from the distance.

"What's this about?" he asked, from eight feet away.

"Can we be civilised for a few minutes?" she asked, remaining seated, afraid to stand up in case her legs gave way. She should have told him on the phone, she thought. It would have been much easier.

"Grace, I'm a busy man. I don't have time for games. You ended it, not me. I'm getting on with my life. So unless you want to try again don't waste my time."

"I'm thirteen weeks pregnant," she blurted out.

"What ... but ... fuck." He put his hand on his head and twirled around. "What the ... I thought we were taking precautions? Jesus Christ, Grace." He sat down on the bench and put his elbows on his knees, holding his head between his hands. After a few moments, he turned towards her. "This is crazy," he muttered, "but I'm going to ask can we try ..."

"No," she said, "if you were going to suggest we try again ... no."

"Why are you telling me then? How do you know it's even mine?" he accused, but she could see the hurt flashing through the anger in his eyes.

"I won't justify that with an answer," she said, her tone loaded with sarcasm. "I wanted to tell you in person. I felt I owed you that. The baby is yours."

"Well it's very simple Grace, either you come back to me or else I don't want anything to do with you or it," he said, looking pointedly at her tummy. "It's up to you." He stood up. She stayed sitting.

"Goodbye, Dirk."

He shrugged his shoulders, turned and walked back the way he had come without a backward glance. Jesus, how could she have been so stupid.

Grace tossed and turned all night. Eventually she gave up trying to sleep. She went downstairs to boil the kettle. What was she going to do? Her baby would never know its father. This wasn't the life she'd hoped for. All those years ago she'd told Jack Leslie she'd make something of herself. She hadn't meant this. She looked out the kitchen window at the October night sky. Some stupid crazy part of her wanted to say yes to Dirk. It would be easier. She wouldn't feel so desperately alone. He wanted her back; could she forgive him?

"Are you okay?" asked Sophia, coming down the stairs, her face filled with concern.

"You're still finding it hard to sleep."

Sophia shrugged her shoulders resignedly and said, "I heard you walking around and thought you might use the company."

"Oh Sophia, you were right; Dirk wants to get back together."

Sophia sat into the stool at the counter and remained silent.

"It would be easier."

Sophia said nothing.

"You told me I was strong. I'm not, Sophia. I don't want to be a single parent. I don't want my child to grow up without a father."

"Do you love Dirk?"

"No."

"So you'll sacrifice the chance of ever finding someone you love because you're scared to be alone."

"Sophia, how can you understand? You found someone who loved you and you loved back. Not everybody is that fortunate. Compromises have to be made."

"Never presume you know another person's story. I was twenty-two years old when I became pregnant with Richard. I brought him up for two years on my own. Someday I will tell you the whole saga but I never sold my soul."

"Are you saying I'd be selling mine?"

"That's a question only you can answer. I'm going back to bed."

Grace watched Sophia as she went back upstairs. Who would have thought? But Sophia was right; she'd end up hating Dirk. The more she thought about everything, the more she realised she was surrounded by a loving family and solid friends. Her baby would have them too. It just wasn't what she had hoped for but it was better than the alternative.

She'd ring Dirk in the morning and ask him to buy her out of the house at the market price. It would be a lot less than they had paid for it but it would be closure. And she could move on with the rest of her life. Her baby needed security. Thankfully Eoghan looked after the finances in the business and the first thing he had organised was that they both took a set figure every month. She'd have to budget tightly but with Sophia's request for her to caretake Rose Cottage rent-free while she returned to New York, Grace could use the rent money to buy all the paraphernalia that went with a baby. If Dirk agreed to the sale of the house she could look for a place to buy or rent and be ready to move in before the baby was born in March.

There was no point in going back to bed; instead she went to the office and switched on her computer. Work would be her saviour.

On Sunday morning Sophia parked her car in the yard at McGraths'. The sky was bright and the air was crisp. She was looking forward to the next few hours. Geoff had invited her to join a group of experienced horseback riders who were on holidays. He was bringing them on a trek through the woods and down to Bayrush Beach. This was what she had vowed to do before returning to New York. Her heart thumped at the thought of cantering along the beach. She had watched the fabulous sight so often. The vision of the sea and the sand being kicked back from behind the powerful animals always caught her breath. And today she was going to be part of it. She had butterflies in her tummy in anticipation. She hadn't had this feeling for years.

Jessie and Geoff had the horses tacked and ready inside the sand arena. There were eight of them.

"Sophia, would you like Caesar as usual?" asked Jessie, bringing the loading block over to the sixteen hands chestnut hunter.

"Perfect, thanks, Jess," she replied, mounting. "I'm anxious today. I must be crazy."

"Caesar is kind, Sophia. Just put his nose behind one of the others and he'll bring you safely down the beach. Don't give him a clear view or he'll think he's in a race. Keep him behind."

"I don't know if that makes me feel better or worse," she replied.

"You'll be grand, relax and enjoy it," said Jessie, walking off with the mounting block. What the hell am I doing, thought Sophia. Leaning forward she patted Caesar's flank, muttering, "Bring me back safe, won't you, boy?"

Moments later Jessie opened the big doors and they set off in a line. Sophia listened to the tourists speaking what sounded like German. The young girl ahead of her turned around. "It is very beautiful here," she said.

"It is," Sophia agreed. "Where are you from?"

"Switzerland," the girl replied.

"So you are used to beautiful scenery."

"Ah, yes, but it is all the yellow. The yellow is everywhere and the sheep."

"Yellow?" Sophia asked, trotting Caesar up next to the girl's horse. She was intrigued about the yellow.

"You will see." Then the girl pointed her whip to the yellow gorse bushes in the hedgerows.

"It's called gorse or furze," said Sophia, delighted to inform.

To the girl's further delight a flock of sheep came into sight. Sophia smiled, thinking what would have been like if they'd come in springtime. The sight of the lambs was a joy to behold.

They began to canter along a quiet road and the clattering of the horse's hooves against the tarmac was like music to her ears. She loved every piece of this. It made her feel so alive.

Half an hour later as they trotted past the racecourse, the excitement within the group grew as the vista of the back-strand, sand dunes and beach of Bayrush came into full view.

"We are so happy. We have never experienced horse-riding on a beach. Our country is land-locked. My friends and I are like little children. You will excuse us … ya," the young girl, shouted above the noise of the hooves as they trotted past the surf club and beachfront shops.

They entered the beach through a well-worn gap in the sandbank. The horses, sensing the excitement, began to get fired up and couldn't wait to let loose. Sophia kept Jessie's advice and pointed Caesar's nose firmly behind Geoff's mount.

"All okay?" he asked; they all agreed. "Stick together and follow my pace, okay?"

And they were off. It was the most incredible feeling, the wind in her face and the power of the horse beneath her. Even being sand blasted by Geoff's horse didn't deter from the exhilaration of it all. Her adrenaline was pumping; she looked across at the young girl who was beaming.

"It's incredible," she called, above the thundering of hooves and panting of the horses.

When they finally finished, Geoff said. "Let the horses walk in the water. They love it."

Geoff turned his horse to be next to Sophia. "Well, did you enjoy that?"

"Fantastic, I want to do this every Sunday. What a buzz! The group loved it, just look at them." The others were chatting and laughing with one another as the horses waded in the ocean.

"I'm afraid we can only do it every two weeks because of the tide. But on the other Sunday we do a two-hour trek around the woods and the lake and we even stop in the local pub for a beer. You should come on that one."

"Sounds like fun," she smiled. They were walking side by side, companionably chatting about this and that when she asked, "How is Jessie?

"She's okay. It's been hard for her both physically and emotionally. She talked with a counsellor and it seems to have helped her. Also she did this thing in Spain, I don't know, some kind of relaxation therapy but it has helped her sleep. She found someone who offers it here."

Sophia was fascinated. Although she loved it in Ireland she still dreaded night-time. She filled her days as much as possible in the hope of exhausting herself but still she found it hard to sleep.

"Do you think I could ask her about it, Geoff?"

"Of course, she'll be around the yard or the house when we get back. You can chat to her then, I'm sure."

Sophia helped untack the horses and said goodbye to the Swiss tourists. Geoff insisted she come in for a coffee. Jessie was in the kitchen making dinner.

"Oh, hi Sophia, will you have a cuppa?" asked Jessie, pushing the big black kettle onto the range hot plate.

"I hope I'm not intruding …"

"I was telling Sophia about the lady you go to … she's interested in that stuff too. So I'll leave ye to it," said Geoff, heading back out the door.

Sam ran through the kitchen when he heard his father's voice and called, "Dad, wait for me! Hey Sophia."

"Hi Sam. Jessie, I can talk to you another time. You're so busy."

"No time like the present, Sophia. And really it's a roast, there's no rush. Tea or coffee?" she asked, taking two mugs from the wooden rack on the worktop. Jessie told her about the doctor prescribing antidepressants and how she hadn't wanted to take them. And about Barcelona and going to talk to the priest she had met at Sophia's house-warming. She had found a lady called Aisling who was a psychologist but had trained in reflexology, acupuncture and a range of other Eastern therapies. She had gone for a couple of sessions and so far it was helping her to sleep.

"I'd like to try it out. Do you have a contact number?" Jessie looked up her mobile and gave the number to Sophia. Sophia appreciated that Jessie didn't pry as to why she would want to see this lady. As Sophia climbed into her car, she thought how easy it had been to chat with Jessie. She keyed the number in there and then. She managed to get a cancellation for the following day.

Wow, thought Sophia as she pulled away from the therapist's house on the outskirts of Bayrush. She had had a wonderful experience but she couldn't describe it. The sound of the pebbles crunching under the tyres as she drove along the avenue to Rose Cottage made her feel comforted. Her mind felt clear for the first time in a very long time. Aisling had recommended that she drink plenty of water for the next few days. She was exhausted and went gladly to bed.

The next morning Sophia and Grace were together in the kitchen. "I miss Richard, I love it here Grace, but I also need to see him. I hoped he'd come but ... he hates flying."

Grace closed the newspaper she was reading and placed it on the breakfast counter. "I can't say I'm surprised. But you hadn't mentioned going home much lately so I thought you'd changed your mind."

"Although I'm aware he's so busy I'll hardly see him but ..." Her voice trailed.

"He's your son," Grace filled in. "You'll be missed, Sophia. When are you leaving?"

"In two days' time."

"Oh." Grace's voice was filled with disappointment. "Well, let's just make the best of your time left here so. Are you and Eoghan going out in the boat today?"

"To be sure, we are," said Sophia, getting up from the kitchen table. "I must get ready."

"Oh God, Sophia, will you ever give up. Your attempts at the Irish accent are getting worse," laughed Grace.

"It is begor." She laughed, running upstairs to change.

"I'll cook dinner for all of us this evening," Grace called after her. She actually dreaded the thought of Sophia leaving and of being alone, really alone.

Later that evening while Eoghan and Sophia sat in the living room, Grace pottered around the kitchen.

"How's the hake coming along?" asked Eoghan from where he sat by the fire, sharing a bottle of Chardonnay with Sophia who sat on the cream couch across from him.

"It's your recipe I'm using so I'll blame you if it all goes wrong. Anyway I'm the pregnant person here. Why am I doing all the work?" She laughed.

"Well it was your idea. Sophia said she'd some news to share and so I'm all ears here," said Eoghan, in great spirits.

"I'm going back to the States for a while."

"Oh." He took a sip but looked quizzically over the glass. "I'm just surprised that's all. I suppose when you rented the house, I figured you were here for the long-haul."

"I'll be back, it's just I have responsibilities and well ... I think it's time I went back to face things."

"You'll be missed," he said, holding his glass up. And then he changed the subject completely. "Is it ready yet, girly?"

"Eoghan Forrester. If you don't behave I'll throw you out," said Grace, but she knew from his demeanour he was saddened that Sophia was leaving. He meant the world to Grace and her life had completely changed the day she met him. He had given her the courage and belief that she could actually set up a business, and he had provided the financial backing she had needed when no bank would support her. She'd have an early night and let them chat, she decided as she plated the dinner.

"Come and get it."

"That smells gorgeous, Gracey!" said Eoghan, getting up to join her at the kitchen counter.

"Come on so, let's tuck in," said Grace. In her heart she wanted Sophia to have plenty of reasons to come back and looking at Eoghan she knew he did too.

Later when Grace had gone to bed, Eoghan and Sophia sat opposite one another in front of the turf fire.

"Grace is going to caretake the cottage while I'm away,"

"Good, it'd be a shame to leave it empty."

"I'm worried about her, Eoghan."

"She has me, Sophia."

"He hasn't acted honourably."

"Sophia, he was always an ass. Excuse the language, but well it wasn't my place to say. We can't always help who we fall for."

She nodded her head in agreement and wondered not for the first time about Eoghan. "I just want to make sure that Grace has a place to stay and that she doesn't make any rash decisions. I'm not prying but I'm very aware that it is a young business, and until they sell the house she will be tied up financially for a while – she might even come out of it owing money."

Eoghan nodded his head in agreement. "It's good of you to offer her this place, Sophia. And I know your friendship has certainly helped pull her through, but she has a good family and friends and we're all here for her so don't worry. Go back and do what you need to do but know that we'll all be looking forward to your return. Now I'll take my leave as they say. Night Sophia and a very safe journey to you," he said, getting up and picking up his coat.

For a moment she was lost about how to say goodbye. He didn't make any attempt to kiss her. So she stood awkwardly and made her way around the couch to the front door. "Goodbye Eoghan." And he was gone.

She closed the door slowly, turned and walked upstairs.

Chapter Ten

*I*t was early December and Jessie was doing her Christmas shopping. She was dreading Christmas. She had dreamed so much about having her babies with them but as Sam was so excited it wasn't fair not to be enthusiastic. She tried so hard not to be sad but sometimes it overwhelmed her. Trying to distract herself, because the last thing she needed was a public outburst, she noticed a poster in the health-food shop window. She stopped and began to read about a series of workshops on self-help. Intrigued, she was about to take out her mobile to insert the number when a lady she knew vaguely said, "Hello."

"Oh hi Vivien," she replied, not too keen to get into a conversation with her. The woman was part of the rowing club set and a notorious gossip to boot.

"How's Grace? I heard the news. She must be devastated, what with being engaged and all … he was always messing around. The whole club knew it."

Jessie could feel the rage inside build up and was doing everything to stop herself from slapping the woman's smug face.

"Well what a wonderful bunch of people you are. I heard that there is no end to the wife-swapping going on up there. But sure you'd know all about it," Jessie said and walked away with her head in the air. That would give her something to think about. It was completely untrue. But she didn't care. If he had been messing around that much, surely one of them would have heard about it. People added legs onto stories. She checked her watch. She was due to meet Kate and Grace for a coffee in Bonita's. Walking into the café she noticed the same poster stuck on the door. This time she stored the number in her mobile.

"What were you looking at?" asked Grace, when Jessie joined them.

"There's a summer camp of workshops going to be held in Clonmel next July. I think I'll try it out."

"What kind of workshops?" asked Grace.

"All self-help stuff. I've no idea but I think I'll try it. It's just I'm sleeping again which is good but there are days I feel so angry I hardly recognise myself, and there's other days when it takes everything to get out of bed. I have to do something about it."

"What about going to Fr. Jim again?" asked Kate, taking a sip from her cappuccino.

"I've nothing left to say."

"Well then sign up for one of the workshops. You've nothing to lose. Is it expensive?" asked Grace.

"No, it seems it is part of a society. All the facilitators offer their services free.

"Wow, that sounds good!" said Grace.

"Which workshop are you going to do?" asked Kate.

"I'm going to look up the website for more detail but, Kate, I'm thinking about trying art therapy."

Grace burst out laughing.

"What's wrong with you?" asked Kate.

"You didn't go to school with her. She couldn't draw a straight line with a ruler."

"Thanks a bunch. You're a fabulous support." But Jessie just smiled; it felt great to be sitting with the two of them bantering, a little bit like the old days.

With less than a week to go to Christmas, Sophia watched her son replying to anybody who spoke to him, noticing that he might as well have been somewhere else for all the interest he took. He had been delighted to see her when she had come back from Ireland. But the light in his eyes had disappeared as quickly as it had come.

"You're a million miles away, Mother," said Richard.

"I'm tired of all the socialising already."

"You're only back six weeks."

Sophia looked around the tables. They were beautifully laid. The people looked fabulous and yet she felt alone. And guilty for not wanting to be part of it all – this was her life. This was what she had always wanted. Success, money, respect. But everything had changed – now all she wanted was a tiny glimmer of happiness for her son. Was it too much to ask?

"Richard, will you spend Christmas with me in Ireland?"

He looked at her. He was stunned. She could see him trying to come up with a million excuses as to why he couldn't. Then he picked up a piece of discarded Christmas cracker and fiddling with it said, "Yes."

"Oh Richard, you will never know how much it means to me. I

couldn't bear the thought of us spending another Christmas just the two of us in the Hamptons like last year." Sophia's eyes filled with tears.

He reached over and touched her hand and her heart felt as though it would burst with the love she felt for him.

Grace was making tea in Rose Cottage when the house phone rang. She picked it up along with her mug and walked into the living area to stretch out on the couch for the long chat she knew was imminent. Sophia was the only person who ever called the house phone.

"Hi Grace."

"Hi Sophia, perfect timing, I've just made a cup of tea. It's great to hear from you. When are you coming back? Eoghan is pining like mad for you."

Sophia laughed at the other end.

"That is exactly why I'm calling. How do you feel about having two visitors to stay with you for the Christmas vacation?"

"Oh Sophia, I'd love it."

"I'll fly in on Wednesday."

"And Christmas Day is Sunday, great! Tell me, who's coming with you?"

"Richard, I've finally convinced him to take some time off. I'm looking forward to showing him around and of course meeting you all. I know he'll love it. How are you feeling? Has your waistline expanded?"

"Of course, I'm like Ten-Ton-Tessie but everybody else says I'm neat. I feel great; all the tiredness is gone. I must say it's true about pregnancy, the hair, nails and skin are all aglow, not that there is anyone to notice it." There was sadness in her voice even though she tried to hide it with glibness.

"Any word from Dirk?"

"Nothing, not even from the auctioneer, he's ignoring my offer to sell the house to him. I can stay with Mam for Christmas, that way you'll have this place to yourselves."

"No Grace, please stay. I'd love you to be with us for Christmas." Grace knew by the sound of Sophia's voice that she really meant it.

"Well in that case I'll be delighted to stay. Thanks, Sophia."

"We'll arrive into Shannon and will be with you just after lunch."

Grace drove up the McGraths' avenue and was met with a visual spectacle. She had forgotten that the McGraths were hosting a sponsored horse ride. She parked and walked across the field to watch the splendid sight of horses and riders dressed in all the finery ready for the off. She'd love to be joining in. Oh well, she thought.

Jessie came walking towards her and Grace was pleased to see her smiling again. She rang at least twice a day to ask how she was doing and if she needed anything. Grace knew she worried about her being alone and she was glad of the support. With the tourist season complete and no social outlet, Grace had begun to write. It was fun to escape into an imaginary world where things could work out the way she wanted them to. She was sad that her little baby wouldn't have a father and sorry for the fact that nobody made her a cup of tea in the evening and asked her how her day was.

"Hey, this is a surprise. It's great to see you, Gracey," called Jessie, walking across the field to join her at the fence.

"Aren't you going out with them?" Grace nodded, in the direction of the assembled riders.

"No, Sam isn't feeling well so I left him for a few minutes. He's lying on the sofa. Come on, let's get some heat into us. It's bloody freezing out here. I hope Geoff doesn't come back with a dose of flu too. I'm delighted you came over, did you bring me any stories?" She linked Grace as they walked back towards the house.

"As a matter of fact, I did." Grace laughed, Jessie was the only one she'd ever share her stories with and she was always encouraging her to join a writers' group but Grace could never seem to pick up the courage.

"Hi Grace," called Sam when she looked in on him sprawled on the sofa watching TV.

"Well, you have the life. Mr McGrath!"

"I'm sick," he said, from under his Liverpool fleece blanket. But he was grinning.

"He'll be sicker in the morning trying to waggle a day off school," Jessie muttered.

"I'd say he'll need a day off," said Grace, grinning at her godchild.

"See I told you, Mom."

"Come into the kitchen Grace Fitzgerald and stop causing trouble."

Grace laughed and winked at Sam who put his thumbs up to her.

Back in the kitchen Grace sat in one of the two armchairs Jessie had placed in the corner of the large room.

"Tea or coffee?" asked Jessie.

Grace calling around was a welcome surprise to Jessie. Grace had become more and more withdrawn since Sophia had gone back to New York. Kate had told her that there were fewer calls and a lot less to do in the off-season which worried Jessie even more. It was the reason she encouraged her to write so much. "Your bump is nice and neat." Jessie smiled, bringing the tea over to join Grace near the window.

"Yeah, I'm in maternity jeans now." She pulled up her top to reveal the elastic waistband. "Six months down, three to go. Oh I have good news … Sophia is coming back for Christmas."

"That's fantastic. I'm delighted. Oh Grace I thought you were going to say you've heard something about the house."

"No, unfortunately," Grace replied, wistfully. "But you know when it does eventually happen I hope to either rent or buy in the countryside. I love it, Jessie. I never thought I would say that."

"I can't believe it. You've spent years calling me 'a country bumpkin'."

Grace was smiling when the back door opened and Geoff walked in, followed by Jack … whose face dropped when he saw Grace.

"Grace, this is a friend of mine, Jack. He's back from Dubai. I don't think you've met."

"We've met before," said Grace.

"Nice to see you again, Grace," said Jack but his face was unreadable.

"And you too," she managed to mutter as Geoff continued talking.

"Jack and I are training a horse together."

"And Geoff wants to call it Jessie's Angel. What do you think Gracey?" Jessie said, clearly pleased.

"That's a great name, I love it," she said, noticing that Jack was staring at her tummy. All she wanted to do was leave, run even.

"So, when is the big day?" Jack asked.

"The 28th of March."

"Congratulations. You both must be over the moon."

There was a momentary silence before Jessie intervened. "Oh sure, it's great news, altogether. Jack, would you like vegetable soup? I made a pot earlier. I'm sure the rest of them will be along in a minute"

"That would be great, thanks Jessie. I'm freezing."

Monique and some of her friends came in and the kitchen was buzzing. Jack came over and sat in the armchair beside her. How could this be happening? She couldn't stop fidgeting and couldn't think of anything to say; even if she could she felt tongue-tied. This wasn't how she had dreamed of meeting him again.

"So how are you?" he asked gently. But before she had time to reply

Jessie came over with a bowl of soup in one hand and a plate of brown bread in the other. "There you are, Jack, tuck in," she said.

"Thanks, Jessie," he smiled.

"I hope ye managed to raise enough money today," said Jessie.

Grace was glad to sit and watch as Jack talked to the McGraths about the turnout and how much they had hoped to make to send two sick people from the parish to Lourdes. He looked great; she thought, there was a healthy glow from him. His cream jodhpurs were splashed in mud. There was even some on his face, making him even more attractive to her if that was possible. Her heart was thumping, making her extremely uncomfortable, antsy even. And his smile. There was no God, she decided. She was six months pregnant and yearning for somebody she could never have. Why wouldn't she feel angry?

"Grace, will you come with me, I want to show you some curtain material I got for Sam's room. I'd like your opinion."

Damn, now I'm going to have to get up and waddle across in front of him. I could kill Jessie.

He smiled and made to help her as she got up. "I'm fine, thanks."

She overheard Geoff saying, "She's usually friendly, but sure it must be the hormones."

"I heard that, Geoff," she called back.

Both men laughed. Monique, Jay and the other teenagers were busy chatting and munching, taking no heed of the adults. Seeing them just served to make her feel worse – fat, pregnant and single.

Jessie brought her into the living room where she had the curtain material still in the shopping bag. "Gracey, you've gone awfully quiet and you're as pale as a ghost."

"I'm just tired. Anyway the material is lovely."

"Thanks."

"I'll head away and leave you to chat," said Grace.

"But your coat is in the kitchen."

"Will you be a doll and get it for me while I say goodbye to Sam."

"He's in the kitchen."

"Oh just get the coat."

"Jesus, you're definitely hormonal."

She smiled. "Ah thanks Jess, I couldn't face waddling back in there."

"And you have another three months to go, girl. You'd better get used to it," laughed Jessie.

"Why did Dad love Ireland so much?" asked Richard.

Sophia paused. Looking out the window as the patchwork quilt of green that was Ireland came into sight, she began to talk. "I've never told you this but when we met, your father's family threatened to disinherit him if he remained with me. I didn't want him to be like me, completely without a family, so I ended it. I lied to him. I told him I didn't love him and that I had met somebody else. He was devastated but had to accept my decision. Two years later I bumped into him in Central Park, you were in a buggy. He bent down, looked at you and knew you were his." A tear rolled down her cheek. "You were always so alike." She paused and, looking across at him, said, "Richard … you don't seem surprised, did he tell you?"

"No, I knew there was something because I found your marriage certificate in Dad's papers after he died. But why didn't you tell me about my grandparents?"

"They did exactly as I had feared and he never spoke to them again."

"But I still don't understand why he loved Ireland so much."

"Because Nana Hannah was Irish – she had been his nanny growing up and she had loved him as though he was her own. When she heard what had happened she moved into the same building as us and insisted on looking after you while we went to work. I don't know what we would have done without her and when she died we were both devastated. You were only six years old."

"I remember her but why didn't you tell me?"

"Why tell you about people who were never going to be a part of our lives? We had you and one another and when you met Heather we were so pleased. And little Billy. Oh Richard I'm so sorry about all that has happened to you. I want so much for you to be happy. Thank you for agreeing to this trip. I know that flying is … well …"

"Let's just try, Mom." He reached across and kissed her on the cheek.

She patted his hand, which rested on the plush upholstery of their Lear jet as they began their descent into Shannon. Bill Wynthrope had certainly provided her with a life she could only have dreamed of. Looking at her son's handsome profile he reminded her so much of him it hurt.

Grace pottered around Rose Cottage cleaning. She wanted everything to be perfect for the impending arrival. Sophia was very easy to live with; it was Richard she was anxious about. She heard a car coming along the pebbled drive. She opened the door and went out to welcome them. "Hi, it's so good to see you, Sophia." They hugged and then Sophia pushed her shoulders back gently to look down to her tummy.

"Let me see you. Oh my, that's a fine bump. You look fabulous. But there's nothing new in that," she added, smiling warmly. "Richard, I would like you to meet Grace."

"Hello." He shook hands formally.

"Hi Richard, it's great to meet you. Sophia told me so much about you."

He raised an eyebrow. "Really?"

Grace felt suddenly very awkward.

"Richard, will you bring in the luggage?" asked Sophia.

This is going to be a nightmare, thought Grace. Although Sophia talked about Richard regularly it was always in relation to his childhood or work. She figured he was in his late thirties. He was tall and dark with a handsome, distant face. Warm wasn't a word to describe him. It occurred to her that maybe he wasn't too pleased to be providing a pregnant woman – who as far as he was concerned was a near stranger to his mother – with free accommodation. That was it, she thought. That's why he was so cool to her. She'd better find somewhere to live after Christmas.

Sophia recognised that Grace had inadvertently said the wrong thing. Richard would think that she had discussed his circumstances with Grace. How could she have thought that two strangers and a middle-aged woman could enjoy Christmas in a pretty cottage on a beach in Ireland?

Richard planted his suitcase at the end of the bed. The downstairs bedroom was small, tiny more like, not that he cared. Why had he agreed to take this trip? And his mother had confided in that woman who would now spend the Christmas vacation feeling sorry for him. His mother's decision to come here to the back of beyond, leaving everything she knew behind, had stunned him.

When she had returned to New York she had told him about cookery courses, horse-riding and music nights in little pubs, and something about going sea-angling with a man called Eoghan. Why had she felt so compelled to rent this place? There wasn't even a bathroom in his room. To shower he had to go upstairs. A couple of days to Christmas and then he was out of here. He would make sure that he got an urgent call – the very next day.

Jack was bored. There was a match on TV but he couldn't concentrate. He had taken a winter lease on a friend's summer house in Kilowen, a large fishing village three miles from Bayrush. At least he was out from under his mother's feet. His mobile rang.

"Hi Abdul. I'm sorry I didn't return your call sooner. I'll be covering maternity leave until March. I'll fly back then and we can take things from there. How does that sound to you?"

As he hung up he knew Abdul wasn't too impressed with him but he didn't want to go back yet. Jesus, what was wrong with him? "She's pregnant with somebody else's child," he said out loud.

Jack lit a cigarette, thinking that he should pack them in. He picked up his phone again. "Fancy a pint,tonight Geoff?" He listened for a moment. "See you in Nutties when you're ready?" He grabbed his jacket and walked out the door.

He sat at the bar looking at the big screen TV. The commentators were analysing the football match between Liverpool and Manchester United when Geoff joined him.

"What are you having?" asked Jack.

"A pint of Guinness, cheers."

The two friends chatted about the game with the barman. After a while the place began to get busy and live music started. Jack said he was going out for a cigarette. The smoking area had high wooden stools and bar tables with a canopy overhead and a wooden and glass wall to the front, with open gaps at either end. There was plenty of heat coming from the gas heaters overhead; even on this cold winter's night it was snug. Geoff joined him although he wasn't a smoker.

"I'd nearly take up the habit, this place is so smart," joked Geoff.

Jack looked around; the place was empty so he decided to ask about Grace. He desperately wanted to talk about her. "How's Grace?"

"She's good. It's hard on her, though."

"What, being pregnant? She looked well to me."

"No, that bit is fine. It's the asshole bit."

"What are you talking about?"

"Dirk. It's over between them. I don't really ask questions, you know yourself."

"What happened?"

"Jack, I don't know … but she's living in Bayrush now. Ah look, she's doing okay. Are you going to the races on Stephen's Day? We're thinking of making a day of it. Do you fancy joining us?"

"Yeah, I might take you up on that. Have you thought about entering Jessie's Angel?"

"Actually I was going to discuss that with you when we go back inside."

"Good idea. It's freezing out here," said Jack, getting up, but his head was in a spin. Grace's relationship was over. He hadn't expected that. But she was heavily pregnant. What was wrong with him? He must be crazy to even think about …"I'll have a whiskey," he said, "It'll get the heat back into me."

"It wasn't that cold out," said Geoff, giving him a sideways look.

When he got home he sat by what was left of the fire. She was in Bayrush; he was in Kilowen, the neighbouring fishing village with only a tiny stretch of coastline between them. There might be some chance for them after all.

"Oh Jess, it's great to have Sophia back, but Richard is a bloody nightmare. I don't know what we are going to do about Christmas Day. He's sooo … serious. I'm so glad we're coming over to you for Christmas dinner." Grace had the phone hanging between her ear and shoulder and was trying to work at the same time.

"I hate to rain on your parade but I'm not exactly Miss Personality at the moment. Let's invite your mother and Kate too. Where is she due to go for Christmas dinner?"

"Lauren invited her ages ago. They are having Sean's parents too. I can't ask her to change at this late stage."

"You're pregnant; any of them would take the stars out of the sky for you at the moment. The only woman to keep things alive is your mother. Is he really that bad?"

"In a word, Jess – yes."

"Ring Lauren and ask her out for the afternoon so that your mother will get to see Lauren's kids too. Sam will be delighted with the company. And we'll invite Eoghan too."

"You're a saviour. I have to go. They're back."

Grace hung up. If she had known how difficult it was going to be she would have moved out for the duration of their stay. It was only Friday morning. Roll on Sunday – Christmas Day.

Grace working at the desk in the upstairs living room when Sophia came in and plopped down on the couch. "We were wondering if you are free for lunch. Surely you must be due a break. You've been working so hard since we came."

I have, thought Grace, more to make myself scarce. It was a great way of getting work done that she had kept putting off. "In actual fact, Kate is on her way. We have some more work to do." As she turned away from the computer screen she saw the disappointment on Sophia's face.

"Tell you what, when Kate comes we'll go for lunch. And after that we can catch up on our work."

"That sounds good to me. How about going to Kilowen? They do a nice pub lunch in Murphy's. It will only take us a few minutes along the coast road."

Twenty minutes later she heard Kate's car on the gravel so she went down to meet her. Kate arrived in her usual flurry, files hanging out of everywhere. "Hi everybody," she called as she clambered across the drive. "Well don't anybody rush to my assistance or anything. No, I'm fine, really."

Grace and Sophia laughed. Meanwhile Richard walked towards her and took a couple of files from her. "Thanks." She smiled up at him.

"You're welcome."

"I love the accent. Say something else."

He smirked at her. "Are you for real?"

"Oh, I love it."

Grace looked at Sophia and turning away they both began to laugh.

"I've missed our chats," Sophia whispered. They hadn't been alone together. Grace nodded in agreement and then called towards Kate.

"Are you okay for time today ? Sophia has kindly asked us to lunch."

"Well, sis, you're the boss. I only obey orders."

"Kate, you've never obeyed an order in your life," laughed Grace.

For the first time in a very long time Richard wanted to know more about somebody. This petite black-haired girl had skin like porcelain and dark eyes a man could get lost in. She had a sapphire stud in her pert nose and a whole load of attitude that he liked immediately. She was so not the type of woman he'd usually go for. He'd had relationships since Heather, but none of them had meant anything.

He felt so guilty about everything. He could have been a better father, a better husband and now he was none of those things. He didn't deserve a second chance.

Twenty minutes later they all piled into the rented Mercedes. Richard drove. Already his mother had insisted on bringing him along every back road in Ireland. "I want you to see the real Ireland," she kept saying, pointing out this old site and that one. He had no interest in castles, towers and portal dolmens. When she wasn't talking history it was geology. His mother was turning into a walking tourism manual. But he had humoured her because she was so taken with it all.

The Kate person kept chatting the whole way along.

"Did you do much shopping when you went back home? I love the outlet stores."

"Not really," his mother answered, shooting him a warning look from the passenger seat. It occurred to him that Kate didn't know how wealthy Sophia was. So that was why she hadn't wanted to fly in more locally. "Grace, I should have offered you the front seat."

Grace laughed. "And really make me feel huge!"

Richard realised that he had been unfair in his judgment of Grace. He saw how hard she worked and he was aware of how self-conscious she was about living in Rose Cottage with them. But he couldn't seem to put things right between them. For all his skills in the boardroom, he was at sea socially. Heather had accepted that about him, it hadn't mattered to her. Stop, he told himself.

He found parking on the wide main street, directly outside the pub. It was a pretty village with lots of fine old townhouses. Back on the cliffs overlooking the sea there was a complex of holiday cottages dotted around. A roadway led to a small fishing harbour beneath it. He thought it was all very beautiful.

Lunch turned into a lively affair with plenty of banter going on between Kate and the waiter, whom she knew from her school days. He was delighted to see his mother relax for the first time since they'd arrived in Ireland. He had been too wrapped up in his own thoughts to notice before. His mother was trying to do what he couldn't do or hadn't even tried to do since Heather and Billy and his father's death. She was trying to move on.

He looked at her across the table. She had always been a strong woman but his father's death had broken her. He had always known how much they loved one another. But now he understood why. What a woman! She had walked away from the man she loved because she had been afraid he'd lose too much for loving her. And she had raised him on her own for the first two years of his life. He had grown up in a steady, loving home considering that they both worked so hard. Now she was trying to guide him, showing him rather than telling him that it was okay to laugh again. Words hadn't worked. Maybe she was right not to tell people who she was. He'd make an effort to enjoy himself for her sake at least. A couple more days and he would be out of here.

"So what are you into?" asked Kate.

"Pardon me?"

"I mean hobbies … you know things that people like to do for fun."

"Nobody has asked me that for years."

"Well then …" She seemed to be waiting for an answer and because he hadn't done anything fun for years he blushed. He hadn't done that for years either. "Watching sport on TV," he muttered.

"Which ones?" She wasn't giving up.

"Superbowl, basketball … you wouldn't be familiar with them."

"Try me …" She had devilment in her eyes.

"Name the LA basketball team?"

"The Lakers and the Clippers. Was that your attempt at a trick question? So lame!" He laughed out loud and his mother smiled across the table at him.

As Jack drove passed Murphy's pub restaurant he spotted Grace being helped into the front seat of a Mercedes by a tall guy with dark hair. He recognised the two other women climbing into the back of the car. One was Sophia and he didn't know the other girl's name.

Jesus, he thought, she didn't exactly let the grass grow under her feet. She was with somebody else already. The guy was making a big fuss of her. Then again who wouldn't? He took in the scene in the few seconds it took to drive by. "Why am I caught up with thinking about her when she is clearly living her life to the full?" he muttered, stopping at the post office to post an application for a herd number to the Department of Agriculture. He had decided to rent some land from Conor to keep some cattle. He was just trying to keep his options open.

Chapter Eleven

"Jess, the major red alert is over. Kate managed to make Richard smile. Maybe it won't be so bad after all," said Grace, sitting down to a cup of tea with Jessie by the kitchen counter in Rose Cottage.

"I always knew I'd be useful for something." Kate laughed.

"Great, so your mother is coming. I met Lauren and she's delighted about the kids going pony trekking after the Christmas dinner," said Jessie. "It's going to be a great day after all. I'll hardly have anything left to do at this stage. Everybody has offered to cook something."

Grace heard a car crunch along the gravel. "It must be Sophia and Richard, they went to the market in Bayrush."

Sophia came in with Richard carrying some shopping bags.

"Hi guys we're just discussing who's doing what for Christmas Day. Let's make a list."

"I'm making a tiramisu for desert. It's a recipe from my cookery course in Cliff Manor," said Sophia proudly.

"Whoooh!" said the girls in chorus.

"All downhill from that!" laughed Grace. "Mam is doing the Brussels sprouts. She fries them with garlic and bacon. They're delicious."

"Yuck, I can't be convinced. Moving on," said Jessie.

"I'm making garlic gratin potatoes and Kate is cooking the ham, which is a small miracle!" said Grace.

"Nigella says all I have to do is place it in a pot and add a bottle of Coke and boil. Ye'll all lick your fingers after it."

They all laughed.

"So that leaves the turkey and I'll boil and roast potatoes. Nora always makes the Christmas cake and pudding," said Jessie.

"Oh great. I didn't know Nora was going to be there too," said Sophia, delighted.

"Of course, Monique and Nora celebrate Christmas with us every year."

"So how many do we have in total, nine adults and Sam?" asked Sophia.

"No, ten, Eoghan is coming," said Grace. Grace noticed Richard, who was reading the newspaper in the living room, look up and smile over at his mother. Sophia had confided in Grace that she had spent last Christmas with just the two of them alone in a house in the Hamptons. She had made Grace promise not to tell the others about her wealth. Grace had previously told Kate about the limo experience, but had gone back on her story and said it was a friend's one. It didn't matter to her one way or the other, and she couldn't really understand why Sophia was so secretive about it. Who cared what she had?

Grace woke to the smell of sausages cooking. She felt a sharp pang of memory. Dirk had always cooked sausages on Christmas morning before they had gone to their respective homes for Christmas dinner. On Richard's first morning here she had cooked sausages and every morning since he began his day with them. She smiled through what could so easily have been tears. She pulled up a pair of leggings and slipped her feet into furry slippers and went downstairs. Ever since their lunch at Kilowen the atmosphere in the house had lifted. She was looking forward to the day, surrounded by all the people she loved.

"You're up. Great, let's exchange presents." Sophia was full of enthusiasm.

"Mom, let's have the sausages while they're hot."

Grace threw her eyes to heaven and pulled the stool out to sit at the counter and be presented with sausages. "Thank God you're going back Richard or I'll be piling on more weight than I already have."

"He's such a fitness freak. I'm amazed by his sudden passion for pig meat," laughed Sophia.

"Eat up," he said, smiling at them. Tucking into her toasted sandwich, Grace smiled as Sophia and Richard did likewise. Who would have thought that she'd be spending Christmas Day with a stranger she'd met on a plane just six months ago? She really hoped Sophia would like her present.

"Come on Sophia," she said, taking her last bite. "I'm dying to give you your pressie."

Sophia came over to join her where she was on all fours pulling a box from under the Christmas tree.

"Get up or you'll hurt yourself," said Sophia.

"Have it," she said, sliding the large box towards Sophia.

Sophia opened it and said, "Oh wow, it's beautiful. Look, Richard."

"It's made by The Handmade Glass Company. And the piece is

called The Gathering Centerpiece, which was a huge tourism campaign to encourage Irish emigrants to come back. I know you don't have Irish blood but I'm just so delighted you came back for Christmas. Sophia, it means the world to me that you're here." Turning to Richard, she said, "Your mother has been so kind to me Richard when I've really needed a friend. I missed you Sophia."

"Thank you so much, Grace. I am so glad that you got that upgrade back in June, I feel like I've known you forever. Come here."

They hugged while Richard stood awkwardly, not knowing where to look. Then Grace handed him a wrapped present.

"I'm afraid …" he began but his mother cut him off.

"We have your present in the shed, Grace. I've been so worried you'd see it." She led the way outside to the little shed at the back of the house. "Open the door, Gracey."

Grace opened the door and peeped in to where she saw two pieces of handcrafted wooden furniture, painted white. One was a large rocking chair with a cushioned seat and the other was a baby's cradle.

"I have the most beautiful Egyptian cotton sheets and covers inside for it. I really hope you like them."

Grace turned with tears in her eyes.

"They're from both of us," said Sophia, beaming.

She hugged Sophia again and then found herself hugging Richard, who was mortified. He kind of patted her on the back the way an old man father-figure type person would.

"Thank you so much. They are beautiful."

Richard carried them to the house. They made such a fuss about where to put the chair he eventually said, "Okay, last call, where am I putting it because I'm going for a walk!" He laughed.

"How about here by the window? I can see the sea from here," his mother exclaimed.

"That's perfect," Grace agreed.

Richard walked along the beach. He couldn't believe that he had felt so much more at ease in the last few days. Grace had given him a copy of Siobhán Creaton's book – *Ryanair: How a Small Irish Airline Conquered Europe*. It only confirmed the fact that Grace had no idea about what had happened. His mother had given him a gift voucher for what looked like a massage treatment. It was booked for the 28th of December, which would have annoyed him a few days ago.

He had been dreading Christmas Day. Every day was hard which was why he worked so much. Work didn't allow him time to think of anything else. He was afraid that he might break down if he thought. He didn't go in for all the psychobabble that people did these days.

He stopped and sat on the break wall. Bayrush, he thought, funny name for the place. Ireland had strange place names everywhere, Kil this and Bally that.

He began to walk out towards the sea. Heather and Billy would have loved it here. "I miss you both so much," he mouthed to the sky. He didn't know if he believed in anything anymore yet he looked upwards. "Merry Christmas, my two beauties." Then he looked down and felt the urge to pick up two cockle shells, one big and one small one. He placed them carefully into his coat pocket. He didn't think about why he did it. It simply felt right. He turned and walked back along the beach to join his mother and her friend for Christmas Mass. He hadn't been inside a church for years. Heather, I'm going to at least try to have a good day today. Hug Billy for me. I love you both, he thought.

There was great excitement in McGraths' house. Sam had woken at six a.m. They had had a lovely morning together which included a trip to Christmas Mass. When they got home it had been all hands on deck. Sam had helped to set the table.

The doorbell rang. It was Nora and Monique.

"Hi Sam, did Santa come?" asked Monique, bending down to him. Jessie smiled; Sam loved her, and she was like a big sister to him. And Nora was a third granny. He led them into the living room to show off all he'd got from Santa. Geoff came up behind her and wrapped his arms around her, nuzzling her ear. "It's going to be a fun day, Jess. I'm so glad we're having a crowd."

"So am I," she agreed; she'd have less time to think about what ifs. He went in to join Nora and the others in the living room. The back door opened and before she knew it, the kitchen was full of people. "Merry Christmas, everyone! What'll ye have to drink?"

"What's burning, Jess?" asking Geoff, arriving back into the kitchen.

"All okay," she answered, laughing. "A minor emergency, don't worry. Let's just say the turkey is well and truly cooked."

Everybody laughed.

A couple of hours later, Grace looked around the table. The plates were all empty and the noise level was incredible. There were conversations going on all around her. She patted her tummy, thinking; little one you'll never be short on family. She noticed that Richard and Kate were deep in conversation; she wondered what they could be talking about. Then again, Kate could make the most mundane things sound fascinating. Geoff got up to clear the places and so did Richard.

"Ah, you have him well trained, Sophia," said Grace's mother, Molly.

"What can I say?" replied Sophia proudly.

In the kitchen Geoff and Richard were putting plates into the dishwasher when Jessie arrived in with more dishes.

"I have to check the horses, Jess. Duke wasn't looking too good this morning."

"No problem, I'll top up everybody's drink. We'll have dessert when you come back."

"I'd like to come with you if that's possible?" Richard asked.

"Sure, put on a pair of those wellies. Thankfully it's a nice, bright day but the ground is still soft."

The two men walked side by side across the cobbled courtyard.

"Do you horse-ride, Richard?"

"I used to when I was younger. My son did."

"Oh, you have kids!"

"There was a plane crash … he was with his mother. They were coming down to join me in Grand Cayman for the weekend. I had been there all week on business. Heather decided to surprise me … I can't explain the shock, Geoff."

Geoff stopped in his tracks. "Oh, Jesus … Richard. I'm sorry." He put his hand on the other man's shoulder. "I'm so sorry."

"It's been three years." Then he turned to look at Geoff. "Thanks for having us here today," he said. "I never talk about it … thanks."

Geoff scratched the side of his head and then walked into the stable. "It's this one, Duke. We've had him a long time. He's one of our first. I reckon it's nothing serious. But I hate to see him sick and he's getting worse."

"Can you call a vet on Christmas Day?" asked Richard.

"I could call a mate of mine. I'm sure he'd dig me out. I'll give it another while, at least let him finish his Christmas dinner. Hey Richard, if you ever want to talk …"

"Thanks, Geoff, I appreciate you saying that."

"No problem. Come on or they'll wonder where we've got to."

Jessie was beginning to serve dessert.

"Come on guys or you'll miss out," Kate called from the table.

"How's Duke doing, Dad?"

"He'll be okay, pal," he replied to Sam, turning to quietly tell Jessie that he would have to ring Jack to come out.

"Ooh," said Molly. "The tiramisu is divine."

"Leave me some," called Geoff, re-joining the table. He noticed Richard winking at his mother. Sophia beamed back at him.

Twenty minutes later a silver Land Cruiser pulled into the yard. Geoff, Sam and Monique headed out immediately.

"Thanks for doing this, Jack. Today of all days."

"Hey, if I couldn't do it for you! Anyway this lad couldn't wait to get out the door."

Jack smiled, noticing both Monique and Garvan turning red with embarrassment.

"Shut up, Jack," Garvan muttered, poking his uncle.

"Lead the way, Sam." Jack laughed. Sam ran ahead. "He's in this one, Jack."

Jack checked Duke over completely as the group of heads watched him over the stable door. Duke's heart was doing okay but he was running a temperature. "A course of antibiotics will clear that up," said Jack.

"I learnt to ride on Duke," said Sam with tears in his eyes.

"Ah Sam," Jack said, putting an arm around him, "he'll be okay. He just has to take it easy from now on. A bit like a granddad, but he won't have a fireside chair, instead he'll have the fields out there to survey all his buddies." Sam started to smile through his tears.

"How about a Christmas drink before we head off trekking?" said Geoff.

"We have a treasure hunt planned along the way. Mum's idea of course," Sam piped up.

"Sounds great, I'm staying," said Garvan.

"Yeah, why not!" said Jack.

"See you inside so," Geoff called, while Jack rang his brother to tell him they were staying.

A couple of minutes later, Jack took off his mucky kickers at the back door and walked into the kitchen. When he saw Grace standing at the island in the middle of the kitchen he wanted to turn around and put them back on and run. She was the last person he expected to see but it was too late, Jessie had seen him.

"Jack, it's great to see you. Thanks a million for checking on Duke for us today especially." She kissed him on his cheek in greeting. Grace was looking at him and he couldn't take his eyes away from hers.

"Hi Grace, Merry Christmas," he said.

"And to you too."

"What will you have to drink, Jack?" asked Jessie.

"A Coke would be great thanks."

Jessie went to get it.

"How have you been?" he asked. His voice sounded funny to his own ears.

"Good, thanks. Busy."

Sam came running over to tell him all about Santa and his presents. He bent down to his level while Sam regaled his story about how he had definitely heard Santa but had pretended to be asleep. "I'm a bit scared of him, really ..."

Grace watched as Jack listened to Sam making animated expressions. Looking at him she wished her life had turned out differently. He was so good with Sam. He would make a great dad. She couldn't look anymore. She walked away, anywhere as long as she didn't have to see him. To see all that they had missed.

When Jack looked up she was gone. He hadn't expected to see such a crowd. Then another family arrived. He hardly knew anybody.

"Ah, a familiar face," he said, greeting Sophia.

"Merry Christmas Jack," she said, brushing her cheek to his. "It's kind of you to do a call out today."

"They're good friends," he smiled. "I didn't expect to see such a crowd."

"Aren't they wonderful to have us?"

"I see Grace's mum is here too."

"Yes and two of her sisters, that's Kate over there." She pointed towards the fireplace where a petite girl with black hair was chatting with Grace's new boyfriend.

"And that's Lauren, she has four kids. We're all going horseback treasure hunting shortly."

Jack noticed Lauren looked very like Grace. She was laughing at something Geoff was saying. Her husband had an arm around her waist and one of her kids was pulling at her skirt. Her hand was gently stroking the little boy's blond hair. It was such a family scene. He was in a room full of people and he felt lonely. It was the strangest feeling.

Sophia was talking to him again and she seemed to expect a reply. He didn't know what she had asked. "I'm sorry. What was that?"

"I asked if you're coming horseback riding?"

"Yes, I think I will." He had to do something. He couldn't stay here. He needed air.

"Okay guys, let's get going. How many for the treasure hunt? We have to organise teams. Let's take it out to the yard. Let some of the oldies relax here."

"The cheek of you, Geoff McGrath," Molly called.

"You're not so young yourself. He's going to be thirty-eight next month," Jessie added. Everybody jeered him.

"Jessie McGrath, you're going to be in big trouble with me later."

Everybody laughed as some of people began to move outside. Jack watched as the "lanky fellow" bent down to talk to Grace. His head was very close to her ear. She smiled up at him. She was staying indoors with her mother and sister Lauren. There was another older woman staying too. He had heard somebody call her Nora.

"We have three teams, okay guys? I divided them as best I could." She began to call out the teams.

"Can I go with Jack, Mum?" asked Sam.

"Of course you can, little man. We make a great team, eh?" said Jack, ruffling his hair.

"The Wanderers are – Geoff, Sophia, Eoghan and Sean with Aoife. The Adventurers are – Jack, Richard and Kate with Sam and Ben. The Seekers are – Garvan, Monique, Tara and Ross."

When he heard whose team he was on, he muttered under his breath, "Some Christmas Day this is turning into."

Jessie finally sent off the last team. "Me and my bright ideas, I'm wrecked, that took more work than I thought."

"It'll be great fun," said Geoff, smiling as he trotted out of the yard.

She walked over to Duke's stable.

"How's my old man?" she said, opening his stable door. He nuzzled her pocket in search of a mint. He knew she was always good for a polo mint. She patted his neck and hugged his face. "What would I do without you?" she whispered into the old chestnut's ear.

She was glad to have a crowd today. It was a distraction from the reality of her life. She still hadn't found the strength to let the babies go as Fr. Jim had advised. Would the emptiness ever really go away? Waking this morning she couldn't help feeling they should be here among their family and friends, being cooed at. "Stop," she said out loud and she walked back to the house and rejoined the party. She sipped wine and listened to Molly and Nora reminiscing about the old days.

"Anyone for chocolates?" she asked. There was a chorus of protest. No, they were all full. She opened a tin of sweets anyway. Soon she smiled as she watched people chat and stretch for a sweet at the same time.

Watching Sam, thoughts of Billy flooded Richard's head. How he wished his life was different. His two most precious memories were of his wedding day and the day Billy was born. Some days he was filled with a rage that simmered within. Work allowed him to keep it at bay; coming here had nearly been his undoing. He had been so annoyed with his mother for asking. His thoughts were interrupted.

"How's the Yank? Are you saddle sore yet?" asked Kate with a hint of mischief in her eyes.

"Why, are you going to take care of me later?" he asked, laughing.

"You cheeky thing! I'm not that kind of girl." She laughed too but Richard noticed Jack giving him a look that could kill him. He wondered if there was something between him and Kate. And then he shrugged it off; he had a habit of putting his foot in it.

Jessie heard the clatter of hooves on the cobbles. "Now the fun begins," she said, dragging herself from the comfortable armchair next to the fire.

When she arrived in the yard Monique and her team had already dismounted. Then Geoff and his gang arrived, followed closely by Jack's team.

"And now for the prize giving. Drum roll! A selection box each." They all laughed as they led their horses to be untacked and brushed down. She left them to it and rejoined the others.

"Jess, I'm going to get some air. I need to stretch my legs," Grace remarked, getting up from the armchair by the fire.

"I'll take your place. I could do with a sit down after all that excitement."

It was getting dark as Grace wandered over towards the sand arena. She could hear the hustle and bustle of everybody settling the horses into their respective stables. Having always lived in the heart of Bayrush it had been hard to get used to the quiet and the darkness of the countryside at first. But she loved it now and hoped someday she'd be able to afford a little cottage.

The air was crisp but she was well wrapped up in a chocolate brown wax jacket. Thankfully the coat was quite flattering to her bump. Jack arriving at the house had disconcerted her. She was glad that he had gone on the treasure hunt. She couldn't have coped with spending today of all days in his company. What was it about him that made her so uncomfortable? She had been so delighted that he wasn't dating that blonde, but what difference did it make? She was clearly not dating material. He was the reason she had come out here, she couldn't be in the same room as him. He had been so kind to Sam earlier that she had nearly cried. God, her hormones were all over the place, she thought.

It was quiet again. They must be all gone back inside. She strolled into the American barn to get in from the chill night air. It was then she saw him looking over Duke's stable door. She was about to turn around but he saw her. Oh no, she thought, but she said, "Hi."

He turned his head while the rest of him remained leaning against the door. "Hi," he answered, his eyes looking deeply into hers. From his body language she took it that he didn't want to talk to her. She felt stupid and awkward so she turned away.

"So, is this how you want it to be, Grace?" he said.

She turned back and with eyes flashing asked. "Want what to be? I spoke to you first." But she hadn't heard him moving and was startled to find him right behind her, so very close she could almost touch him, and God did she want him to touch her, to feel his arms around her, holding her and telling her it would all be okay.

"You told me before that we couldn't be friends. What do you expect from me? The day we met in Jessie's kitchen you practically took my head off. Earlier you turned and walked away. And now you're doing the same thing. What did I ever do that you can't stand to be in my company? You know what, you are right. We can't be friends."

His face was so close. His green eyes burned into hers. She had never wanted anyone as much in her life. He must have seen it in her eyes. "Can't we …" she began and then he was kissing her – a kiss that she matched with as much longing as him. It seemed to last forever. And then he pulled away just as abruptly as he had begun.

"Oh Jesus, Grace. I'm so sorry. I shouldn't have. Oh God." She was frozen to the spot. She could feel her cheeks burning with the sheer embarrassment of it all.

"I feel awful, you're pregnant and I took advantage of you. Oh my

God, I am so sorry Grace. Please forgive me."

"Forget it Jack. It was nothing." She turned and she was so blinded by the tears that filled her eyes that she nearly tripped.

"Grace ..." he said, making to help her.

"I'm fine," she managed to say as she virtually ran back towards the house, as much as a pregnant woman could. She felt dirty. What kind of a person was she? Kissing a man while she was carrying another man's child; she hated what she had become.

A few minutes later Jack walked into the kitchen. There was no sign of Grace. He found Geoff and told him he had to get back to Conor's where there was a card game awaiting him. He couldn't stand the thought of seeing her with that asshole. He felt sick that he had taken advantage of her. What kind of person was he?

As he drove away he realised he'd actually forgotten Garvan in his haste to leave. The last thing he wanted to do was play cards. He racked his brain for an excuse not to but then thought better of it. He was going to get drunk, very drunk – anything to blot out what he had done.

Grace went straight to the bathroom. She couldn't face seeing Jack again. Why hadn't she pulled away first? Because she couldn't. She hadn't wanted him to stop. She was sick inside. She had dreamt of that moment, wished and longed for it and now it was tainted. His face said it all. He was horrified, disgusted with himself. How could she face him? She prayed he'd be gone when she went back downstairs. Composing herself, she opened the bathroom door and from the landing window she saw Jack's jeep speeding down the avenue. She took a deep breath and walked downstairs as if nothing had happened, when the truth was her life had just fallen apart.

Sophia saw Grace coming back into the living room. She knew immediately that something was wrong. She tried to catch her attention but Grace pretended not to notice her.

Where was Jack, Sophia wondered? Garvan, Monique and the other kids were in the other room. Oh well, thought Sophia. Looking around the room she noticed how well Kate and Richard were getting along. She hadn't expected that. A part of her had thought that Grace and Richard might have hit it off had the circumstances been different, but maybe that had been her wishful thinking.

"Will I top you up?" asked Geoff, breaking her reverie.

"Do, please," she answered, holding out her glass.

He poured and then sat on the empty seat beside her.

"Thanks for making us all so welcome today, Geoff."

"Oh Sophia, you'll never know how much I appreciate the crowd. Jessie's parents are gone to Spain to be with Cliona for Christmas and we always go to my parents for Stephen's Day so it was perfect really."

"Life is not easy."

Geoff nodded in agreement. "But we have to make the best of it. Take a look over there. She is the best thing that ever happened to me. We were only sixteen when we met but I knew she was the one. And we have Sam. So what more can I say?"

"You're a very lucky man, Geoff."

"And so are you Sophia. He's a great guy." Geoff nodded in Richard's direction.

Sophia could feel a lump forming in her throat and had to excuse herself. Eoghan noticed and followed her to the kitchen.

"Sophia, are you okay?" he asked kindly.

The kitchen was empty thankfully, she thought. "I just needed air."

"Did Geoff say something to upset you?"

"No, no. It's Christmas Day, Eoghan. I … can't bear it. I want to be here but I want the day to end. There are just so many memories. So many good times but for the past three years this day has been awful."

"But I thought you said you only spent last year without your husband?" He was confused.

She slumped into the kitchen chair. He went to the counter and retrieved a bottle of brandy and poured one for each of them.

Grace walked in and taking in the sight of them, she asked, "Can I have one of them?"

They both chorused. "No."

Eoghan went over to boil the kettle. "Cup of tea coming up for you, girly!"

"I hate Christmas Day," declared Grace, plopping onto the chair as the other two raised their glasses in agreement.

"I'm going to the races tomorrow if you'd like to come along?" said Kate.

"Sure thing. What kind of races?" asked Richard, with a twinkle in his eye.

She laughed. "It's amazing that we speak the same language and yet you don't seem to understand half of what I say."

"You have me nailed. I like the sound of you though."

"Touché," she said, clicking her glass to his. "Horse racing, hurdles to be exact. It's always a great day out."

"Sounds fun."

"Great, I'll pick you up so."

"No offence but do we have to go in your car?"

"Well the cheek of you. If you want to come to the races with me – yes we do. If you want to invite me somewhere then we can use your transport."

Richard threw his head back and laughed.

"What's so funny?"

"Nothing," he said and then added, "So where are we going the following day then?"

"How about the mountains?"

"Cool, the mountains it is."

The next morning when Grace came into the kitchen Sophia was already sitting in the rocking chair in the corner holding a cup of coffee.

"Morning," she said. "Richard left you some sausages under the grill."

"You're kidding," smiled Grace.

Sophia laughed. "Kate came and picked him up. They're off to the races."

Grace raised her eyes. "Really?" She looked under the grill. "Will I, won't I?" and then she popped one into her mouth and poured herself a cup of tea. She sat on a stool next to the counter.

"So are you going to tell me what happened?" asked Sophia.

"Was it that obvious?"

"No, just to me."

"Oh Sophia, I'm a slut."

"What?"

She told Sophia what had happened outside in the yard. She didn't spare the detail. "Sophia, I am in love with somebody who I can never be with. How can I ever look him in the eyes again? I thought I loved Dirk, but nobody has ever made me feel the way Jack Leslie does. And now that I actually kissed him, I know for sure that I have never ever felt anything like that before. I am pregnant with another man's child. How much more complicated can my life get?" She rested her head in her hands.

"For once in my life Grace, I have no words of wisdom for you only to say, he kissed you first, which says to me that he has feelings for you too."

"Really … do you really think that? Why did he run then? He knows I've broken up with Dirk."

"How can you be sure?"

"Because he's around Jessie's place a lot and surely Geoff must have mentioned it."

"Maybe, but I wouldn't be so sure."

"Where did he think Dirk was?"

"How I am supposed to know? But I can tell you that he has feelings for you. I knew it from the moment I met him in the garden at your mother's house. And don't tell me you didn't notice. You were so … unsettled that you went to the beach that evening."

"Really?"

"Really. Grace, I don't know what you are going to do. I don't have the answers."

"He walked away, Sophia. He obviously wants nothing to do with me."

Sophia sighed and got up. She put her mug in the dishwasher. Passing Grace, she rubbed her back and said, "How about the races? Come on, let's wrap up warm."

"Awww."

"Don't be lazy. Come on. It beats sitting here moping."

Grace dragged her feet as she climbed the stairs. Sophia was right. She'd have to get on with her life. The past was the past.

Chapter Twelve

I'm glad you changed your mind, Geoff. The ground is perfect for Jessie's Angel, not too soft," said Jack, running his hand along the horse's flank. "She's in great condition."

"Hey Geoff," said Kate, coming over to the horsebox where Jack and Geoff had just unloaded the young horse. Jack was surprised to see Richard beside her yet again.

"Are Grace and Sophia coming?" asked Jack. The question came out of his mouth before he had time to think about how it sounded.

"Yes, as a matter of fact, I just got a text," Richard answered, but he was smiling at Kate.

"Great, she must be feeling better. Oh wow, she's looking good," said Kate, walking around the horse.

"Sure, we'll give her a run anyway. I'm not expecting much, it'll be good experience for her and for Jay too," said Geoff, patting Jay on the back. We've walked the course already ..."

But Jack had stopped listening. He couldn't figure it out. Was he with Kate or Grace? He had a hangover from hell after drinking way too much and ending up crashing out at Conor's house. He desperately wanted to see Grace and yet he didn't. He was a grown man acting like a teenager. He shoved his hands into his coat pocket and realised he had left his phone in the jeep, which was in the car park.

"I'll be back in a few minutes," he called to Geoff who was too engrossed with Jay to notice. He walked through the crowds, saying hello to people he recognised from years back. It was good to be at a race meeting, he thought. God he'd missed the buzz of it all. Bayrush was a far cry from the tracks he was used to but the atmosphere certainly made up for it. With a Christmas feeling in the air and a spring in his step, his day was looking up. He dashed across the road through the traffic.

"OMG there he is. Duck!" said Grace, trying desperately to hide her face. She was in the passenger seat of Sophia's car when she saw Jack making his way through the car park.

"For goodness sake, Grace, we can't ignore him. He's walking right towards us."

Grace was purple-faced. "I can't believe this is happening."

"It's Bayrush, not New York," laughed Sophia, obviously finding it incredibly amusing. To add to it Sophia was rolling down the window to speak to him. Oh, it was just too much.

"Hi ladies," he said leaning down. Grace didn't know where to look she was so embarrassed.

"Hi Jack, there seems to be a great turnout," said Sophia.

"Absolutely, I've been inside already. Just forgot my phone and you know yourself – I'd be lost without it. I met Kate and Richard inside. They're expecting ye."

"Oh, em, I'm just dropping Sophia. I'm not staying. Richard knows that," said Grace. Sophia went to object but Grace continued. "You know how hard parking is around here. I offered Sophia a lift." Sophia looked from Grace to Jack and back.

"Em yes, that's right Jack. Em …"

"Out you get," said Grace firmly, "Give me a call if you need a lift home." Sophia opened the car door in a state of confusion.

"I'll just go and get my phone, Sophia. We can walk back together," said Jack. "See you around, Grace."

"Not if I see you first," she muttered under her breath.

"What the hell is going on?" said Sophia, amused.

"Just get out quick and let me into the driver's seat. I want to be gone before he turns around. Oh Sophia, I'm mortified and I'm like a beached whale. Move, woman."

Sophia burst out laughing. "You are a crazy woman."

Grace could hardly get around the car into the driver's seat fast enough. She fired the engine and was gone in seconds. There was no way she could spend the afternoon in his company. Absolutely no way!

"She's in a mad hurry," remarked Jack.

"It's her hormones," laughed Sophia. "Come on, aren't we blessed with the weather?"

Jack laughed. "Where are you going with that terrible attempt at an Irish accent? Brutal."

"Oh stop it, you're nearly as bad as Grace." She laughed and linked him as they walked along the road towards the entrance.

Sophia took a sideways look at him. Even unshaven and a tad

under the weather, Jack was handsome. But more than that he was good humoured and funny. There was something irresistible about him. How would it all end, she wondered? Although she had been amused by Grace's reaction it also pulled at her heart. Life was so unfair. These two were perfect for one another but what chance did it have? Grace was heavily pregnant and he was obviously going through a marriage break-up. The ring mark was still on his finger the day she'd met him in Molly's garden. What a dilemma!

Two days later Grace was sitting in the rocking chair by the window in Rose Cottage. "Where is Richard off to?" she asked, as the tyres of his car crunched down the avenue.

"This could be a disaster," said Sophia, who was sitting at the counter in the kitchen.

"Why?"

"I arranged an appointment with Aisling, the complementary therapist."

Grace looked at her incredulously. "Is he into that kind of thing?"

Sophia paused and then said, "No, but neither was I. Since Richard arrived here he's opened up in ways I never thought possible. He's smiling and I've even heard him laugh out loud a few times since he came here. Oh Grace, it has been so hard since the accident."

Grace remained still as Sophia began to talk about Heather and her grandson Billy.

"Oh my God, Sophia. You both have been through so much. I can't imagine what you must be feeling. I'm lost for words. Maybe it will be good for him, Sophia. It has helped Jessie and I've noticed that you seem to be sleeping a little better."

"I really hope so."

At a loss for what else to say and seeing how worried Sophia looked, Grace got up. Waddling to the kettle, she asked, "How about a cuppa?"

"That would be lovely. Will we watch an episode of *Castle*?"

"Good idea," said Grace, thinking a distraction was exactly what Sophia needed.

Richard should have read the information leaflet his mother had given him with the voucher. He had no idea what he had let himself in for. The lady was very pleasant and was going through the medical checklist with him. He didn't like to be rude by asking too many questions. What was she going to do next?

"Richard, can I ask why did you come here this evening?"

"I guess I thought it was for a massage."

"So many people end up here through well-meaning family and friends. Their hearts are in the right places but it wouldn't be fair to you or me if I proceeded."

"Well then, now that I'm here, tell me a little about what it is that you do."

So she sat on a stool beside the plinth and explained that she was a clinical psychologist who had developed an interest in looking at people in a more holistic way. She advocated medication but also held the view that often a person can store what she called "issues in our tissues." An example of that can be that when a person is continually worried it can affect the stomach, or with tension across their shoulders people say things like, "they have the weight of the world on their shoulders." "Well we do in Ireland, anyway," she smiled and continued. She held the view that people are all innately aware of this. Another example is that people hold fear in their kidneys. How many times do we hear of people having "accidents" when they're afraid?

"It does all sound a bit wacky. But I'd like to try it. What do I have to do?"

"Lie on the plinth, fully clothed, and I will place a blanket over you. Close your eyes and let me work away."

Richard decided to be open; after all he was here and nobody knew him. His mother was more positive than he remembered in a very long time. She was trying to help herself – why couldn't he?

After a few moments he completely relaxed. He let the woman do her work. She held points around his head and back, which supposedly released blocked energy. An hour later, he emerged from his relaxed state.

"Ideally go to bed early. You may find that your body will continue to process some concerns that you are holding on to. Drink plenty of water to hydrate your system and flush out toxins. And, Richard, if you are willing, please follow up this treatment in the States. There are many therapists like me around. We're not all weird. Many are qualified medical professionals using complementary therapies to help people to help themselves. Look up some information on the internet. Kinesiology, acupuncture, reflexology, massage, are all widely regarded as being hugely beneficial for personal well-being. There are other energy therapies too. I am not saying that any one of them is a cure-all. But remember Richard, the best person to help you is you. We only have one shot." Then she smiled, adding, "Although some people might dispute that."

He thanked her and for the first time in a long time he planned on doing exactly what someone had told him to do.

When Grace had said that Richard wasn't expecting her, it had led Jack to believe they were most definitely an item. He had such a hangover he had only stayed long enough to see Jessie's Angel running. She had come fourth, which they were pleased about since it was her first race, other than a few outings at the point to points. That Richard guy had bugged him, and nor did he want to bump into the rest of the gang again over the holidays. Last night he had rung his pal Charlie in Galway and made plans to spend a few days up there. Getting away from Bayrush was exactly what he needed and Charlie being a party animal guaranteed he'd have a good time. He revved the jeep and turned up Bruce full blast and settled back for the long drive ahead.

On the 30th of December, Grace stood on the stone step in front of the cottage waving Richard and Sophia off. She would miss them. The house had been complete with them around.

Kate hadn't turned up to say goodbye. Grace had noticed how Richard had kept watching for her. She knew how much Kate hated goodbyes especially since she had spent months as a young child sitting on the floor in the hall waiting for their father to come home. She feared that maybe Kate, her fun-loving sister, had lost her heart to Richard, a man way older than her with loads of extra baggage. But she supposed there was little any of them could do when it came to matters of the heart. Men, never again, she thought. Walking back upstairs she was looking forward to getting back to her writing. It was holiday time and she had nothing else to do. Sometimes the loneliness overwhelmed her and made Dirk's offer worth considering. At least her baby would have a mother and father …

"Imagine, it's the end of February already," remarked Jessie, tucking into a Caesar salad, in a quaint coffee shop in the old Viking district of Waterford city.

"I must admit I'm so glad January is over. The evenings are brighter and everything is starting to grow," Grace said.

"Sounds like you might like to come to the Grow Your Own group with me."

Grace threw back her head and laughed. "Jessie, I can't keep up with you. Every week you're at a different talk, workshop or display."

"Oh Grace, I don't know. It's like I'm searching for answers that I'll never find. I can't sit still because if I do my mind goes to a place I can't go back to …"

"I know the feeling … Anyway, tell me about the latest one."

"Reiki. People from all walks of life take part. Some are in the beauty industry. Others are in sports injuries or physiotherapy. I had a preconceived notion that everybody would have gypsy skirts and millions of crystals hanging out of them and would talk about the universe at every opportunity," said Jessie, smiling.

"In fairness, it does sound wacky when people talk about auras and chakras and the like. And if they start going on about past lives, that's when most of us tune out." Grace smiled.

"I know but there is much to be learnt from the ancient world."

Grace laughed. "If you're not careful I will buy you a gypsy skirt and crystal ball for your next birthday."

"What's wrong with taking the best of both worlds? Anyway to change the subject – what about Kate? How is she doing?"

"She often stays over in the room Richard slept in. I'm really worried about her."

"Ah, Gracey."

"She's usually the one flitting in and out of romances without a care in the world. Not this time."

"It happens to us all. Remember the time I wouldn't get out of bed for a week over Stephen O'Connor. I saw him the other day and he hasn't a hair on his head. Lucky escape it turned out to be. You know me about hair. I'd be filing for divorce."

Grace burst out laughing. "I remember coz you had me crying with you too, you big eejit."

"But seriously Grace, do you think Richard will come back? I thought they were just friends, did you?"

"Yes, I did too until she didn't turn up to say goodbye and he kept watching out for her. She said nothing happened but I think there's more to it. But where can it go? There's an ocean between them, in more ways than one. He told me that Geoff knows about his family. I met him one morning walking on the beach. I don't think he had actually planned on telling me – it just happened. Nor do I know if he told Kate. She never mentions him and it's certainly not something I'd bring up with her. It's none of my business anyway."

"Grace, I have no idea what you're talking about."

"Oh Jessie, I presumed Geoff told you. Please don't mention this again. I would hate Richard to think we were talking about him."

"Look Grace, you haven't told me any details. Everybody has secrets. I don't want to know. If Richard told Geoff something in confidence you can be sure it will stay that way. But I do want to know … now, without getting chewed up and spat out, you and Jack?"

"What makes you ask?" Grace smiled. She had wondered how long it would take Jessie to ask.

"Let's say it's my womanly intuition. You act all funny when he's around … I can't put my finger on it …"

"Jess, I promise I'll tell you over a bottle of wine some night. It's the only thing I never told you about. It's insignificant really. The only priority I have now is this." She patted her bump affectionately. "Good things come out of bad."

Since Richard had returned to New York he had been busy. He hadn't tried to contact Kate. He had been hurt that she hadn't come to say goodbye. But what could he offer? She deserved more. She didn't need the complications of being involved with a 'dead man walking', which was how he felt about himself. The fact that he was actually thinking about something other than work was an improvement.

He had invited his mother for dinner and had actually cooked, which was something he hadn't done for a very long time. As he walked over to join her on the L-shaped nubuck couch he thought how well she looked. Something had changed in both of them on their trip to Ireland but he couldn't define it.

"Why did you go to that part of Ireland? You'd never been there with Dad," he asked, holding his glass of red wine.

She swirled her wine around the crystal glass and then looked him straight in the eye. "Honestly?" He nodded, "I wanted out. I'd had enough of New York. Previously I had met Grace on a flight. She had been upgraded unexpectedly and it was the first time in years that I had spoken to somebody who didn't have an agenda. She was so natural and driven about a presentation she was preparing to make later in the day that she reminded me of what it was like starting out in business. And as it turned out she was from the south-east of Ireland and I'd never been there before so I decided to visit her. I meant to stay for a few days, a week maybe …"

"I had no idea … how sad and lonely you were feeling."

"You're busy Richard, you like your life that way."

"I'm sorry, Mom," he said, genuinely.

"Oh Richard, I'm not telling you to make you feel guilty. We all need to make our own choices. I made a decision back in August that changed everything for me. I don't think I could live full-time in Ireland, but it has helped me. As much as I had company I also spent time alone. I read more than I had done in years. I joined the local library and spent hours there. I even took some Irish speaking classes. There's a Gaeltacht area along the coast from Bayrush."

"Mom, you really should work for the Irish Tourist Board," he laughed.

She smiled. "I nearly drove you crazy at first, didn't I? Talking about castles, but I'd like to think you enjoyed Christmas overall."

"I did," he said, looking down into his wine glass.

"She's lovely, you know."

"She's too young."

"You're right; it's none of my business."

"What kind of books did you read?" he asked, changing the subject.

It was like pressing a button; she was off. She began to talk about human behaviour and how people mirror what they admire unconsciously. "Just as children do – we copy what we see." She noticed his look of confusion. He didn't know what she was talking about. So she asked him who he had admired as a child. He couldn't think of anyone.

"Maybe a character in a book or an actor."

"Darcy, from Pride and Prejudice.

"What did you admire about him?" she asked.

"His intolerance of trivia, his independence, the way he helped people without needing recognition for it. And I suppose I liked his quiet, passionate way." He smiled, took a sip of wine and added, "And he made an ass of himself socially."

Sophia smiled knowingly.

"Am I being counselled unwittingly?"

She laughed, but then he smiled, realising that he had actually described himself. Nice one, mother, he thought.

It was a Saturday morning and as always the harbour was thronged with tourists ready to board the ferries for Ellis Island and the Statue of Liberty. Sophia was filled with apprehension. She rang the bell to gain access to the converted loft. She took the lift to the second floor and was greeted by a woman with brown cropped hair and a friendly smile. She relaxed immediately. There were twelve chairs in a semi-circle in a corner of the room where the winter sunlight streamed in.

"Come on in, I'm Julie."

"Hi Julie, I've never been to this kind of workshop before."

"And so you're very welcome. We're always glad to have new people. Help yourself to some tea or coffee," she said, pointing towards a table laden with a range of herbal teas and a pot of freshly brewed coffee. She chose raspberry and sipped, watching as others arrived.

"You are all very welcome today. My name is Julie. Today is an introduction to Alfred Adler, the Austrian psychologist, and his theories." And so she began …

Sophia took it all in. When she had read about him in Ireland she had become quite fascinated by his psychology. He believed in holism, treating people as a whole person rather than just the disease or incapacity they suffered from. If a child had a challenge, then rather than the parent concentrating on what the child "can't do", Adler believed that they should concentrate on what they "can do". Act "as if" the problem doesn't exist – let the child develop strategies to cope.

Sophia felt a lump rise in her throat. Oh, how Heather would have loved to have known about him. She had dedicated so much of her time trying to firstly find a diagnosis and then to understand the challenge Billy had. It was called dyspraxia and Heather had been finally getting a handle on how to help, when they were taken. It was so dreadfully unfair. Feeling her emotions welling inside, Sophia slipped out of her seat and made her way to the bathroom through tear-filled eyes. She leaned against the bathroom door and took deep breaths; this might be "the something" she was searching for. There must be so many parents out there, like Heather had been, trying to find ways to help their loved ones. Minutes later, and having regained her composure, she returned to her seat.

"Another aspect of his psychology was that of bridging all sections of the community," continued Julie. "Adler spent a considerable amount of time in cafés discussing his theories with people from many different professional and social backgrounds. His was a psychology of valuing all human beings."

Sophia's mind wandered. She had been so lost when she arrived in Ireland. She had questioned everything about her life. What had she contributed to the world? If she died what would be her legacy? Yes, there was a magazine empire, and they had always been charitable with their money. But spending time in Ireland had made her realise that she was alive, healthy and had much to offer. A seed had planted in her mind. It was a familiar feeling, one that she hadn't felt in years. Maybe it was time to do something about it. But first she was returning to Bayrush around the middle of March. She wouldn't miss the birth of Grace's baby for anything.

Grace's mobile rang. She looked at the screen. Her stomach lurched. It was Dirk's number.

"Hello."

"Hello Grace. I was thinking of you."

"Really, how nice," she said with a tone loaded with sarcasm.

"Ah don't be like that."

"Dirk, you're on very thin ground that I even answered this call so don't tell me what I should or shouldn't be like. Why you are calling me after all these months?"

"We have a buyer for the house. But I miss you, Gracey. Can't we just try again?"

"You must be joking. Are you for real?"

"Why do you think I reacted so badly to the baby? You didn't want me, Grace. I was an asshole. I made mistakes. Don't you think I've paid enough of a price already by not having you in my life? I miss you like crazy. We were together for three years and how many times did I ask you to marry me? You were the one with the 'commitment' issues. I stayed. I made a mistake. Okay ... I made a few mistakes. But there are plenty of guys going off to goddamned brothels and the like. God only knows what diseases they are bringing back to their wives. Their wives Grace, the thing you would never agree to be. I love you. I have loved you since the first time I saw you."

She was standing in the kitchen. The rain was pelting down outside and she was so lonely. She hadn't wanted to be a mother, and certainly not a single one. She listened as he pleaded but felt nothing. She would rather be alone than with someone who had so little respect for her. Yes, it would be easier to accept his offer and she wouldn't have to worry about money again. One of the biggest exhibitions in the Cruising Industry was on in Miami in March and she could lose a significant amount of business by not being represented there. But even if it meant going on social welfare, she wouldn't go back to Dirk.

"Accept the offer. Whatever it is! Goodbye Dirk."

"Wait, Grace."

"What?"

"Let me help with the baby. I'll accept that it's over and final. But please Gracey … Let me try to be a father."

There was a prolonged silence.

"I'll think about, it Dirk. It's come as a shock to hear from you. I'm due in less than four weeks."

"I'm an asshole."

"I know."

"Ring me … please."

"Bye, Dirk."

"That hunky vet was over in McGraths' today," said Kate, stretching over to take some crisps from the bowl on the coffee table in Rose Cottage.

"Really."

"Mmm, he's gorgeous."

"I didn't think he'd be your type."

"He was asking for you. If I didn't know better I'd say you are his type."

"What do you mean?"

"Well you're preggers, but it was the way he was asking about you. I was wondering if he'd even noticed. Have ye met before?"

Grace flushed and she changed the subject quickly. "Kate, it's probably a lot to ask but would you go to the Cruise Fair in Miami this year?"

"I'd love to, but what about Eoghan, doesn't he want to go?"

"He's not a sales person and he said he'd be delighted if you went instead. You know the business and you've been there before."

"But I was with you. Are you sure you want to risk sending me? What if I make a mess?"

"Kate, I'd be lost without you. And when the baby comes I'll convince Eoghan we need to take you on full-time."

"When is it on?"

"The 18th of March for four days."

"The baby is due on the 28th. I don't want to miss that. But I suppose I'll be more useful in Miami. Go on, you've twisted my arm. A freebie to Miami, why not?" she laughed. "What will we watch?"

"CSI – I'm not watching any more of Sophia's old movie collection with you. Find yourself another victim."

Kate laughed as she refilled the crisp bowl and searched for CSI on the planner.

Grace smiled as her mother went about the cottage cleaning and tidying.

It was a sure sign she was anxious. As her due date drew nearer it seemed she and Kate were determined not to leave her alone. The excuses they made to stay over had eventually worn thin and her mother had finally declared firmly that she was moving in until the baby was born. Most nights she was surrounded by both of them. It was a nuisance because when she went to look for something her mother would say "it's over there, I thought that was a better place to keep it." Molly was worse since Sophia had called to say she was coming back for St Patrick's Day, which was only a few weeks away.

Grace watched her mam as she tucked into the pasta carbonara she had made for her.

"Well, what do you think?"

"Now I wouldn't like to offend you, but the Italians can keep it. Give me meat and two veg any day."

"Ah Mam."

"'Tis grand. I'm eating it, aren't I?"

"Struggling though."

"I like the garlic bread."

Grace laughed. They alternated making dinner. Grace cooked some of her favourites and Molly cooked the dinners Grace had grown up with.

"I loved the chicken stir-fry the other day," her mother said as a consolation.

"You did to be fair. So what's for dinner tomorrow?"

"Ribs and cabbage. I'll ring Kate, she'll be delighted," said Molly, beaming. "Kate loves them."

Grace threw her eyes up to heaven. Her mother still treated Kate like the baby. "Mam, I'm glad you learned to drive. I love having you here."

"Go on outta that," said Molly, picking up her plate and bringing it across to kitchen. But Grace knew she was pleased she'd said it. "You'll be giving out in a minute when you can't find something."

Grace burst out laughing. "Sooo true. Remember the day Gerry finally got the old Fiat started up? He had been working on it for weeks."

"Yeah and that Mamie Somers from 29 shouting down the street. 'Thanks be to God, I thought that pile of rubbish was never going to be moved, good riddance. It'll probably break down and they'll have to walk home.' She's still as crotchety as ever. Imagine I was fifty-four learning to drive."

"I know, Mam, I was so proud of you."

"I didn't get the same chances as you, Grace. That's why I was always pushing you to study. I had to leave school early to take care of my mother. Ah sure, it's all in the past now."

"I know, Mam, you did great. We're all fine."

They both looked down at her bump and then her mother laughed. "Thirty-six! I get you to thirty-six …"

"Don't start again!" laughed Grace.

At two in the morning, Conor had phoned Jack. He was having trouble delivering a calf. In the end Jack had to perform a Caesarean section on the cow.

Afterwards they were both wrecked and sat in the kitchen chatting over a cup of tea. Conor asked him how he was and everything poured out. He couldn't believe that he finally voiced all he had felt for the past few months.

Conor listened without interruption and when Jack finished, he said, "You must be screwed in the head to get mixed up with a pregnant woman! Jesus, it's enough to cope with a new baby – never mind a baby that's not yours."

"Weren't you listening? She's with somebody else."

"Aren't you lucky then! Move on boy. Go back to Dubai where you've a thriving practice and sort things out with Lynda one way or another."

"Do you think?" said Jack, sighing heavily.

"Look Jack, what you're doing here is wasteful. Driving all over the place covering maternity leave, treating cattle, sheep, pigs, dogs and cats, when really you should be working with horses."

"The maternity leave is up after St Patrick's Day. Maybe you're right. I should go back. Thanks for the chat."

"No probs." Then he punched him, and laughing, said, "Could you imagine the mother's face if you walked in with a pregnant woman whose baby wasn't yours? Jaysus, I wouldn't be wishing for you."

Jack laughed and, turning away, he put on his coat. It was never meant to be. Timing had always been against them.

Chapter Thirteen

O h look, they're so cute!" said Sophia as a troupe of Irish dancers followed the bag pipers.

"If you say the words 'cute' or 'quaint' again, I swear …" said Kate, pretending to thump Sophia who just laughed.

"Give her a break, Kate. She's used to New York's St. Patrick's Day parade, and let's face it Bayrush's effort is a bit of a comedown," said Jessie, who was linking Geoff, Sam with huddled in between them. They looked so happy today, thought Grace, feeling every minute of her pregnancy.

"Penny for them," whispered her mother, linking her. It was a particularly cold March day and standing around had seemed like a good idea earlier but now Grace wished it was all over.

"Will we slip away to the hotel?" said Grace. "I'm freezing."

"You're a girl after my own heart," smiled her mam. "They can follow us. What time is lunch booked for?"

"One-thirty," said Grace, as they made their way through the crowds lining the street.

She spotted Dirk in the crowd with a dark-haired girl, whom she recognised as the events co-ordinator from his hotel. She must be about twenty-five, thought Grace miserably, remembering the girl had a sexy French accent to boot. Could the day get any worse? Even though she didn't want to be with Dirk, it still hurt. The house sale had fallen through so she was still up in the air about her plans. Sophia had assured her that she was happy to have her stay at the cottage indefinitely but Grace knew that it wasn't fair to outstay her welcome. Dirk waved. She waved back. What was the point in being unpleasant about it?

"Look at him. That little article. Look at the smug head on him," remarked her mother.

"Shush, somebody will hear you."

"I don't care," she said, indignantly.

"Hello Mrs Fitzgerald," said a voice, coming from behind. Grace turned at the same time as her mother to be met with the sight of Jack Leslie beaming at them.

"Well hello … Jack. Isn't it lovely to see you? We're going in for a drink to heat us up. Would you like to join us?"

OMG, thought Grace, this can't be happening. "Mam, I'm sure Jack hasn't got time …"

"I'd love to." He cut across her, smiling as he led her mother up the steps to the entrance of the harbour front hotel.

"There's a perfect spot," he said, guiding her mother to a table at the window. "What would you like to drink?" he asked.

"I'll have a sherry, thank you very much, Jack."

Grace threw her eyes to heaven wondering what exactly her mother was playing at.

He turned towards her, raising his eyebrows. "And yourself?"

"Tea, would be lovely, thanks." He smiled; her heart melted. It so wasn't fair. He disappeared into the crowded bar.

"He's a lovely boy. Did you go with him when you were young?"

"Mam!"

"I'm only asking."

"Is that why you asked him to join us? What are you like? Haven't you noticed I'm pregnant?"

"It doesn't seem to bother him, nor did your engagement ring," her mother retorted. "Anyway I just wanted 'that article' to see that you're not without suitors."

"You are the limit at times."

"Hello Jack," said Sophia, with a smile that could light up Ireland, and then she nudged Grace when he wasn't looking. What was it with Sophia and her mother? thought Grace, happy to look up and see the McGraths and Kate too. There was safety in numbers.

Kate was surprised to see the handsome Jack sitting with her mother and sister in one of the cubicles.

Jack stood up as the McGraths' greeted him. Kate shot a questioning look in Grace's direction but she knew her sister was pretending not to notice. What was going on? wondered Kate.

Jack went to help Geoff at the bar while their mother filled in Sophia and Jessie about how she had seen "that article". Kate gave her sister a sympathetic look. Grace looked wrecked and Kate couldn't help feeling that having Jack around wasn't exactly helping things. She went over to the bar where the two men were chatting.

"Are ye going to the races today?" she asked.

"As a matter a fact yes," said Jack.

"What time is the first race?"

"One-thirty, we're just staying for a quick coffee and heading away then," said Geoff.

"Me too," said Jack. "I'm glad you decided to hold Jessie's Angel back today, Geoff. She's coming on well and it would be great to be placed in her next race. I should mention I'm going back to Dubai."

"Kate, will you order another pot of tea, please?" called Molly, making her miss the rest of the conversation. The two lads were talking about the horse again. The handsome vet was going back to Dubai. Well how about that, thought Kate.

By nine-thirty on St. Patrick's night, Sam was tucked up in bed. Jessie had had a great time at the races. Jack had introduced them to his brother Conor and his wife Marie and they had all come back to the house for drinks. She got up to get some more wine to top up Marie's glass and Jack followed her to the kitchen.

"Just popping out for a smoke."

"I'm delighted that we met your brother and Marie. They're good fun," said Jessie, taking the bottle from the fridge.

"Yeah, he's ten years older than me. There's just the two of us. We've always been close." He smiled.

He had a great smile. His eyes twinkled and the skin around them kind of crinkled up in a really cute way and he had perfect white teeth. She wondered if they were real or capped. She had heard all about the glamorous world he lived in from Monique. Garvan had told her. Jack was definitely Garvan's hero. In fairness you would need to be dead not to think he was cute, happily married though she was. He said something that she completely missed because she had been so busy thinking.

"I'm sorry. What did you say?"

"I was wondering how Grace is."

"Didn't you see her today? Oh, em." Jessie was confused. Grace still hadn't talked about whatever had happened between them.

"I just thought she looked tired."

"She doesn't have long to go. She's bound to be tired."

"Tell her I hope everything goes well for her. Did Geoff tell you I'm going back to Dubai?"

"No, no, he didn't mention it. I'm not surprised though. The grapevine has it that you were hugely successful over there. How could you possibly stay here after working with some of the best horses in the world?"

"The vet I was covering for is back from maternity leave and there isn't enough work to keep me on. But to be honest, I miss my practice and it isn't fair to my partner Abdul. He has been very good about me taking a leave of absence but it's time I get back to my life. Lynda wants to talk; we've been married for nine years …"

Not wanting to seem inquisitive, Jessie said, "Well Jack, I can only wish you the best of everything, I hope it works out for you. I know the value of happiness. And if you believe it's worth fighting for, go for it."

"Thanks, Jessie. I'll go outside for a smoke. I'm trying to pack them in again."

"Good on you," she said, going back to join the others in the living room.

Just after three a.m. they waved everyone off and then Geoff kissed her and declared, "That was a great day, love."

It had been a long time since they had had a few drinks together.

"Come on, honey," she said, linking him up the stairs.

"Ah, I'm okay now. I'll be grand in a minute when the world stops spinning. Do I make your world spin, honey?"

"You do pet," she said. Geoff was fast asleep in minutes. She was happy to see him so relaxed. They were finding their way again. He had been so supportive of her. Sometimes she felt his feelings had been overlooked. Men weren't given sympathy in the same way. But she knew how heartbroken he had been too.

She tossed and turned, trying to find a comfortable position. But Jack's revelation about him going back to Dubai had unsettled her. What had happened to his marriage? She wouldn't have thought he was the wandering type. Maybe nobody had wandered anywhere. Why did she think he would be perfect for Grace? With that she turned over, tucked her head into her pillow and fell fast asleep.

"Now are you sure Jessie is calling over?" asked Sophia, hovering at the door of Rose Cottage.

"Sophia, Mam will be waiting. The cookery demonstration will be over by the time ye get there at this rate."

"We'll both have our phones on silent. Just in case."

"Go …" called Grace, from where she was already sitting by the fire. She was looking forward to catching up alone with Jessie. She stretched to add more crisps to the bowl and heard Jessie's jeep coming up the pebbled drive. They must have literally passed one another in the driveway, she thought.

"Hello the house," called her friend, stepping into the little tiled porch.

"Come on in. I've just sat down. Oh Jess, I'm as big as a house and I can't stop eating," Grace said, patting her very large bump.

"At least you have an excuse," said Jessie, dropping into the couch opposite her. "But sure, you only have a week or so to go."

"Jessie, I need to talk to you before Sophia gets back. God knows Mam and herself made such a fuss about going she'll probably be back in less than an hour."

"What's the matter ... what's going on?"

"It's Dirk, he rang."

"He never!"

"He did. About a month ago."

"What, and you're only telling me now! I hope you told him to sling his hook."

"I thought you were of the opinion never to speak ill of a person's ex. For all you know the friend will go off and marry him. Bye, bye friend, that's what you used to say."

"Did I really say that? Well I wasn't talking about you. I am allowed to have an opinion about you."

"Okay, okay, some perspective please. Listen to me and don't interrupt or make any of those stupid faces you make when you're dying to butt in."

"But I need a coffee first," said Jessie, getting up to boil the kettle. "This really is a beautiful place. I just love the open plan. Now, I'll shut up." She sat back down with the steaming cup of coffee and listened intently as Grace told her what Dirk had asked for.

"Okay. What do you want to do? What's in your heart?"

"I want my baby to have a mother and a father even if we don't live together."

"Well, honey, that's it. Your decision is made and don't let anybody deter you from it."

"But Jess, what do you think?"

"Dirk is who he is. He's not a bad guy, just foolish. I think it would be awful to stand in the way of their future relationship. And I think you are a great person, Grace Fitzgerald."

Grace hugged her. That's what she wanted to hear. She couldn't spend her life hating Dirk. It would take too much energy. He made a mistake but was she really blameless?

"Any other news?" Grace asked, filling up the crisp bowl again.

"Actually yes, Jack Leslie is going back to Dubai. I got the feeling he's been having trouble in his marriage … I didn't like to pry but I think he's going back to work it out."

"Oh … really."

Grace's heart lurched. He was going back. She had known how silly it was to hope but in the dead of the lonely nights she had dreamed that maybe someday they could find a way to be together. And now he was leaving.

"Gracey, does he mean something to you, tell me? And please don't fob me off again."

"I met him the summer you met Geoff at Irish college. Things had been particularly bad at home. Dad had left. And oh Jess, he was so kind. We hung out together for ten days and he helped me through the worst days of my life."

"You never really talked much about home back then."

"And I didn't with Jack either. But he seemed to understand …" She told her about how she couldn't stop thinking about him. She left out the bit about "the kiss". Then she added. "But that's life – some things are never meant to be. We make choices. We all have roads to go. So Jess, here I am alone. Thirty-six years old, pregnant and in love with a married man who's about to go back to his wife in Dubai. How, in God's name, did this happen to me? Oh, Jessie, I don't mean the baby. I want my baby so much now. I didn't feel like that at first. I was so angry with myself for being so bloody stupid to get pregnant in the first place. I thought about an abortion, Jess. I can't explain the shame I feel about that."

"Grace, we're not perfect. Nothing can be gained by berating yourself about that. The point is you didn't go. I'm not going to debate the abortion issue here. There are circumstances and choices that people make. Who are any of us to stand in judgment of another?"

Grace told her about the grotto and the sick baby. She often thought about the girl and the baby.

"I'm sure they are both fine," Jessie assured her. "Gracey, I think you need to go to bed. You look worn out, honey. I'll stay until Sophia comes home."

"You're right Jess, I won't argue. I am tired."

"Come on," she said, helping her up. "That bump of yours is dropping, girly. I'll come up and check on you when you're settled. Now don't forget to brush your teeth."

"Funny, ha, ha, mother hen," said Grace, smiling as she gladly climbed the stairs.

*

Jessie sat back into her comfortable position by the turf fire. Staring into the flames, she thought she hadn't expected that admission from Grace. She had imagined that Grace might say that she had "shifted" Jack when they were young. And that there might have been some cringe-worthy story but nothing that a good glass of wine and a right old laugh about it wouldn't have sorted. Timing was definitely against them. She felt awful for her friend.

After about ten minutes she went upstairs to check on Grace. Thankfully she was fast asleep and she looked so peaceful. How am I ever going to cope when Sam grows up? Falling in and out of love, I'll want to choke any girl who might hurt him. Please God and the angels help my friend, she thought.

Grace heard Jessie coming up the stairs. She closed her eyes so that her friend wouldn't worry about her. How could she possibly sleep? It had been hard enough to cope when she thought he was just a few miles away. But he was leaving, and going back to his wife. There was no hope for them now.

Over the past few months she had begun to daydream, little fairy tale dreams about how when the baby was born she might bump in to him at Jessie's place. He would think that the baby was so cute and then realise that it was her – them – that he wanted to spend the rest of his days with. She imagined them walking on the beach like something from the movies. The only problem with the little dream was that she couldn't decide if the child was a boy or a girl playing at the water's edge while the two of them sat on the sand looking on. The sun was always shining and the beach was always empty except for them in her little story. It was all white shirts and jeans rolled up and all three of them bare-footed. But tonight she was bereft. She felt cold inside. Nothing had ever made her feel pain like this before.

Around eleven Sophia opened the front door. When she saw Jessie sitting in semi-darkness with just the flames of the fire and the distant light coming from the kitchen area and Barbra playing in the background, she asked, "Where's Grace?"

"Thankfully she's sound asleep. She's tired now that it's coming close. She works so hard too. I suppose it's the joys of being self-employed. No such thing as maternity leave to look forward to. I told her to go to bed, that I would stay until you got back. We'll be on twenty-four hour watch for the next while."

Sophia sat down opposite her. "She's so lucky to have such a good family and solid friends, Jessie."

"You get back what you give."

"That's such a simple analogy but so very, very true."

"I'm a psychologist in the making." Jessie smiled.

"You are that – people pay millions for that piece of advice." Sophia smiled.

"You don't have to answer this. But what drew you to Ireland, Sophia?"

"I'll sound like a corny American when I say, the people."

"Really … I suppose we never truly value what we have or who we are. Everybody thinks the grass is greener on the other side."

"Not everything is as it seems."

"Oh, Sophia, you have lost me there. I'm tired tonight."

"People in Ireland still care about their neighbours. They'd generally notice if they don't appear outside for a few days. You may call them nosy but I wouldn't. I see it as a person who cares. In New York I felt lonely even in the most crowded places, with people whom I thought were my friends. When I came here first I was truly alone. I booked into a bed and breakfast and I had a lovely time. I chose Bayrush because I was inspired by a girl on an aeroplane. My circumstances remain the same but I'm coping better. Grace included me in her life and over just a short space of time I've been invited to a variety of places with people from many different social backgrounds." She sighed and continued, "Jessie, I'm not blind. I can see that there is a huge social divide here as in any other country. Grace is special. She works hard and is so proud of where she's from. God knows there are many who come from nothing and quickly forget and take enjoyment from looking down their noses at others."

"What can I say, Sophia? You have given me a new perspective. It is so easy to knock things about our country but I wouldn't live anywhere else."

"That's not the first time I have heard somebody say that."

"On that note I'm off home."

"Goodnight Jessie. See you tomorrow."

The two women kissed cheeks as Sophia showed Jessie out.

"Thanks, Sophia, for caring so much about her. She needs you now more than ever."

"I'll be here."

*

Kate walked through the dining room of one of Miami's finest hotels, looking for her place. She hoped she wouldn't trip. It had been easier last time because she had been Grace's support. She felt huge responsibility to get things right. Wouldn't it be great to arrive home with a new contract? She was determined to network as much as possible. She looked for some familiar faces in the crowded room. Thankfully she was part of an Irish contingent, which included members of the Port Authority and the Tourist Board, so she wasn't completely alone.

"Hi Kate, you look fantastic," said Joe from the Port Authority, pulling out the chair for her.

"Thanks, Joe," she said, waiting for his wisecrack, but it didn't come. She had always got on well with him. They spent most of their time slagging one another off. Joe introduced her to the others at the table, a mixture of cruise industry types and travel-trade writers. The evening was being hosted by Pal Pacific.

There was a good buzz of conversation going on all around her. The guy next to her mentioned that a new small cruise company were very keen to break into the Northern European market. She made a note of the name of the company in her head. Tomorrow she'd go to their exhibition stand to talk to their marketing people. Joe said something to her but she missed it. She was distracted by a conversation between two of the writers. "Sorry Joe, just a sec," she said, listening to what was being said beside her.

"The big boss is in town."

"You mean Wynthrope himself?" asked the other guy. The first guy nodded sagely.

"Excuse me," said Kate. "Which magazine do you write for?"

"*Cruise News*," he answered, not in the least impressed that she hadn't known already. It can't be Richard, she thought. They hadn't spoken about work or for that matter anything personal.

"How many magazines do they own now?" asked the other writer. "They're buying up everyone, what's his name again …?"

"Richard, that the son's name."

Kate had been about to take a sip from her water glass when she nearly spilled it with shock.

"Jeez, lucky escape there," laughed Joe.

"Shhhh," she said, trying to hear what else was being said.

"You're great craic tonight," said Joe sulkily, turning to talk to the person next to him. She felt awful for being rude to him but she could hardly believe her ears.

"He took over completely after the old man died," continued Mr Writer. "He had been running the business for a number of years before that. But it was the mother who was a force to be reckoned with. She encouraged such strong sales at its inception in the sixties. Without her Wynthrope Communications wouldn't be what it is today." Mr *Cruise News* writer was practically bursting with pride.

What the hell was going on? Why was her sister living in a house owned by a "force to be reckoned with"? Did Grace even know? thought Kate.

As soon as the dinner was over she excused herself. She went up to her hotel room, took out the laptop and googled Wynthrope Communications Inc. She found out it was a holding company for fifty magazines or so with headquarters in New York. Richard was the CEO. There were photographs of him, Sophia and his father and information about him professionally on their website. There was nothing about him personally. Did he have a girlfriend, a wife, an ex-wife? She drew a blank. She decided to go back to the bar; maybe she could pick up with the guys again. She touched up her make-up. She would have to step it up to worm her way back in with Mr Writer. He had been seriously put out by her blunder earlier and she wasn't in Joe's good books either.

When she arrived down to the huge lobby bar, Joe waved over to her.

"Sorry about earlier," she muttered to him.

"Ah forget it," said Joe, never one to hold a grudge. Mr Writer was in company with him and in high spirits. He had obviously had a few more since dinner.

"Hi there, honey. Come on over and join us. What would you like to drink?" he said.

"A martini, thanks, that would be lovely."

"I love the way you Irish talk. I'm gonna call you 'Irish', okay, Irish." He laughed at his own joke. Whatever, Kate thought, as long as it wasn't "honey". Anyway one drink and she would have her information. She was hoping to find out where Richard was staying.

"So, you mentioned you write for *Cruise News*."

"That's right, Irish."

"You must get to travel a lot. What a great way to earn a living."

He was off. The guy was in his fifties, bearded with mismatched clothes. As he ranted on about his travels, she wondered what it was about journalists that they loved facial hair and were quite colour-blind. After much smiling and nodding in the right places, he paused for a breath and she said, "You mentioned that Richard Wynthrope is in town!"

"That's right, he's staying with friends. These guys have friends everywhere."

Shite, she had hoped he'd know which hotel. But then one of his colleagues interrupted. "He's staying here."

"What?" said Mr Writer.

"Yeah, I saw him at the reception desk earlier. I presume he was checking in."

She nearly jumped for joy. "Thanks, guys," she said, hopping off the bar stool.

"Wait, you haven't finished your drink."

"You must have lost your touch, Chad." Some of the group started laughing at him as he knocked back her martini. "No point in wasting it."

Kate went to reception. No, they didn't have a Richard Wynthrope staying at the hotel. She began to describe him. The receptionist stood behind the desk looking at her as if she was crazy. Her eyes darted from one side of Kate to the other, looking for another customer to come to rescue her from this mad person.

"You have a nice day, now," said the receptionist.

"It's eleven-thirty at night," Kate replied, completely frustrated, walking away towards the lift. She had had enough drama for one evening. Richard was here, so was she, and she couldn't find him.

Grace walked into the coffee shop. Dirk was sitting in the bay-window seat wearing a designer rugby shirt. It was pink. Another guy wouldn't be seen dead in pink, but not Dirk.

He stood up, making to chaperone her into the bay-window seat. The baby was due in five days and the size of her bump made manoeuvring through the small tables an impossible task. They were attracting glances from staff and customers alike.

"Let's just sit here, Dirk," she said, pointing to a small table with chairs facing one another. He retrieved his coffee and newspaper and joined her at the new table. She ordered a latte; finally her taste for coffee had returned.

"So," she said after the waitress had disappeared.

"It's good to see you, you look great," he said.

She laughed. "Yeah right, Dirk. You could always talk it up. You haven't lost it."

"Are we going to start a slanging match here, or what?" he asked. His eyes were a mixture of anger and hurt.

"Okay, I'm sorry … it's my hormones, okay? So as you were saying on the phone, you would like to be involved with the baby."

"Yes, Grace I really would."

He looked straight into her eyes. Then he hung his head. "Is it … is it really too late for us, Gracey?"

"Yes." It was a cold yes spoken with no regret in it. Over the months since they had broken up she had realised that she had been unfair to him too.

"Look, Dirk, I'm sorry. It was my fault too. I thought … oh I don't know, I thought I loved you but if I did why did I keep avoiding setting a date? You deserve more, Dirk. We both do. We had some really good times, didn't we? We can again in a different way."

"So, it's a yes to the baby and a no to me. Grace, are you sure? I love you, Grace. I want to be a father to the baby no matter what. I'm not walking away from my responsibilities. Who has the perfect relationship? Can't we at least try again?"

She shook her head and said, "I can't live a lie, Dirk. I don't love you anymore."

He was silent for a moment and then he said, "Thanks, Grace. Thanks for being straight, even if it's hard to take. I think we can be good parents, don't you?"

She smiled, really smiled for the first time.

"Grace, I promise I won't mess this up. I want to be a good father."

"These days, Dirk, there are all kinds of family units. Ours will be different but just as long as we have the best interests of our baby at heart, that's what counts."

He picked up his coffee cup, held it up and said, "Cheers!"

She clicked her latte glass to his, adding, "It's all going to be okay."

After leaving Dirk, Grace saw that there were three missed calls on her mobile from Kate, so she rang her back. Miami was four hours behind. It was lunchtime in Ireland. It rang out. Kate was probably in one of the morning workshops.

Grace was concerned though; it must be something important. She was due to meet Sophia for lunch in Bonita's in Bayrush so she walked back to the underground car park. When she reached the bottom of the escalator, she felt a sharp pain across her stomach. She inserted coins in the parking meter and began to walk towards the car when the pain came again.

Jesus, she thought, as she leaned against a parked car. That was sore. She tried to ring Sophia on her mobile but she was out of coverage. She needed to go back up the escalator. A woman passed by and seeing her distressed state she asked kindly, "Are you okay?"

"No," she managed to say, holding the mobile in her hand. The woman caught her other hand.

"Hold on to me. Now breathe, you'll be okay."

Another person stopped and she heard the woman ask the stranger, "Will you call an ambulance?" The woman had such a kind reassuring voice and was taking control.

"I think I am in trouble. I need to contact my friend ..." Grace passed out.

When she came around she was in an ambulance.

"We're near the hospital and they're expecting you. No need to worry, love," the medic assured her. Lifting the oxygen mask, Grace said, "But my friend is waiting in a restaurant ... she'll be worried sick."

"The lady who called us also rang the last number you tried to call, so your friend will probably be at the hospital when we get there. Relax, everything will be fine."

"Thank you." What a woman, Grace thought. An earth angel; she smiled thinking of Jessie who believed the world was full of them. The ambulance door opened and there was Sophia. She was never so glad to see anyone.

"Jessie is on her way," said Sophia. "I didn't call your mother."

"Thanks, Sophia, I don't want her to worry."

The obstetrician confirmed Grace was in labour and the nurse brought her to the antenatal ward, and the waiting began.

Chapter Fourteen

Kate tried Grace's mobile again but there was no answer. She tried Jessie's mobile. Geoff answered.

"Hi Kate, I just found Jessie's phone on the ground outside Beauty's stable."

"I'm looking for Grace. I've tried Mam too but neither answered. Is there any news?"

"They're probably just busy. I'm sure one of them will call you back soon."

"Okay, thanks Geoff." But talking with Geoff did nothing to assuage her fears. Maybe Grace had gone into labour. She clicked Eoghan's number next.

"Hi Sophia, have you seen Jessie? I found her mobile in the stable. Kate has been trying to contact Grace or Molly but nobody is answering. Please tell me you know where my wife is," said Geoff, light-heartedly.

"Yes, she's right here beside me. We're in the hospital. It's started."

"Well sure isn't that great news."

"I don't think Grace would agree," said Sophia and he could hear Grace's distant retort. "Are all men the same – totally thick!"

"She's not exactly herself at the moment," Sophia explained, half whispering and half laughing.

"Look, tell Jess I found her phone and we'll expect her when we see her."

"I must have dropped it in the rush to get here. See you later, honey," Jessie called from across the room.

"Concentrate," said Grace.

"Jesus if I'd known I was going to be abused I'd have told you to shove it. It's a wonder any relationship survives this."

"Ahhh."

"Grace, you're not even in full labour yet."

"I was just practising." They all laughed.

But hours later Grace was in agony. Jessie hadn't been able to put

Molly off coming to the hospital so the three of them sat around the bed in the ward.

"For Christ's sake, somebody should have told me. You," she said, glaring at Jessie. "You're supposed to be my friend; you should have told me."

Sophia and Jessie passed looks over the top of the bed where Grace lay.

"Come on, get up, let's go walking, we'll walk it out. If there was a window to clean I'd get you at it," said Molly.

Sophia and Molly were asked to leave. Only Jessie as the birthing partner was allowed to stay. It was one o'clock in the morning and Grace still had not progressed sufficiently and was complaining of pains that seemed to be more than labour pains. Jessie was getting more concerned by the minute. The nurse began to prep Grace for an emergency Caesarean section. She suggested taking an epidural, that way Grace would be alert enough to see the baby immediately.

Jessie wondered why she had agreed to come here, what if something went wrong. She tried to push all the memories away. But if Grace had asked somebody else she'd have been so cross. Her friend needed her to be strong.

"Can you make sure that the screen is high enough? I don't want to be able to see," said Jessie to the nurse as she led her into the surgical ward to join Grace.

"Don't worry, you wouldn't unless you want to look."

But just in case, Jessie virtually crawled in the door, afraid to raise her head for fear of what she might see. Grace was very anxious.

"Excuse me, I can feel that. Please don't start yet. I don't think that anaesthetic is working."

Jessie noticed there were looks exchanged around the room.

"Relax, Grace," said the nurse in a reassuring voice and then Grace fell asleep.

"I'm sorry but we had to up the anaesthetic I'm afraid. Can you wait outside please?" said the head nurse, leading Jessie out.

Jessie joined Molly and Sophia. She explained what had happened but played it down to allay Molly's fears, but she could see that Sophia was thinking the worse too. Oh please, God let them both be okay, she prayed.

Around one-fifty a nurse came out and they all looked up expectantly but she kept on walking. Another ten minutes passed. Jessie thought her heart would burst she was so afraid. Molly and Sophia were pacing up and down the corridor. Finally the door opened and the doctor emerged.

"Can I speak to Grace's closest family member?"

"I'm her mother, but I would like you to speak with all of us. I'm very nervous, Doctor. What is happening?"

"Mrs Fitzgerald, your daughter is going to be fine. We had to give her a general anaesthetic. So it will be a while before she comes around fully. She had a baby boy ..."

"Oh, that's wonderful. What a relief!" Jessie held Molly's arm.

"However, there are some complications. The baby will need surgery. I will be in a better position to explain this when Miss Fitzgerald comes around. It's not imminent but it is something we will have to address."

"Can we see them, Doctor?"

"The baby has been brought to the neonatal unit. He will have to be monitored. Unfortunately you will only be able to look at him through the glass wall. I don't know how the mother will feel about you seeing the baby yet. She may well want to be the first to see him."

"Yes Doctor, thank you, I think we will wait," said Molly. They all nodded in agreement.

"Molly, I think you need to sit down," said Jessie, concerned. There was so much to take in. Molly began to cry. Not a sobbing cry, just tears rolling slowly down her face.

Jessie's heart ached for the elderly woman. Please, please God, she thought, let the baby be okay. Whatever it is, let them both be okay. They would handle it together, just don't take this baby. We all need this baby.

"There, there, Molly, everything will be fine," assured her.

Seeing Sophia taking over, Jessie excused herself and walked towards the lift. She needed air and she needed it fast. She exited the hospital through the casualty area out into the cold March night. She walked a small distance from the exit and then she heard herself howl into the night sky.

"Please God, I know you're up there. Don't take this baby. You don't need any more babies. You have enough babies."

She needed a cigarette badly. She hadn't had one for years. She heard a voice coming from behind. She got such a fright that she jumped.

"Are you okay, love?" asked the security guard.

Looking into his kind, wise face, she asked, "You wouldn't have a cigarette by any chance?"

He reached into his jacket pocket and produced a box and lighter. They lit up.

"Bad news, eh?"

"Yeah."

She was grateful he didn't ask any questions. They stood smoking in silence. The silence was so comfortable she wondered if maybe it was a regular occurrence in his line of work.

"Come on, love. Come back inside. It's freezing out here. Have a cup of tea. It will all be all right."

She let him walk her back inside. She felt stupid and melodramatic. She needed to pull herself together. Her friend needed her. She told him kindly that she was okay and thanked him for being so nice.

"The nurses suggested we go home," said Sophia. "Grace is in the recovery room and there's nothing we can do."

Jessie nodded in agreement. She followed Sophia's car to Molly's house as it was nearest to the hospital. It was two-forty in the morning. They made tea. Always tea in a crisis, thought Jessie.

"There are fresh sheets in the hot press, Jess," said Molly, pouring the tea. "I'd already made a bed for Sophia. Had I known ..."

"It's fine Molly ... Grace and the baby are going to be fine too," she assured her.

"I'll set the clock for seven-thirty. Do you think they'll let us in that early?" asked Molly.

"I doubt it but you could ring," said Jessie, feeling lost without her phone. She'd love to talk to Geoff.

At ten o'clock the next morning the doctor came in to speak with Grace. She had been fortunate to get a private room and was surrounded by Jessie, Sophia and her mother. He asked if he could speak to her with just one person in the room.

Grace told him that it was important to her that all three stayed. He conceded and began the process of explaining that she had given birth to a baby boy but there were complications.

"The baby has a hole in his heart which needs to be dealt with. Thankfully, it is a common enough procedure but like any procedures there can be complications. We have to do further tests. I'm sorry."

Grace turned away towards the window. She couldn't believe what he was telling her. Her baby, her little baby boy had a hole in his heart. After a minute she asked the question she was terrified of an answer to. "Are you telling me that he might not survive ...?"

"Thankfully we have the knowledge and skills to address the issue. Your little baby has a good chance, but there are always risks."

"Jessie, will you contact Dirk for me?"

*

Sophia sat with Jessie in the coffee shop in the lobby of the hospital. Jessie had contacted Dirk who said he was on the way. Sophia's mobile rang.

"What's going on?" asked Kate, her voice filled with exasperation.

"Oh, Kate ... it's Grace."

"Tell me."

"She's had the baby. When are you coming home?"

"The day after tomorrow. But that's good news ... isn't it? Sophia, what's going on? Grace and the baby are okay, aren't they?"

"Yes, of course." Sophia was stalling. "Can I call you back in a few minutes? Everything is okay. What hotel are you staying at?

"I'm in the Woodmore."

Sophia hung up. She told Jessie that it was Kate and that she hadn't known what to tell her but that she couldn't leave the poor girl in limbo.

But Jessie was hardly listening. Sophia realised that it had been a long night for all of them but most especially Jessie after all she had been through only recently.

"There's Dirk," said Jessie. Sophia watched as Dirk walked through the lobby of the hospital. She couldn't help feeling sorry for him under the circumstances. She looked at her watch. It was twelve-thirty which meant it was eight-thirty in the morning in Miami.

"I just remembered Richard is in Miami. He could go to Kate then she wouldn't be alone. I can explain everything to him."

"That's a good idea," Jessie answered absentmindedly as Sophia clicked Richard's name.

Kate opened the hotel room door and couldn't believe her eyes. "What are you doing here? Richard, please don't tell me it's bad news." She turned and walked back into the room, and standing at the window looking out across Miami Bay, she waited. Richard still hadn't spoken a word. "Will you for God's sake just tell me Richard?"

He began to stammer. "Sh, sh ... She's okay, so is the baby. It's ju-ju-just that there are some ... complications."

"Richard, would you ever just get it out? I never realised you were so ... Oh I don't know ... What complications?"

"The baby has a hole in his heart. The little baby ..." With that he sat down on the bed and put his head in his hands. Then he added. "He has a hole in his little heart. They can't operate until he is stronger. They have to keep him in the neonatal unit."

Kate sat on the bed next to him. She didn't know what to make of all this. Nor did she know who was consoling who any more. She had a hugely important meeting to attend in approximately four minutes in the lobby downstairs. She had managed to speak to the marketing people from Cel Cruise. It would be fantastic for the business if they could close a deal.

"Okay," she said. "Come on. I have to meet these guys from Cel Cruise in the lobby, like now. So come on. I have to do this for my sister. And, prat and all as you are at delivering news, I need you more than I ever needed anyone in my life. So get it together. I am going to get this contract if it's the last thing I ever do. You can pretend you work with me, okay?"

He stood up and followed her out the door.

Richard could see the contingent weren't impressed. These guys were never kept waiting but Kate switched it on. They got the full blast of her charm and within minutes she had them laughing. She said something about when Americans build hotels they build virtual cities and sure how could a girl not expect to get completely lost. It lightened the mood. Richard sat quietly listening to her sales pitch. Then one of the men asked him his opinion of Ireland.

"It's a wonderful place with a beautiful coastline, mountains, monasteries, castles, towers and old world pubs with traditional music and dance. And some fine restaurants too. Ireland for Real also offers golf, fishing, shooting, and for the more active, horse-riding and other more adventurous water sports activities like sailing, surfing, and kite surfing …" Then he added, looking at a gobsmacked Kate, "To me, its most special feature is … the people. They are wonderfully, warm and welcoming."

"Wow, sounds like our passengers will just love it. What do you think?" Hank Catonia turned to the other two guys who both nodded in agreement.

"I think, Miss Fitzgerald, we might have ourselves a deal. I'll have my people contact yours in the next few weeks. We can thrash out the finer details."

"Thank you," she said, looking individually at the three men in front of her. "Thank you so much, you will never know how much this means to us. Your passengers will love Ireland."

They shook hands. When they were out of sight, Kate flopped back into the couch and breathed a huge sigh of relief. She closed her eyes and when she opened them he was standing in front of her.

"Come on, up you get," he said.

"Where are we going?"

"Home."

"What do you mean?"

"Let's just check out. I'll make some calls and we'll be back in Ireland in no time at all. We can wait with everyone else."

Richard hadn't done anything spontaneous in years. He felt alive again. He realised that he needed her and no matter what the obstacles were, he hoped with all his heart that she felt the same.

Checking out, Kate discovered that Richard's reservation was booked under *Cruise News*. Why hadn't she thought of that?

Richard had organised the company jet to fly them to Ireland. Editor my ass, she thought. He'd have to explain that and everything else to her. But now was not the time.

Molly left the room when Dirk came in. Grace noticed the colour draining from his face as he looked at her. She was so weak she could hardly move and she was devastated because she wasn't strong enough to see the baby.

He stood awkwardly for a moment and then pulled a chair up beside the bed. Touching her hand, he asked gently. "How are you feeling?"

She smiled weakly and then tears trickled down her face. She explained what she had been told so far. She could see he was devastated but was trying his best to hold it together.

"Jessie will bring you to see him, that's if you still want to."

"Of course I want to, it changes nothing. I am his father. I promise you Grace I will do everything I can to be a good father. Do you think so little of me … you think because he's got something wrong that I wouldn't want him? God, Grace …" But then he paused and said, "I know I've been a bastard. I deserved that but, Grace, can we put it behind us and move forward from here? I want to see him." She just nodded because even after everything that had happened between them she knew he genuinely meant what he was saying.

Jessie saw Grace's text.

"Grace wants me to bring Dirk to see the baby. I'll be back shortly."

"Good," said Sophia. "I'm so glad."

Jessie saw Dirk coming out of Grace's room. Molly was in the corridor waiting, and Jessie overheard Molly speaking to Dirk. "Grace is allowing you into the baby's life but if you hurt them again, Dirk, you'll have me to deal with." Then Molly turned and smiled towards Jessie as though she hadn't said a word. "Ah there's Jessie now."

Jessie couldn't help feeling sorry for the poor guy. He was pale and anxious-looking and having to deal with Molly too.

"Hi Dirk, come on, I'll lead the way. We'll have to be gowned up."

"Thanks, Jessie," he said gratefully as Molly went back into Grace's room.

The baby was in an incubator with wires coming in and out of it. Jessie watched Dirk as he sat next to it and just gazed at his son.

"He's beautiful," he whispered, "Jesus, Jessie it's terrifying. If there is a God, which I doubt, but if there is, please don't let anything happen to my child."

Standing behind him, she could hear the lump in his throat. He was trying hard to stop the tears that were so close.

"Take some pictures on your phone for Grace," she said, trying to lighten the moment. "She'll be delighted to have them."

"Good idea." He began to take some shots and then he sat down and put his hand into the incubator and touched his baby for the first time. "Imagine," he said, "I have a son."

Jessie walked back with him to say goodbye to Grace.

Closing the door behind her she heard Dirk saying, "He's so beautiful. He looks just like you Gracey although he has my mother's mouth."

Jessie knew that would amuse Grace even though she was too sore to laugh. She was glad to be heading home to her own two boys.

Jessie drove into the yard and was greeted by Sam who hugged her and ran off to join Monique in the yard. Geoff walked towards her and took her in his arms. He squeezed her tight.

"The doctors said that the baby has to be stronger before they can do anything but luckily he is a good weight already and is showing strong vital signs so far."

"Well that is positive news. Thank God. We'll just have to wait and see. I'm so proud of you, Jess."

He wrapped his strong arms around her again. She needed it. Last night had brought everything back again. "Geoff, do you think we'll ever really get over it?"

"No, honey, we won't, but we'll learn to live with it. I must admit I was worried when you agreed to be Grace's birth partner but I figured you knew best."

"I wanted to be. If she had asked somebody else I would have had murder."

Smiling, he agreed. "I know and Grace knew it too. The baby will be okay. That is quite a common enough problem and as you said, the baby is a little fighter already. Come on, there's some soup and rolls inside."

"Geoff."

He turned around. "Yeah."

"I love you."

"Me too."

"I hate that."

"What?"

"Me too – like it means you love yourself too."

"Of course. Sure that's what I meant." She laughed and threw her eyes to heaven, walking in the back door behind him.

The aeroplane touched down at Waterford Airport. It was the nearest airport to Bayrush. Kate felt like royalty. It was all so surreal. They had talked the whole way over. Richard had told her about his wife and child. She couldn't imagine what he must have gone through. But being her usual self she had stupidly said, "You picked a fine time to tell me about the plane crash."

He had smiled at the paradox of it all but she was annoyed with herself for saying it. Sometimes she wished her mouth didn't run off with her the way that it did. She was so glib at times. It was her protection. She felt so confused and she was upset about Gracey and the baby. Why couldn't things be simple? Why was everything a big drama in her life? She had turned twenty-seven last month. Why couldn't she fall for somebody straightforward? He seemed to just find her amusing – smiling in that way of his at her sometimes rather stupid jokes.

Well, Kate Fitzgerald, the best thing you can do is to get on with your life, because there is not a chance in hell that a man like Richard could love someone like you, she thought as she sat in the passenger seat of the hired Mercedes.

"Kate?" Her heart nearly missed a beat.

"Yes."

"Don't mention how you got home to anyone."

"Why didn't you tell me you own a huge communications company?"

"You never asked."

"True but ..."

"Look, my mother would prefer if you didn't mention anything you might know about her, even to her. Will you respect her privacy?"

"Of course, Richard."

After dropping Kate to her mother's house, Richard drove up the gravel drive to Rose Cottage. Why hadn't he told her how he felt about her? She was wonderful. Everything about her made him smile but he couldn't verbalise it. Sometimes the guilt overwhelmed him. Why was he still here when Heather, who was a much better person than him, wasn't? He didn't deserve a second chance. He wasn't good enough. He reversed the car out of the drive and called the airport.

"I need to get back to New York urgently."

Kate Fitzgerald deserved the best and he wasn't worthy of her. She had opened his heart again, and made it possible for him to think that he could care about somebody else again; for that he could be grateful.

The baby had to remain in the neonatal ward, which Grace found very difficult. Dirk sat beside her as they waited for the doctor to speak with them about how he planned to proceed. She had chosen the name Finn, after Finn Mac Cool, the Irish Warrior, and Dirk had been in total agreement. She looked at her beautiful baby boy who was wearing a special cotton hat her mother had knitted for him. Molly had said it was nice to do something to help, and she and Nora had offered to knit more for other babies.

Thankfully Finn was gaining strength by the day. She put her hand into the incubator and touched his tiny body with her fingertips. She couldn't explain the overwhelming feeling of love she had for this tiny being. No words could explain it.

She turned as Dirk said, "It's an incredible feeling isn't it? Imagine he's our baby, Grace."

She smiled and just nodded with tears in her eyes. "We did something good."

Dirk smiled as the door opened and the doctor drew up another chair.

"Guys, let me just explain. Approximately 500-600 babies are born in Ireland every year with a congenital heart defect. It seems that Finn had ventricular septal defect, VSD, which is an opening that exists between the two lower chambers of the heart. If the opening is small, it will not strain the heart and only requires a heart catheterisation procedure.

But if the opening is large, I would recommend open-heart surgery. The surgeon won't know until he operates, so you will have to grant permission in advance. It will be done in Dublin. I understand there is much for you both to consider."

"Will there be other side effects?" asked Dirk.

Grace couldn't think straight: "open-heart surgery".

"Some babies with a large ventricular septal defect can become undernourished and also have growth problems. They may develop severe symptoms or high blood pressure in their lungs. Repairing a VSD with surgery usually restores the blood circulation to normal. The long-term outlook is good, but he will require long-term follow up."

"Grace, he'll be okay," said Dirk, leaning over and squeezing her hand. She was grateful to him. And she was seeing another side to him.

"We won't be proceeding until Finn is stronger. We'll take it a day at a time. I believe you're being discharged today. And visiting will continue to be restricted to just immediate family. It minimises the risk of infection, so we ask you to please adhere to it."

"Of course," said Dirk. "Although I'm finding it difficult to keep my mother away."

"There is a God," Grace muttered under her breath.

"I heard that," said Dirk, smiling. The doctor grinned.

"If you have any questions I'm around, just ask."

"Thank you, Doctor," said Dirk.

Kate called to Rose Cottage, hoping to see Richard. She had been so busy rushing between the office and the hospital that she hadn't had time to see Richard. Stupidly she hadn't asked for his cell number. There was no sign of his hired car but Sophia's was there along with Eoghan's. She got out of her car and was about to knock when Sophia opened the door.

"There's coffee in the pot," said Eoghan, from where he was sitting at the counter.

"Great. I'd murder one," she said, sitting on the stool beside him. She looked around hoping to find evidence that he was here, which was pointless because his car wasn't. So she asked, "Sophia, is Richard here?" She could see a strange look pass between her and Eoghan.

"No," said Sophia.

"Is Richard coming back?" asked Eoghan.

Kate was confused.

"Not that I've heard," said Sophia

"Oh …" It was then that the penny dropped. With all the panic nobody had asked how she had managed to come back so quickly. So she hadn't had to lie. But surely Sophia knew. Obviously not.

Sophia continued, "I spoke to him yesterday and he never mentioned that he was planning to visit."

"I thought I saw his jacket, my mistake." Both Sophia and Eoghan looked around. "Don't mind me, I'm just jet-lagged."

"Don't go filing today or we'll never find them again," laughed Eoghan. "Anyway I'm glad Gracey is getting out today …"

"But Eoghan, she'll be devastated having to leave little Finn. Dirk has been wonderful."

"I agree," said Kate, "and I'm not his biggest fan."

"Well I just hope she doesn't take him back," said Eoghan firmly. "He's not good enough for her. I never had much time for him."

Sophia and Kate looked at one another. It was so unlike Eoghan to make such a comment. "I'm just saying." He took a sip from his mug as if to say that was the end of the conversation.

Six weeks later Grace was exhausted physically, mentally and emotionally. It was two in the morning. She was lying awake in bed in a hostel connected to the hospital in Dublin. Finn was scheduled to be operated on in the morning. Hopefully a catheter procedure was all that was required. If not, the surgeon would have to proceed immediately with open-heart surgery. Grace was trying desperately to stay positive. Dirk was staying in a hotel across the road. He was proving to be a great support but she was surer now than ever that she didn't have any feelings for him in that way.

From the first moment she saw Jack again, the truth was that she could never love anyone the way she loved him. She thought of him every single day. What was he doing? When he had kissed her had he realised what a big mistake he'd made? Was it the reason he had gone back to his wife in Dubai? She turned and gathered a pillow, clutching it in an effort to fill the physical void she felt inside. "Please God in Heaven, keep my little Finn safe. He is my world and all that matters," she prayed. Eventually she slept.

Sophia sat in Molly's kitchen waiting for *the* phone call from Grace. The doorbell rang. Molly got up to answer it.

"Come in, Jessie."

"Any word yet?"

"Nothing yet," said Molly, going to the kettle.

Jessie sat down. Sophia heard the front door open. It was Kate calling from the hall.

"Any news?"

"None," said Molly, setting out mugs as Kate joined them.

The front door opened again, this time it was Lauren. "Well?" she asked.

"Nothing."

She sat down and so it continued as more of the family arrived until there was no more room left in the kitchen. All of Grace's brothers and sisters were now waiting and Eoghan was there too. Grace hadn't wanted anybody to travel with her. She had said that she and Dirk would go together. It wouldn't be fair to swamp him with her family. So not by any pre-arrangement they all arrived at Molly's house around the time the operation was scheduled for.

Sophia was overcome by emotion. She could see the pure love and care that these people had for one another, not a soppy love, just a sense of family and of what family was about. The phone rang.

"Grace ..." said Molly

There was complete silence as Sophia watched Molly's face. Molly listened intently. It was like they had all taken a joint intake of breath.

"Oh Gracey ... That's wonderful."

The relief was palpable. Whatever it was, it was good news. There was a cheer from some of the men. Molly explained that everybody had come along to wait for the news at her house and that was why there was so much noise.

"Shush everybody, Grace says to say thank you to you all, and that little Finn is going to be fine. They were able to fix his little heart with you know that cat-a-thingy so he's going to be just fine."

This time everybody cheered.

Chapter Fifteen

The July sunshine almost blinded Jessie as she drove along the picturesque road from Waterford to Clonmel. She was filled with apprehension but was looking forward to attending the July summer school she had read about before Christmas. She had no idea what to expect.

"Mom, do I have to go? I won't know anybody else," said Sam from the backseat.

"It'll be fun and you'll make friends easily. It's good to try new things." She didn't know whether she was talking to him or herself. Since the babies, she had attended so many talks from baby bereavement groups, angel meetings, even a gardening group. She was searching for something, anything to fill her mind. She was uneasy in the world but mostly she was glad she had Sam and Geoff because if she didn't she wondered if would she bother getting out of bed.

Why was it so hard? The complementary therapy sessions with Aisling helped to keep the darkness away. But she still couldn't verbalise how she felt. Who wants to hear? She couldn't imagine how a parent felt who had lost a child that had lived and that they had known and loved. Stop Jessie, she said firmly, afraid that she would change her mind entirely and drive back home.

"Here we are," she said, in a cheerful voice for Sam's benefit.

He let out a big sigh. "I can stay with Dad tomorrow. I can help around the yard," he said earnestly.

"Honey, you're going to have great fun. It's an adventure."

"But I can have adventures at home."

She threw her eyes to heaven, thinking he's definitely my son. She must be crazy to come here. The sun was shining and they were going into a school for the day. "How about we give it a try for today and if we don't like it we won't come back tomorrow?"

He nodded reluctantly and climbed out of the jeep. She took his hand and walked up the avenue towards the entrance.

*

Kate sat on the storm wall on Bayrush Beach. She was unsettled. She had recently read an article in a magazine about goal setting. And it occurred to her that she had never taken control of her life except when she managed to get clean from drugs. Since then she had spent most of her time patting herself on the back and not thinking about what she should be doing with her life. It occurred to her that Grace and Jessie had spent so much of their time and energy helping her and over the past few months she had been able to give back to them when they had needed her.

She was working full-time for Ireland for Real and still helped out at weekends at Jessie's place. But it wasn't her dream. She picked up her sketchpad and it opened on the page she had sketched the day after she and Richard had gone to the mountains. She had watched as he walked around the peak taking photographs in all directions. She had been surprised that he was such a keen photographer. It was just a pencil sketch of his face. She ran her finger along his jawline. God, she missed him. How could she miss a man she hardly knew? She flicked the page over and began to draw. When she drew time disappeared.

The sun streamed in the bedroom window. The tide was in and Grace could see people already out kayaking. The surfers would be disappointed; it was way too calm. She was lying in bed and had taken to leaving the curtains open so that she could enjoy the glorious view in the mornings. But these days she was more often woken by a little cry from the cot beside the bed. It was hard to believe her little man was three months old and doing well after such a nerve-wrecking start.

Initially feeding had been a very anxious time but Finn had settled now. She had plenty of help and support from her mother and Kate. And Jessie had been her lifeline to bounce things off and to blow off to when it all got too much.

Grace had been over protective, always correcting Dirk, and so he had finally lost his cool with her and told her to lighten up and give him a chance. She had and had even let him take Finn for a few hours between feeds to see his mother and his family. Grace stretched as she got out of bed. All in all, life was good.

She managed to work at home in between feeds and nappy changing. On the days the cruise ships were in her mother took care of Finn, showing him off to all her friends and neighbours.

The sale of the house had fallen through so she had missed out on putting an offer on a tiny rundown cottage she'd seen. Thankfully Sophia had insisted she stay on at Rose Cottage until they agreed a sale. She was so grateful to her. She wasn't near achieving her goal of doubling the business. But they had been able to offer Kate a full-time job because an opportunity to coordinate the cruise ships at other Irish ports had come through.

She was happy with her life to a point. Late at night while Finn slept, she wondered if she would she ever find love again or if she was destined to be alone. She was writing again. It was her escape because sometimes it was hard not to wallow in self-pity.

Finn began to stir.

"Hello, little one. Look at you!" she gushed at the little face looking up at her. She picked him up and said, "I wonder does everybody think their baby is the best thing since sliced bread." She laughed as she walked over to the window. "Let's go for walk on the beach. Maybe Sophia will come too."

"Are you free today, because if so, it's a perfect day for sailing!"

"But you don't have a sail boat," laughed Sophia. She was sitting in the rocking chair in Rose Cottage.

"But I know a man who does," Eoghan chuckled on the other end of the phone. "I'm at the marina in Bayrush so get here as soon as you can. It'll be a great day."

"Okay, I'm on my way."

Grace came downstairs. "I heard you laughing."

"I'm actually going sailing. Eoghan knows a man who owns a sail boat."

"Cool."

"Let me hold him. Come here little man," said Sophia. Taking Finn in her arms she cooed at him. "Who's the best little fellow?"

She loved having both of them living with her. And she secretly dreaded the day they'd move out. Sophia knew that Grace was anxious to get on with her life and that she had been disappointed when the sale of the house fell through. Sophia planned to go back and forth to the States for the foreseeable future and it was perfect to know that Rose Cottage was being lived in.

"Sophia, don't you have to get to Bayrush?"

"I know, I lose time just looking at his beautiful face."

Grace smiled, taking him back. "Go or Eoghan'll leave without you. What do you fancy for dinner tonight?"

"I'm easy, whatever is going."

"Great, enjoy," said Grace.

"Good morning," said a pretty young girl from behind a desk in the entrance hall.

"My name is Jessie McGrath and this is my son Sam."

The girl looked down her list of names. "Perfect, there you are. I'm Sandy." She ticked the names and said, "Come on, let's show you where to go. You'll have great fun," she said to Sam. "You'll be doing art, drama, and playing games outside. I'm glad you have a cap because it's a glorious day. We plan to have a picnic too."

"That's sounds like fun," said Jessie. Sam perked up when he heard they were going outside. "Sam's an outdoor guy, aren't you honey?"

He smiled and nodded. Great, thought Jessie, at least one of us is happy. "I'll pick you up at break time and you can tell me all about it."

"Okay Mom, see you later."

Sandy gave her directions to the room designated for art therapy. There was a large circle of chairs in the middle of the room. Jessie was greeted by an elderly lady with a beautiful smile.

"You're very welcome today. I'm Miriam and I'm just waiting on everybody to arrive."

She sat in one of the free chairs and looked around. She caught an eye here and there; people smiled and she smiled back. She wondered if they all felt as self-conscious as she did. Grace had been right. She couldn't draw a straight line with a ruler. Oh God, what have I let myself in for?

Sophia parked her car on the dockside and joined Eoghan at the gate leading to the gangplank. She didn't mention that she hadn't been on a sailboat since before Bill died. If she had time to really think about it she probably would have declined.

"Are we going alone?" she asked.

He was already aboard and was about to help her on. "Well, em, yes, if that's okay with you." She nodded, taking his proffered hand as she climbed on board the small sailboat. "It's small but it should be fun if we can get some speed up."

"Eoghan, I'm not twenty, you know."

"Ah sure you're never too old for an adrenaline rush. You said you can sail, so let's do it."

"Oh my God, what have I let myself in for?"

He laughed and untied the little boat from the dock – they were off.

She noticed it had a motor board and was thankful. She didn't fancy depending on weather she knew little about. She trusted Eoghan and had gone out in his fishing boat once before; he was after all a member of the sea rescue team.

They tacked out to sea and within minutes she was back to her old form. The wind whipped her face and she felt alive and free again. It was strange how Ireland brought out feelings of youthfulness in her. The world was filled with possibilities again. She looked across and caught Eoghan looking at her in a way that made her feel young and attractive but he looked away again quickly. Had she imagined it? The girls joked so much about the two of them that she was beginning to believe it. She laughed at her stupidity.

"What are you laughing at?" he shouted, above the noise of the wind and the sea.

"It's exhilarating ... I'd forgotten how much I missed it." They did some gibing and turning and managed to get a rhythm going.

"I'm impressed," he said twenty minutes later when they took a break and let the sail at half-mast.

"It's like riding a bicycle. You never forget except how good it feels." She looked across at him and wondered about his past. The girls didn't know anything more than that he was originally from Dublin and he had retired to Bayrush six years ago. He didn't wear a wedding ring and he never mentioned anything about family besides a brother who visited now and then. Eoghan opened a rucksack he had stored in the hold and began to pour coffee from a flask. Handing it to her his fingers brushed against hers. She jerked and she spilt some coffee. It was like an electric shock back to reality – what was she playing at?

"Thanks, Eoghan, I'm sorry to be so badly co-ordinated."

"You certainly showed no signs of that earlier. I'm mightily impressed."

"I've enjoyed it. Thanks for arranging it but I'd like to get back." She didn't feel comfortable anymore. She couldn't think straight. She had noticed he was quite handsome that first day she had met him at the harbour, but now that she had got to know him it was much more ... God, she needed to get back to dry land fast.

"Sure thing," he said, reaching to take the cup back but instead she placed it in the rucksack – minimum touching.

He gave her an odd look but she pretended not to notice. I'm fifty-nine years old and behaving like a teenager, she thought. The sooner I get back to New York the better.

*

Jessie tucked Sam in. He was wrecked after the day.

"I can't wait for tomorrow. Sandy said we're making puppets and we're going to do a show for the parents at the end of the week."

"How cool is that?" said Jessie. She was wrecked too. "Now go to sleep, sweet dreams." She leaned down and kissed him on the forehead. "Night night, I love you."

"I love you too, Mom." And then he turned over on to his side. He'd be asleep in no time, she thought, as she went to the computer in one of the bedrooms they had set aside as an office. The art therapist had suggested that writing a journal might be very helpful. It was a four-day course and so much had happened already. She decided to take her advice. But sitting in front of the computer looking at a blank white screen she didn't know where to begin. She searched for a diary or notebook. Nothing. To hell with it she thought, she'd buy a nice little notebook tomorrow. She stood up and turned off the computer. Stopping at the door, she knew she was just putting off the inevitable. And so she turned the computer back on and began to type.

"The christening ceremony was perfect, Gracey. You're the best boy ever," said Kate, holding little Finn in her arms. "And you didn't even squeal."

"Give me a little hold," said Jessie, stretching out her arms.

"No," said Kate, cuddling him all the more.

"Grace, tell her to give him to me. I'm his godmother."

"Will you two give it a rest and help? I have a full house here. Kate, go out and rescue Sophia from Dirk's mother. And you keep my mother away from Dirk," she said, looking at Jessie while taking Finn from Kate. "Hey, little man, you're the best." Grace planted a big kiss on his plump cheek. "And check on the older kids; just make sure there's an adult on the beach too."

"God you're bossy," laughed Kate, heading out the back door. "I'll check the kids first."

"At least Dirk didn't bring his girlfriend after all," said Jessie.

"I'd say his mother warned him not to."

"Listen," said Jessie, as she cocked her ear towards the garden. "If she mentions The Meadows Golf and Country Club again, I'd say Sophia will want to hit her with one. And I mean an actual golf club," said Jessie, putting on a posh voice. "God bless Sophia she has the patience of a saint to be still listening to her."

"Sophia will just let her rabbit on and probably tell us something good about her, making us feel terrible for bad-mouthing her. Sophia is fair-minded to a fault."

"How anybody could find a good point about that woman, I'll never know," laughed Jessie.

"We need more cutlery out there," said Kate, coming back into the kitchen.

"Here," said Jessie, picking up a basket full of cutlery wrapped in serviettes as Grace put Finn in his carrycot. "How are all the kids doing on the beach?"

"Gerry and Joe have organised a game of football. My lovely sister Marilyn is looking after the smaller ones."

"Ouch," said Grace.

"I can't be perfect all the time, sis. She really pushes my buttons. Did you hear the carry-on of her at the church?"

"You're worse to pay any attention to her," said Grace, adding, "Ah Kate, will you please go out and rescue Sophia? I can see the poor woman wilting."

"Anything for you, sis," said Kate, sauntering back outside. Kate had a way about her that even Violet Fleischer seemed to soften to, snob and all that she was. She just wished their older sister Marilyn would lighten up on Kate.

"Jess, it's going well, isn't it? ... I just wish my life was normal."

"What's normal anymore? Look, Kate has Violet smiling already. It's a great day," said Jessie, giving her a squeeze. "Stop worrying."

But Grace could feel the tears coming behind her eyes. It was hard not to be emotional today. She wished her baby could be brought up with a mother and father who loved one another and lived in the same house, but that wasn't how it was to be.

"Will I top you up?" asked Sophia getting up to retrieve the bottle of red, open on the coffee table.

"Yes please, I'm exhausted. It was a great day but I'm really glad they are all gone. I love this room," Grace remarked, looking around the upstairs living room. "It's like a hidden gem."

Sophia poured the red liquid into her glass. "It was a lovely day. It all went off very well."

"Dirk's mother even enjoyed herself. She's probably glad that I'm not going to marry her beloved Dirk after all. That's what made her so happy all day," Grace remarked from her curled up position on the couch.

"She's a strange old fish, but she's not the worst," Sophia commented.

Grace smiled. "We nearly took bets today that you would say something positive about her."

"Am I becoming that predictable?"

"Yes."

Sophia laughed. "Well then I have some news for you too and if you're so clever – start guessing."

"Ah, would you give me a break. It's late. Anyway don't be getting all sulky because I think you're so fair-minded."

Sophia laughed again. "I suppose it's my age, the older I get, the wiser I get."

"I should think so."

"Don't be such a smart ass over there or I'll change my mind about telling you my news."

"Ah go on, tell me, have you and Eoghan like …" Grace was sitting up now, waiting.

"No, I have not. You must be kidding." Sophia guffawed.

"Well then, what is it? Where are you going?" she called after her as Sophia disappeared out the door. Moments later she came back with a large brown envelope in her hand.

"These are for you. Well for Finn to be exact."

Grace asked, "What's this about?"

"Just take it," she said, handing the envelope to Grace who began to open it.

Grace read down through the enclosed papers and after a couple of minutes said, "You can't do that, Sophia. This is too much. I mean really, I appreciate that you would even think of it. But no, you can't do that."

"It's not for you. It's for Finn. You can't honestly deny me this, Grace."

"But the house … you love this house, Sophia. When did it go up for sale? My God …"

"I put in an offer and they accepted. Grace, the house is bricks and mortar. I love you and that little baby more. It's for Finn. Now you have to accept it. Please."

Grace started to cry.

"Oh, come here will you, it wasn't supposed to make you cry, you silly goose."

"I'm just … I'm overwhelmed … I don't know what to say … I can't believe that you would do this." She knew it was pointless arguing. Sophia had bought the house for Finn. "Thank you, thank you so much. You know how much I love it here and I know Finn is going to love it too."

"You are very, very welcome. Let's open a bottle of champagne to celebrate. And for goodness sake, stop crying."

Grace hadn't drunk so much in a very long time. She was blown away by it all. Imagine, her dreams of bringing up Finn beside the sea had come true. She would never leave this house. She loved it so much. And she wouldn't have to worry about the future so much because no matter what happened they would always have a place to live. How lucky they were! But more importantly it assured her that they would always have Sophia in their lives. So much had changed in just over a year.

Sophia lay in bed. She was thrilled that Grace had accepted her gesture. She had so much money it seemed crazy not to give something to a person who was very important to her. But to do it she had had to think very carefully. Sometimes gestures like that can cause offence and that was last thing she wanted to do.

Sophia worried about Grace. She had known feelings of isolation bringing up Richard alone for the first two years of his life. The emptiness she had felt inside and the utter joy the day she met Bill in Central Park. It had made them stronger.

She supposed Grace had become like the daughter she never had. They were very similar in many ways. She often wondered about Jack. Had he gone back to his marriage? She had really liked him and so had Grace. Life was strange and never easy. She put the book she had intended to read back on the bedside locker and turned out the light.

Jessie was washing down Ollie, a chestnut gelding, when Jack Leslie walked across the cobbled stones towards her.

"You must be preparing for a show." He smiled that deadly smile of his.

"Well, I'll be," she said, standing up straight. "This is a surprise! It's great to see you."

Monique heard Jessie's voice and turned around. "Hi Jack, welcome back," she called out.

"Hey Monique, he's looking good," said Jack, nodding towards the grey horse she was busy grooming.

"Does Geoff know you're back?" asked Jessie when he reached her.

"No, I decided to come home at the last minute for a week's holiday. Catch up with the family and get away from all that hot weather." He laughed.

"Don't rub it in now. The weather has been so changeable here. At least it's not raining, I suppose. Listen to me ranting on here. How about a coffee? Geoff should be back shortly. I'll just finish this lad."

"No rush, I'll take a look at Jessie's Angel."

"She's in the well field," she called after him. OMG he's back, she thought. I wonder if his wife is here too. She looked towards his jeep. No, maybe she's gone shopping. Oh don't be so nosy, Jessie McGrath, she admonished herself.

Later as she made the coffee, she was dying to ask about his marriage, but she didn't dare. He chatted about this and that and nothing at all. She wished he'd ask about Grace or maybe bring up something so she could follow a line of questioning. She was worse than Miss Marple. He talked about his work. He said he had to travel a lot. Normally she'd be interested in talking about horses forever but not today. "So, that must be difficult!"

"How so?"

"You know, you told me you were going back to your ... eh." *Oh shite, she thought.*

"Oh yes, Lynda. It didn't work out. I knew when I got back. It wasn't meant to be."

She tried to hide a smile; so there might be a chance for them.

"How are Conor and Marie?"

"Great, Mark their second guy is starting university shortly. It's an expensive business here, especially putting two of them through at the same time."

"It is. We'll probably have to re-mortgage by the time Sam starts."

"How is he getting on?"

"He's doing well. Sam loves horses but he's good at his schoolwork too. Believe it or not I'm starting a course too."

"Well done, you. What are you going to study?"

"It's a psychology course. I'm really looking forward to it."

He started to laugh.

"What are you laughing at?" she asked, smiling at him.

"You, psychology, it will suit you. You have me twigged, so I'm going to finally ask, how is she?"

She laughed and said, "I couldn't have been more obvious. Grace is great; she has the most beautiful little boy. She called him Finn and I'm his godmother," Jessie declared proudly. "She's doing well now. We had a scare at the beginning ..."

"I heard all about it from Conor. Garvan told him. I wanted to contact her but you know how it is." He paused. "Is she, you know, like really happy?"

"She's not back with Dirk. If that's what you're asking?"

"No, not him, the American guy. The fellow she was with at Christmas."

"What American guy? Do you mean Richard? He's Sophia's son."

"But I thought he was with Grace."

"Grace?" she asked incredulously. "More like Kate you mean. What made you think he was with Grace?"

"Ah, nothing! I must have got my wires crossed."

"Look Jack, uncross them. We only get one chance in life, just one shot. If you care about her enough – do something about it. If you're going back to Dubai, please don't contact her because she is trying to get her life back on track and she could do without the setback."

"Jessie, are you saying you think I have a chance?"

"I'm not saying anything. But you'll have to deal with me if you hurt her. Think carefully about what you want, Jack."

Geoff arrived in and so the two men talked horses.

"I better get back to work or else I'll be sacked from my own yard," Jessie said. "Why don't you come over for dinner tomorrow evening after the event in Colcone?"

"Thanks, Jessie, I'd love to."

Jack drove to Bayrush beach and parked the car. He got out and started to walk along the shore. She had never been with Richard! He had replayed that kiss in his mind a hundred times. She hadn't pulled away. How could he have been so stupid?

Every moment he'd seen her played like a movie in his head. Seeing her at McGraths' over the stable door, then bumping into her in the yard, the afternoon in her mother's garden, on the beach with Sam, the Viking night, the day the cruise liner had arrived in Bayrush, in the kitchen at Jessie's after the sponsored ride, Christmas day, he cringed, the races the next day. St. Patrick's Day. No wonder she had hardly spoken a word to him that day. He had pulled away from her. He had hurt her.

But did he really want to be with her? She had somebody else's baby. Could he accept that? Could he give up his practice in Dubai? Conor had been right, he loved working with horses. He hadn't been happy with the work here. She couldn't leave Ireland with the baby. The father of the child wouldn't want that. Anyway, why was he thinking about that? She loved her work and Ireland. He wouldn't expect her to move. But that would mean he would have to come back. His head was in circles. He stopped in his tracks and looked out to sea. He could see

Everest Rock in the distance. When had he forgotten how beautiful Ireland was? When had he started to miss it so much? God he'd love a cigarette. He had packed in the habit six months ago.

He walked back along the beach towards the jeep. He passed a newly built dormer-style cottage with a thatched roof and a pretty garden with a gate directly on to the beach. He could hear music playing. It sounded like Barbra Streisand. An aroma of barbeque wafted in the air, reminding him that he was hungry. He could hear the sound of voices and laughter carried in the quiet of the evening. The next house along was a wooden log house. It was all very dark and quiet. It was years since he had walked the beach. Geoff had told him she lived somewhere in Bayrush. He wondered where exactly.

"Who's for more chicken?" asked Grace, turning the meat on the barbeque. She had invited the girls over because her friend Lisa was home on holidays from Manhattan. And she was delighted that Anna, Paul's wife, had come too. Lisa was in the middle of one of her stories. Being an events manager in Manhattan, she often had them all cracking up with laughter. Grace loved when she was home. It was a perfect excuse to have a girlie evening. Kate kept complaining about the music. Anna passed her plate over.

"Shut up, you can have a turn in a while. I like *Barbra*," Jessie insisted. "And I was here first, so tough."

"Well she's my sister and I often stay here so I win."

"Will the two of ye give it a rest or I'll turn the music off altogether," said Grace. "Ye're worse than ten children at times."

"Thank goodness for the gas heater," said Lisa, "it's getting chilly."

"Will we take it inside?" asked Grace, picking up the coleslaw dish to refill it.

"Ah no, we'll be inside long enough. You'll just have to toughen up, Lisa. You're getting too used to the good life," remarked Kate, changing the CD to Lily Allen.

"If only, girly," laughed Lisa.

Anna followed Grace inside. "I'm glad it's worked out for you both. I was so worried we'd lost you as a friend, Grace. And Paul is thrilled about being Finn's godfather."

"I'm so happy Dirk chose him because it will ensure that you'll both always be in Finn's life no matter what happens in the future. Promise me that, Anna."

Anna hugged her. "Of course we will, Grace."

Chapter Sixteen

"So Sophia is in Killarney with Eoghan, Nora and the rest of their bridge club group ..." Kate remarked, putting plates into the dishwasher. "What do you make of that?"

"What?" asked Grace, wiping down the granite counter.

"Sophia and Eoghan."

"They're just friends."

"I think Eoghan would like to be more than friends. Fancy another glass of wine, sis?" Kate asked. "I might as well stay over. I really enjoyed the evening. Lisa is great craic."

"Great. Pour away, I'll just check on Finn, back in a sec." Grace had noticed Sophia and Eoghan but she didn't want to get into that conversation. She was afraid they might end up hurting one another. He wasn't aware of Sophia's secret wealth and Grace wasn't sure how he would react if he found out.

Nothing gave her joy like looking at her baby. She still couldn't explain the depth of feeling that she had for this little person. She bent down and gazed at the sleeping figure in the half-light of the room. She listened to hear his breathing and couldn't help thinking of Jessie. Losing her beautiful babies had changed so much for her. She was different in many ways. She put on a good front but Grace knew she was still very raw. The one-year anniversary was coming up soon. They were all different because of it. After a few minutes she stood up and went to join her sister downstairs. Kate had The Script on in the background and was curled up on the sofa.

"How is our little cutie doing?"

"Fast asleep, I reckon he'll sleep until around seven."

"He's great. I'm a bit clueless about babies, but it seems to me that Finn is an advert for them."

Grace smiled in agreement. "Well Kate, how are you doing?"

"Am I that obvious?"

"Yes."

"I don't know what's wrong with me. I'm not interested in going out socialising anymore. I'm twenty-seven and I can't think of anything I've done to be proud of."

"If I was a fairy godmother who could grant you your heart's desire what would you want?"

"If only you were," she replied wistfully.

"Humour me for a minute. Say it out loud. Voice it. It may not be as hard to have as you think."

"I wish … Okay, I wish that … Don't get me wrong, Gracey. I love working for you, it's just …"

Grace finished for her. "It's something you fell into. Kate, I want you to be happy. You need to follow your dreams. Life is too short for regrets. You have been a fantastic support to me, more than any person could ever wish for. Kate, please don't feel stuck on my account. I am fine. I am making decisions for me and Finn. You need to make decisions for yourself."

"I know but you've always been so good to me. I really screwed up, didn't I? Grace I'm so ashamed of that time. When I see Marilyn she reminds me of how badly I feel … about me."

"And she's perfect … I don't think so. We're all trying here. Shit happens. All we can do is learn from it, that's about it. It's the person who never learns – they are the ones I worry about. Yes, you made mistakes but look at yourself. You're a breath of fresh air to everyone around you. Everybody loves you. Even Dirk's mother has a soft spot for you. Follow your heart Kate. I bet we're talking about a certain guy here too?"

Kate looked very sheepish. "Gracey, I can't believe it myself. In a million years I would not have picked Richard. I suppose that's why I was so relaxed around him at Christmas. I didn't think of him that way. Yeah, I wouldn't have minded a bit of a fling but we didn't even kiss. Yet I was desperate to see him when I heard he was in Miami. I made a complete prat of myself with the receptionist in the Woodmore. Then when he turned up at my bedroom door, I nearly died. But when he told me why he was there, everything went to the back of my mind. He told me about his wife and child, I don't know if he told you. But it was awful …"

"He told me."

"And Gracey, at Christmas he was vague about what he worked at, something about being an editor of a magazine. It turns out he is the CEO of an International Communications company. Did you know that too?"

Grace nodded. "But that's not for people around here to know.

Sophia would not be too pleased about that."

"You needn't worry. I haven't told anybody. But Grace, it just puts him so out of my league. I'm a former drug addict. That's what I mean. That's why I'm feeling so shite! I can't possible tell him that. What would he think of me? I'm so ashamed. Anyway it doesn't matter because there is no future in it. He's too old anyway." She was talking herself into and out of the relationship all at once.

"Kate, the first thing you have to do is work at what you get some satisfaction from. Believe in yourself. If you want Richard – go after him. Tell him. Risk it. The worst thing he can do is reject you. If you are working at something that makes you happy you can bury yourself in your work while your heart mends if it doesn't work out. Then you will be able to get on with your life. If you don't try you will never know. He's not going to be around for long, mark my words."

Grace was thinking of her own lost opportunity. If only she had taken her own advice maybe things would be different. The man she loved was in another woman's arms.

"Thanks, Grace, for everything. I did think of flying over and just turning up at his office. But I thought I was just being my ridiculously whimsical self. But now I think I will."

"Christ Kate, I'm not quite sure myself now that you're agreeing with me. Don't take me quite so to heart."

"Ah sis, you really are a chicken at times. What about the vet on Christmas Day? I saw the way he kept looking at you. He's a fine bit of stuff. Do you know him? I thought it was a bit weird that he seemed to fancy you even though you were as big as a house."

"I wasn't that big. But did you really notice that he was looking at me?"

"A blind man could see it."

"It's a long story, Kate. Maybe in another lifetime things would have been different. I knew him years ago. And yes, I fancied him big time, then. He went back to Dubai." Then she added quietly, "To his wife."

"Oh God, sis, I'm sorry, I didn't know. Maybe you are right. Sometimes we just have to take a risk if we really want something. I have some savings and maybe Lisa will lend me the keys of her apartment. I think I'll book a ticket to New York."

"OMG Kate Fitzgerald, you really are a crazy lady," laughed Grace. There was no point in putting her off; if Kate wanted to do something nothing would stop her.

*

Sophia and Eoghan sat in the hotel lobby in comfortable armchairs. Piped music played gently in the background. They had left the rest of their group in the pub down the road where a ballad session was in full flow. She had been tired and Eoghan, ever the gentleman, had insisted on walking her back to their hotel. When he asked if she fancied a nightcap she had accepted. She enjoyed his company. She knew so little about him, and yet they talked about everything and anything but never the personal. She realised that was why she liked him so much. He was easy to be around. Her glass was nearly empty. He nodded towards it. "Another?"

"I shouldn't …" But she wanted to stay chatting. She smiled.

He looked around and caught the attention of the night porter.

"Could we have the same again?"

Minutes later the porter placed two Baileys with crushed ice on the table.

"You're right. It does taste of more."

He smiled and clicked his glass to hers. "Are you staying this time?"

"In Ireland?" she asked, raising her eyebrows. "No, I don't think I could live here permanently. Oh I do love it, but Richard is in New York and he's all I've got now …"

Her voice trailed away. He sipped his drink and waited.

"I lost my grandson and his mother." She began to tell him about the accident and he sat quietly and listened as she talked for the first time in a long while about how it happened and how she felt. And then she said, "Billy had a learning difference called dyspraxia or DCD." She looked into the glass and watched as the chipped crystals swam in the milky liquid. She had never talked about this to anyone besides her family.

"What is it?"

"It's a motor co-ordination problem. It's often called 'the hidden handicap' because it's not obvious, but it affected every area of his life. He found it difficult to play because he couldn't catch a ball, or understand the rules of play like turn-taking. Riding a bicycle was nigh on impossible for him. Schoolwork was a nightmare because it would take him longer to find the page number or take down information from the board. Handwriting takes such co-ordination. I suppose I never thought about it until it happened in our family. Oh Eoghan, poor Billy found many ordinary day-to-day activities so hard. And Richard couldn't understand it. Heather, his mother, researched as much as she could and was determined to make life easier for him. She had even taught him to ride his bicycle and the joy the day he cycled for the first time without supports was incredible. And then we lost them and I might as well have lost Richard too. And then Bill dying …" A tear rolled slowly down her cheek. She didn't wipe it away, instead she sipped her drink. "I'm sorry we're away for an enjoyable weekend and I'm burdening you with my tales of woe."

He smiled and stretched his feet in front of him. "Am I running away?"

"Thank you," she said. "I'm looking forward to tomorrow. A boat trip to see Fungie the dolphin. Sounds like fun." She needed to lighten the air.

"You can't beat the Kerrymen for their ingenuity. If only we could get a Fungie of our own in Bayrush, eh." He laughed. "I love coming down here. It always makes me feel proud to be Irish. Even in the middle of the winter they manage to get the tourists in."

"You're really passionate about the work you do in the tourism industry."

"If I hadn't met Grace that day in the coffee shop I often wonder would I have followed a different path? I had taken early retirement but I wasn't quite ready to put my feet up, that's why I'm involved with the sea rescue as a volunteer. These days I'm busier than I was when I worked full-time. Not that I'm complaining."

"I'd like to find a project to feel passionate about."

"You will, now that you know you are looking." He smiled knowingly.

She smiled and said, "It's past my bedtime. Goodnight, Eoghan, and thank you."

"You're welcome," he said, standing as she got up. There was an awkward moment where neither of them knew what to do. So she walked away quickly towards the lift, pressing the button and waiting for the door to open. When she stood in and looked back towards where he had sat back down, she wondered for the first time what it would be like to be with another man. She flushed as the lift door closed.

Jessie, Geoff and Sam set off for the gymkhana at Colcone. It was a big event on the circuit and Jessie was thankful it was another fine, bright day. The field being used for parking was nearly full already. But they still had plenty of time to walk around. They checked the schedule. Sam was due to jump at eleven-fifteen.

"Hi guys," she heard a familiar voice calling.

"Oh look Mum, it's Gracey!" said Sam. "She came to see me."

Jessie turned around. Grace looked fantastic, wearing skinny jeans, fabulous black leather boots with a tan brown trim and a sleeveless wax jacket. Her long blonde hair fanned her beautiful face and she was sporting a pair of black Jackie O style sun-glasses. Her figure was completely restored. She had little Finn in a baby sling in front of her. Jessie looked around. The amount of admiring glances she was getting was unbelievable. She was like a model.

Sam ran over to her to give her a hug and coo at baby Finn, who was beginning to grow some hair. It was so blond for a long time he looked bald at a distance. And he had his mother's eyes – the most beautiful shade of dark blue. He was a smiley little fellow!

"Hi honey," Grace said, bending down to Sam. "I wouldn't miss today for the world. Are you looking forward to it?"

"Yes, I can't wait, Bubbles is great. He'll help me get over the jumps."

"No bother to you, Sam. Sure you're great at it. The most important thing is to enjoy it."

"I know, that's what Mum says too."

She ruffled his curly red hair as they walked together to the coffee caravan, chatting and laughing.

"Can I go over to Oliver?"

"Yes," said Jessie, waving at Oliver's mother as Sam ran towards them with Buzz waddling along behind him.

"He's not a bit nervous," remarked Grace, just as Jessie spotted Jack in the distance.

"Let's go back and sort out the pony," said Jessie. *Please God Jack will make the right decision*, she thought.

Grace turned and could have sworn she saw Jack. Nobody had mentioned he was back. Maybe it was her imagination or just wishful thinking. Whoever it was had his back turned and was wearing a striped red and navy polo shirt and jeans. She stared but the guy didn't turn around. Oh imagine if it was him! But if it was – that was probably his wife standing next to him; the woman was leaning into him. It couldn't be him. Jack was thousands of miles away. It was probably all the wine she had last night making her wistful.

It was a bit of fun, a diversion from reality to think he might be here. Grace became distracted because Jessie asked her to find Geoff – she needed him to help unload Bubbles and get him warmed up. The gymkhana at Colcone was a big show and it attracted a large attendance. Both Jessie's and Geoff's parents had arrived too.

About twenty minutes later a man with a West-Brit accent announced across the PA system that it was time for the under eights novice jumps – Sam's group. A young lad opened the gate to let Bubbles in and then the buzzer went and they were off over the first sixty-centimetre jump. And then the next, no problems. Sam led the little pony over the double-barred jump. Grace watched as his two grandmothers looked away. They were so nervous for him. Grace looked towards Jessie, whose face was bursting with pride. Sam was still going clear coming up to the last fence and then it was complete … the applause from their corner was rapturous. Grace wouldn't have missed this for the world. Sam jumped down. He was grinning from ear to ear and Geoff picked him up and swung him around.

"Dad, put me down. Not cool, Dad, not cool at all," Sam muttered at his father. Everybody patted Sam on the back and told him well done. And then Grace heard a familiar voice join in the congratulations.

"Hey Sam, that was terrific, well done."

"That's my son, Jack." Geoff ruffled Sam's helmet-free head.

"Dad, that's just the first round."

"I know. I know. Just take your time. Don't get hung up about the clock. Just enjoy it."

"I will. Stop saying that, Dad."

Jack patted Geoff on the back, saying, "He did really well."

"Don't I know it!"

Jessie stood close to Grace and whispered in her ear, "Breathe, don't forget to breathe."

"Feck off," Grace whispered back.

"And for God's sake, be nice to him."

After a few minutes she caught his eye. He smiled that smile of his; her knees nearly buckled. He came over and stood next to her, lowering his head to see Finn in the baby sling to her front. She could smell his hair, he was so close.

"Hello Finn," he said to the baby, gently catching his little fingers. "I've heard all about you. You're a little cutie, just like your mommy."

Jesus, she thought, she would need oxygen if she didn't get away from him. Why did she always feel like running when he was near? He turned his face; it was so close to hers she felt as though there was nobody else around them. One slight move and their lips could touch. And then he asked, "How've you been?"

She was in a field full of fresh air and she could hardly breathe. She managed to squeeze out, "Good."

"I'm glad." He smiled again. That blasted smile of his.

"Look, I was only here for Sam's jump. I have to go. Jessie," she called out, putting distance between them. "I'll call around later. Well done Sam, that was brilliant. Enjoy the rest of the day."

"Okay, I'll see you later," Jessie called after her.

She waved goodbye to everybody and set off across the field to her car. *Shite*, she thought, *I was really looking forward to spending the day and having a picnic with everybody. If his wife had come over she'd die of shame. I can't share the same sky as him, I just can't.* These thoughts raced through her head as she fastened Finn into his car seat. She heard somebody calling her name.

"Grace, wait, hang on, will you?"

"What ... what do you want?" She was angry now, angry with him for messing up her day. Goddamn it, for messing up her life.

He reached the car, looked straight into her eyes and said simply, "You."

"Have you forgotten – you're married. Now if you'd please let me pass I have somewhere I need to be."

"I don't know why I bother. You're such a hot head. I don't think I could put up with you for any more than a day. What do you think? Can we spend one day together without fighting? We used to be able to. Can it be that hard for you to be your pleasant self with me? You manage it with everybody else. Why not me?"

"Because ..." She couldn't think straight, his beautiful eyes were pleading.

"Look, can't we try to be friends? One lousy day out of your life! That's all I am asking for. Let's just call it quits for the day!"

Her head said no but her heart couldn't resist. She didn't have any other plans. Obviously his wife wasn't with him. She had Finn with her. What harm could it be?

"Okay, quits so. From this moment on we are going to be pleasant to one another until seven o'clock this evening, then the day is over, okay?"

"Okay."

"Get in."

"Yes sir." He laughed. "What about my jeep?"

"I'll drop you back for it later."

"Sounds good to me!"

She drove down the long winding lane back towards the main entrance to the estate, passing the big old house.

"Wow, it's fabulous, isn't it?" he remarked.

"Mmm," she replied, thinking not half as fabulous as him. God, she needed to get a grip if she planned on getting through the day.

Kate had slept like a log for the first time in months. She had finally made some decisions. It was after twelve when she emerged from the little downstairs bedroom in the cottage. She took the stairs two at a time and logged onto the internet. She booked a flight to New York for Tuesday morning and back on Thursday.

Then she began to search the web for college courses in art and design. While scrolling she rang Lisa on her mobile and asked if she could stay in her apartment in Manhattan.

"No problem, you'll have to change the sheets and ignore the small bit of chaos I left behind me but you're more than welcome to use it."

"Do you fancy going for a bite to eat and a few drinks on me later?" said Kate, pressing print.

"Yes sounds good, but let's go Dutch!"

"Cheers Lisa, how about meeting in Nuttie's at eight and then Casa Luigi, it's a lovely tapas bar across the road, my favourite actually. See you then."

She continued her search on the internet for another hour. Then she went downstairs, got dressed, picked up her sketch book and headed for the beach. She felt as if the weight of the world had lifted from her. She was following her dreams. She felt free.

At first Grace didn't know where to go. Tourism was her game and yet she couldn't think straight she was so flustered. Thankfully she had everything she needed for a day out with Finn. Finally her thoughts settled on the mountains. There was a footpath all the way from the car park right up to the waterfall. She'd be able to push the buggy along it. She had suggested that they go back to her house to arrange a picnic but Jack thought it might be nice to go for lunch somewhere along the way.

She talked about the weather, and Finn's sleeping and feeding habits. He chatted about his nephews and what they were studying and about Ireland and all the changes over the last few years. She felt comfortable and yet flustered being around him. She was glad that she was driving because it kept her occupied.

Jack was so happy that if she had suggested a trip to the town dump it was fine by him. He looked at her sideways profile while she concentrated on driving. Everything about her just fitted, at least it did in his eyes. He turned to look at little Finn in his car seat. He could do this. He could accept this little baby. If only she would give him the chance. His future hinged on this day. He had until seven o'clock.

Sam's final was called. Jessie watched as her son took each jump. She had to remind herself to breathe. Her mother stood beside her and put her arm around Jessie just as Sam was jumping the last fence, rushing to beat the clock. Yes, his time put him in the lead.

"Mum, I could never understand why you were so nervous about me racing in the point to points but I think I'd have a fit if Sam suggested it. I nearly stopped breathing through that." They both laughed.

"Jessie, you were as hard to stop then as you are now. I'm glad you never let anything hold you back. I know the past year has been hard on you all. We never talk about the babies but that doesn't mean we don't think about them. I want you to know I'm very proud of you and of the way you have picked yourself up and got on with your life. I never tell you these kinds of things. I suppose it's the way I was brought up. Don't give your kids a big head. Maybe it was a generation thing, but whatever it was, I want to tell you today and every day of my life I am proud of you and I love you."

Jessie was frozen to the spot.

"Mum, have you being watching too much Oprah?" she joked, through tear-filled eyes.

"Will you go away outta that Jessie McGrath? Look over there, your son is waving at you, what kind of a mother are you at all?"

"Thanks, Mum," she said, leaning over and kissing her mother's cheek. "Thanks for saying that. I love you too." Her mother beamed at her and Jessie thought that for the rest of her life she would treasure this moment.

It was a great day. She hoped Grace's day would be too. She had seen Jack follow her.

Grace pushed the buggy along the footpath towards the waterfall. She had given Finn his bottle in the car. Thankfully she was no longer breast-feeding, otherwise she would never have agreed to this. Her heart was thumping; she didn't want this day to ever end. She stole a sideways glance. He was everything to her. Had he really meant what he had said at the car earlier? Had she misheard him? He had said "you". Maybe she had misunderstood.

Finn was contented and was about to fall asleep with the motion of the buggy. Although the car park had been busy, the walk was long enough not to be crowded. People passing every now and then meant that there were no deep meaningful conversations which suited her. She didn't want to know about his wife or life in Dubai. She just wanted this day. She could have it to add to her little daydreams about them. How pathetic was she? The truth was if he whisked her behind one of those huge rock boulders she would do the business and worry about the consequences later. Thankfully he couldn't read her mind; she blushed as an elderly couple passed and nodded a greeting.

"My, aren't they a handsome-looking family. They look so happy. It's nice to know romance is not dead."

"What was that, love?" the old man asked.

"Nothing, forget it," the woman half-roared back at him.

"Poor auld divil, must have a hearing problem," Jack laughed, adding, "Nothing is ever as it seems, eh!"

She smiled but didn't say anything, wishing that it was as it seemed. When they arrived at the waterfall, she found a flat rock to sit on. She always loved listening to the sound of the water gushing down the rock-face. Some children paddled in the stream a short distance from them while older ones attempted to climb up the rocks along with some athletic type dads. Jack sat opposite her. She noticed a young couple lying side by side nearby. The girl was looking up at the sky while the guy leaned up on his elbow and tickled her nose with a piece of long grass. Embarrassed, she looked away. It was so peaceful even though it was quite populated. Finn woke. She took him up immediately.

"Can I? " Jack asked, surprising her.

"Yes, sure." She passed her little son into his arms.

"He's so small. I'm afraid I'll hurt him," he said nervously.

"He's tougher than he looks. He's my little warrior. Aren't you, honey?" she gushed at Finn. Finn granted her a big smile.

"Ah, look at him. I've never held a baby before – even my nephews. I wasn't around much when they were babies. I'm all fingers and thumbs but it feels great."

She actually thought she was going to cry with the realisation of how strongly she felt about him. She didn't want the day to end. She wished she could stop time.

It was nearly twenty-one years to the day she had first met him. And at seven tonight she'd have to say goodbye again. She must have been crazy to agree to this. She had the urge to run again. She muttered something and walked away.

*

Jack watched her. She had said something about dropping something. He could see she was upset. He wanted to walk after her but he couldn't because he was actually terrified to move. Imagine that a baby could frighten a grown man so much. As soon as he could he would tell her everything. He would move back if she wanted him to. He could work as a vet again. He didn't give a shit if he never worked with horses again. But why had she been so mad with him earlier? He had to get to the bottom of that but he didn't want to make a complete fool of himself either.

"We better head back. Are you hungry?" she asked.

He wanted to answer "no, only for you". But he'd sound like a fool. So he said, "Yeah, my stomach thinks my throat is cut."

She laughed. "I thought you'd have forgotten all the local slang. You've been away so long."

"There are some things a person never forgets," he said as she took Finn gently from his arms and placed him back into the buggy. Finn was still smiling.

"Does he ever cry? Babies get such a bad rap. I haven't heard a whimper."

"He's very good humoured. He takes after his mother that way." She laughed.

"Oh, I don't know about that. I know another side to that same woman." As he said it he poked her side.

"Funny, ha, ha." She smiled at him.

God, she's beautiful, he thought. *Please stop the bloody clock.*

Kate finished sketching. It was getting cooler so she went back to the cottage to get ready for her evening out. She loved Casa Luigi. Luigi who owned it was a good friend of hers. She was into music and Luigi's often held dinner and music sessions with well-known musicians as a "kind of audience with" idea. Tonight they had Viv O'Connor playing. She was really looking forward to it.

On her way she planned to call to her mother's house. She'd tell her she was going to Dublin for a few days. She had no intention of telling anyone but Grace where she was really going. It was okay to be rejected as long as nobody else heard about it. She had less than forty-eight hours to wait. The night out would take her mind off what she was about to do.

Chapter Seventeen

*F*inn was due another feed so driving down the mountain Grace suggested that she could cook for Jack at Rose Cottage. It would be so much easier with Finn.

"You're determined to get me back there. That's the second time in one day you've offered to bring me to your place. What kind of a girl are you at all?"

"Okay, smart ass. That's the last time I will ever ask you."

"I'm kidding, you know, it's a joke."

"You're such a patronising ass at times," she quipped.

"No really, I'd love to go to your house but only if I can help to cook. I don't want you to go to any trouble on my account."

"Okay, you can cook."

"I said help."

"I know but I said cook."

"Now who's the smart ass?"

She laughed; it felt so good, just like it used to be.

Jessie and Geoff were unloading the horses in the yard when Geoff said, "You asked Jack over for a bite with us this evening."

"Ah don't worry. We won't be seeing him this evening, I hope."

He looked at her with a confused expression.

"I'll tell you later," she said, nodding in the direction of some of the girls still in the yard. She didn't want to be overheard.

"Right so, whatever."

Sam had won his competition and Jessie was on a high. Tonight she and Geoff would celebrate. Romance wasn't dead in Bayrush Stables, she thought.

Jack laughed when she turned into the drive of the cottage.

"What's so funny?"

"I actually walked past this house last night. I heard voices; you had a barbeque going on."

"Were you spying on me, or what?"

"You wish. That's some big head you've got. Of course I wasn't. I didn't even know where you lived until now."

"That's what you're telling me."

"Look, it's only after five, we're not allowed to argue until after seven. So there."

She laughed, realising that it had been a long time since she had felt as relaxed. Kate's car was in the drive. Finn was due to be fed and changed. Grace took him out of his car seat and walked across the pebbled drive towards the cottage. The door opened. Kate's jaw dropped when she saw Jack. Grace stifled a laughed at the look on Kate's face.

"You remember Jack, don't you? Jack, my sister Kate."

"Of course, nice to meet you again, Kate."

"And you." Kate mumbled, "Well guys I'm off, I'm going to town. I'll probably stay over ... in town." It was absolutely loaded with, "don't worry I won't walk in on you".

"Jack is staying for dinner but he's leaving at seven," Grace replied.

"Goodbye Kate," he said, as Grace asked him to get the baby bag from the car. When he came in he placed the bag on the counter. Grace smiled at him. He didn't smile back. She looked at him questioningly.

"What's the matter ...? What's wrong?"

"What's wrong ... are you serious? If you find me so hard to put up with I'll order a taxi now."

"I'm sorry ... did I say something to offend you? I thought ... you'd want to leave at seven. Not be stuck with me and ..." She could feel the colour drain from her face as she clutched Finn in her arms.

"Gracey," his voice softened. "Can I take Finn while you get out some food? I'll cook. I'm absolutely starving. I get irritable when I'm hungry."

"Sure," she replied, passing Finn into his arms. It was all she could manage to say. Her heart had lurched when she thought he was leaving. How was she going to cope when the time came? Hopefully Finn would be settled by then. She could curl up in bed with her pillow and neither Sophia nor Kate would be there. She could cry to her heart's content.

"Do you like pasta?" she asked.

"Great, thanks," he replied.

She took out some fresh pasta, smoked salmon, prawns, crabmeat, mushrooms, tomatoes, fresh garlic and cream and some ciabatta bread. She opened a bottle of Chardonnay. She poured two glasses and took a big gulp from one.

*

He could see her from the living area. She was visibly shaken. He had hurt her. He felt awful. He looked down at Finn who was gurgling up at him. Why did they always misunderstand one another, he wondered? She placed a glass of wine beside him. He passed Finn into her arms with confidence this time; he had made his decision. He hoped it would match hers.

He worked efficiently in the kitchen while she became more subdued by the minute. He took a few mouthfuls from the glass of wine she had given him and continued to prepare the food. After a few minutes he asked, "Grace, where is your CD player?"

"There, beside the window."

He walked over and flicked through the CD collection and found the one he was looking for.

"I didn't know you were a Barbra fan," said Grace.

He smiled, and pouring the water from the pasta, he said, "It'll be ready in five."

"I'm just going to put Finn to bed," she called to him, walking upstairs.

"No problem, take your time."

Finn had fallen asleep in her arms; she placed him gently in his cot and whispered, "Night night, sweetheart, sleep tight."

He could hear her voice through the baby monitor. It warmed his heart all the more. Minutes later she came downstairs. He noticed she had freshened up, brushing her hair and adding lipstick. As far as he was concerned she didn't need any of it.

"I thought we'd eat at the dining table. I'm glad Kate lit the fire," he commented.

"Wow," Grace said when she saw Jack had lit the many candles she had dispersed around the room. The last thing she wanted was food. It was six-forty-five, there wasn't much time left.

He carried the two plates of pasta to the table. He walked back to collect the wine and the breadbasket. He refilled both glasses and finally sat down and smiled at her. "Enjoy," he said, raising his glass in a toast.

She lifted hers to chink it. He talked about horses. She pushed her food around, hardly able to eat.

"Is my cooking that bad?" His eyes crinkled the way she just loved.

"No, it's beautiful, really, it's just … I suppose I was over-hungry. It's been … a long day. I'm tired."

"Gracey, can I ask you something?"

"Sure." Her heart lurched. There was so much she wanted to ask of him. *Please don't say you're leaving*, she pleaded silently.

"Listen to this song especially the first four lines." He got up, walked to the kitchen window and turned the CD to a duet with Bryan Adams and Barbra Streisand, "I've Finally Found Someone". Grace froze. Could this be real, all she had dreamed and hoped for? He felt the same. She could feel tears coming.

He stood by the window in the kitchen, waiting. Her heart was pounding as she walked towards him. He held her face in his hands and looking into her eyes he said, "I've always been lousy with words. While I was waiting for you, I heard that song. It sums up how I feel." He was the most serious she had ever seen him. Then he whispered, "Grace Fitzgerald, you're exceptional, I can't wait for the rest of my life."

Running his hands through her hair, he tilted her face slightly and kissed her gently. She had dreamed of this moment for so long. She was terrified he would stop again, but he didn't. Instead he swept her off her feet, as though she were no weight, and carried her into the living room. He placed her on the rug in front of the fire. Her body was filled with anticipation, the light from the fire flickered as he began to slowly undress her. They made love gently at first and on and on into the night exploring one another. Laughing, because later he ran out to the kitchen to get some more wine and food and he set up a picnic in front of the fire. She was starving not having eaten properly earlier. No matter what happened she'd treasure this night forever.

Jessie woke at seven a.m. She slipped out of bed quietly. She and Geoff had had a wonderful evening together. It had been like the old days. Something had shifted in her since doing the art therapy workshop. She had peeled layers off her emotions without having to talk about it. She pulled up a pair of jodhpurs and put on a rugby shirt. As she passed Sam's bedroom, she peeped in and saw his tousled head. He was still fast asleep. She smiled and thought how blessed she was. Oh, how she hoped everything would work out for Grace. She truly believed she and Jack were perfect for one another.

She tacked up Jessie's Angel, the young, grey gelding Geoff had named for her. Breathing in the smell of her, she thought how grateful she was for the life she lived. Working with horses had always been her and Geoff's passion and recently Angel had brought them luck. She had won two races since St. Patrick's Day – minor races but they were wins.

As she trotted out of the yard, she thought of her babies. They were never far from her mind but today was special. It was their first anniversary. She often thought about Fr. Jim and his suggestion about letting the babies go but she hadn't found the strength to do it. She began to canter through the woods towards the highest point on their land. When she reached it, she hopped down and tied Angel to a tree. She walked towards a big rock and sat looking out across the forests and fields towards the ocean. She could see the town of Bayrush in the distance and the church perched high on the hill overlooking the sea. She hardly went to the graveyard because she hated to think that her babies were in a hole in the ground. She looked up. The blue sky was dotted with fluffy clouds. She imagined her babies sitting on them but then wondered if they had grown up or if the remained the same in heaven. It was a mystery.

She took out a photograph from the pocket of her red sleeveless jacket and looked at it. It was the one Sam had insisted on taking with the teddy bears on either side of the babies. Tears rolled down her cheeks.

"I know you are up there and someday I hope to be there with you. But for now I have to let you both go. Fr. Jim says that you came for a reason. I haven't quite figured that out yet, maybe it's about making me a better person. Maybe I'm supposed to do something more with my life. I'm certainly less black and white about things. I'd like to think I learned something over the past year. He said if I let you go, you'll come back tenfold. So this is probably the most selfish thing I will ever do."

She stood up and said. "Anthony and Geoff, my beautiful boys, this is not goodbye. I am setting you free so that we, your earthly family, will feel the love you have for us. I live in the hope that I will see you both again. For now watch over us, especially your big brother here, he needs you. Thank you for being in our lives even if it was such a short time. I love you both."

She turned away then and untied Angel from the tree and hopped up. As she walked Angel back down the trek, she felt an overwhelming sense of peace.

Everything sounded wonderful in the dead of the night, thought Grace. He had said he'd move back. She hadn't told him about Rose Cottage. It was too complicated to explain. He was moving way too fast for her.

She made breakfast and they sat outside. He was talking a mile a minute about their future. She needed him to slow down. She couldn't get a word in.

"Stop," she said. "Listen to me. I have a son, Jack. Can you really accept another man's child? He will always come first. I'm sorry."

She got up to take the dishes back inside. She had to tell him the truth. She couldn't let him throw away a career he loved to come back to Ireland to her.

When she turned around he was behind her.

"Come here," he said gently, taking her in his arms. "I'll slow down. Let's just take it one day at a time, okay?"

"I want to get to know you, Jack. A lifetime has passed since we met. We're not the same. I've had to grow up and so have you. We have baggage."

"Okay, I get it. I'm overwhelmed and tired. Is this the way it's going to be for the rest of our lives – arguing and making up? I'll love the making up," he said, putting his strong arms around her.

"If you think you're having your wicked way with me again, you can forget it." She laughed.

"Do you think …?" He nodded in the direction of the stairs. "What time is Sophia due back?"

"Any minute. And I want you gone, Mister."

He ran his hand up her back and nuzzled her ear, muttering, "That's not what you said last night."

"Your mother will be wondering where you've got to!"

"Funny, ha, ha!"

"Well honey, can you fit the bill? Can you romance me, or what?"

"Just watch me, by the end of the week you will be burning for me."

"You're going back on Friday. We only have four nights."

"It's more than we thought we had yesterday, Grace. And we have the rest of our lives. It will work out. It's just going to take time."

"Jack, I want you to be happy, and working with horses is your life's ambition. I can't move. It wouldn't be fair to Dirk. And if I'm honest I don't want to live anywhere else!"

He hugged her close to him. "We'll work it out and for now romance it is. Can you get a babysitter for tonight? I want to spend this evening with just you and me. The days can be the three of us, but I'm being selfish for just one evening." As if on cue, Finn cried. He kissed her eyelids. "You're so tired, honey. I'm really sorry I kept you up all night."

She laughed and punched him gently as she made to break away to go upstairs.

"Do you know that you're worse than ten children?" she said, running upstairs.

She heard him singing in the kitchen. That's a talent he doesn't have, she smiled as she took Finn up.

"Will you drop me over to collect my jeep?" he asked, when she arrived back with Finn in her arms.

"Are you going already?"

"Course not, but I think it will look a bit odd parked in the middle of an empty field."

"Of course, I'll pop this little guy in the car seat and we'll go now."

She was thrilled he planned to spend the rest of the day with them.

Sophia had had a wonderful time. The boat trip in Dingle was fun. Fungie had given a great display. Eoghan had joined a group of swimmers but she had been more than happy to watch from the comfort of a large boat. The Irish were hardy souls as far as she was concerned. The pebbles crunched under the wheels of the car as she drove up the avenue to Rose Cottage. She loved the sound; she was home. She noticed a jeep parked outside and wondered briefly who owned it.

She took her travel bag from the truck and was about to enter the house when the door opened.

"Hi Sophia, did you have a good time?" said Grace, looking particularly glowing.

"It was fab," said Sophia, trying to see who was behind her.

"Hi Sophia," said Jack, coming out to greet her.

"Hello Jack, this is a pleasant surprise."

"Jack called around to say hello," offered a blushing Grace.

"Really … you're back for good?"

"No, no, just a holiday."

"Oh that's too bad," said Sophia, smiling; there was so much being left unsaid. She was quite amused by them. It was like they had been caught out. The chemistry between them was almost tangible.

"How about a cuppa?" said Grace, walking towards the counter.

"I'd love one. I'll join you in minute," she said, continuing upstairs. She couldn't help beaming. Oh how she had hoped for this moment. There was nothing like a new romance. To see Grace's face flushed was worth a million dollars. She put her travel bag on the bed and went down to join them.

"So tell me. Did I miss anything?" she asked.

They both burst out laughing.

"Where do we start?" said Jack.

"The beginning is always a good place," said Sophia, beaming as she rested her chin in her hand and listened as they told her about their day together, leaving out the finer details, of course.

"Guys, I'm so happy for you both," said Sophia, just as Finn let out a squeal of delight from his bouncer.

Grace went to get his changing bag as there was an aroma emerging from the little man. Sophia took the opportunity to have a quick word.

"Jack, take care with her. She deserves the best. She's been through so much already. Please don't make her promises you can't keep."

"Sophia, I won't. I'll do my very best to make her happy."

Sophia could see the sincerity in his face but wondered if they were promises he could keep. After all, he was living in Dubai and she had heard from Geoff that he had a thriving practice over there. Long distance romance was never easy.

On Tuesday the aeroplane taxied along the runway. Kate wondered if she was crazy. Maybe the drug-taking in her youth had, in actual fact, caused some brain damage. But if she had been sure on Sunday of her decision, seeing Grace with Jack made her certain. It was worth the risk. Although she was glad she had submitted a portfolio of her art to a college in Dublin, just in case things went terribly wrong. At least she'd have an art course to look forward to. She walked into the Headquarters of Wynthrope Communications Inc.

"Hi." She smiled pleasantly at the receptionist. "I wonder if it is possible to speak to Richard Wynthrope?"

"Do you have an appointment?" the receptionist asked, eyeing her disdainfully from her head to her toes.

"No," she answered, twirling the button on the jacket her friend had knitted. Kate loved it, and clearly this woman did not.

"Let me take a contact number. I will ask his PA to contact you. It may be towards the end of October."

"What? It's August. No. If you could just tell him that Kate is here. It's just for a few minutes. I actually need to tell him something really important."

The receptionist looked at her as if she was stark raving mad. It felt like ground-hog day – she had difficulties dealing with receptionists once again. It seemed an appointment with the Pope would be an easier achievement.

The tipping point came when she asked what time he'd be going to lunch; that was when the receptionist asked her to leave. Fair enough, Kate thought, she was beginning to sound like a stalker. Kate slunk out of the building onto the sidewalk. She'd try his apartment, surely he had to go home at some point. She sent Grace a text for Richard's address.

To kill some time she decided to take the subway to an outlet store at the harbour and then she'd spend the remaining time in the Metropolitan Museum of Art. It would be a perfect way to while away the afternoon. She'd go to his apartment at six.

After a busy few hours exploring some of the finest works of art she had ever seen, she arrived at his building with her holdall slung across her back, carrying a couple of outlet store bags. She asked the doorman if Richard Wynthrope had arrived home yet. The man looked at her as if she was mad.

"I can't discuss residents' business with you, lady," he said.

"I only asked a simple question," she replied, with matching indignation in her voice.

"Are you Irish?"

"Yeah, and I'm wrecked tired too. I just got here, my flight landed at twelve and I've spent the afternoon wandering around the outlets and the Met. This is some city, there's never a dull moment. I love it."

He started to chuckle. He was a big, huggy-bear looking man. She reckoned he was in his mid-fifties. Kate smiled, as his whole body seemed to rock under his doorman's attire. He must be roasting in all those clothes, she thought.

"Look lady, there's a café at the end of the block. Grab yourself a coffee. If he comes along I'll tell him where you are. How's that sound?"

"Thanks a million. That'll be grand," she replied.

She found a window seat in the coffee bar. Fair play to the doorman, he could have told her to get lost like the receptionist had, she thought. After about three quarters of an hour, a limousine pulled up. A young girl climbed out. Then a man who could have been her father emerged but from the way he was putting his hand around her, he most certainly wasn't.

Another ten minutes passed until she spotted a black town car. This time she saw Richard. When the door opened he was on the phone. She grabbed her holdall and shopping bags and ran out the door and down the street. He was standing on the street talking to the doorman. That was when she saw a pair of long, slim legs appear from the car. Richard looked up the street in the direction the doorman was pointing. His face said it all. These were no ordinary pair of legs – they were the legs of the "new person" in his life. The rest of her became visible and she was stunning.

Kate stopped dead in her tracks. She turned on her heel and ran up the street. She was heartbroken. How could she be so stupid? Fuck love. She had been so high on love in the last thirty-six hours, she'd lost her grasp of reality. What in God's name had she been thinking? The most hurtful thing was the look on his face when he saw her. It was so far from what she had expected. She was so glad she had the keys to Lisa's place.

She got on the subway. It was rush hour. She was pushed and shoved around for thirty minutes. After which she walked for ten minutes to Lisa's apartment door where she dumped her bags inside and locked it again. She went to the corner store and bought a big tub of ice cream, a bottle of vodka, tonic water and chips as the Americans called them. The guy serving at the counter kept staring at her.

"Have I got something on my face?"

"No, it's cute."

She threw her eyes to heaven, paid and walked back up the street. She always loved New York, but now it was tainted. She would never come back.

Richard told Jane that he didn't feel well and asked if he could take a rain-check on the theatre. He knew she was disappointed.

"Is it something to do with that small dark-haired girl running up the street?" She spoke in such a haughty manner it irritated him.

"What girl?" he replied dismissively. "Sean will drop you home."

"Fine, see you at the office tomorrow."

He nodded as she kissed him lightly on the lips. She was beautiful, and they had been dating for a couple of months. She worked as a legal advisor for the Corporation. Brains and beauty, but she wasn't Kate.

Ten minutes later, he walked around his penthouse with his cell phone in his hand. His mother still hadn't answered. He'd try her again.

"Hi, Richard," she said in a cheery voice.

"Mom, how is everything over there?"

"Great, I'm at Sally's birthday party."

"Who is Sally?"

"Jessie's friend, Ollie's mother, you met them when you were here!"

Richard threw his eyes to heaven. "Mom, I met so many people and I can't keep up. Do you know where Kate is?"

"Grace said she was away for a few days. She's starting an art course in Dublin. Isn't that wonderful for her? She's so talented, Richard. Did you ever see her work?"

"No. I didn't know that but there's much I don't know about her. Are you sure she's in Dublin?"

"Hang on, I'll ask Grace. She's here with Jack. Oh I have so much to tell you …"

"Mom, it's okay," he cut across quickly. He could hear her laughing at the other end and trying to find Grace. Shit, he thought. "Mom, forget it. I'll talk to you tomorrow."

"I can't find her. Eoghan is looking for her."

Richard was completely exasperated. "Mom, have you been drinking?"

"Oh, just a glass or two of wine. Grace said Kate has been on such a high for the last few days. The course is something she has always wanted to do. How's em …"

"Jane," he filled in for her. "Fine, I'll call you tomorrow."

"Don't you want …"

He cut her off in mid-sentence. What was he going to do? The doorman said she was Irish. He saw her with his own eyes and yet he couldn't believe she was in New York. And what about the art course in Ireland? She had never mentioned art to him.

He poured himself a brandy and threw himself down on his trendy nubuck corner suite. He looked around. It was so different from his home with Heather and Billy. He hated suburbia. It held nothing but memories. He could never live anywhere but his beloved Manhattan. He walked over to the floor to ceiling glass wall; Central Park was in darkness. He could see the lights of the city twinkling all around it. Central Park was his backyard, the only piece of countryside he needed. He sent a text to his mother to apologise, blaming a bad connection for cutting her off.

Kate danced around the apartment to Gloria Gaynor's "I will survive". She loved that Grace's friends had loads of old music. Although, she thought, that Barbra had a lot to answer for. It was Sophia's fault for constantly playing *The Essential Barbra Streisand* when she was home. It was funny how she thought of Bayrush as Sophia being home. That bloody duet where Barbra sings with Celine Dion, "Tell Him".

"Tell him my arse," she said out loud. She was glad the doorman had been such a nice fellow. She would have been in a right pickle if she had been standing right outside the building. It was all Sophia's fault. If it hadn't been for her she would never have laid eyes on him.

*

Sophia watched as Grace and Jack danced. They looked perfect together. So happy. She wished nothing but the best for them. She thought of Bill and all the happy years they had shared. Taking a sip of her wine, she wondered what that call from Richard was about. Why had he wanted to know about Kate? He was dating a girl called Jane and it seemed that she was becoming a regular in his life.

"Would you like to dance?"

She looked up to see Eoghan standing over her with an outstretched hand. It would be rude to refuse. It was a lively number so where was the harm, she thought.

"Why thank you, I would." She felt happy. Maybe it was the wine or the atmosphere or both. Eoghan was a great dancer and she was thoroughly enjoying being led in a waltz around the floor. Then the music changed and she found herself in his arms slow dancing to Martina McBride singing Kris Kristofferson's "Help Me Make It Through the Night". It felt wonderful to be held. She was so lonely and, well, Eoghan was very attractive. God, the wine most definitely had gone to her head. She was totally absorbed in the words of the song and so was he from the way he was looking at her so intently. The moment the song ended she broke away, embarrassed by the thoughts in her head.

She sat back down at her table where Grace, Jack and a few others were bantering with one another. She noticed Eoghan didn't join them. She looked around for him and saw him leaving. She picked up her glass and took a large slug. She never drank much but tonight it had certainly gone to her head.

Grace had spent every moment of the last four days with Jack. Even while she worked, he looked after Finn. Sophia had offered to babysit to let them spend their evenings together. Grace had had butterflies in her tummy waiting for him to collect her that first night. It was like being a teenager going on a first date.

All week she had lived only for the moment, not daring to think of what the future would hold for them. And now it was over. The time had come to say goodbye.

And again Sophia had come to the rescue. She had taken Finn to visit Molly. Grace couldn't face a public goodbye at the airport so they were walking along the beach holding hands. He had virtually moved in to Rose Cottage for the last four days. The bed was going to feel so empty without him. They had no idea of what lay ahead. His divorce, his work; she knew how hard it would be to leave a successful practice and, by her recollection of Dubai, a very glamorous life behind. The weather alone was hard to beat.

What could she offer here, life in rainy Ireland with a five-month-old baby and a recession?

He stopped and looked out towards the sea. She looked at his side profile and thought how handsome he was as he watched kite surfers twirling through the air above the sea.

"I'd love to try that," he said, putting his arm around her shoulders. "When I come back it's something I'm going to do."

Would she have to wait until next summer to see him again, she wondered. He turned and taking her in his arms, he held her close and said, "I'll be back, Grace just as soon as I can. It's the only promise I can make at this moment."

With his thumb, he wiped a tear that escaped from her eye and then he kissed her where it had been, and, trailing kisses along her face, his lips found hers. She kissed him back passionately, as she could not voice the depth of her emotions.

They walked back to the house. His jeep was in the drive and it was time to go. Conor had offered to drive him to the airport. He planned to leave his jeep at his mother's house.

"Did you notice I didn't sell it?"

"Why not?"

"I suppose I hoped that there was always going to be a chance for us and now there is, so don't you give up on me, okay? I'm like Arnie – I'll be back." He laughed and hugged her. He climbed in and drove off.

She stood watching as the jeep crunched its way down the drive until moments later the brake lights flashed and he got out. Before she knew it, she was running towards him. He picked her up and swung her around as if she was no weight at all, and landing her feet back on the ground she said, for the first time in her life, "I love you," to a man and really meant it.

"I love you too." He laughed.

"Did you forget something?" she asked.

"No, but I'm glad I stopped. I was going to tell you first but you beat me to it."

She laughed and said, "I'm a true feminist." She kissed him again. "Go before I want to drag you back inside."

"Promises, promises! See you soon on Skype, honey."

She could only nod as she watched the jeep disappear. She walked towards the oak tree in the middle of the garden and sat on the rope swing hanging from its branches. There was nothing she could do but wait and hope that somehow they'd find a way to be together.

But as she swung back and forth she couldn't stop the negative thoughts from creeping in. Nobody can have it all, life just wasn't like that, nor was she foolish enough to think that he'd give up everything he had worked for to come back to a place he had wanted to leave so badly twenty years ago. "Oh stop, Grace," she said out loud. "I'll always have beautiful memories of these last four days."

Chapter Eighteen

*J*essie's mind was working overtime as she cantered to the sounds of the birds wakening and the lake water lapping gently against the shore. Losing her baby boys had brought her on a journey, forcing her to open up to new ways of thinking. She had read many books, way beyond what she used to. The experience had made her see the world more clearly and she realised that only she could change her destiny. She could choose to remain in a dark hole or choose to live her best life. Over the past while she had being brewing an idea that she intended to share with two people who were very important to her, the Fitzgerald girls.

She was so happy for Grace. She had finally found "the one". And Finn was getting stronger with each passing day. The only blot on the horizon was that Jack couldn't get out of his partnership in Dubai yet. Kate had confided about her disastrous trip to New York, but at least she had followed her heart, even though it hadn't work out. Kate's art course was going well, so who knew what the future held for her?

Jessie had liked Richard. Geoff had eventually told her about his wife and son. She couldn't imagine what he must have gone through. It also made her realise that everybody had a story. And poor Sophia had had more than her fair share of loss.

She hosed down Caesar and spent the rest of the morning tidying around the yard before going inside to prepare Sunday lunch. Ten minutes later she heard a car outside. She felt strangely nervous. What if they didn't like her idea? Would she do it anyway?

"Where's my lunch?" Kate called, coming in the back door and pinching Jessie in the sides.

"If you're not careful you won't be getting any," Jessie laughed.

"You're mad having us for lunch; you get so little time off," Grace remarked, placing a chocolate cake and treats for Sam on the kitchen counter. "Where is the little man?"

"Geoff brought him to a gymkhana. So it's just me, and now that Kate won't be around so much I thought I'd cook for her today, even though she drives me nuts when she is here." Jessie laughed when Kate punched her gently.

"I always knew you'd miss me the most."

"That's pushing it," said Jessie, bending down to gush at Finn in his carry-tot. "He's getting so big, you little cutie."

They sat around the butcher block table chatting and laughing. It was lovely that everybody was in such good form. Over coffee Jessie finally broached the subject.

"Girls, you know I've being doing courses and workshops and how interested I am in looking at things in a different way."

"Yeah," they both chorused. Kate started to yawn dramatically.

"Just listen ... how did I manage to land two cynics for friends?"

"We keep you grounded." Grace laughed. "Okay, on with the story." Grace winked at Kate.

"Grace, Kate ... me and Geoff, we need to create another source of income. Livery isn't cheap and with the numbers dwindling, we have to come up with other ideas. I'd like to blend some of my new experiences with work here at the yard. I'd like your opinion about converting the old barn into training rooms and making the outbuildings into self-catering units?"

"Well, I've always said agriculture and tourism are our greatest strengths," said Grace. "And you have a great location, with the woods, beach and mountains all nearby. When you say blend ... explain?"

"Oooo she's sounding all official now. Next she'll be looking for a business plan," said Kate.

"I will too," said Grace. "Go on, Jessie."

"I'd like to start with two units to see if there is an uptake, but ultimately I would love to have a training venue where we could host workshops and have more people stay on site."

"Like art therapy?" said Kate, enthusiastically.

"Shush Kate, let Jessie explain," said Grace.

"Exactly, and other workshops like yoga, meditation, Reiki, bereavement counselling, kinesiology, reflexology, but also gardening, photography, art classes ..."

"Who would host them?"

"I'd invite people who are specialists in their fields. They could stay free and at first people could come and stay in the area but eventually I hope to provide enough self-catering that people can stay on site. Also there is enough land to provide space for camping and caravanning or build log cabins, and local people could attend, of course."

"But how do you plan to make an income?"

"I was thinking the workshops would be held in the winter months. And I would let the apartments out in the summer to families and couples."

"Why are you so keen about a training centre?"

Jessie sighed and said, "I'd love to provide a place where every other weekend there was something different happening. Since losing the babies my mind has been opened, and I've landed in places I never thought I would go to. I've gained something."

"Now you're talking airy fairy again," said Grace, "If you plan to go to a bank and put yourself and your family under more financial pressure than you already are, you'd better get your head out of the clouds."

"God, sis, you can be brutal at times," said Kate, getting up to refill the kettle.

"Jessie, I'm not saying it's a bad idea, but you need to be clear about what you want."

Jessie put her head in her hands and said, "I am clear, but I can't explain it properly. I have so many ideas and plans but it all gets muddled up. Let's change the subject, I'm feeling like my bubble has been burst."

"I'm really sorry, Jess," said Grace, "but you already work the rounds of the clock."

"Look I'm no business brain," said Kate, "but I like the sound of your idea and I've seen you working with the special needs kids who come here on Saturdays for their riding lessons. I'd image that a family with a child with needs would love to spend longer here. And if there were a few units and a large space indoors and outdoors to play, sure wouldn't they have a ball?"

"But Kate, that would cost a fortune! There would be fire regulations and disability access needed and all kinds of costs," said Grace.

"I'm just saying ..." said Kate, wanting to make Jessie feel better.

"Let's forget about it for the moment," said Jessie. She had had enough. She had hoped for a much better reception. Grace was right. They didn't have that kind of money; the only thing she could do was play the lotto and dream.

As Grace walked back to her car she looked around. The sun was setting behind the oak trees whose branches were beginning to lose their leaves. She heard a horse neighing and walked towards the American barn where the horses' heads perched out over the stable doors. It was here that Jack had kissed her for the first time. It was only two weeks since he had gone back to Dubai but she missed him – so much at times she couldn't breathe.

Looking at the bales of hay and shavings, she realised how expensive it was to keep all the animals fed, bedded and vetted. It was a way of life, not a job, she thought. The McGraths worked twenty-four seven and they didn't complain about it. Jessie considered she was lucky to be working with horses. It had always been her passion. But since losing the babies she had changed in many ways. She so desperately wanted to do something worthwhile. Jessie was laughing again which was a huge relief and now she was dreaming. Grace wouldn't fault her for that. Hadn't she herself visualised that, one day, big beautiful cruise liners would anchor in the harbour and bay of Bayrush, and it had happened. She would do all in her power to help Jessie make her dream come true. Grace was already bringing groups to Bayrush for golf and fishing. She'd do some research into the activities Jessie had mentioned. She patted Caesar's nose and then turned and walked towards the lake where the derelict barn and outhouses Jessie had been talking about were located.

"Hi Aisling, thanks for coming out here to meet me," said Jessie, resting the pitchfork she'd been cleaning out a stable with against the wall. "We'll take a walk down to the lake and the old buildings and I'll talk you through what I'm thinking of."

"Sounds good," said Aisling. She had worked in complementary therapy for twenty years and had told Jessie she was intrigued by her idea and would like to visit the site.

It was a week since Grace had grilled Jessie about her idea. It had spurred Jessie on to research and talk to people to gather opinions.

Aisling had been a lifeline in Jessie's dark times and she valued her opinion dearly. She also appreciated how pragmatic she was, being a trained psychologist but also seeing the benefits of alternative therapies. It was all about blending. That was Jessie's guiding line – to use the best of all worlds. Every day she woke up with more ideas. She'd ring Grace and say things like, "What about growing a vegetable garden to teach kids about plants?" Then. "How about an adventure park for team building?" and "Maybe we'll have a variety of cookery classes." She was driving Grace crazy. She needed to steady up and focus.

The two women walked along the lane towards the site until the view of the lake appeared in the distance.

"What do you think?" asked Jessie, bursting with anticipation for Aisling's initial reaction.

"The view is fabulous, and I love all the old stonework and even how it forms a natural courtyard, but Jessie, it will cost a fortune."

Two emotions flashed through her; elation and disappointment collided.

"Look Aisling, let's pretend I won the lotto. Look at the possibilities of what we could achieve here."

"In that case I see endless opportunities. You could have a large training room in the barn, and smaller therapy rooms for hire on a daily basis to a variety of therapists, acupuncturists, reflexology, massage, kinesiology, life-coaching and many more. You'd be amazed by what's out there and because you'll have accommodation, people from all over the world could come and stay on site presenting their therapies. Wow, it's really peaceful here," she said, looking across the lake with the mountains as a backdrop. She took out the dousing rods Jessie had asked her to bring and began to walk around the site checking for radon lines. After a few minutes, she said, "It's completely clear."

"And that's a good thing. Now all I need is a lotto win," laughed Jessie.

"Dreams do come true, Jessie. If you really want something and believe in it – it can happen."

Thank God I didn't bring Grace today, thought Jessie. If she saw me walking around with someone with dousing rods she'd have me checked in.

Later that evening she rang Fr. Jim, who had been so helpful and kind. She had discovered he hosted workshops all around Ireland using beautifully carved wooden pieces to explain how people processed emotional issues. She was so excited she could hardly sleep for thinking of all the wonderful workshops and therapies that could help people, and it could happen in her beloved Bayrush.

Sophia stretched her legs. She was sitting in her armchair in the upstairs living room reading to the sounds of Grace's keyboard clinking. She had watched as Grace and Jack had fallen head over heels and worried about where it was all going to end. Every evening after Grace settled Finn, Grace went online to chat with Jack, and then Sophia would hear the sounds of her keyboard as she went back to her writing. Grace had confided in Sophia that writing had kept her sane while she was pregnant.

Sophia smiled when she saw Grace glance at her phone again; she was worse than a teenager making sure her phone was nearby at all times. If it wasn't all so heartbreaking it would be funny, thought Sophia.

She picked up her book to resume reading just as her own cell phone rang. She smiled when she saw the name on the screen.

"Are you free tomorrow? I managed to get a loan of the sailboat again."

"Oh Eoghan, I'm sorry but I'm going back to New York tomorrow."

"Oh, you never mentioned it." He sounded so disappointed. "Another time, eh! Safe journey!" And the phone went dead.

She sat looking at the phone. Had she imagined it or was Eoghan a little put out with her for not telling him she was going back sooner?

A few days later, Grace invited Jessie over to Rose Cottage to chat about her idea.

"And I thought you had dismissed it out of hand," said Jessie, dropping into the comfortable couch placed perfectly with a view of the beach.

"I spoke to an event manager, she believes that there may be a niche market for what you plan to offer with both companies for team building and even hen parties looking for something different."

"Hen parties!!!"

"Massage, yoga, trying out pottery or art, total switch-off stuff."

"What happened to Learner driver signs and nurses' outfits …?"

"You'd be amazed at how the market has changed."

"Clearly I am."

"Anyway, all I am saying is that your idea could be viable if you research, focus and draw up a business plan. There are grants available specifically for tourism and because you also want the local community to benefit from what you want to create, they may look kindly towards it. Jessie, you've been running a successful business for ten years. That will stand to you when you go to talk to these people."

"So, you definitely didn't dismiss it."

"I never dismiss anything you say. I have great faith in you, I've been thinking about it nonstop, so much so that I'd like to write a story about it, maybe we might even get some publicity if I could get it published."

"Oh wow Grace, wouldn't that be fantastic?" Jessie jumped up. "I'm so excited. I have so much I want to tell you that there might even be enough for a novel. And the way you write you could make a romantic story out of it, just like you used to when we were young."

"Oh Jess …"

"No, Grace. I know you think I'm crazy sometimes but listen to me, you could do it."

Grace laughed. "Now who's encouraging who!"

"Try, give it a shot. Humour me."

"Okay, you're on, and if I can do it, I promise any money made from it will go to funding the project."

"Okay, I want a novel from you, not a short story. We need money and publicity."

"You're a hard taskmaster. I brought you over here today to tell you what I wanted you to do, not the other way around."

"We're in this together, partner. Two heads are better than one," said Jessie, laughing.

"Let's contact an architect. You need to apply for planning permission and now that Dirk has decided to buy me out of the house, I'll have some money to invest too. That is if you and Geoff agree."

"Wow Grace, that would be fantastic," said Jessie, hugging her.

"It isn't much Jess, now that the market has deflated."

"I don't care, Grace. The fact that you believe in me and the idea is enough."

Jessie's excitement was infectious. She was walking around the room talking nonstop, ideas flowing from her.

"Jess, slow down, give me a chance to write down all you're saying," laughed Grace, turning back to the computer.

"Hurry up so. Partner," she said, whooping with delight.

October had rolled in and Rose Cottage was quiet since Jack and Sophia had left. With Kate gone to Dublin, Grace was often lonely. The season had ended, leaving a gap in her otherwise crazy life, so she was thankful to have her writing. Most evenings, after her nightly call to Jack, she wrote. She lost herself in her characters and their stories, not knowing where they would lead her to next. It was fun and it filled the lonely evenings.

It would have been so much harder and too expensive to talk everyday had it not been for the internet. But sometimes it was difficult to look at Jack and not be able to touch him. Lynda, his wife, was making things difficult since her affair had ended. She was becoming increasingly bitter. She had even refused to sign the divorce papers, and Jack was getting stressed out by it all. Grace signed in; he was already online, waiting for her.

"Hey there," he smiled, "how's the little man? Is he all tucked up?"

"Fast asleep already." She smiled; she loved that he always asked after Finn. She heard his doorbell.

"Sorry about this, I'm not expecting anyone," he said, getting up. "I won't be a sec."

"No probs," she replied, looking into the living room of his rented apartment. It was so bland, she thought, and then she heard a woman's raised voice.

"I won't sign those fucking papers. You're trying to cut me out. Only for me that business of yours would be nothing. Nothing. It was my contacts. Me – I'm the one who made you here."

"Lynda, can you please calm down? Let the solicitors handle it, okay? I told you I'm not speaking with you unless there is a solicitor present. I've had enough."

Grace was frozen to the spot. She felt like a voyeur.

Lynda marched into the living room. "What have we here?" she said, staring into the computer. "So you're the little Irish whore! Rana told me about her," she screamed at Jack. She came up closer to the screen and hissed. "You're the one in the photograph I found in his pocket. I have evidence that he's been seeing you all the time we've been married."

Her face was distorted-looking she was so close. Grace was shaking. The woman was crazy.

"What the hell are you talking about? Get out of my apartment. Don't speak to Grace like that!" said Jack. Grace had never heard him so angry.

"Jack, I'll talk to you later," Grace said and clicked off before Lynda could say another word. Her stomach was in turmoil. No wonder Jack was so stressed. What photograph? She went to the drinks cabinet and poured herself a brandy. Why did everything have to be so complicated for them? She flopped onto the sofa.

The computer blipped. She was still so shaken she was afraid to go near it. But then she thought of Jack. How must Jack feel? She got up and pressed the keys.

"I'm so sorry, Grace. I can't believe she's dragging your name into it."

"What photograph is she talking about, Jack?"

"The one we had taken in the photograph booth in Bayrush twenty years ago. I gave you two and kept two."

"We were kids, for God's sake," said Grace, remembering the day vividly. She had treasured hers and had them in her bedside locker. "And you kept them all these years?"

He nodded. "I thought I'd lost them but she must have taken them. Oh Grace, this is all just one hell of a crazy mess. She plans on naming you in the divorce …"

Grace shook her head in disbelief. "What does she want, Jack?"

He put his head down and muttered, "She wants to get back together."

Grace sat in silence. Confused. Was that what he wanted, she wondered? Terrified, she asked, "Jack, what do you want?"

"I don't want your name dragged through muck. She's bad-mouthing me everywhere. What she is saying isn't true. If it continues it will affect the business and I wouldn't be able to attract anyone to buy my share. Abdul doesn't have the finance to buy me out."

She sighed. "I don't know what to say, Jack. When you told me she was bitter I had no idea how much. I'll understand if you want to go back to her. Maybe the truth is that we were never meant to be. Our timing ... well our timing has always been lousy." She smiled through the tears she was desperately trying to hide. "Goodbye Jack ..."

"Wait ..." he said, stretching in towards the screen, but she had already clicked the button off.

The tears streamed down her face. Her mobile rang – Jack's photo appeared. She ignored it. What was the point? It was too complicated. It was over. She went to her room and threw herself down on the bed. Who would have thought that a stupid picture taken in a photo booth could cause this heartbreak? She sobbed into the pillow.

Sophia was already seated in one of New York's finest restaurants when Richard and Jane arrived. She must be important for him to want to formally introduce her. The girl was stunning. Tall with blond bobbed hair and by all accounts she had brains to match her beauty. Sophia could see the attraction for him. Her son was terribly intelligent; sometimes it made him rather dry and serious.

She stood up as they approached and for the first time in a long while she was glad of her height. It's true what they say about making judgments about people within the first thirty seconds of meeting them. Instinctively Sophia did not like this girl. It was going to be a long evening.

Richard was even more stilted than normal. Jane oozed confidence. She had every right to, but it was too much. She was brusque with the waiters as if she was doing them a favour by honouring them with her presence.

Oh beam me up, Scottie, Sophia thought and began to smile. Richard asked, "Is everything okay, Mother?"

"Yes, of course. Could you both excuse me for a moment, please?"

She made her way to the restroom. It was Kate's voice that had popped into her head. She used to say "beam me up" when she wanted to get out of something. If Richard was making plans this was going to be the biggest mistake of his life and all she could do was watch and wait.

She pushed open the door. Thankfully the restroom was empty. She stood looking at her image in the mirror. Next month it would be two years since Bill's death. She had never wanted to be with anyone else, not that the opportunity hadn't arisen over the years for both of them but she had never been tempted and neither had Bill. She knew that absolutely, which made her feel worse about what had happened between her and Eoghan recently. If she were honest it was the reason she had left Ireland so suddenly. No wonder he had been curt with her on the phone. Her face flushed at the thought. Maybe Richard was like her ... lonely. She'd have to accept his choice but the truth was she wished it was Kate.

She had to get through this evening. She would talk to Richard privately; maybe then she could ascertain the depth of it all. She touched up her already perfect make-up.

Was she turning into an interfering mother?

Richard knew from the moment he introduced them that it was a disaster. How could he possibly think that his lively, passionate mother could connect with Jane? She was Ivy League. His mother was a mixture of everything, not least Italian.

Sometimes he wondered where his temperament fitted. His father had been a gregarious, outgoing man, the life and soul of a party. Richard possessed none of the traits he so loved in other people. The problem was that those types didn't like to be around him so much.

Why shouldn't he settle now? Jane was easy to get along with and the sex was good. What more did he want? There wasn't a man in the room who wouldn't want to be with her. His mother would have to get over it, but it felt like the longest dinner of his life.

Afterwards Sean, his driver, dropped his mother at her building on Park Avenue and continued to his place. He stood beside Jane as the lift took them to his penthouse; there was an obvious distance between them. He offered her a drink. She accepted a vodka martini. He poured himself a large brandy.

"Your mother is very nice," she remarked, from where she sat on the couch.

"Yes, she is," he said, handing her the crystal glass. He sat in the armchair opposite.

"She's very protective of you."

"That's what they do!"

"Cindy invited us to the Hamptons this weekend. I was hoping you could join us."

He noted the change of subject. He always feigned work as an excuse to get out of things he didn't want to do but it was becoming increasingly difficult because Jane knew his schedule. He had noticed she was particularly warm to Colleen, his personal assistant. It hadn't bothered him until now. She walked towards him and straddled his lap. This Ivy League girl often surprised him with her forwardness. She never had a problem initiating. He wasn't in the mood. He didn't react. He wondered fleetingly what was wrong with him.

"I'm sorry ..." He made to move. She was highly offended. It was alien to somebody as beautiful as her to be rejected. She was too much of a lady to rant but he could see she was doing all in her power not to lose control. In that moment he knew he was wasting his time. Jane was the wrong woman. And the truth was if his mother had even slightly encouraged him he had been prepared to pop the question, to get it out of the way.

She picked up her jacket and walked out the door – slamming it behind her. He turned on the TV. He could get the sports results now, in comfort. But why did images of a petite, black-haired, smiling Irish girl keep popping into his head, he wondered? "Shit."

Grace woke to the sound of the doorbell ringing. She jumped up, fully clothed, and realised she must have fallen asleep. Glancing at the alarm clock, she saw that it read one a.m. Finn lay fast asleep in his cot next to her bed. She rushed downstairs, wondering who would call at this hour. Peering through the peephole, she saw Jessie.

"What is God's name are you doing here?" she asked, swinging the door wide open.

"Why didn't you answer your phone? I've been trying it and so has Jack. He's worried sick about you. He rang to ask me to come over to check on you," said Jessie, following her into the kitchen where Grace began to fill the kettle.

"It's never straightforward for me, Jessie. I'm a disaster when it comes to men. I don't know why I never learn. I shouldn't have allowed him into my life. I'm such a fool." She slumped onto the stool.

"Grace, he's worried sick about you. Please just ring and tell him you're okay and that you'll talk tomorrow. Everything will seem better in daylight. I don't know what's going on but I do know he really loves you and that has to be worth fighting for."

She picked up Grace's phone and handed it to her. Reluctantly Grace texted Jack to say she'd talk to him in the morning. Seconds later a reply came. It had a big X on it.

Jessie smiled. "Grace, you'll work it out together. I know you said Lynda was giving him a hard time."

"Oh Jess, you won't believe what happened earlier." She began to tell Jessie. Jessie, being Jessie, had her smiling about it by the time she got to the end of the story.

"Imagine he actually kept the photos. That is just so sweet," said Jessie, getting up to put her mug in the dishwasher. "Now get some sleep." She squeezed Grace's shoulders as she walked towards the door.

"Thanks, Jess," Grace called from the doorway as Jessie got into the jeep.

Chapter Nineteen

*I*t was a Friday evening in November and Kate was driving home through a fog listening to "The Coronas". She was two months into her art course and loving every minute of it.

She had bundles of energy day and night, so much that she had volunteered at a drug rehab centre in Dublin. They were very open to her ideas around art helping with the healing process.

Grace had been right when she had said that the quickest way to mend your heart was to work at something you love, but it hadn't stopped Kate hoping that someday she would meet Richard again. When she eventually saw the "Welcome to Bayrush" sign she felt the familiar pang for home. She was really looking forward to catching up with the girls over the weekend. She couldn't afford the petrol money to come home too often.

"Thank you, George," said Sophia, alighting from the black limousine outside of Wynthrope Communications Inc headquarters. She walked through the circular glass doors and was greeted immediately by the receptionist. "Good morning, Mrs Wynthrope, it's so nice to see you."

"Why, thank you," she said, walking straight to the lift which went directly to Richard's floor. When the doors opened she noticed he had redecorated. It was three years since she had last visited his floor. She'd been to board meetings, but after retiring she and Bill had taken a back seat, leaving all of the decision-making to Richard. She hadn't seen him since that awful dinner and she was anxious to talk to him. He was avoiding her calls and she knew it. She hoped to either take him to lunch or order in.

"Hello Mrs Wynthrope, how are you?" said Colleen, smiling warmly. Colleen had been with the company for fifteen years and had been Richard's personal assistant for the past ten.

"I'm fabulous thanks, and you? I hope he's treating you well," Sophia smiled.

"He's a gent! But don't tell him I said that. Is he expecting you. He never said."

"No, I thought I'd surprise him. Surely he eats!"

"On the run most of the time," laughed Colleen, "but I can fix it for you. Let me juggle his timetable."

"I always knew I could count on you," said Sophia, sitting in one of the comfortable armchairs opposite Colleen's large desk.

"He's in a meeting at the moment," she said, nodding her sandy-coloured head in the direction of the walnut door.

"That's grand. It will give us time to catch up."

"You've even picked up the local lingo," said Colleen. Both Colleen's parents were Irish; her father hailed from Donegal and her mother from Cork. "Did you enjoy Ireland?"

"Oh Colleen, it's wonderful. I know it rains a lot but it's truly beautiful."

"I'm hoping to bring my daughter there some day. I'd like her to see where her grandparents came from."

"Speaking of which, how is Fay? She must be eight or nine now ..."

"Eight, well do you want the long or the short version?"

"I've all the time in the world."

Colleen began to pour her heart out about how Fay had recently been diagnosed with both dyspraxia and a speech and language disorder. Sophia could hardly believe her ears; she felt as though she had been guided to come here today as she listened intently to Colleen. "There's huge awareness about dyslexia, but dyspraxia is little known and so hard to explain. People often correct me by saying 'don't you mean dyslexia?'."

As Sophia listened, she thought Colleen could have been talking about Billy. Her grandson had experienced all of the same difficulties, lack of co-ordination, poor social skills, talking off point, but he had also had a huge empathy and gentleness of nature, and an ability to do almost anything as long as the task was explained in more detail.

"Mrs Wynthrope, mostly people with dyspraxia are of average to above average intelligence and the evidence suggests that they become early school leavers because they begin to believe they are stupid and just don't 'get it' like others do. I'm sorry, I'm on a rant."

"Colleen, will you please call me Sophia?"

"I know, but it's hard to break the habit. I'll blame my mother." She laughed. Her face was round and jovial with a smattering of freckles across the bridge of her nose. And although she was born and bred in New York, she sounded Irish at times.

"Richard's son was diagnosed with dyspraxia ..."

"I knew that. I suppose that's why I feel I can talk to you. I remember Heather being so worried. She told me about it one day when she was particularly upset. She was such a wonderful mother. Oh God, I'm sorry I'm upsetting you."

"It's good to talk, Colleen. Maybe you should get in touch with an association or go online. I'm sure there are lots of other parents out there looking for answers and finding solutions."

"Sometimes I'm too exhausted to know where to begin."

"It's not easy working full-time and bringing up a family."

The walnut door opened and Richard emerged, smartly dressed in a light grey suit. He was accompanied by a small, rotund man in his fifties whom Sophia didn't recognise, and a tall, dark-haired woman whose age was hard to tell. It *was* New York, thought Sophia.

Richard was surprised to see her but hid it well amidst the fond farewell handshakes. They both acknowledged her as they left through the glass doors.

"Hi Mom, this is a surprise," he said, kissing her cheek.

"Lunch?" she enquired.

"You should have called. I'm flat out."

Looking sheepish, Colleen called from her desk, "You have an hour."

"Are you two plotting?" He smiled, knowing how fond his mother was of Colleen.

"Would we?" Colleen feigned innocence, adding, "Will I order in?"

"Perfect, surprise us," said Sophia, leading Richard back into his large corner office. She paused and turned back to Colleen. "I'd love to meet Fay …"

Looking up from her desk, Colleen smiled and said, "I'd love that too." Colleen wrote her cell number on a yellow post-it and handed it to Sophia. "Give me a call and thank you, Sophia."

The office had a fabulous view over Manhattan and the Hudson. She went to the burgundy-coloured leather couch and made herself comfortable. "Soooo," she said.

"You're so obvious, Mother," he said, walking to the drinks cabinet and taking the crystal top from the brandy decanter. He didn't ask but simply poured two brandies into Waterford crystal tumblers. He placed one in front of Sophia and dropped into the leather armchair opposite her.

"To what do I owe the pleasure?" he asked.

"Jane was nice."

"Nice is good, I think."

"Nice is … non-descript."

"Ouch …"

"Okay, I'll give her intelligent."

"Harvard," he offered.

"Mmmm." But she sensed he was playing with her.

"Nice and intelligent, that's all you can come up with for my future wife."

Sophia was stunned; even though she had feared it, she honestly didn't think he would be so …

"Gotcha."

"Oh Richard, that's so not funny," she said, taking a gulp of brandy and then laughing.

"You're right, it isn't, and I'm not getting married, quite the opposite actually."

"Oh, what a shame!"

"Your sincerity knows no bounds, Mother."

She laughed loudly and said, "Thanks be to God."

"Do you know that you're beginning to sound more Irish than the Irish?"

"I'm sure the lads wouldn't agree with ye."

"Oh God, I can't take anymore. When are you going back?"

They were laughing when Colleen arrived with an array of delicious delights from Richard's favourite deli.

Grace sat in the rocking chair at Rose Cottage holding Finn who had fallen asleep in her arms. She looked at his little face and wondered would he ever have a brother or sister. Everybody should have a Kate, she thought, thinking of her beloved sister. She missed having her around. *Oh stop*, she told herself, *stop being so maudlin*. Ever since the awful incident with Lynda, Jack had tried his best to assure her that everything would work out. But she couldn't help worrying. He was extremely busy at work and had saved a very valuable race horse by performing a major operation on its leg. She had been pleased for him but it hadn't allayed the fears she had. How could he possibly settle back to a run of the mill life in Ireland? Stuck with her, Finn and no job and penniless because Lynda was determined to take him for all he was worth.

God, you never make it simple for me. Why couldn't I fall for somebody straightforward? she thought. Some days she wondered if she should leave everything to be with Jack like he was prepared to do for her. But how could she? Dirk was entitled to see Finn regularly. It wasn't an option. She longed to see Jack, even if it might be for the last time. It was still better than nothing. Her heart was heavy. She felt she was slowly losing him.

Jack rushed to the airport. He barely made it before they closed the gate. Since he and Grace had got together he had been back to his whirlwind life, Paris for the Priz de L'Arc, Melbourne for the Melbourne Cup. Abdul had been extremely good to him, allowing him some space when his marriage had fallen apart. And just when they were making it to the top in Dubai he wanted to leave. He couldn't blame Abdul for being upset.

How many hours and days had he spent on aeroplanes over the past twenty years, he wondered as he put the head phones on, just as Michael Bublé sang, "I just wanna go home". Jack wondered where in the hell was his "home". Where had it ever been?

Things had been stilted with Grace since the Lynda episode. Trying to communicate over the phone, text, email and Skype was difficult, especially when he could see all that he was missing. He couldn't explain that. Sometimes he'd say he had to go even when he hadn't.

He was exhausted and fell asleep with the earphones on.

Around two a.m. Grace woke startled. She could hear the sound pebbles crunching under the wheels of a car. She got up, filled with terror, and peeped around the curtains. She could hardly believe the sight before her. Jack was getting out of his silver jeep. But he hadn't said he was coming. Being such a sceptic she was terrified. Was he here to break up with her – face to face? Why did she have to analyse everything? Why couldn't she just run out and jump into his arms and worry about the consequences after? She walked downstairs slowly and opened the door, shaking with trepidation.

He was already walking across the drive. His face was pale and drawn and he had lost weight. But it was the look in his beautiful eyes that said everything. She knew it was going to be okay. He smiled and she walked into his arms before he got inside.

"Hey, honey, I'm home." he said into her hair. "So you better let me in."

She touched his face tenderly. "You look exhausted. Are you hungry?"

"Only for you." She threw her head back and laughed.

"Jeez that works with all the other women," he joked. "Boil the kettle so while I take a peek at the little man."

She began to make paninis and tea, chuffed that he wanted to see Finn. In that act alone she loved him more than words could ever say.

Climbing into bed she cuddled into him and both of them slept like babies. He was home, even if they only had seventy-two hours before he left again.

She woke to the sight of Jack with Finn in his arms. "Look at those brave lads. Up, up. Wow. Are you going to be a little kite surfer, eh? I'm going to give it a go. They're a hardy bunch all the same. It's the end of November."

She laughed. "I'm not letting you out of my sight. Come here."

He leaned down and kissed her. "Will we walk up to Bonita's for a dirty big fry-up?"

"I can make you one."

"Ah no, let's just chillax and have it handed to us. We can walk it off us then. God, I love that beach even on a winter's day. Let's buy a house around here."

"Jack, it'll be a long time before either of us can afford a house around here." She felt awful but she couldn't tell him that the house was in Finn's name. She had promised Sophia that her secret was safe with her. "You really are considering a life here again!"

"I am doing my best to come up with a solution." He sat on the bed next to her while Finn gurgled in his arms. "It might mean commuting but Grace I'm not going anywhere. You and Finn are my life now. You have to start believing that."

"What about Lynda?"

"I have made it abundantly clear that there will be no reconciliation. Also Rana, Abdul's wife, reminded her that it was she who had an affair and although they are friends she would stand as a witness to that. Rana is convinced as soon as Lynda finds a new man she'll sign the papers."

"Jack." She didn't quite know how to say it. "Jack, em, I've never been … well … keen on marriage …"

He looked at her in amazement. "You were engaged when I met you."

"I know but … well it wasn't really by choice."

"Did he put a gun to your head?" He smiled.

She laughed, "It's just not important to me. All I want is a real commitment. Rings and bits of paper well … what are they worth … mine ended in a mess and well, so did yours. I just want to be with you. So if she never signs the papers, so what?"

"Well. I'll be damned and I thought you were an old-fashioned girl," he said, putting Finn back into his cot.

"Come here," she said, pulling him onto the bed. "Breakfast can wait."

Sophia sat on a park bench in Central Park with Colleen. "Thanks for agreeing to meet."

"I was delighted you rang and that you're interested in learning more about dyspraxia. It's lonely, sometimes I feel I'm the only mother in the world with this worry."

Sophia just nodded in agreement.

As Sophia listened to Colleen she watched Fay and her two cousins and noticed how difficult the little girl found the climbing frame. She couldn't manage the swing at all and in the end she had retreated to the sand pit.

"Do you see the stepping stones? They are impossible. Because she is so badly co-ordinated she can't play hopscotch or skip. All of this excludes her. When it comes to board games she can't understand the rules or turn-taking so she ends up annoying people. The professionals use words like auditory processing problems, spatial awareness challenges, and wait for this: proprioceptive problem. I'd never heard of some of those words." Colleen let out a big sigh and added, "She's always the one on the outside. I know I should be grateful, look at her, she's beautiful, kind and so loving, but why does it have to be so hard?"

"Okay, I'm hearing all the challenges and I saw it first hand with Heather and Billy, but let's look at what interventions are successful. What has helped?"

"Occupational therapy certainly helps. And there are a few books and manuals written about dyspraxia. These have certainly helped me get a handle on it. Since Fay started the exercises a few weeks ago I've seen improvements already."

"So you're saying it's not that Fay can't do things, she just needs more time to have things explained to her."

"Exactly, but can you imagine how embarrassed she'd be if I went over and showed her how to swing in front of the other kids or where to step next on the climbing frame?"

"But that's what you'll have to do."

"I have done it. But the last time I was here a woman remarked snidely, 'has she never been to a park before?' I could have cried. After that Fay made me promise not to help again. The hidden handicap, DCD, dyspraxia, clumsy child syndrome, are all names given to the same condition. I know that it's not as bleak as other difficulties but it's so frustrating for her. I've been advised to make sure to build her self-esteem because, if not, it will become a psychiatric problem. And as I've already told you, school dropout rates are very high across the world for teens with this condition." Colleen's eyes had filled but she got up and went over to Fay. "Will I give you a push on the swing, pet?" Fay nodded.

Fay reminded Sophia so much of Billy. She remembered vividly the day Heather had cried when she came back from seeing him off on his school tour. None of the kids had wanted to sit with him on the bus. Sophia had cried that evening thinking of her grandson.

"What would you like to see for Fay in the future?" she asked Colleen, joining her at the swing.

"More public awareness of the condition. I'd love to talk to other mothers and maybe find a place to meet where kids with dyspraxia could socialise with other children doing activities where the steps can be broken down to suit their ability to learn. I always tell Fay you can do it. It just takes you a little longer than others."

Later, as they walked through the park towards the exit nearest her building, Sophia's mind was working overtime. The three girls were busy enjoying the ice-creams Sophia had bought them. What about creating a place where families could holiday together and take part in fun activities with instructors who appreciate the challenges the kids and teens have? She wasn't going to make any idle promises until she was sure about what she could contribute. She turned towards Colleen and said, "Thanks for meeting me with Fay today. She's a wonderful child, so pleasant and mannerly."

"She has brought us so much joy."

Seeing the look of sadness sweep across Sophia's face, Colleen hugged her and said, "I know how much they meant to you. They were two very special people."

Sophia couldn't speak. Instead she nodded and called, "Goodbye," to the girls and left before the tears came.

With just ten days to go to Christmas, Sophia sat on a chaise longue reading the newspaper with her half-moon reading glasses perched on the end of her nose. She heard the front door opening.

She took off her glasses and smiled. "Hi Richard, this is a surprise."

"Yes, I thought I'd stop by to say hello. Are you leaving soon?" Richard asked.

"Not until Friday ..."

"Oh, I thought it was sooner. I was thinking I might join you. I could do with a break."

She raised her eyebrows in disbelief and then said, "That would be wonderful. Did I mention Eoghan, Nora, Molly and I are off to Europe in April? We're going to drive and stay wherever we fancy."

"You still haven't told them?" His tone was accusing.

"No, I haven't," she answered, equally forcefully.

"So you're going to keep this up forever?"

"I will tell who I want when I want, Richard. Eoghan is planning this trip. I am certainly not going to ruin it for him."

"You have been to nearly every city in Europe. Have you told them that?" She didn't answer. "So you're going to stay in crap hotels all over Europe just because you can't tell your friends the truth!"

"Richard, you are such a snob. It doesn't matter where I stay. In actual fact it's none of your business."

"Fine! Don't call me when you've been robbed or mugged because you stayed in the wrong part of town."

"Did you come here to have a row? Well today is not a good day for one. I am choosing to live my life the way that I want to. Can you say the same?"

That was low. Almost as soon as she said it she regretted it. He turned on his heel and slammed the door in his wake.

"I am so sorry," she said, into the empty space.

Richard was so angry with her. But why had he antagonised her? What was going on with him? He had called because he'd changed his mind. Previously she had asked him to spend Christmas in Ireland but he told her he planned to go skiing with Jane and some friends.

His mother was right – it was her life. Who was he to tell her how to lead it? He walked through Central Park. Although it was cold the sun shone. He loved this city and he didn't know if he could leave it. But he couldn't stop thinking about Kate. Even that awful jacket she had worn the day he'd seen her in New York made him smile. He needed to hear her voice again, that husky, sexy voice, and her laugh.

Grace was on the phone while Jessie made coffee in the kitchen in Bayrush.

"That's good. I'm glad for him. Okay, we'll see you next Saturday then. I'm looking forward to catching up." She hung up.

"So who's coming? I gather there is more than Sophia from your conversation." Jessie placed the mugs on the counter.

"Richard."

"That's good news, isn't it?"

"You must be joking. Kate will be home for Christmas. She's getting her life back and now this …"

"But Gracey, if it's to be, it will be."

"Jessie, will you give me a break? She's my little sister. It's not fair. Kate doesn't fit into a box. She's a free spirit. That's who she is. He's too old for her and well he's so …"

"You sound like your mother. Listen to yourself. I'll take that back, your mother wouldn't say that. She'd say if you love somebody then it will work out. Better to have loved and lost then never have loved at all."

"What did you do before you came out today? Swallow a book full of meaningless quotes!"

"I'll have you know those are fabulous words of wisdom that I am spouting."

"Well, if you're not going to talk sense, don't bother talking at all."

"Are you pregnant again? Is that why you're getting so … contrary?"

Grace laughed. Jessie, she was so "live and let live" these days.

"Welllllll …"

"No, of course I'm not pregnant. The cheek of you."

"Look Gracey, on a serious note don't stand in the way. Don't lie to Kate. You don't have to say Richard is coming."

"You're right, Jessie. Maybe she won't be around. I think she's dating one of the guys on the art course. She doesn't say too much. But I have a feeling there's something going on. He's younger than her. Talk about extremes but that's Kate for you."

"She might as well. If it was the guy I met the last time I wouldn't blame her. He was cute."

"Yeah, if you're into scruffy looking, arty types!"

"Jeez, I pity poor Finn. He'll have his work cut out with you as his mum. Nobody will get past the front door."

"Look who's talking!"

They both laughed.

Chapter Twenty

S o, how's everybody?" Sophia asked as Richard brought the suitcases in from the car.

"Do you have a couple of hours?" Grace replied, smiling. "I'll start with my news, Finn has regular check-ups and the doctors are very pleased with his progress. It's hard to believe he's nine months already. And Jack is home for Christmas, he'll be back shortly. He's picking Finn up from Dirk. He and Abdul have taken on another partner so he still commutes but he's in Europe more often. It's not ideal but we're getting there."

"My goodness that all sounds ... very civilised."

"Dirk's happy I'm in a relationship because ... guess what ... he's getting married. I wanted to save the news to see the look on your face."

"OMG, to the French girl?"

Grace nodded. "Sophia, I couldn't be happier for him because ... even better, he's offered to buy my share of the house. Alleluia," said Grace, doing a twirl around the kitchen. Sophia and Richard laughed. "And I'm busy with Ireland for Real. Cel Cruise, the company Kate secured for us, will arrive here in April for the first time."

"Speaking of Kate, how is she?" Richard asked quickly.

Grace exchanged a knowing look with Sophia as Richard busied himself fiddling with the sugar bowl. "Great, she's in the middle of an art course in Dublin. She intends to study art therapy next."

"I wondered ... is she around?" He continued playing with the sugar bowl.

"I'm not sure, you know Kate, she's a wander-luster."

"A what?"

"That's what I call her. The wander-luster, she comes and goes as she pleases. I suppose you Americans would call it a free spirit."

Sophia spluttered and intervened. "How's Jessie?"

"Oh Sophia, we are working on a project together."

"Really?" Sophia perked up. "What kind of project?"

"Jessie and Geoff are planning to build self-catering holiday houses down by the lake around the old barn. It will be for tourists, but she plans to offer a range of speciality weekends of all kinds. Anything from art and craft classes to angel therapy. Where would Jessie be without the angels?"

Sophia was intrigued. Maybe they would allow her to become involved. This might be the something that she had been looking for. "They have helped me along my way too."

"I've never heard you talk about angels." Richard looked at her quizzically.

"There are many things I don't talk about, Richard. Does she have any plans drawn up?"

"As a matter of fact, the architect has promised to have them to her before Christmas."

"I can hear Jack's jeep," said Sophia, getting up. "I'm just dying to see the little man." She opened the front door and rushed across the drive, bending down to where Finn sat in the carry-tot Jack had just taken from the jeep. "Hello, my little cutie."

"I knew you were fond of me but not in front of you know who …" laughed Jack, nodding in Grace's direction where she stood in the doorway, laughing.

"You're a rascal, Jack Leslie," laughed Sophia, and then she kissed him on either cheek. "It's good to see you again. Come and meet my son Richard."

"Hi, Richard, it's nice to meet you again," said Jack, stretching out his hand.

"Likewise. We're gonna crowd you guys out a bit. Maybe I should check in somewhere in town," said Richard, shaking hands.

"No way, mate. We're all set up here!" Jack replied.

Later, Sophia held Finn in her arms as Grace poured some wine for her. She was trying to listen in on Jack and Richard's conversation. She just didn't want Kate to be hurt again. They were talking about New York. Jack said it was the best city in the world. He was telling Richard about how he and Kate could spend hours talking about it. "I'm surprised she didn't get a holiday visa years ago and spend some time living there. I suppose that's life, that's the way it goes."

"Is she around?"

"Yep," said Jack, finishing his beer bottle. "Want another beer?"

Richard smiled. "Sure." Grace was pleased they were getting on well. Jack had suggested staying at his mother's while they were here but she had firmly told him no way unless he wanted her and Finn in his mother's with him.

"Girls, come on over and join us," said Jack, taking two beers from the fridge.

"I'll just make up a bowl of nibbles," said Grace, as Sophia carried Finn into the living room, still cooing and beaming at him.

"Hi Jessie, I thought I heard your voice," said Sophia, coming downstairs the following morning.

"I just dropped around to say welcome back," said Jessie as Sophia kissed her on the cheek while Grace put another mug on the counter.

"I miss this when I'm in New York – popping over to one another's houses for coffee. So Jessie, Grace told me about your project. Sounds like a great idea."

"We hope to apply for planning soon. We've got so many ideas. And with Grace's marketing head, I feel we can create something really positive for the area."

"And please God and the angels that Jessie's Angel will win at the races on St. Stephen's Day because Geoff and Jack have offered to put the winnings towards it," said Grace, beaming.

"You are crazy ladies," laughed Sophia, and looking towards Jessie she added, "I can't believe that Grace is talking about angels."

"Sure I hang around with you two. Eventually it had to rub off," laughed Grace.

"But seriously girls, you can't be pinning hopes on a horse."

"No that's just one iron in the fire. We're working on a business plan. As you know, Jessie owns the land and buildings so that's a real benefit."

"And Grace has finished a first draft of a novel."

"My goodness, you never said. Well done you," said Sophia.

"It's still in a raw state but I loved the experience. Of course Jess is very excited about it. But … well, what would I know about writing …"

"Give it to Sophia to read, ah please Gracey. Wouldn't it be nice to get another opinion since you think mine is so biased," pleaded Jess and then she added, "Sophia, I talked about the babies and how I felt. Losing the babies made me challenge myself in ways that I never thought possible. You and I often talked about 'the meaning of it all'. I wasn't like that before. I never had it hard. I was so dammed lucky I didn't even know it. Nothing was a challenge. I met Geoff and fell in love, married young. We travelled the world together, came home. Settled down, had Sam. Hey, happy days. There was therapy in being able to talk to Grace about everything and the rest was our friend Gracey's vivid imagination."

As Sophia listened it struck her how much these two friends gave to one another unconditionally. Theirs was true friendship, unselfish and inclusive.

"Can I read it?" Sophia asked.

"Ah, Sophia, I'm nervous about giving it to you. It's not that I don't want you to read it but there's a fair amount of heartbreak and loss it in and I don't want to upset you."

"Grace that is what life is all about. Did you ever hear the story about the woman who begged Buddha to bring her young son back to life?" Jessie and Grace looked at her intrigued as she continued. "He told her to knock on all the doors in the village and ask if any of them had not suffered from loss. Needless to say the woman did not find one. We have all lost someone we love and if we haven't yet, we are going to. Awful as that may sound!"

"Sophia, you really know how to liven up a conversation," muttered Jessie. "There's your answer, Grace. Give Sophia your book."

Sophie burst out laughing at Jessie.

"In that case, I would be honoured if you read it," said Grace.

"By the way, what's it called?"

"It's called 'After It All.'"

"Odd choice." Sophia looked quizzically from one to the other.

"Sure, we're odd people."

Grace had uploaded the book to her tablet and Sophia had read it through the night. It was seven o'clock in the morning. Sophia went downstairs and boiled the kettle. Taking a cup of peppermint tea in her hand and with her dressing gown wrapped tightly around her, she walked to the red gate at the end of the garden. She hadn't accounted for the morning dew. Her slippers were soaking but they didn't bother her. She stood looking out to sea. The sun was just beginning to rise and the light glistened across the water as tears trickled down her cheeks.

The novel dealt with loss through death and separation, and the ensuing grief. But more importantly Grace had managed to make the characters believable. It had left her feeling inspired and uplifted.

Sophia thought of her little grandson Billy and his beautiful mother Heather, and then of her beloved Bill. She treasured them with all her heart. She was richer for having had them in her life. It was time. She had to move on, push forward until it was her turn to go. And there was nothing surer, that day would come. Until then she was going to cherish every moment. Europe, here I come. She was going with new friends who strangely felt like old ones. How could that be? A chance meeting on an aeroplane had changed everything for all of them.

"This book is going to be published," she said, aloud.

Grace looked out the kitchen window. Sophia was outside in her dressing gown. She opened the back door. "Come in or you'll have your death end."

"I don't even know what that means," smiled Sophia, walking back up the path.

"It means you'll get the flu. I've just boiled the kettle but I see you've had one already. I'm off to Jessie's for a hack."

"Can I come too, but I'd also love to see the site."

"Of course. I'll pop some toast on while you go change."

At the site Sophia became more excited. As she walked around, she wondered how they'd feel if she were to become involved. She thought about Fay and how Colleen had said she'd love to visit Ireland. Imagine if Jessie's place offered holidays to families whose children had dyspraxia. They could meet others from all over the world and share their experiences. There could be fun activities planned for the kids and information talks for parents along with relaxation therapies.

Just listening to Jessie was fun. She was brimming with ideas that were all very viable. She talked about growing vegetables and a herb garden, with an emphasis on teaching adults and kids gardening and cooking. There was space to develop an adventure park. She could suggest that some of the equipment could take into consideration children with co-ordination problems. Oh, but there was so much she'd like to contribute too. If it took off she could visualise log cabins dotted around and even an area for camping or caravanning. She was apprehensive about asking, especially because Jessie didn't know how wealthy she was. Richard was right. She shouldn't feel she had to hide things from her friends, but it would sound extremely arrogant of her to say, "Oh by the way, I forgot to mention I'm a multi-millionaire."

"Do you have any serious ideas about how you plan to fund it?" asked Sophia.

"Geoff and I hope to apply for European funding to develop a tourism product mixed with agriculture, equestrian and horticulture. Also the training programmes that we will offer will be open to the local community too. If it takes off, we'd love to have a coffee shop using local produce and displaying local art and craft. And even the possibilities of renting out workshop space for artists, and craftspeople to work and sell from here."

"How did that idea come about?"

"When we spoke to the Enterprise people, one of them mentioned our proximity to the main route from Rosslare to Kerry. There is a significant passing trade. It wasn't something we had considered before. But it could make the place more sustainable year round. Also crafts people could hold workshops or summer schools."

"Wow!" said Sophia. She was relieved that they had certainly researched.

"Also one evening while I was out walking I met some young girls from Holland. They were lost and looking for directions. I walked them back to where they were staying in a big old house with a beautiful garden. They told me they were staying there free in return for weeding the elderly owner's large garden. What a great idea! A working holiday with an opportunity to learn English and volunteer in some capacity for your keep."

"So it's becoming more than a training centre. Each day you seem to add thoughts and ideas," said Sophia as she took in the size of the half empty barn. Geoff had big round straw bales stacked neatly on one side. "I'm imagining barn dances, parties or even weddings," said Sophia.

"That's another great idea. It's awful really, Sophia. Every time I come down here I get carried away with myself. There are endless possibilities."

"I think that a place like this could be great for children with learning differences. You could host summer schools. I have a particular interest in a condition called dyspraxia," said Sophia, hoping it might be something the girls would consider.

"Oh my God, wouldn't that be great. Maybe other associations or charities might want to use it for their weekend breaks too," said Grace.

"I also have some friends involved in psychology and they hold events and are always looking for the right kind of venue," Sophia continued.

"Those are exactly the kinds of things I want to happen here. I want it to be a place of peace, creativity and fun. Learning mixed with lightness. Oh am I mad?" said Jessie, swinging her hands around. "It all means so much to me. It will take years to do all that I dream of and it will have to sustain itself enough for us to make a living and pay back the borrowings."

"What will you call it?" asked Sophia.

"Butterfly Barn," Grace and Jessie chorused and Sophia laughed at their enthusiasm.

"How do you feel about having an investor?"

"Who?" asked Jessie, looking confused, but Sophia noticed Grace smiling broadly at her.

"Me."

"Oh my God, Sophia, would you really consider investing in it?" said Jessie, just as Geoff's tractor arrived into the courtyard.

"Absolutely!"

"Did you hear that guys? Sophia would like to invest in Butterfly Barn."

"It's a deal," called Sam, as he climbed down from the tractor cabin. "Coz my mom has no money and big dreams."

"Now who did he hear that from?" laughed Jessie, looking towards Geoff, who pretended to look behind.

"I've no idea," he answered, grinning from ear to ear.

Sophia shook hands with Sam and tousled his curly red hair.

"You're like the three musketeers, all for one and one for all," he said, running over to where his mother had said was a good place to build therapy rooms. "Sophia, the puncture person can go here and the reflex person here and …" He jumped from one spot to the next.

"Come on, Sammy boy," laughed Geoff, "I'm dying for a coffee."

"Why the name Butterfly Barn?" asked Sophia as they strolled back along the lane towards the house.

"Well there's a barn and to me a butterfly signifies change. It breaks out of its chrysalis to become something colourful, beautiful and free and just like my babies, butterflies have a short life span. And although their leaving brought me great sadness, Anthony and Geoff's presence in this world has brought our family on a journey we would never have experienced. They have opened my mind and my heart and shown me the true goodness of the people around us. Now tell me about … dyspraxia, I've never heard of it?" asked Jessie.

Sophia felt a lump form in her throat as she began to share with her two new friends the learning challenges her beautiful grandson had struggled with.

"Okay, Grace, what's the problem?" Sophia asked, putting her pottery mug down on Jessie's butcher block table. "Why can't it be published?"

"Because Sophia, in case you have somehow forgotten, I AM NOT A WRITER."

"What is that supposed to mean? Speak English, for God's sake you wrote a book and now you're talking crap."

"Sophia, how very unbecoming of you – using language like that," laughed Jessie.

"She is making me cross," declared Sophia.

"And you are making me feel about two years old," Grace retorted.

"Will the two of you give it up?" Jessie said, getting up to cut some ginger cake and placing it in front of them. "Eat!"

Sophia and Grace laughed.

But within seconds, Sophia resumed. "What is wrong with you, Grace?"

"You're making in all sound so real, and that it is possible."

Sophia looked at Jessie. "What do you think?"

"You're scaring the daylights out of me too."

"I can't believe we are having this conversation and that you both have such a low value of your abilities. Grace, you wrote a book. And Jessie, don't you figure it's a bit selfish not to share what you have learnt?"

"Ouch!" said Grace. "I felt that – did you, Jessie? She's changing her plan of attack."

"If she doesn't get us one way, she's trying another." Jessie laughed.

"Okay Sophia, you are the expert when it comes to publishing. If you really think it can be done ..." Grace paused, looking at Jessie to gauge a reaction.

Jessie shrugged her shoulders and said, "Why not try, Gracey! You wrote a good story. And I think that it's only the beginning for you."

"Girls, I want you to feel comfortable," said Sophia, sipping her coffee.

"Hang on a second ... what's this about you and publishing, Sophia?" asked Jessie, frowning.

"Oh, it's just Sophia used to work as a journalist so she'd have some contacts. That's all I meant," said Grace, getting up to pour more tea and feeling awful for lying.

Sophia just smiled. "A long time ago, but there might be someone I know who can help."

Kate drove up the pebbled avenue to Rose Cottage. There was a Mercedes in the drive.

"Great, my friend Sophia from New York is here, you'll get to meet her," she said to Philly, her friend since the first day of art college, but it had become a little more recently. He was fun. Jessie thought he was cute. Grace had thrown her eyes to heaven and called him "Eye candy".

They got out and had begun to walk across the pebbles when the front door opened. She stopped in her tracks and stared in amazement at Richard. He was clearly as shocked as she was.

"Hi," he said, looking from her to Philly in a questioning way.

"Hi. I thought ... I didn't know ..."

"They're not here."

"I'll call back later. Bye."

But Richard had already turned away and was walking towards the garden gate which led to the beach. She got back into the car.

"Who's yer man?" Philly asked.

"Ah, nobody," she replied, trying to reverse as fast as she could. She was so upset she could hardly speak.

Later that evening, Grace, Jack, Sophia, Richard and Geoff sat around Jessie's dining-room table as Jessie began to clear the plates. Richard got up to help and followed her to the kitchen. "Jessie, I heard about your plan."

She looked at him in amazement. "You did!"

"I think your idea for a holiday retreat – I suppose that's what you'd call it – is a good one. When you get it up and running I can advertise it in the States, if you'd like."

"Are you for real? I thought you worked for a fashion magazine ..."

"I know a few people. You know how it is. I can see what I can do."

His mother would kill him if he told her the array of magazines they owned. Evading, he added, "I think grief touches everybody at some stage in life and information on some of the wonderful therapies available has to reach ordinary people like you and me."

He knew by the look on her face that she was dying to ask more questions but was holding herself back. "Create a website where people can view the holiday homes and the range of weekends available. Talk to the experts and associations and get them to link to your site. Now I need a beer. And I also want to know if Grace's sister is in love with that teenager?"

Jessie burst out laughing. "Here's the beer, and no, she's not. I'll let you in on a little secret." He leaned towards her. "She's in love with you but if you tell anybody I told you, I will murder you myself. Get your finger out, Richard. Both of your lives are passing you by. Now get that into you. Tomorrow is a new day."

The next morning Kate parked her car at the far end of the beach and began to walk along the seashore. It was only seven-thirty in the morning. She couldn't sleep. She hadn't been able to function properly since she had seen Richard yesterday. She had music playing in her ears to drown out the thoughts exploding in her head. What was she going to do? Never one to deliberate, she was more of an impulsive person. Why had she put that bloody song on her playlist? There was a lot to answer for being friends with Jessie McGrath; she smiled. But she listened to every word while looking out to sea towards Everest Rock. When it was over she muttered, "You know what Barbra, you are right. I will 'Tell him' – what have I got to lose? I'll know once and for all."

She started to run in case she'd change her mind. She ran to the sounds of the pebbles and sea shells crunching under her feet. She reached the red cast-iron garden gate and flung it open. Knocking on the French doors, she could see Grace having breakfast with Finn and Jack, who got up to open the door.

"I know we like having visitors but ..." he laughed, pretending to look at his watch.

"Is he up yet?" she asked Grace, ignoring him in her fluster.

"How did you know he was here?"

"Long story. Same room?"

Grace nodded and turned to Jack. As she rushed passed them, Kate heard her say, "I'd love to be a fly on that bedroom wall."

Richard was in bed.

"What the ...!"

"Look," she said. "I am only ever going to say this once." She took a deep breath. "I love you, you plonker!"

"Only once!" he joked.

"Only once. Okay, I'll only call you a plonker once. Oh no – that was twice. Ah, what the hell!"

"Come here, you big eejit ..." he said, making a miserable attempt at her Irish accent. "I love you, Kate Fitzgerald."

"I'm a recovered drug addict."

"I was born out of wedlock."

"No, I'm serious."

"So am I and so what!" Then he added, "Kate, I don't care. We all make mistakes. Show me a perfect human being. If I met one I'd be bored stupid. Now come on, we're wasting valuable time."

As she jumped onto the bed, she whispered, "Thank you, Barbra."

"What did you say?"

"Oh, I just wanted to say thank you."

"To who?"

"To the world. To everyone. To Sophia for having you". Then she laughed as she pulled her top off. "Out of wedlock ... well who would have thought?"

"You know, you're a crazy woman. What am I letting myself in for?

I know one thing for sure – it won't be a quiet life."

"Stop talking and start doing." She laughed again.

"It's been a magical Christmas so far," said Grace, snuggling into Jack who was lying in bed beside her. Sometimes she wanted to pinch herself to check that she wasn't dreaming. Instead she pinched him.

"Ouch. That hurt!" He yelped.

"You're such a baby," she laughed, getting up. "Come on or we'll be late for the races. We've a two-hour drive ahead of us. And you have to help Geoff load up Jessie's Angel."

He groaned, turned over and said. "Just give me five more minutes."

Finn was still asleep. She went to the bathroom and while in the shower she heard the door open and there was Jack. For a fleeting second she thought of Dirk. And then she began to cry.

"What's the matter, honey?" asked Jack, his voice filled with concern. She stepped out of the shower and wrapped her dressing gown around her and blurted out, "I set the date with Dirk in the shower."

Jack laughed, wrapping a towel around him. "And that made you cry. It'd make me cry too if I thought I had to marry him."

"It's not funny Jack …" But she was smiling through her tears.

"Grace, does this mean that the shower is out of bounds coz you set a date in it? Come here." He took her in his arms. "We both have a past. That's life but we have one another now and nothing is going to come between us again. I promise – although it might take me years to get a divorce."

"Jack, I told you before how I feel about marriage."

"But I didn't tell you how I feel about it. I want you to make an honest man of me. I want to be Finn's legal guardian. I want you both in my life forever. Can you hack that?"

She nodded from where she had sat down on the toilet lid.

"By the way, this is a ridiculous place to be having this conversation." He laughed, kissing the top of her head as he stepped back into the shower. "Nah, nah, nah, nah, nah, I got here before ya."

"You are such a big baby," she said, going out to pick up Finn who had begun to wake.

"Richard was so excited about the race he could hardly sleep," said Kate, from where she sat in the back seat of Sophia's car.

"I'm glad we're travelling together because if I had to listen to another word about racing and form and all the other lingo that goes with it, I'd scream," said Grace.

"So true," agreed Sophia. "We're nearly there. Eoghan said he'll ring when he's parked. He has Monique and Nora, and even your mother asked if he had room for one more."

"What? My mother is coming?" said Grace in disbelief. "My father spent so much time in the bookies, she once told him he should move his bed down there. Can you believe it, Kate?"

"It's gas that she didn't tell us."

"She's a star for making the effort. There's a parking place over there, Soph," said Grace.

"Perfect," said Sophia, gliding the car in comfortably. Richard had travelled with Jack to help, making it the first time in three days that Kate had been apart from him. Grace looked towards her sister and smiled. She was already on her mobile asking Richard where exactly they were. Kate was positively glowing. Grace wondered would they become like her and Jack – a long distance relationship? But it didn't matter; as long as he was "the one" everything was possible. With the crowds flooding into the place, Grace was thankful that Dirk had taken Finn for the day. She was glad they were finding their way. She and Dirk still had their moments, but it was important to her that Finn would always have a relationship with his father. And thankfully she liked his fiancée.

Sophia came up beside her and linked her as they walked along. "I'm so happy," she whispered, nodding in Kate's direction. "It's been the best Christmas is a long time."

"Absolutely."

"Hey, girls, over here," called Jessie from where Jack had arranged seats for all of them on the pavilion.

"Dad couldn't sleep a wink last night," said Sam, obviously repeating what Geoff had said.

"He wasn't the only one. It's so exciting," said Grace. "Here's Eoghan and the rest of the gang."

Sam ran over repeating his line. And then he spotted his grandparents and ran towards them.

"You know win, lose or draw, this is a great day," Jessie whispered to Grace as they both sat down. "Just take a look around. Everybody came to support us, even your mother who is so anti-gambling."

"Jess?"

"Mmm …"

"I think your babies, Anthony and Geoff are here too."

Jess placed her hand over Grace's and smiled. "Thanks for saying that because I feel them around me every day of my life."

Grace's eyes filled with tears as she said, "I think they will help us make Butterfly Barn come true."

THE END

Acknowledgements

The great thing about writing a book is that you get a chance to thank people. Because without the love and support I'm surrounded by, this crazy dream of mine would never have come true. So here I go. I apologise in advance if it sounds like an Oscar speech, but I just can't resist.

This book came from the many wonderful experiences I've been blessed to have in my life. Beginning with my fantastic and hugely supportive parents, Nancy and Paddy Galvin, both of whom never stopped believing in me. To my sister, Yvonne, and my brother, Alan, thank you both for your support and encouragement always. Growing up in our house is where I got my inspiration to write about the bonds of family. To my parents-in-law, Eugene and Siobhán, for all the love and kindness they have shown me over the years, I am truly blessed. My sisters-in-law, Eleanor Galvin, Fionnuala Galvin, Una O'Dwyer, Edel Pattyn, Siobhán Campell and Isabel O'Neill, have given me even more inspiration about what family means. A special thanks goes out to Issy for, well, everything. I'm honoured to share my life with my friends, Mary and William Harrington, Siobhán Millea, Deirdre Power, Fiona Redmond, Noeleen Bresnan, Siobhán Power, David and Ann Veale, Denise Keogh, Denise Ryan Sherman and Roseline Dalton. When I was disheartened you were all there to buoy me up again. I know I wrecked your heads at times, but ye love me anyway. Thanks, girls, William and David.

Little did I know that Seán Power's idea to bring cruise liners into the beautiful city of Waterford would inspire the career choice of my lead character, Grace Fitzgerald. Thank you, Seán, for being a great mentor and friend over the years.

Thanks to Vanessa O'Loughlin from Writing.ie, who saw some merit in my work and encouraged me to find an editor. Also to Patricia O'Reilly, whose advice was hugely beneficial. Thanks to Jim Nolan and Damian Tiernan for encouraging me to learn more about the craft of writing.

Without my editor, Grace Wells, I would never have found the courage to follow my dream. She kept me focused and structured, because I can spend so much time up in the clouds – hence the book cover. Thank you, Grace. A big thank you to Margaret Organ, the Arts Officer, Waterford City & County Council; the day I became a member of Artlinks was a defining moment for me. It allowed me to believe that all of this might be possible.

Thanks to Catherine Fitzpatrick, another new friend, for telling me about Words at the Arthand, run by a fantastic couple called Seán and Miranda Corcoran. Set high on the cliffs of our beautiful Copper Coast, it's a place where poets, writers and people who simply love words gather once a month to share their work. On a wet and cold winter's night in January, I shared the first pages of Butterfly Barn. Without having that experience, I honestly don't think I would be writing this acknowledgement today. The writing community in this county is fantastic; thank you all so much.

A huge thanks to Frank McQuillan, Patricia Daly and all the team in the Business Training Centre, Kilmacthomas, part of the Waterford Wexford ETB. Without their mentoring, suggestions and guidance, I would never have embarked on this self-publishing journey. To Kieran McCarthy for my website and for offering to produce a film clip for me. It was one of the most terrifying experiences ever, but thank you, Kieran. Thanks to Louise Buggy, David Hennessey, Deirdre Mooney, Claire Bowman and all my Kilmac buddies for their help, chats, feedback, input, ideas and laughs in the Workhouse. And did we come up with some crazy ideas at times … What about the Viking?!

Thank you to John Foley, my brilliant photographer friend, for my profile photograph and for posting fantastic shots from around the country to *Butterfly Barn*'s Facebook page.

When I decided to self-publish, I became a member of the Alliance of Independent Authors. Through it I learnt that I should find a group of beta readers, people who would read the book and give an unbiased opinion. This search led me to make many new friends and to connect again with old ones. I would like to thank all of them for their time and encouragement. Without their input I would not have done this. So here they are: Valerie Lyons, Mary Ní Bhreacháin, Kate Murphy, Marie Waldron, Sheila Shanahan, Orla Byrne, Suzanne De Barra, Clíodhna Campbell, Catherine Kavanagh and Bernie Vaughan. A special thanks to Emma Tobin, Mags O'Connor, Christine Casey,

Gráinne Delaney and Sinéad Fitzpatrick for reading my very first draft eight years ago and for encouraging me to follow my dream. I know, girls, it took me a long time to find the courage. I'd like to thank Dara Ní Bhreacháin, she knows why!

When it came to social media, I hadn't a clue where to begin. Without Siona Stokes, the Butterfly Barn Facebook page wouldn't exist and the book would still be in the closet. Siona, you're a star and another great new friend. Thanks also to Edrina Briscoe and Judy O'Brien both of whom have their work cut out trying to explain to me how it all works. And to all my Facebook and Twitter friends, thanks for passing the word around and for all your support since the beginning.

Thanks to Chenile, Robert and the team at Kazoo Independent Publishing Services, who made this journey an enjoyable experience. Their knowledge and expertise around publishing is second to none. I really appreciate your commitment to this book.

Thanks to The Book Centre, Waterford, for hosting my book launch. As a self-published author, I could only have dreamed of being launched in a bookshop, but Maeve Ryan and her team made it happen for me. Thank you so much. Thanks also to Lucy and the team in Eason, Dungarvan for giving me the opportunity to host a second launch in the west of the county.

To the people who read this book, I really hope you enjoy it. If you do, please pass the book on to your friends. The reason I write is to tell stories that affect people's lives. Maybe there's an issue I address that you are interested in. Regarding the learning challenge called dyspraxia, thank you so much to Harry Conway at the Dyspraxia Association of Ireland, for his commitment to making people aware of it, and also for his great friendship and support. I recently became aware of a not-for-profit organisation called Féileacáin, who are doing wonderful work to support anyone who has been affected by the death of a baby during pregnancy or shortly after. It's lovely to know that there are so many people out there willing to lend a helping hand. A special thanks also to Fr Jim Cogley for his great kindness, both back when I needed it and more recently when I was researching this book. If these or any other issues have struck a chord with you, please visit my website. Who knows, maybe someday a place called Butterfly Barn will come true.

And finally, the biggest thanks of all goes to my husband, Michael, who has travelled this rollercoaster called life with me. Without his love, encouragement and unwavering belief in me, I'd be lost. We have been blessed with the two nicest people I know, our daughter, Aisling, and our son Eoghan.

Love and many thanks,
Karen.

14340556R00162

Printed in Poland
by Amazon Fulfillment
Poland Sp. z o.o., Wrocław